SILHOUETTE BOOKS

THE GIFT

ISBN-13: 978-0-373-28153-4

Copyright © 2007 by Harlequin Books S.A.

The publisher acknowledges the copyright holder of the individual works as follows:

HOME FOR CHRISTMAS
Copyright © 1986 by Nora Roberts

ALL I WANT FOR CHRISTMAS
Copyright © 1994 by Nora Roberts

GABRIEL'S ANGEL
Copyright © 1989 by Nora Roberts

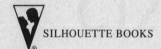

Recycling programs for this product may not exist in your area.

Praise for #1 *New York Times* and *USA TODAY* bestselling author

NORA ROBERTS

"Roberts' bestselling novels are some of the best in the romance genre. They are thoughtfully plotted, well-written stories featuring fascinating characters."
—*USA TODAY*

"There's no mystery about why Roberts is a bestselling author of romances and mainstream novels: she delivers the goods with panache and wit."
—*Publishers Weekly*

"Nora Roberts is among the best."
—*Washington Post Book World*

"Some estimates have [Nora Roberts] selling 12 books an hour, 24 hours a day, 7 days a week, 52 weeks a year."
—*New York Times* magazine

"Roberts is deservedly one of the best known and most widely read of all romance writers."
—*Library Journal*

"A superb author…Ms. Roberts is an enormously gifted writer whose incredible range and intensity guarantee the very best of reading."
—*Rave Reviews*

"Romance will never die as long as the megaselling Roberts keeps writing."
—*Kirkus Reviews*

Dear Reader,

What do you get when you take two Nora Roberts Christmas novellas and add *Gabriel's Angel,* Nora's much loved tale of a modern-day Ebenezer Scrooge? The perfect Christmas gift for the romance lover, that's what!

With the holiday season just around the corner, we are delighted to bring you *The Gift,* a heartwarming 3-in-1 volume of classic Nora Roberts romances, each encapsulating the spirit of Christmas. And, as an extra-special bonus, we've also included three of Nora's favorite holiday recipes!

In *Home for Christmas,* prizewinning reporter Jason Law returns to New Hampshire after years of travel, eager to see Faith Monroe, the girl he left behind. But Faith didn't wait for him as she'd promised, and Jason has a lot of work to do if he wants to win her back.

All I Want for Christmas is the story of identical twins Zeke and Zach, who send their Christmas list to Santa early. The only things on it: new bicycles and a mom. Now they just have to get their dad to cooperate.

And in *Gabriel's Angel,* reclusive artist Gabriel Bradley thinks he's found the perfect hideaway—a remote mountain cabin—until a beautiful pregnant woman shows up seeking shelter from a snowstorm…and changes his life forever.

We hope you have a wonderful holiday season and that you enjoy this very special collection of stories.

Best wishes,

The Editors

Silhouette Books

NORA ROBERTS

THE *Gift*

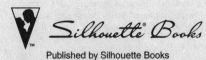

Silhouette Books

Published by Silhouette Books

America's Publisher of Contemporary Romance

CONTENTS

NORA ROBERTS'S
HOLIDAY RECIPES

POP'S PANCAKES

A longtime tradition in my family is Christmas breakfast. My parents' home was always crowded and noisy, and everyone lent a hand—watching the light on the waffle iron, holding their plates out for more. We were allowed to fry the bacon or flip the pancakes on the griddle. But nobody—nobody—made the pancake batter except my pop. There were two huge bowls of it to feed the horde before we got down to exchanging gifts and ripping colored paper to shreds. Because there were so many of us, we often ate in shifts, crowding around the dining room table and spilling over to the breakfast bar. Wherever I sit, the first bite takes me back to childhood.

6 eggs, beaten
1 can evaporated milk
¼ cup butter or margarine, melted
1½ cups regular milk (1 cup for waffles)
3 cups flour
6 tbsp baking powder

Combine ingredients in the order listed. Mix well. Let stand for 10 minutes to rise. For pancakes, spoon batter onto hot griddle. Be patient—don't flip until bubbles appear.

Enjoy!

PLAIN OR PAINTED HOLIDAY COOKIES

Baking helps put me in the mood for the holidays. There's nothing like a little flour on your hands to start "Jingle Bells" ringing in your head. The tradition in my house goes this way: first put on an album of Christmas music. It isn't possible to work over a hot oven without the proper setting. Gather your ingredients:

¾ cup shortening
1 cup sugar
2 eggs
1 tsp vanilla extract
2½ cups flour
1 tsp baking powder
1 tsp salt
Optional: evaporated milk, food
coloring, small paintbrush, colored
sugar or sprinkles

If you have kids, this is the time to step back and let them do some of the work. It makes it fun, and the mess is almost worth it. Let one of them mix the shortening and sugar together. Let another one crack the eggs into the bowl. Then you can help by picking out the pieces of eggshell. Add the vanilla extract and mix thoroughly. Blend in flour, baking powder and salt. Cover and chill for at least an hour.

Preheat your oven to 400°F. Now comes the time when the kids fight over who rolls out the dough. See that it's rolled to about an 1/8" thick on a floured board. If you don't have cookie cutters in cute little Christmas shapes, you should. We generally stick to the tried-and-true angels, Santas and trees.

When you cut the cookies, make sure to dip the cutter into flour now and then or you'll end up with a jammed-up Santa. Place cookies on an ungreased cookie sheet. Now you can either sprinkle them with plain or colored sugar and be done with them, or if you're feeling adventurous you can use that little paintbrush. Divide small amounts of evaporated milk into several cups, along with a little food coloring in each. Then go ahead and paint. Remember, it doesn't matter if Santa's blue or the Christmas tree is red. And just add a little water as the mixture thickens.

Bake for six or seven minutes. Break off a couple of times to sing a round of "Deck the Halls." You'll feel better. You should have about four dozen cookies, but then, if you have children, forget it. When your husband comes home and asks what's for dinner, shove a cookie in his mouth!

OLD-FASHIONED BREAD PUDDING

I do a lot of complicated baking at this time of year—time-consuming treats that keep me in the kitchen for hours. I really don't mind, but there's something to be said for simplicity. One of my men's favorites is an old family recipe handed down through the Scottish branch of my family, through my father to me. It's wonderfully simple and old-fashioned, something that can literally be tossed together when you discover unexpected holiday visitors are coming to call. Best of all, since it's made in one dish, there's little to clean up. I should warn you, most of the measurements are estimates. Experiment. It's that kind of dish.

6 to 8 slices bread, torn into pieces
3 to 4 eggs, lightly beaten
¼ cup margarine, melted
¼ to ⅓ cup sugar
3 to 3½ cups milk
About ¼ cup raisins (it's up to you)
Cinnamon to taste (I like a lot myself, maybe 3 tbsp or so.
I really don't measure—I go by how it looks.)

Preheat oven to 400°F. Mix all ingredients, gently but thoroughly, in a casserole dish. Pop it into the oven for 1 hour. Can be eaten warm or cold.

HOME FOR CHRISTMAS

Chapter 1

So much can change in ten years. He was prepared for it. All during the flight from London and the long, winding drive north from Boston to Quiet Valley, New Hampshire, population 326—or it had been ten years before when Jason Law had last been there—he'd thought of how different things would be. A decade, even for a forgotten little town in New England, was bound to bring changes. There would have been deaths and births. Houses and shops would have changed hands. Some of them might not be there at all.

Not for the first time since Jason had decided to visit his hometown did he feel foolish. After all, it was very likely he wouldn't even be recognized. He'd left a thin, defiant twenty-year-old in a scruffy pair of jeans. He was coming back a man who'd learned how to replace defiance with arrogance and succeed. His frame was still lean, but it fitted nicely into clothes tailored on Savile Row and Seventh Avenue. Ten years had changed him from a desperate boy determined to make his mark, to an outwardly complacent man who had. What ten years hadn't changed, was what was inside. He was still looking for roots, for his place. That was why he was heading back to Quiet Valley.

The road still twisted and turned through the woods, up the mountains and down again, as it had when he'd headed in the opposite direction on a Greyhound. Snow covered the ground, smooth here, bumpy there where it was heaped over rocks. In the sunlight trees shimmered with it. Had he missed it? He'd spent one winter in snow up to his waist in the Andes. He'd spent another sweltering in Africa. The years ran together, but oddly enough, Jason could remember every place he'd spent Christmas over the past ten years, though he'd never celebrated the holiday. The road narrowed and swept into a wide curve. He could see the mountains, covered with pines and dusted with white. Yes, he'd missed it.

Sun bounced off the mounds of snow. He adjusted his dark glasses and slowed down, then on impulse, stopped. When he stepped from the car his breath came in streams of smoke. His skin tingled with the cold but he didn't button his coat or reach in his pockets for his gloves. He needed to feel it. Breathing in the thin, icy air was like breathing in thousands of tiny needles. Jason walked the few feet to the top of the ridge and looked down on Quiet Valley.

He'd been born there, raised there. He'd learned of grief there—and he'd fallen in love. Even from the distance he could see her house—her parents' house, Jason reminded himself and felt the old, familiar surge of fury. She'd be living somewhere else now, with her husband, with her children.

When he discovered that his hands were balled into fists he carefully relaxed them. Channeling emotion was a skill he'd turned into an art over the past decade. If he could do it in his work, reporting on famine, war, and suffering, he could do it for himself. His feelings for Faith had been a boy's feelings. He was a man now, and she, like Quiet Valley, was only part of his childhood. He'd traveled more than five thousand miles just to prove it. Turning away, he got back in the car and started down the mountain.

From the distance, Quiet Valley had looked like a Currier and Ives painting, all white and snug between mountain and forest. As he drew closer, it became less idyllic and more approachable. The tired paint showed here and there on some of the outlying houses. Fences bowed under snow. He saw a few new houses in what had once been open fields. Change. He reminded himself he'd expected it.

Smoke puffed out of chimneys. Dogs and children raced in the snow. A check of his watch showed him it was half past three. School was out, and he'd been traveling for fifteen hours. The smart thing to do was to see if the Valley Inn was still in operation and get a room. A smile played around his mouth as he wondered if old Mr. Beantree still ran the place. He couldn't count the times Beantree had told him he'd never amount to anything but trouble. He had a Pulitzer and an Overseas Press Award to prove differently.

Houses were grouped closer together now, and he recognized them. The Bedford place, Tim Hawkin's house, the Widow Marchant's. He slowed again as he passed the widow's tidy blue clapboard. She hadn't changed the color, he noticed and felt foolishly pleased. And the old spruce in the front yard was already covered with bright-red ribbons.

She'd been kind to him. Jason hadn't forgotten how she had fixed hot chocolate and listened to him for hours when he'd told her of the travels he wanted to make, the places he dreamed of seeing. She'd been in her seventies when he'd left, but of tough New England stock. He thought he might still find her in her kitchen patiently fueling the woodstove and listening to her Rachmaninoff.

The streets of the town were clear and tidy. New Englanders were a practical lot, and Jason thought, as sturdy as the bedrock they'd planted themselves on. The town had not changed as he'd anticipated. Railings Hardware still sat on the corner off Main and the post office still occupied a brick building no bigger than a garage. The same red garland was strung from lamppost to lamppost as it had been all through his youth during each holiday season. Children were building a snowman in front of the Litner place. But whose children? Jason wondered. He scanned the red mufflers and bright boots knowing any of them might be Faith's. The fury came back and he looked away.

The sign on the Valley Inn had been repainted, but nothing else about the three-story square stone building was different. The walkway had been scraped clean and smoke billowed out of both chimneys. He found himself driving beyond it. There was something else to do first, something he'd already known he would have to do. He could have turned at the corner, driven a block and seen the house where he grew up. But he didn't.

Near the end of Main would be a tidy white house, bigger than most of the others with two big bay windows and a wide front porch. Tom Monroe had brought his bride there. A reporter of Jason's caliber knew how to ferret out such information. Perhaps Faith had put up the lace curtains she'd always wanted at the windows. Tom would have bought her the pretty china tea sets she'd longed for. He'd have given her exactly what she'd wanted. Jason would have given her a suitcase and a motel room in countless cities. She'd made her choice.

After ten years he discovered it was no easier to accept. Still, he forced himself to be calm as he pulled up to the curb. He and Faith had been friends once, lovers briefly. He'd had other lovers since, and she had a husband. But he could still remember her as she'd looked at eighteen, lovely, soft, eager. She had wanted to go with him, but he wouldn't let her. She had promised to wait, but she hadn't. He took a deep breath as he climbed from the car.

The house was lovely. In the big bay window that faced the street was a Christmas tree, cluttered and green in the daylight. At night it would glitter like magic. He could be sure of it because Faith had always believed so strongly in magic.

Standing on the sidewalk he found himself dealing with fear. He'd covered wars and interviewed terrorists but he'd never felt the stomach-churning fear that he did now, standing on a narrow snow-brushed sidewalk facing a pristine white house with holly bushes by the door. He could turn around, he reminded himself. Drive back to the inn or simply out of town again. There was no need to see her again. She was out of his life. Then he saw the lace curtains at the window and the old resentment stirred, every bit as strong as fear.

As he started down the walk a girl raced around the side of the house just ahead of a well-aimed snowball. She dived, rolled and evaded. In an instant, she was up again and hurling one of her own.

"Bull's-eye, Jimmy Harding!" With a whoop, she turned to run and barreled into Jason. "Sorry." With snow covering her from head to foot, she looked up and grinned. Jason felt the world spin backward.

She was the image of her mother. The sable hair peeked out of her cap and fell untidily to her shoulders. The small, triangular face was dominated by big blue eyes that seemed to hold jokes all of their own. But it was the smile, the one that said, *isn't this fun?* that caught him by the throat. Shaken, he stepped back while the girl dusted herself off and studied him.

"I've never seen you before."

He slipped his hands into his pockets. *But I've seen you,* he thought. "No. Do you live here?"

"Yeah, but the shop's around the side." A snowball landed with a plop at her feet. She lifted a brow in a sophisticated manner. "That's Jimmy," she said in the tone of a woman barely tolerating a suitor. "His aim's lousy. The shop's around the side," she repeated as she bent to ball more snow. "Just walk right in."

She raced off holding a ball in each hand. Jason figured Jimmy was in for a surprise.

Faith's daughter. He hadn't asked her name and nearly called her back. It didn't matter, he told himself. He'd only be in town a few days before he took the next assignment. Just passing through, he thought. Just cleaning the slate.

He backtracked to walk around the side of the house. Though he couldn't imagine what sort of shop Tom could have, he thought it might be best to see him first. He almost relished it.

The little workshop he'd half expected turned out to be a miniature of a Victorian cottage. The sleigh out in front held two life-size dolls dressed in top hats and bonnets, cloaks and top boots. Above the door was a fancy hand-painted sign that read Doll House. To the accompaniment of bells, Jason pushed the door open.

"I'll be right with you."

Hearing her voice again was like stepping back and finding no solid ground. But he'd deal with it, Jason told himself. He'd deal with it because he had to. Slipping off his glasses, he tucked them into his pocket and looked around.

Child-size furniture was set around the room in the manner of a cozy parlor. Dolls of every shape and size and style occupied chairs, stools, shelves and cabinets. In front of an elf-size fireplace where flames shimmered, sat a grandmother of a doll in lace cap and apron. The illusion was so strong Jason almost expected her to begin rocking.

"I'm sorry to keep you waiting." With a china doll in one hand and a bridal veil in the other, Faith walked through the doorway. "I was right in the middle of..." The veil floated out of her hand as she stopped. It waltzed to the floor with no sound at all. Color rushed away from her face, making the deep-blue eyes nearly violet in contrast. In reaction, or defense, she gripped the doll to her breast. "Jason."

Chapter 2

Framed in the doorway with the thin winter light creeping through the tiny windows she was lovelier than his memory of her. He'd hoped it would be different. He'd hoped his fantasies of her would be exaggerated as so many fantasies are. But she was here, flesh and blood, and so beautiful she took his breath away. Perhaps because of it, his smile was cynical and his voice cool.

"Hello, Faith."

She couldn't move, forward or back. He trapped her now as he had so many years before. He didn't know it then, she couldn't let him know it now. Emotion, locked and kept secret for so long struggled against will and was held back. "How are you?" she managed to ask, her hands like a vise around the doll.

"Fine." He walked toward her. God, how it pleased him to see the nerves jumping in her eyes. God, how it tormented him to learn she smelled the same. Soft, young, innocent. "You look wonderful." He said it carelessly, like a yawn.

"You were the last person I expected to see walk through the door." One she'd learned to stop looking for. Determined to control herself, Faith loosened her grip on the doll. "How long are you in town?"

"Just a few days. I had the urge."

She laughed and hoped it didn't sound hysterical. "You always did. We read a lot about you. You've been able to see all the places you always wanted to see."

"And more."

She turned away, giving herself a moment to close her eyes and pull her emotions together. "They ran it on the front page when you won the Pulitzer. Mr. Beantree strutted around as though he'd been your mentor. 'Fine boy, Jason Law,' he said. 'Always knew he'd amount to something.'"

"I saw your daughter."

That was the biggest fear, the biggest hope, the dream she'd put to rest years ago. She bent casually to pick up the veil. "Clara?"

"Just outside. She was about to mow down some boy named Jimmy."

"Yes, that's Clara." The smile came quickly and just as stunningly as it had on the child. "She's a vicious competitor," she added and wanted to say *like her father,* but didn't dare.

There was so much to say, so much that couldn't be said. If he had had one wish at that moment it would have been to reach out and touch her. Just to touch her once and remember the way it had been.

"I see you have your lace curtains."

Regret washed over her. She'd have settled for bare windows, blank walls. "Yes, I have my lace curtains and you your adventures."

"And this place." He turned to look around again. "When did all this start?"

She could deal with it, she promised herself, this hatefully casual small talk. "I opened it nearly eight years ago now."

He picked a rag doll from a bassinet. "So you sell dolls. A hobby?"

Something else came into her eyes now. Strength. "No, it's my business. I sell them, repair them, even make them."

"Business?" He set the doll down and the smile he gave her had nothing to do with humor. "It's hard for me to picture Tom approving of his wife setting up a business."

"Is it?" It hurt, but she set the china doll on a counter and began to arrange the veil on its head. "You always were perceptive, Jason, but you've been away a long time." She looked over her shoulder and her eyes weren't nervous or even strong. They were simply cold. "A very long time. Tom and I were divorced eight years ago. The last time I heard he was living in Los Angeles. You see, he didn't care for small towns, either. Or small-town girls."

He couldn't name the things that stirred in him so he pushed them aside. Bitterness was simpler. "Apparently you picked badly, Faith."

She laughed again but the veil crumpled in her hand. "Apparently I did."

"You didn't wait." It was out before he could stop it. He hated himself for it, and her.

"You were gone." She turned back slowly and folded her hands.

"I told you I'd come back. I told you I'd send for you as soon as I could."

"You never called, or wrote. For three months I—"

"Three months?" Furious, he grabbed her arms. "After everything we'd talked about, everything we'd hoped for, three months was all you could give me?"

She would have given him a lifetime, but there hadn't been a choice. Struggling to keep her voice calm, she looked into his eyes. They were the same—intense, impatient. "I didn't know where you were. You wouldn't even give me that." She pulled away from him because the need was as great as it had always been. "I was eighteen and you were gone."

"And Tom was here."

She set her jaw. "And Tom was here. It's been ten years, Jason, you never once wrote. Why now?"

"I've asked myself the same thing," he murmured and left her standing alone.

Her dreams had always been too fanciful. As a child Faith had envisioned white chargers and glass slippers. Reality was something to be faced daily in a family where money was scarce and pride was not, but dreams weren't just for nighttime.

She'd fallen in love with Jason when she'd been eight and he ten and he'd bravely vanquished three boys who'd tossed her into the snow. It had taken three of them. Faith could still look back on that with a sense of satisfaction. But it had been Jason fiercely coming to her rescue and sending her opponents scattering that she remembered best. He'd been thin, and his coat had been too large and mended at the elbows. She remembered his eyes, deep, deep brown under brows drawn close in annoyance as he'd looked down at her. Snow had coated his pale blond hair and reddened his face. She'd looked into his eyes and fallen in love. He'd muttered at her, hauled her up and scolded her for getting into trouble. Then he'd stalked off with his ungloved hands thrust into the pockets of his too-big coat.

Through childhood and into adolescence she'd never looked at another boy. Of course she'd pretended to from time to time hoping it might make Jason Law notice her.

Then when she'd been sixteen and her mother had sewn her a dress for the spring dance at the town hall, he'd noticed. So had several other boys, and Faith had flirted outrageously, with one goal in mind: Jason Law. Sulky and defiant, he'd watched her dance with one boy after another. She'd made sure of it. Just as she'd made sure she looked directly at him before she'd stepped outside to take the air. He'd followed her, just as she'd hoped. She'd pretended to be sophisticated. He'd been rude. And he'd walked her home under a fat full moon.

There'd been other walks after that—spring, summer, fall, winter. They were in love as only the young can be, carelessly, heedlessly, innocently. She told him of her longings for a house and children, for lace curtains and china cups. He told her of his passion to travel, to see everything, and write it down. She knew he'd felt trapped in the small town, hampered by a father who gave him no love and little hope. He knew she dreamed of quiet rooms with flowers in crystal vases. But they were drawn together and tangled all the dreams into one.

Then one night in the summer when the air was sweet

with wild grass they stopped being children and their love stopped being innocent.

"Mom, you're dreaming again."

"What?" Up to her elbows in soapy water, Faith turned. Her daughter stood at the doorway to the kitchen, snugly wrapped in a flannel gown that came up to her chin. With her hair freshly brushed and her face scrubbed clean, she looked like an angel. Faith knew better. "I guess I was. You've finished your homework?"

"Yeah. It's dumb having homework when school's nearly out."

"Don't remind me."

"You're grumpy," Clara declared and eyed the cookie jar. "You should go for one of your walks."

"Just one," Faith said, easily outguessing her daughter. "And don't forget to brush your teeth." She waited while Clara rooted through the jar. "Did you see a man this afternoon? A tall man with blond hair?"

"Uh-huh." Mouth full, Clara turned back to her mother. "He was walking up to the house. I sent him to the shop."

"Did he—say anything to you?"

"Not really. He looked at me kind of funny at first, like he'd seen me before. Do you know him?"

While her heart began a slow, dull thud, Faith dried her hands. "Yes. He used to live here a long time ago."

"Oh. Jimmy liked his car." She wondered if she could talk herself into another cookie.

"I think I will take that walk, Clara, but I want you in bed."

Recognizing the tone, she knew the cookie would have to wait. "Can I count the presents under the tree again?"

"You've counted them ten times."

"Maybe there's a new one."

Laughing, Faith gathered her up. "Not a chance." Then she grinned and carried Clara into the living room. "But it won't hurt to count them one more time."

The air was brittle when she stepped outside and it smelled of snow. There was no reason to lock the doors in a town where she knew everyone. Bundling her coat closer, she glanced back at the second-story window where her daughter slept. Clara was the reason why the house wasn't cold, why her life wasn't empty when both things could easily have been true.

She'd left the tree burning and the lights around the door sent out festive color. Four days until Christmas, she thought, and the wonder of it came home again. From where she stood, the town looked as pretty as a postcard with the strings of lights, the tree with its star in the town square, the street lamps burning. She could smell smoke from the chimneys and the bursting scent of pine.

Some might find it too settled, others would find it dull. But Faith had made it a home for herself and her daughter. She'd altered her life to suit her, and it fitted her well.

No regrets, she promised with one last glance at her daughter's window. No regrets at all.

The wind picked up a bit as she walked. There'd be snow for Christmas. She could feel it. She'd look forward to that, not back any longer.

"Still fond of walking?"

Chapter 3

Had she known he'd find her? Perhaps she had. Perhaps she'd needed him to. "Some things don't change," she said simply as Jason fell into step beside her.

"I've found that out in one afternoon." He thought of the town that had stayed so much the same. And of his feelings for the woman beside him. "Where's your daughter?"

"She's sleeping."

He was calmer than he'd been that afternoon, and determined to stay that way. "I didn't ask you if you had other children."

"No." He heard the wistfulness in her voice, just a sigh of it. "There's only Clara."

"How did you pick the name?"

She smiled. It was so like him to ask questions no one else would think of. "From the Nutcracker. I wanted her to be able to dream." As she had. Dropping her hands in her pockets she told herself they were simply two old friends walking through a quiet town. "Are you staying at the inn?"

"Yeah." Amused, Jason rubbed a hand over his chin. "Beantree took my bags up himself."

"Local boy makes good." She turned to look at him. It was easier somehow walking like this. Odd, she realized, she'd seen the boy when she'd looked at him the first time. Now she saw the man. His hair had darkened a bit but was still very blond. It was no longer unkempt, but cut in a carelessly attractive style that had it falling over his brow. His face was still thin, hollow at the cheeks in the way that had always fascinated her. And his mouth was still full, but there was a hardness around it that hadn't been there once. "You did make good, didn't you? You made everything you wanted happen."

"Most everything." When his eyes met hers she felt all the old longings come back. "What about you, Faith?"

She shook her head, watching the sky as she walked. "I never wanted as much as you, Jason."

"Are you happy?"

"If a person isn't, it's their own fault."

"That's too simple."

"I haven't seen the things you've seen. I haven't had to deal with what you've had to deal with. I am simple, Jason. That was the problem, wasn't it?"

"No." He turned her to face him and slid his hands up to her face. He wore no gloves, and his fingers warmed against her skin. "God, you haven't changed." As she stood very still he combed his fingers up through her hair, then down to where the tips brushed her shoulders. "I've thought about the way you look in the moonlight countless times. It was just like this."

"I've changed, Jason." But her voice was breathless. "So have you."

"Some things don't," he reminded her and gave in to the need.

When his mouth touched hers, he knew that he'd come home. Everything he remembered, everything he thought he'd lost was his again. She was soft and smelled of springtime even when snow dusted the ground around them. Her mouth was willing, even as it had been the first time he'd tasted it. He couldn't explain, even to himself, that every other woman he'd held had been nothing but a shadow of his memory of her. Now she was real, wrapped in his arms and giving him everything he'd forgotten he could have.

Just once, she promised herself as she melted against him. Just once more. How could she have known her life had such a void in it? She'd tried to close the door on the part of her life that included Jason, though she'd known it wasn't possible. She'd tried to tell herself it was only youthful passion and girlish fancy but she'd known that was a lie. There'd been no other men, only memories of one, and wishes, half-forgotten dreams.

She was holding no memory now but Jason, as real and urgent as he'd always been. Everything about him was so familiar, the taste of his lips on hers, the feel of his hair as her fingers raked through it, the scent of man, rough and rugged, that he'd always carried with him even as a boy. He murmured her name and drew her closer, as if the years were trying to separate them again.

She wrapped her arms around him, as willing, as eager and as in love as she'd been the last time he'd held her. The wind whipped around their ankles, puffing up clouds of snow while the moonlight held them close.

But it wasn't yesterday, she reminded herself as she stepped back. It wasn't tomorrow. It was today, and today had to be faced. She wasn't a child any longer without responsibilities and a love so big it overshadowed anything else. She was a woman with a child to raise and a home to make. He was a gypsy. He'd never pretended to be anything else.

"It's over for us, Jason." But she held his hand a moment longer. "It's been over for a long time."

"No." He caught her before she could turn away. "It isn't. I told myself it was, and that I'd come back and prove it. You've been eating at me half my life, Faith. It's never going to be over."

"You left me." The tears she promised herself she wouldn't shed spilled over. "You broke my heart. It's barely had time to mend, Jason. You won't break it again."

"You know I had to leave. If you'd waited—"

"It doesn't matter now." With a shake of her head she backed away. She would never be able to explain to him why it hadn't been possible to wait. "It doesn't matter because in a few days you'll be gone again. I won't let you whirl in and out of my life and leave my emotions in chaos. We both made our choices, Jason."

"Damn it, I missed you."

She closed her eyes. When she opened them again they were dry. "I had to stop missing you. Please leave me alone, Jason. If I thought we could be friends—"

"We always were."

"Always is gone." Nonetheless she held out both hands

and took his. "Oh, Jason, you were my best friend, but I can't welcome you home because you scare the hell out of me."

"Faith." He curled his fingers around hers. "We need more time, to talk."

Looking at him, she let out a long breath. "You know where to find me, Jason. You always did."

"Let me walk you home."

"No." Calmer, she smiled. "Not this time."

From the window of his room, Jason could see most of Main Street. He could, if he chose, watch the flow of business in Porterfield's Five and Dime or the collection of people who walked through and loitered in the town square. Too often he found the direction of his gaze wandering to the white house near the end of the street. Because he'd been restless, Jason had been up and at the window when Faith had walked outside with Clara to see her off to school with a group of other children. He'd seen her crouch down to adjust the collar of her daughter's coat. And he'd seen her stand, hatless, her back to him, as she'd watched the children drag themselves off for a day of books. She'd stood there a long time with the wind pulling and tugging at her hair, and he'd waited for her to turn, to look at the inn, to acknowledge somehow that she knew he was there. But she'd walked around the side of the house to her shop without looking back.

Now, hours later, he was at the window again, still restless. From the number of people he could see walk back to the Doll House, her business was thriving. She was working, busy, while he was standing unshaven at a window with his portable typewriter sitting silent on the desk beside him.

He'd planned to work on his novel for a few days—the novel he'd promised himself he'd write. It was just one more promise he'd never been able to keep because of the demands of travel and reporting. He'd expected to be able to work here, in the quiet, settled town of his youth away from the demands of journalism and the fast pace he'd set for himself. He'd expected a lot of things. What he hadn't expected was to find himself just as wildly in love with Faith as he'd been at twenty.

Jason turned away from the window and stared at his typewriter. The papers were there, notes bulging in manila envelopes, the half-finished manuscript pages. He could sit down and make himself work through the day into the night. He had the discipline for it. But in his life there was more than a book that was half-finished. He was just coming to realize it.

By the time he'd shaved and dressed, it was past noon. He thought briefly about walking across the street to Mindy's to see if she still served the best homemade soup in town. But he didn't feel like chatty counter talk. Deliberately he turned south, away from Faith. He wouldn't make a fool of himself by chasing after her.

As he walked, he passed a half a dozen people he knew. He was greeted with thumps on the back, handshakes and avid curiosity. He'd strolled down the Left Bank, up Carnaby Street and along the narrow streets of Venice. After a decade of absence he found the walk down Main Street just as fascinating. There was a barber pole that swirled up and around and back into itself. A life-size cardboard Santa stood outside a dress shop gesturing passersby inside.

Spotting a display of poinsettias, Jason slipped into the store and bought the biggest one he could carry. The saleswoman had been in his graduating class and detained him for ten minutes before he could escape. He'd expected questions, but he hadn't guessed that he'd become the town celebrity. Amused, he made his way down the street as he had countless times before. When he reached the Widow Marchant's, he didn't bother with the front door. Following an old habit, he went around the back and knocked on the storm door. It still rattled. It was a small thing that pleased him enormously.

When the widow opened the door, and her little bird's eyes peered through the bright-red leaves of the flowers, he found himself grinning like a ten-year-old.

"It's about time," she said as she let him in. "Wipe your feet."

"Yes, ma'am." Jason scrubbed his boots against the rough mat before he set down the poinsettia on her kitchen table.

No more than five feet tall, the widow stood with her hands on her hips. She was bent a bit with age and her face was a melody of lines and wrinkles. The bib apron she wore was covered with flour. Jason smelled cookies in the oven and heard the majestic sound of classical music from the living-room speakers. The widow nodded at the flowers.

"You always went for the big statement." When she turned to look him up and down, Jason found himself automatically standing tall. "Put on a few pounds I see, but more wouldn't hurt. Come, give me a kiss."

He bent to peck her cheek dutifully, then found himself

gathering her close. She felt frail; he hadn't realized it by looking at her, but she still smelled of all the good things he remembered—soap and powder and warm sugar.

"You don't seem surprised to see me," he murmured as he straightened up.

"I knew you were here." She turned to fuss at the oven because her eyes had filled. "I knew before the ink dried where you signed the registration at the inn. Sit down and take off your coat. I have to get these cookies out."

He sat quietly while she worked and absorbed the feeling of home. It was here he'd always been able to come as a child and feel safe. While he watched, she began to heat chocolate in a dented little pan on the stove.

"How long you staying?"

"I don't know. I'm supposed to be in Hong Kong in a couple of weeks."

"Hong Kong." The widow pursed her lips as she arranged cookies on a plate. "You've been to all your places, Jason. Were they as exciting as you thought?"

"Some were." He stretched out his legs. He'd forgotten what it was to relax, body, soul and mind. "Some weren't."

"Now you've come home." She walked over to put the cookies on the table. "Why?"

He could be evasive with anyone else. He could even lie to himself. But with her there could only be the truth. "Faith."

"It always was." Back at the stove, she stirred the chocolate. He'd been a troubled boy, now he was a troubled man. "You heard she married Tom."

And with her, he didn't have to hide the bitterness. "Six months after I left I called. I'd landed a job with *Today's News*. They were sending me to a hole in the wall in Chicago, but it was something. I called Faith, but I got her mother. She was very kind, even sympathetic when she told me that Faith was married, had been married for three months and was going to have a baby. I hung up, I got drunk. In the morning I went to Chicago." He plucked a cookie from the plate and shrugged. "Life goes on, right?"

"It does, whether it tows us along with it or rolls right over us. And now that you know she's divorced?"

"We promised each other something. She married someone else."

She made a sound like steam escaping from a kettle. "You're a man now from the looks of you, not a bullheaded boy. Faith Kirkpatrick—"

"Faith Monroe," he reminded her.

"All right then." Patiently, she poured heated chocolate into mugs. After she set them on the table, she seated herself with a quiet wheeze. "Faith is a strong, beautiful woman inside and out. She's raising that little girl all alone and doing a good job of it. She's started a business and she's making it work. Alone. I know something about being alone."

"If she'd waited—"

"Well, she didn't. Whatever thoughts I have about her reasons I'm keeping to myself."

"Why did she divorce Tom?"

The old woman sat back, resting her elbows on the worn arms of her chair. "He left her and the baby when Clara was six months old."

His fingers tightened around the handle of the mug. "What do you mean, he left her?"

"You should know the meaning. You did so yourself." She picked up her chocolate and held it in both hands. "I mean he packed his bags and left. She had the house—and the bills. He cleaned out the bank account and headed west."

"But he has a daughter."

"He hasn't laid eyes on the girl since she was in diapers. Faith pulled herself out. She had the child to think of after all, if not herself. Her parents stood behind her. They're good people. She took a loan and started the doll business. We're proud to have her here."

He stared out the window to where the boughs of an old sycamore spread, dripping with snow and ice. "So I left, she married Tom, then he left. Seems Faith has a habit of picking the wrong men."

"Think so?"

He'd forgotten how dry her voice could be and nearly smiled. "Clara looks like Faith."

"Hmm. She favors her mother." The widow smiled into her mug. "I've always been able to see her father in her. Your chocolate's getting cold, Jason."

Absently, he sipped. With the taste came floods of memories. "I hadn't expected to feel at home here again. It's funny. I don't think I felt at home when I lived here, but now…"

"You haven't been by your old place yet?"

"No."

"There's a nice couple in there now. They put a porch on the back."

It meant nothing to him. "It was never home." He set the chocolate down and took her hand. "This was. I never knew any mother but you."

Her hand, thin, dry as paper, gripped his. "Your father was a hard man, harder maybe because he lost your mother so young."

"I only felt relief when he died. I can't even be sorry for it. Maybe that's why I left when I did. With him gone, the house gone, it seemed the time was right."

"Maybe it was, for you. Maybe the time's right to come back again. You weren't a good boy, Jason. But you weren't so bad, either. Give yourself some of that time you were always so desperate to beat ten years ago."

"And Faith?"

She sat back again. "As I recall, you never did much courting. Seems to me the girl chased after you with her eyes wide open. A man who's been all the places you been oughta know how to court a woman. Probably picked up some of those fancy languages."

He picked up a cookie and bit into it. "A phrase or two."

"Never knew a woman who wouldn't flutter a bit with some fancy language."

Leaning over he kissed both her hands. "I missed you."

"I knew you'd come back. At my age, you know how to wait. Go find your girl."

"I think I might." Rising, he slipped into his coat. "I'll come back and visit again."

"See that you do." She waited until he opened the door. "Jason—button your coat." She didn't pull out her handkerchief until she heard the door close behind him.

Chapter 4

The sun was high and bright when he stepped outside. Across the street a snowman was rapidly losing weight. He found the streets as he'd found them yesterday on his drive in—full of children fresh out of school. He felt the surge of freedom himself. As he headed north, he saw a girl break away from a group of children and come toward him. Even bundled in hat and scarf he recognized Clara.

"'Scuse me. Did you use to live here?"

"That's right." He wanted to tuck her hair into her cap but stopped himself.

"My mother said you did. Today in school, the teacher said you went away and got famous."

He couldn't stop the grin. "Well, I went away."

"And you won a prize. Like Marcie's brother won a trophy for bowling."

He thought of his Pulitzer and managed, barely, not to laugh. "Something like that."

To Clara he looked like a regular person, not someone who bounded around the world on adventures. Her eyes narrowed. "Did you really go to all those places like they said?"

"That depends on what they said." In tacit agreement they began to walk together. "I've been to some places."

"Like Tokyo? That's the capital of Japan, we learned that in school."

"Like Tokyo."

"Did you eat raw fish?"

"Now and again."

"That's really disgusting." But she seemed pleased all the same. She bent and scooped up snow without breaking rhythm. "Do they squish grapes with their feet in France?"

"I can't say I ever saw it for myself, but I've heard tell."

"I sure wouldn't drink it after that. Did you ever ride a camel?"

He watched her bullet the snowball into the base of a tree. "As a matter of fact, I did."

"What was it like?"

"Uncomfortable."

It was a description she readily accepted because she'd already figured it out for herself. "The teacher read one of your stories today. The one about this tomb they found in China. Did you see the statues?"

"Yes, I did."

"Was it like *Raiders?*"

"Like what?"

"You know, the movie with Indiana Jones."

It took him a minute, then he laughed. Without thinking he tipped her cap over her eyes. "I guess it was, a little."

"You write good."

"Thank you."

They were standing on the sidewalk in front of her house. Jason glanced up, surprised. He hadn't realized they'd come so far and found himself regretting he hadn't slowed his pace a bit. "We have to do this report on Africa." Clara wrinkled her nose. "It has to be five whole pages long. Miss Jenkins wants it in right after Christmas vacation."

"How long have you had the assignment?" It hadn't been that long since his school days.

Clara drew a circle in the snow at the edge of her lawn. "Couple of weeks."

No, he realized with some pleasure, it hadn't been so very long. "I guess you've started on it."

"Well, sort of." Then she turned that quick, beautiful smile on him. "You've been to Africa, haven't you?"

"A couple of times."

"I guess you know all kinds of things about climate and culture and stuff like that."

He grinned down at her. "Enough."

"Maybe you should stay for dinner tonight." Without giving him a chance to answer, she took his hand and led him around to the shop.

When they walked in, Faith was boxing a doll. Her hair was pinned up in the back and she wore a baggy sweatshirt over jeans. She was laughing at something her customer had said. "Lorna, you know you wouldn't have it any other way."

"Bah, humbug." The woman put a hand on her enormous stomach and sighed. "I really wanted this baby to make an appearance before Christmas."

"You still have four days."

"Hi, Mom!"

Faith turned to smile at her daughter. As she spotted Jason the spool of ribbon in her hand spun in a red stream to the floor. "Clara, you didn't wipe your feet," she managed to say, but kept her eyes on Jason.

"Jason! Jason Law." The woman rushed over and grabbed him by both arms. "It's Lorna—Lorna McBee."

He looked down into the pretty round face of his longtime neighbor. "Hello, Lorna." His gaze drifted down, then back up. "Congratulations."

With a hand on her stomach she laughed. "Thanks, but it's my third."

He thought of the scrawny, bad-tempered girl next door. "Three? You work fast."

"So does Bill. You remember Bill Easterday, don't you?"

"You married Bill?" He remembered a boy who had hung out in the town square looking for trouble. A few times Jason had helped him find it.

"I reformed him." When she smiled, he believed it. "He runs the bank." His expression had her giggling. "I'm serious, stop in sometime. Well, I've got to be moving along. This box has to go into a locked closet before my oldest girl sees it. Thanks, Faith, it's just lovely."

"I hope she likes it."

To keep her hands busy, Faith began to rewind the spool of ribbon. A puff of cold air came in, then was cut off as Lorna breezed out.

"Was that the bride doll?" Clara wanted to know.

"Yes, it was."

"Too fussy. Can I go over to Marcie's?"

"What about homework?"

"I don't have any except that dumb Africa report. He's going to help me." Jason met her smile with a lifted brow. "Aren't you?"

Jason would have dared any man within a hundred miles to resist that look. "Yes, I am."

"Clara, you can't—"

"It's okay 'cause I asked him to dinner." She beamed, almost sure her mother would be trapped by the good manners she was always talking about. "There's no school now for ten whole days so I can do the report after dinner, can't I?"

Jason decided it wouldn't hurt to apply a little pressure from his side. "I spent six weeks in Africa once. Clara might just get an A."

"She could use it," Faith muttered. They stood together, looking at her. Her heart already belonged to both of them. "I guess I'd better start dinner."

Clara was already racing across the yard next door before Faith pulled the door of the Doll House shut and turned the sign around to read Closed.

"I'm sorry if she was a nuisance, Jason. She has a habit of badgering people with questions."

"I like her," he said simply and watched Faith fumble with the latch.

"That's nice of you, but you don't have to feel obliged to help her with this report."

"I said I would. I keep my word, Faith." He touched a pin in her hair. "Sooner or later."

She had to look at him then. It was impossible not to. "You're welcome to dinner, of course." Her fingers worried the buttons of her coat as she spoke. "I was just going to fry chicken."

"I'll give you a hand."

"No, that's not—"

He cut her off when he closed his fingers over hers. "I never used to make you nervous."

With an effort, she steadied herself. "No, you didn't." He'd be gone again in a few days, she reminded herself. Out of her life. Maybe she should take whatever time she was given. "All right then, you can help."

He took her arm as they crossed the lawn. Though he felt her initial resistance, he ignored it. "I went to see Widow Marchant. I had cookies right from the oven."

Faith relaxed as she pushed open the door of her own kitchen. "She has every word you've ever written."

The kitchen was twice the size of the one he'd just left and there were signs of a child in the pictures hanging on the front of the refrigerator and a pair of fuzzy slippers kicked into a corner. Moving with habit, Faith switched on the burner under the kettle before she slipped out of her coat. She hung it on a peg by the door, then turned to take his. His hands closed over hers.

"You didn't tell me Tom left you."

She'd known it wouldn't take him long to hear it, or long to question. "It's not something I think about on a daily basis. Coffee?"

She draped his coat over a hook and turned to find him blocking her way. "What happened, Faith?"

"We made a mistake." She said it calmly, even coolly. It was a tone he'd never heard from her before.

"But there was Clara."

"Don't." Fury came into her eyes quickly and simmered there. "Leave it alone, Jason, I mean it. Clara's my business. My marriage and divorce are my business. You can't expect to come back now and have all the answers."

They stood a moment, facing each other in silence. When the kettle let out a whistle, she seemed to breathe again. "If you want to help, you can peel some potatoes. They're in the pantry over there."

She worked systematically, he thought angrily, as she poured oil to heat in a skillet and coated chicken. Her temper was nothing new to him. He'd felt the brunt of it before, sometimes deflecting it, sometimes meeting it head-on. He also knew how to soothe it. He began talking, almost to himself at first, about some of the places he'd been. When he told her about waking with a snake curled next to his head while he'd been camping in South America she laughed.

"I didn't find it too funny at the time. I was out of the tent in five seconds flat, buck naked. My photographer got a very interesting roll of pictures. I had to pay him fifty to get the negatives."

"I'm sure they were worth more. You didn't mention the snake in your series on San Salvador."

"No." Interested, he put down his paring knife. "You read it?"

She arranged chicken in the hot oil. "Of course. I've read all your stories."

He took the potatoes to the sink to wash them. "All of them?"

She smiled at the tone but kept her back to him. "Don't let your ego loose, Jason. It was always your biggest problem. I'd estimate that ninety percent of the people in Quiet

Valley have read all your stories. You might say we all feel we have a stake in you." She adjusted the flame. "After all, no one else around here's had dinner at the White House."

"The soup was thin."

Chuckling, she put a pan of water on the stove and dumped in the potatoes. "I guess you just have to take the good with the bad—so to speak. I saw a picture of you a couple of years ago." She adjusted a pin in her hair and her voice was bland. "I think it was taken in New York, at some glitzy charity function. You had a half-naked woman on your arm."

He rocked back on his heels. "Did I?"

"Well, she wasn't actually half-naked," Faith temporized. "I suppose it just seemed that way because she had so much more hair than dress. Blond—very blond if my memory serves me. And let's say—top-heavy."

He ran his tongue around his teeth. "You meet a lot of interesting people in my business."

"Obviously." With the efficiency born of habit she turned chicken. Oil hissed. "I'm sure you find it very stimulating."

"Not as stimulating as this conversation."

"If you can't stand the heat," she murmured.

"Yeah. It's getting dark. Shouldn't Clara be home?"

"She's right next door. She knows to be home by five-thirty."

He went to the window anyway and glanced at the house next door. Faith studied his profile. It was stronger now, tougher. She supposed he was, too, had had to be. How much was left of the boy she'd loved so desperately? Maybe it was something neither of them could be sure of.

"I thought of you a lot, Faith." Though his back was to

her she could almost feel the words brush over her skin. "But especially at this time of year. I could usually block you out when I had work to do, deadlines to meet, but at Christmas you wouldn't let go. I remember every one we spent together, the way you'd drag me through the shops. Those few years with you made up for all the times as a kid I woke up to nothing."

The old sympathy welled up. "Your father couldn't face the holidays, Jason. He just couldn't handle it without your mother."

"I understand that better now. After losing you." He turned back. She wasn't looking at him now but bent industriously over the stove. "You've been spending Christmas alone, too."

"No, I have Clara."

She tensed as he walked to her. "No one to fill the stockings with you, or share secrets about what's under the tree."

"I manage. You have to alter life to suit yourself."

"Yeah." He took her chin in his hand. "I'm beginning to believe it."

The door slammed open. Wet and beaming, Clara stood dripping on the mat. "We made angels in the snow."

Faith raised a brow. "So I see. Well, you've got fifteen minutes to get out of those wet things and set the table."

She struggled out of her coat. "Can I turn on the tree?"

"Go ahead."

"Come on." Clara held out a hand for Jason. "It's the best one on the block."

Emotions humming, Faith watched them walk out together.

Chapter 5

They were still humming when the meal was over. She knew her daughter was a friendly, sometimes outrageously open child, but Clara had taken to Jason like a long-lost friend. She chattered away at him as though she'd known him for years.

It's so obvious, Faith thought as she watched Clara stack dishes. Neither of them noticed. What would she do if they did? She didn't believe in lies, yet she'd been forced to live one.

The other two paid little attention to her as they settled down with Clara's books. In the easy, flowing style he'd been born with, Jason began to tell her stories about Africa—the desert, the mountains, the thick green jungle that teemed with its own life and its own dangers.

As their heads bent together over a picture in Clara's book Faith felt a flood of panic. "I'm going to go next door," she said on impulse. "I have a lot of work backed up."

"Mmm-hmm." With that, Jason dismissed her. A laugh

bubbled in her throat until it ached. Grabbing her coat, Faith escaped.

They were more than toys to her. They were certainly more than a business. To Faith the dolls who filled her shop were the symbol of youth, of innocence, of believing in miracles. She'd wanted to open the shop soon after Clara had been born, but Tom had been adamantly set against it. Because she'd felt indebted, she'd let it pass, as she'd let so many other things pass. Then when she'd found herself alone, with a child to support, it had seemed the natural thing.

She worked long hours there, to ease the void that even the love for her daughter couldn't fill.

In her workroom behind the store were shelves filled with pieces and parts of dolls. There were china heads, plastic legs and torsos. In another section lay the ones she called the sick and injured. Dolls with broken arms or battered bodies were brought to her for repair. Though she enjoyed selling and found a great creative thrill in making her own dolls, nothing satisfied her quite so much as taking a broken toy that was loved and making it whole again. She turned on the light and her radio and set to work.

It soothed her. As time passed, her nerves drained away. With crochet hook and rubber bands, with glue and painstaking care she replaced broken limbs. With a bit of paint and patience she brought smiles back to faceless dolls. Some were given new clothes or a fresh hairstyle, while others only needed a needle and thread plied by clever fingers.

By the time she picked up a battered rag doll she was humming.

"Are you going to fix that?"

Startled, she nearly stabbed herself with the needle. Jason stood in the doorway, hands in pockets, watching her. "Yes, that's what I do. Where's Clara?"

"She nearly fell asleep in her book. I put her to bed."

She started to rise. "Oh, well I—"

"She's asleep, Faith, with some green ball of hair she called Bernardo."

Determined to relax, Faith sat down again. "Yes, that's her favorite. Clara isn't much on ordinary dolls."

"Not like her mother?" Interested, he began to prowl the workroom. "I always thought when a toy broke or wore out it got tossed away."

"Too often. I've always thought that showed a tremendous lack of appreciation for something that's given you pleasure."

He picked up a soft plastic head, bald and smooth, that grinned at him. "Maybe you're right, but I don't see what can be done about that pile of rags in your hand."

"Quite a lot."

"Still believe in magic, Faith?"

She glanced up, and for the first time her smile was completely open, her eyes warm. "Yes, of course I do. Especially at Christmastime."

Unable to help himself he reached down to run a hand over her cheek. "I said before that I'd missed you. I don't think I realized how much."

She felt the need shimmer and the longing plead inside her. Denying both, she concentrated on the doll. "I appreciate you helping Clara, Jason. I don't want to keep you."

"Does it bother you to have someone watch you work?"

"No." She began to replace stuffing. "Sometimes a concerned mother will stay here while I doctor a patient."

He leaned a hip against the counter. "I imagined a lot of things when I was coming back. I never imagined this."

"What?"

"That I'd be standing here watching you stuff life back into a rag. You may not have noticed, but it doesn't even have a face."

"It will. How did the report go?"

"She needs to do the final draft."

Faith glanced up from her work. Her eyes were wide with the joke. "Clara?"

"She had the same reaction." Then he smiled as he leaned back. The room smelled of her. He wondered if she knew. "She's a bright kid, Faith."

"Sometimes uncomfortably so."

"You're lucky."

"I know." With quick skillful movements, she pushed the stuffing into place.

"Kids love you no matter what, don't they?"

"No." She looked at him again. "You have to earn it." With needle and thread she began to secure the seams.

"You know, she was out on her feet, but she insisted on stopping at the tree to count the presents. She tells me she had this feeling there's going to be one more."

"I'm afraid she's doomed to disappointment. Her list looked like an army requisition. I had to draw the line." Putting down the thread, she picked up her paintbrush. "My parents already spoil her."

"They still live in town?"

"Mmm-hmm." She'd already gotten a sense of the doll's

personality as she'd worked with it. Now, she began to paint it on. "They mumble about Florida from time to time, but I don't know if they'll ever go. It's Clara. They just adore her. You might go by and see them, Jason. You know my mother was always fond of you."

He examined a slinky red dress no bigger than his palm. "Your father wasn't."

She grinned at that. "He just didn't quite trust you." She sent him a quick, saucy smile. "What father would have?"

"He had good reason." As he walked toward her, he saw the doll she held. "I'll be damned." Charmed, he took it, holding it under the light. What had been a misshapen pile of rags was now a plump, sassy doll. Exaggerated lashes spiked out from wide eyes. Curls had been sewn back into place so that they fell teasingly over the brow. It was soft, friendly and pretty as a picture. Even a full grown man could recognize what would make a small girl smile.

She felt a ridiculous sense of accomplishment at seeing him smile at her work. "You approve?"

"I'm impressed. How much do you sell something like this for?"

"This one's not for sale." Faith set it in a large box at the back of the room. "There are about a dozen little girls in town whose families can't afford much of a Christmas. There are boys, too, of course, but Jake over at the five-and-dime and I worked a deal a few years back. On Christmas Eve, a box is left on the doorstep. The girls get a doll, the boys a truck or a ball or whatever."

He should have known. It was so typical of her, so much what she was. "Santa lives."

She turned to smile at him. "He does in Quiet Valley."

It was the smile that did it. It was so open, so familiar. Jason closed the distance between them before either of them realized it.

"What about you? Do you get what you want for Christmas?"

"I have everything I need."

"Everything?" His hands cupped her face. "Aren't you the one who used to dream? Who always believed in wishes?"

"I've grown up. Jason, you should go now."

"I don't believe that. I don't believe you've stopped dreaming, Faith. Just being with you makes me start again."

"Jason." She pressed her hands to his chest, knowing she had to stop what could never be finished. "You know we can't always have what we want. You'll leave in a few days. You can walk away and go on to a hundred other things, a hundred other places."

"What does that have to do with right now? It's always right now, Faith." He drew his hands through her hair so that pins scattered. Rich warm sable tumbled over his fingers. He'd always loved the feel of it, the smell of it. "You're the only one," he murmured. "You've always been the only one."

She closed her eyes before he could draw her close. "You'll go. I have to stay here. Once before I stood and watched you walk away. I don't think I can bear it if I let you in again. Can't you understand?"

"I don't know. I know I understand I want you so much more now than I ever did. I'm not sure you can keep me out, Faith." But he backed away, for both of them. "Not for long anyway. You said before I didn't have a right to all the answers. Maybe that's true. But I need one."

It was a reprieve, it was space to think. She let out a long breath and nodded. "All right. But you promise that you'll go now if I answer?"

"I'll go. Did you love him?"

She couldn't lie. It wasn't in her. So her eyes were direct and pride kept her chin high. "I never loved anyone but you."

It came into his eyes—triumph, fury. He reached for her but she pulled away. "You said you'd go, Jason. I trusted your word."

She had him trapped. She had him aching. "You should've trusted it ten years ago." He swung from the workroom and into the frigid night.

Chapter 6

Quiet Valley bustled with Christmas energy. From a jerry-rigged loudspeaker on top of the hardware store roof carols rang out. An enterprising young man from a neighboring farm got a permit and gave buggy rides up and down Main Street. Kids, keyed up with lack of school and anticipation, shouted and raced on every corner. The skies had clouded over, but the snow held off.

Jason sat at the counter in the diner and sipped coffee while he listened to town gossip. Word was the Hennessys' oldest had the chicken pox and would be scratching himself through the holidays. Carlotta's was selling Christmas trees at half price and the hardware store had a sale on ten-speeds.

Ten years before Jason would have found the conversations mundane. Now he sat content, sipping his coffee and listening. Maybe this was what had been missing from the novel he'd been trying to write for so long. He'd been around the world, but everything had always been so fast paced, so urgent. There had been times when his life as well as his story had been on the line. You didn't think about it when it was happening. You couldn't. But now, sitting in the warm diner with the scent of coffee and frying bacon he could look back.

He'd taken assignments, a great many of them dangerous, because he hadn't given a damn. He'd already lost the part of himself he'd valued. It was true that over the years he'd built something back, inch by gritty inch, but he'd never found the whole—because he'd left it here, where he'd grown up. Now he just had to figure out what the hell to do with it.

"Guess they serve almost anybody in here."

Jason glanced up idly then grinned. "Paul. Paul Tydings." His hand was gripped by two enormous ones.

"Damn it, Jas, you're as good-looking and skinny as ever."

Jason took a long look at his oldest friend. Paul's hair was thick and curly around a full, ruddy face offset now by a bushy moustache. His bull-like frame had assured him a starting place on the offensive line. Over the years, it had thickened into what was politely termed a successful build. "Well," Jason decided. "You're as good-looking."

With a roar of laughter, Paul slapped him on the back. "I never expected to see you back here."

"Nor I you. I thought you were in Boston."

"Was. Made myself some money, got married."

"No kidding? How long?"

"Seven years come spring. Five kids."

Jason choked on his coffee. "Five?"

"Three and a set of twins. Anyway, I brought my wife back for a visit six years ago and she fell in love. Had a jewelry store in Manchester, so I opened one here, too. I guess I've got you to thank for a lot of it."

"Me? Why?"

"You were always filling my head with ideas. Then you took off. It made me think I should try my hand at seeing a few places. In about a year I was working in this jewelry store in Boston and in walks the prettiest little thing I ever laid eyes on. I was so flustered I never imprinted her credit card. She came back the next day with the blank receipt and saved my job. Then she saved my life and married me. Never even would have met her if it hadn't been for you talking about all the places there were to see." Paul nodded as his coffee was served. "Guess you've seen Faith."

"Yeah, I've seen her."

"Throw a lot of business her way being as three of my kids are girls and all of 'em are brats." He grinned and added two packages of sugar to his coffee. "She's as pretty as she was when she was sixteen and dancing in the town hall. Settling in this time, Jason?"

With a half laugh he pushed his cooling coffee aside. "Maybe."

"Come by the house and meet the family, will you? We're just south of town, the two-story stone place."

"I saw it driving in."

"Then don't go out again without coming in. A man doesn't have many friends who go back to red wagons with him, Jason. You know—" he glanced at his watch "—seems to me Faith breaks for lunch about now. I've got to get back." With a last slap on the back, Paul left him at the counter.

Thoughtfully, Jason sipped at his coffee. He'd been away ten years, a long time by any standard, yet everyone in town he ran into saw him and Faith as a couple. It seemed it was easy to blink away a decade. Easy for everyone, he added, but for himself and Faith. Maybe he could brush away the years, the time lost, but how could he ignore her marriage and her child?

He still wanted her. That hadn't changed. He still hurt. That hadn't eased. But how did she feel? She'd told him the night before that she'd never loved another man. Did that mean she still loved him? Jason dropped a bill on the counter and rose. There was only one way to find out. He'd ask her.

The Doll House was crowded with children. Noisy children. When Jason walked in shouts and laughter bounced off the walls. Helium-filled balloons hugged the ceiling and cookie crumbs littered the floor. In the doorway of the workroom was a tall cardboard castle. Just in front of a shiny white curtain stood a puppet of Santa Claus and a green-suited elf. With a lot of chatter and exaggerated effort, they loaded a glittering golden sleigh with colorful boxes. Twice the elf fell on his face while lifting a box and sent the children into peals of laughter. After a great deal of confusion, all the presents were loaded. With a belly-bursting *Ho-ho-ho!* Santa climbed into the sleigh. Bells jingling, it rocked its way through the curtain.

To the clatter of applause, a series of puppets crossed

the stage for bows. Jason saw Mrs. Claus, two elves and a reindeer with a telltale red nose before Santa took the stage with a ringing "Merry Christmas!" He didn't even realize he was leaning back against the door and grinning when Faith popped around the castle for a bow of her own.

But she saw him. Feeling foolish, she took another bow as the children clambered up. With the ease of a veteran kindergarten teacher, she maneuvered them toward the punch and cookies.

"Very impressive," Jason murmured in her ear. "I'm sorry I missed most of the show."

"It's not much." She combed her fingers through her hair. "I've been doing it for years now without much variation." She glanced over at the group of children. "It doesn't seem to matter."

"I'd say it does." He took her hand and brought it to his lips while a group of girls giggled. "Very much."

"Mrs. Monroe." A little boy with carrot-red hair and a face full of freckles tugged on her slacks. "When's Santa coming?"

Faith crouched down and smoothed at his hair. "You know, Bobby, I heard he was awfully busy this year."

His bottom lip poked out. "But he always comes."

"Well, I'm sure he'll find a way to get the presents here. I'm going to go in the back in a minute and see."

"But I have to talk to him."

The pout nearly did her in. "If he doesn't make it, you can give me a letter for him. I'll make sure he gets it."

"Problem?" Jason murmured when she straightened up again.

"Jake always plays Santa after the puppet show. We give out a few little things, it's nothing really, but the kids depend on it."

"Jake can't make it this year?"

"He caught the chicken pox from the Hennessy boy."

"I see." He hadn't celebrated Christmas in years, not since...since he'd left Faith. "I'll do it," he told her and surprised himself.

"You?"

Something in her expression made him determined to be the best St. Nick since the original. "Yeah, me. Where's the suit?"

"It's in the little room off the back, but—"

"I hope you remembered the pillows," he said before he sauntered away.

She didn't think he'd pull it off. In fact, five minutes after he walked away, Faith was sure he'd changed his mind altogether and continued out the back door. No one, including the group of kids with mouths full of cookies was more enchanted than she when Santa walked in the front door with a bag over his shoulder.

He had the chance for one booming "Merry Christmas" before he was surrounded. Too stunned to move, she watched the children bounce and jump and tug.

"Santa needs a chair." Jason sent her a long intense look that had her swallowing before her feet could move. Dashing into the back room, she brought out a high-backed chair and set it in the center of the room.

"Now you have to line up," she began, scooting children around. "Everyone gets a turn." Grabbing a bowl of candy canes, she set them on a table beside the chair. One by one, the children climbed up on Jason's knee. Faith needn't have worried. She'd had to school Jake to make the right responses, and most importantly, not to promise and risk disappointing. After the third child had climbed down, Faith relaxed. Jason was wonderful.

And having the time of his life. He'd done it just to help her out, perhaps even to impress her, but he got a great deal more. He'd never had a child sit on his lap and look at him with complete faith and love. He listened to their wishes, their confessions and complaints. Each one was allowed to reach in the sack he carried and pull out one gift.

He was hugged, kissed with sticky mouths and poked. One enterprising boy had a good grip on his beard before Jason managed to distract him. Happy, they began to file out of the shop with their parents or in groups.

"You were great." Faith turned her sign around after the last child had left to give herself a chance to catch her breath.

"Want to sit on my lap?"

Laughing, she walked to him. "I mean it, Jason, you were. I can't tell you how much I appreciate it."

"Then show me." He pulled her down onto his lap where she sank into pillows. She laughed again and kissed his nose.

"I've always been crazy about men in red suits. I wish Clara could have been here."

"Why wasn't she?"

With a little sigh, Faith let herself relax against him. "She's too old for all this now—so she tells me. She went shopping with Marcie."

"Nine's too old?"

She didn't speak for a minute, then moved her shoulders. "Kids grow up fast." She turned her head so she could look at him. "You made a lot of them happy today."

"I'd like to make you happy." Reaching up, he stroked her hair. "There was a time when I could."

"Do you ever wish we could go back?" Content, she let herself be cradled in his arms. "When we were teenagers, everything seemed so simple. Then you close your eyes for a minute and you're an adult. Oh, Jason, I wanted you to carry me away, to a castle, to a mountaintop. I was so full of romance."

He continued to stroke her hair as they sat, surrounded by dolls and the echo of children's laughter. "I didn't have enough of it, did I?"

"You had your feet on the ground, I had my head in the clouds."

"And now?"

"Now, I have a daughter to raise. It's terrifying sometimes to realize you're responsible for another life. Did you...?" She hesitated, knowing the ground was dangerous. "Did you ever want kids?"

"I haven't thought about it. Sometimes I have to go into places where it's tough enough being responsible for your own life."

She'd thought of that—had nightmares about it. "It still excites you."

He thought of some of the things he'd seen, the cruelty, the misery. "It stopped exciting me a long time ago. But I'm good at what I do."

"I suppose I always knew you would be. Jason." She

shifted again so that her eyes were level with his. "I am glad you came back."

His fingers tightened when she rested her cheek against his. "You had to wait until I was stuffed like a walrus to tell me that."

With a laugh, she wrapped her arms around his neck. "It seems to be the safest time."

"Don't bet your life on it." He pressed his lips to hers and felt hers tremble. "What's so funny?"

Choking back the laugh, she drew away. "Oh, nothing, nothing at all. I've always dreamed of being kissed by a man in a beard wearing a red hat and bells. I've got to clean up this mess."

When she rose, he hauled himself up. "The timing has to click sooner or later." She said nothing as she gathered up bits of colored paper. Jason picked up his sack and glanced inside. "There's one more box in here."

"It's for Luke Hennessy. Chicken pox."

He looked at the box, then back at her. Her hair curtained her face as she pulled a sticky candy cane from the carpet. "Where does he live?"

Still holding the candy, she stood up. Some might say he looked foolish, padded from chest to hips, wrapped in red and with his face half-concealed by a curly white beard. Faith thought he'd never looked more wonderful. She walked to him to pull the beard down to his chin. Her arms went around him, her mouth found his.

Her kiss was warm as it always was, full of hope and simple goodness. Desire raced through him and settled into sweet contentment. "Thank you." She kissed him again in friendship. "He lives on the corner of Elm and Sweetbriar."

He waited a moment until he was steady. "Can I get a cup of coffee when I get back?"

"Yeah." She adjusted his beard again. "I'll be next door."

Chapter 7

He had to admit, it had given him a kick to walk through town. Kids flocked after him. Adults called out and waved. He was offered uncountable cookies. The biggest satisfaction had been the awe on the young Hennessy boy's face. That had topped the wide-eyed shock of his mother when she'd opened the door to S. Claus.

Jason took his time walking back, strolling through the square. It was strange, he discovered, how easy it was to take on the personality of a set of clothes. He felt…well, benevolent. If anyone he'd ever worked with had seen him now, they'd have fallen into the snow in a dead faint. Jason Law had a reputation for being impatient, brutally frank and quick-tempered. He hadn't won the Pulitzer for benevolence. Yet somehow, at the moment, he felt more satisfaction in the polyester beard and dime-store bells than he did with all the awards he'd ever earned.

He was ho-hoing his way along when Clara stepped out

of the five-and-dime. She and the little brunette at her side went off in peals of giggles.

"But you're—"

One narrow-eyed stare from Jason did the trick. Cutting herself off, Clara cleared her throat and offered her hand. "How do you do, Santa?"

"I do very well, Clara."

"That's not Jake," Marcie informed Clara. She stepped closer to try to recognize the face behind the puffs of white.

Enjoying himself, Jason sent her a wink. "Hello, Marcie."

The brunette's eyes widened. "How'd he know my name?" she whispered to her friend.

Clara covered another giggle with her hand. "Santa knows everything, don't you, Santa?"

"I have my sources."

"There isn't any Santa really." But Marcie's grown-up sophistication was wavering.

Jason leaned over and flicked at the fluffy ball on top of her cap. "There is in Quiet Valley," he told her and nearly believed it himself. He saw Marcie stop looking beyond the beard and accept the magic. Deciding against pressing his luck, he continued on down the street.

It wasn't easy for a fat man in a red suit to slip into a door inconspicuously, but Jason had had some experience. Once he was in the back room of Faith's shop, he shed the Santa clothes. He wanted to do it again. As Jason slipped into his own slim slacks, he realized he hadn't had so much fun in years. Part of it had been the look in Faith's eyes, the way she'd warmed to him, if only briefly. Part had been the simple act of giving pleasure. How long had it been since he'd done something without an angle? On an assignment there was constant bargaining. You give me this, I'll give you that. He'd had to toughen himself against sympathy, against compassion to find the truth and report it. If his style had a hard edge, it was because he'd always gone for the story that demanded it. It had helped him forget. Now that he'd come home it was impossible not to remember.

What kind of man was he really? He wasn't sure anymore, but he knew there was one woman who could make or break him. Leaving the suit in the closet, he went to find her.

She had been waiting for him. She was ready to admit she'd been waiting for him for ten years. Throughout the rest of the afternoon, Faith had made her own decisions. She'd made a success of her life. Though the search hadn't always been easy, she'd found contentment. Confidence had come with the years and she knew she could go on alone. It was time to stop being afraid of what her life would be like when Jason left again and to accept the gift she'd been offered. He was here, now, and she loved him.

When he came into the house he found her curled in a chair by the tree, her cheek resting on the arm. She waited until he came to her. "Sometimes at night I sit like this. Clara's asleep upstairs and the house is quiet. I can think about little things, enormous things, just as I did as a child. The lights all blend together and the tree smells like heaven. You can go anywhere, sitting just like this."

He picked her up, felt her yield, then settled in the chair with her on his lap. "I remember sitting like this with you at Christmastime in your parents' house. Your father grumbled."

She snuggled close. There was no padding now, just the

long lean body she knew so well. "My mother dragged him into the kitchen so we could be alone for a little while. She knew you didn't have a tree at home."

"Or anything else."

"I never asked where you live now, Jason, whether you found a place that makes you happy."

"I move around a lot. I have a base in New York."

"A base?"

"An apartment."

"It doesn't sound like a home," she murmured. "Do you put a tree in the window at Christmas?"

"I guess I have once or twice, when I've been around."

It broke her heart, but she said nothing. "My mother always said you had wanderlust. Some people are born with it."

"I had to prove myself, Faith."

"To whom?"

"To myself." He rested his cheek on top of her head. "Damn it, to you."

She breathed in the scent of pine while the lights danced on the tree. They'd sat like this before, so long ago. The memories were nearly as sweet as the reality. "I never needed you to prove anything to me, Jason."

"Maybe that's one of the reasons I had to. You were too good for me."

"That's ridiculous." She would have shifted, but he held her still.

"You were, and still are." He, too, stared at the tree. The tinsel shimmered in the lights like the magic he'd always wanted to give her. "Maybe that's why I had to leave when I did—maybe it's why I came back. You're all the good things,

Faith. Just being with you brings out the best parts of me. God knows, there aren't many."

"You were always too hard on yourself. I don't like it." This time she did shift so that her hands were on his shoulders and her eyes were directly on his. "I fell in love with you. There were reasons for it. You were kind though you pretended not to be. You wanted to be considered tough and a troublemaker because you felt safer that way."

He smiled and ran a finger down her cheek. "I was a troublemaker."

"Maybe I liked that, too. You didn't just accept things, you weren't afraid to question."

"I nearly got kicked out of school twice because I questioned."

The old anger stirred. Had no one understood him but herself? Had no one else been able to see what had been racing and straining inside him? "You were smarter than anyone else. You've proved that if you needed to."

"You spent a lot of time defending me, didn't you?"

"I believed in you. I loved you."

He reached for her face in an old gesture that melted her heart. "And now?"

She had too much to say and not enough ways to say it. "Do you remember that night in June, after my Senior Prom? We drove out of town. The moon was full and the air was so sweet with summer."

"You wore a blue dress that made your eyes look like sapphires. You were so beautiful I was afraid to touch you."

"So I seduced you."

She looked so pleased with herself he laughed. "You did not."

"I certainly did. You would never have made love with

me." She touched her lips to his. "Do I have to seduce you again?"

"Faith—"

"Clara's having dinner next door at Marcie's. She's going to spend the night. Come to bed with me, Jason."

Her quiet voice raced along his skin. The touch of her hand to his cheek seared like fire. But tangled with his need for her was a love that had never grown old. "You know I want you, Faith, but we're not children now."

"We're not children." She turned her face to press her lips into his palm. "And I want you. No promises, no questions. Love me the way you did on that one beautiful night we had together." Rising, she held out her hand. "I want something for the next ten years."

With their hands linked they walked up the stairs. He pushed away all thought of the other man she'd chosen, of the other life she'd lived. He, too, would block out ten years of loss and take what was offered.

Night came early in the winter so the light was dim. In silence she lit candles so that the room glowed gold and shifted with shadows. When she turned back to him she was smiling, with all the confidence and knowledge of a woman in her eyes. Saying nothing, she came to him, lifted her mouth and offered everything.

Her fingers were steady as she reached for the buttons of his shirt. His trembled as he reached for hers. Murmuring, she waited for the brush of his hands against her skin, then sighed from the sheer glory of it. They undressed each other slowly, not tentatively, but with the quiet understanding that every moment, every instant would be treasured.

When he saw her, as slim, as lovely, as unexplainably

innocent as she'd been the first time, his head spun with needs, with doubts, with desires. But she stepped to him, pressed her body against his and dissolved all choices. She was stronger than she'd been. He could feel it, not in muscle but in spirit. Perhaps she had changed, but the longings that were racing through him were the same as they'd been in the boy on the brink of manhood. As heedlessly as the children they'd once been, they tumbled onto the bed.

They didn't relive the experience. It was as fresh, as wildly thrilling as the first time. But they were man and woman now, more demanding, hungrier. She drew him closer, running her hands over him with an urgency just discovered, with a turbulence just released. She'd waited so long, so very long and wouldn't wait a moment longer.

But he took her hand and brought it to his lips. He quieted her tumbling breath with his mouth.

"I hardly knew what to do with you the first time." Gently he nuzzled at her throat until she moaned in frenzied anticipation. Raising his head, he smiled at her. "Now I do."

Then he took her places she'd never been. Higher, still higher he drew her, then just as suddenly plunged her deep where the air was thick and dark. Trapped in the whirlwind, she clung. She'd wanted to give, but he left her helpless. Tender, soft, easy, his fingers caressed until her body shuddered. He drank in her sigh with lips abruptly urgent, ruthlessly demanding, then patiently soothed her again. Sensations rocketed inside her, leaving no room for thought, for reason or even for memories.

When they came together it was everything for both of them. Time didn't slip back but trapped them and held them close in the here and now.

He kept his arms tightly around her and they were quiet. With her eyes closed, she absorbed the unity. She loved, and for the moment there was nothing else. For him both ecstasy and contentment were troubled with questions. She was so warm, so free with her emotions. She loved him. He needed no words to know it and never had. But the loyalty he'd always understood as an intrinsic part of her had been broken. How could he rest without knowing why?

"I have to know why we lost ten years, Faith." When she said nothing, he turned her head toward him. Her eyes glistened in the shifting light but the tears didn't fall. "Now more than ever I have to know."

"No questions, Jason. Not tonight."

"I've waited long enough. We've waited long enough."

On a long breath, she sat up. Bringing her knees to her chest, she wrapped her arms around them. Her hair cascaded down her back. He couldn't resist taking a handful. She'd been his once, completely. No one else had ever touched her as he had. He knew he had to accept her marriage, and that her child belonged to another man, but he needed to understand first why she had turned to someone else so soon after he'd gone away.

"Give me something, Faith. Anything."

"We loved each other, Jason, but we wanted different things." She turned her head to look at him. "We still want different things." She took his hand and brought it to her cheek. "If you had let me I would have gone anywhere with you. I would have left my home, my family and never looked back. You needed to go alone."

"I didn't have anything for you," he began. She stopped him with a look.

"You never gave me a choice."

He reached for her once more. "If I gave you one now?"

She closed her eyes and let her forehead rest on his. "Now I have a child, and she has a home I can't take away from her. What I want doesn't come first." She drew back far enough to look at him. "What you want can't come first. Before somehow I never thought you'd really go. This time I know you will. Let's just take what we have, give each other this one Christmas. Please."

She closed her mouth over his and stopped all questions.

Chapter 8

Christmas Eve was magic. Faith had always believed it. When she awoke with Jason beside her, it was more than magic. For a while, she simply lay there, watching him sleep. She'd imagined it before, as a girl, as a woman, but now she didn't need the dreams. He was here beside her, warm, quiet, and outside an early-morning snow was falling. Careful not to wake him, Faith slipped out of bed.

When he rolled over, he smelled her—the springtime scent her hair had left on the pillowcase. For a few minutes, he lay still and let it seep into his system. Content, he lay back and looked at the room he hadn't been able to see in the dark.

The walls were papered, ivory, with little sprigs of violets. At the windows were fussy priscillas. There was an antique rosewood bureau cluttered with colored bottles and boxes. On a vanity was an old-fashioned silver-handled brush and comb. He watched the snow fall and smelled the pot-pourri on the stand beside the bed. The room was so like her—charming, fresh, and very, very feminine. A man could relax there even knowing he might find stockings draped over a chair or a blouse mixed with his shirts. He could relax there. And he wasn't letting her go again.

He smelled the coffee before he was halfway down the stairs. She had Christmas music on the stereo and bacon frying. He hadn't known it would feel so good just to walk into a kitchen and find your woman cooking for you.

"So you're up." She was wrapped from head to foot in a bright flannel robe. Desire dragged quietly at his stomach muscles. "There's coffee."

"I could smell it." He went to her. "I could smell you the moment I woke."

She rested her head on his shoulder, trying not to think that this was the way it might have been—if only. "You look as though you could have slept for hours. It's a good thing you didn't or the bacon would be cold."

"If you'd stayed in bed a few more minutes, we might have—"

"Mom! Mom! It's snowing!" Clara burst through the door and danced around the kitchen. "We're going to go caroling tonight in the hay wagon and there's snow all over the place." She stopped in front of Jason and grinned. "Hi."

"Hi yourself."

"Mom and I are going to build a snowman. She says Christmas snowmen are the best. You can help."

She hadn't known just what reaction Clara would have to finding Jason at the breakfast table. With a shake of her head, Faith began to beat eggs. She should have known Clara would be willing to accept anyone she'd decided to like. "You have to have some breakfast."

Clara fingered the plastic Santa on her lapel, tugging on the string so that the nose lit up. It never failed to please her. "I had cereal at Marcie's."

"Did you thank her mother for having you?"

"Yeah." She stopped a minute. "I think I did. Anyway we're going to build two of them and have a wedding and everything. Marcie wanted the wedding," she added to Jason.

"Clara would prefer a war."

"I figured we could have that after. Maybe I should have some hot chocolate first." She eyed the cookie jar and calculated her chances. Slim at best.

"I'll fix it. And you can have a cookie after the snowman," Faith told her without bothering to turn. "Hang your things by the door."

Scrambling out of her coat, she chattered at Jason. "You're not going back to Africa, are you? I don't think Africa would be much fun at Christmas. Marcie's mother said you'd probably be going to some other neat place."

"I'm supposed to go to Hong Kong in a few weeks." He glanced at Faith. She didn't turn. "But I'll be around for Christmas."

"Do you have a tree in your room?"

"No."

She gave him a wide-eyed look. "Well, where do you put your presents? It's not Christmas without a tree, is it, Mom?"

Faith thought of the years Jason had grown up without one. She remembered how hard he'd tried to pretend it didn't matter. "A tree's only so that we can show other people it's Christmas."

Unconvinced, Clara plopped into a chair. "Well, maybe."

"She used to say the same thing to me," Jason told Clara. "In any case, I don't think Mr. Beantree would like it if I left pine needles all over the floor."

"We've got a tree, so you can have dinner with us," Clara declared. "Mom makes this big turkey and Grandma and Grandpa come over. Grandma brings pies and we eat till we're sick."

"Sounds great." Amused, he looked over as Faith scooped eggs onto a plate. "I had Christmas dinner with your grandparents a couple of times."

"Yeah?" Interested, Clara studied him. "I guess I heard somewhere that you used to be Mom's boyfriend. How come you didn't get married?"

"Here's your hot chocolate, Clara." Faith set it down. "You'd better hurry, Marcie's waiting."

"Are you coming out?"

"Soon." Grateful that her daughter was easily distracted, she set the platter of bacon and eggs on the table. Ignoring the half-amused lift of brow from Jason, she took her seat.

"We need carrots and scarves and stuff."

"I'll take care of it."

With a grin Clara gulped down chocolate. "And hats?"

"And hats."

A snowball hit the kitchen window. Clara was up like a shot. "There she is. Gotta go. Come soon, Mom, you make the best."

"Soon as I'm dressed. Don't forget your top button."

Clara hesitated at the back door. "I've got a little plastic tree in my room. You can have it if you want."

Moved, he only stared at her. Just like her mother, he thought, and fell in love a second time. "Thanks."

"'Sokay. Bye."

"She's quite a kid," Jason commented as the door slammed behind her.

"I like her."

"I'll give her a hand with the snowman."

"You don't have to, Jason."

"I want to, then I've got some things to take care of." He checked his watch. It was only Christmas Eve for so long. When a man was being offered a second chance, it wasn't wise to waste time. "Can I get an invitation for tonight?"

Faith smiled but simply pushed the food around on her plate. "You've never needed one."

"Don't cook, I'll bring something."

"It's okay, I—"

"Don't cook," he repeated, rising. He bent to kiss her, then lingered over it. "I'll be back."

He took his coat from the hook where it had hung beside Clara's. When he was gone, Faith looked down at the toast she'd crumbled in her hand. Hong Kong. At least this time she knew where he was going.

The snow people in the side yard grinned at him as he struggled past. Boxes balanced, Jason knocked on the back door with the toe of his boot. The snow hadn't let up a whit.

"Jason." Speechless, Faith stepped back as he teetered inside.

"Where's Clara?"

"Clara?" Still staring, she pushed back her hair. "She's upstairs getting ready for the hayride."

"Good. Take the top box."

"Jason, what in the world have you got here?"

"Just take the top box unless you want pizza all over the floor."

"All right, but..." As the enormous box in his arms shifted, she laughed. "Jason, what have you done?"

"Wait a minute."

Holding the pizza, she watched him drag the box into the living room. "Jason, what is that thing?"

"It's a present." He started to set it under the tree then discovered there wasn't enough room. With a bit of rearranging, he managed to lean the box against the wall beside the tree. He was grinning when he turned to her. If he'd ever felt better in his life, he couldn't remember it. "Merry Christmas."

"Same to you. Jason, what is that box?"

"Damn, it's cold out there." Though he rubbed his hands together now, he hadn't even noticed the biting wind. "Got any coffee?"

"Jason."

"It's for Clara." He discovered that feeling a bit foolish didn't dim the warmth.

"You didn't have to get her a present," Faith began, but her curiosity got the better of her. "What is it?"

"This?" Jason patted the six-foot box. "Oh, it's nothing."

"If you don't tell me you don't get any coffee." She smiled. "And I keep the pizza."

"Spoilsport. It's a toboggan." He took Faith's arm to lead her out of the room. "She happened to mention when we were building the snowman that some kid had this toboggan and it went down Red Hill like a spitfire."

"Spitfire," Faith murmured.

"And snow like this is just made for going down Red Hill like a spitfire, so..."

"Sucker," Faith accused and kissed him hard.

"Put that pizza down and call me that again."

She laughed and kept it between them.

"Wow!"

Faith raised a brow at the noise from the living room. "I think she saw the box."

At full speed, Clara barreled into the kitchen. "Did you see? I knew there'd be one more, I just knew. It's as tall as you are," she told Jason. "Did you see?" She grabbed his hand to drag him back. "It has my name on it."

"Imagine that." Jason picked her up and kissed both cheeks. "Merry Christmas."

"I can't wait." She threw her arms around his neck and squeezed. "I just can't wait."

Watching them, Faith felt her emotions tangle and knot until her bones ached with it. What should she do? What could she do? When Jason turned with Clara, the lights from the tree fell like wishes over their faces.

"Faith?" He didn't need words to recognize distress, pain, turmoil. "What is it?"

Her hands were digging into the cardboard of the box. "Nothing. I'm going to dish out this pizza before it's cold."

"Pizza?" Delighted, Clara bounced down. "Can I have two pieces? It's Christmas."

"Monkey," Faith scolded gently, tousling her hair. "Set the table."

"What is it, Faith?" Jason took her arm before she could follow her daughter into the kitchen. "Something's wrong."

"No." She had to control herself. She'd managed everything for so long. "You overwhelmed me." With a smile she touched his face. "It's happened before. Come on, let's eat."

Because she seemed to need to keep her thoughts to herself, he let it go and followed her into the kitchen where Clara was already peeking into the cardboard box. He'd never seen a child plow through food with such unrestrained glee. He'd never known Christmas Eve could be special simply because there was someone beside him.

Clara swallowed the last of her second piece. "Maybe if I opened one present tonight there'd be less confusion in the morning."

Faith seemed to consider. "I like confusion," she decided and Jason realized the conversation was an old tradition.

"Maybe if I opened just one present tonight, I could get right to sleep. Then you wouldn't have to wait so long to creep around and fill the stockings."

"Hmm." Faith pushed aside her empty plate and enjoyed the wine Jason had brought. "I like creeping around late at night."

"If I opened—"

"Not a chance."

"If I—"

"Nope."

"But Christmas is just hours and hours away."

"Awful, isn't it?" Faith smiled at her. "And you're going caroling in ten minutes, so you'd better get your coat."

Clara walked over to tug on her boots. "Maybe when I get back, there'll be just one present that you'll figure isn't really important enough to wait until morning."

"All the presents under the tree are absolutely vital." Faith rose to help her on with her coat. "And so are the following instructions. Stay with the group. Keep your mittens on, I want you to keep all your fingers. Don't lose your hat. Remember that Mr. and Mrs. Easterday are in charge."

"Mom." Clara shifted her feet and sighed. "You treat me like a baby."

"You are my baby." Faith gave her a smacking kiss. "So there."

"Jeez, I'll be ten years old in February. That's practically tomorrow."

"And you'll still be my baby in February. Have a good time."

Clara sighed, long-suffering and misunderstood. "Okay."

"Okay," Faith mimicked. "Say good-night."

Clara peeked around her mother. "Are you going to stay until I get back?"

"Yeah."

Satisfied, she grinned and pulled open the door. "Bye."

"Monster," Faith declared and began to stack plates.

"She's terrific." Standing, Jason helped clear the clutter. "Little for her age, I guess. I didn't realize she was almost ten. It's hard to—" He stopped as Faith clattered dishes in the sink. "She'll be ten in February."

"Umm. I can't believe it myself. Sometimes it seems like yesterday, and then again…" She trailed off, abruptly breathless. With studied care, she began to fill the sink with soapy water. "I'll just be a minute here if you'd like to take your wine into the living room."

"In February." Jason took her arm. When he turned her, he saw the blood drain from her face. His fingers tightened, bruising without either of them noticing. "Ten years in February. We made love that June. God, I don't know how many times that night. I never touched you again, we never had the chance to be alone like that again before I left, just a few weeks later. You must have married Tom in September."

Her throat was dry as bone. She couldn't even swallow, but stared at him.

"She's mine," he whispered and it vibrated through the room. "Clara's mine."

She opened her mouth to speak, but there seemed to be nothing she could say. Lips trembling, eyes drenched, she nodded.

"God!" He had her by both arms, nearly lifting her off her feet before he backed her into the counter. The fury in his eyes would have made her cringe if she hadn't been willing to accept it. "How could you? Damn you, she's ours and you never told me. You married another man and had our baby. Did you lie to him, too? Did you make him think she was his so you could have your cozy house and lace curtains?"

"Jason, please—"

"I had a right." He thrust her away before he could give into the violence that pushed him on. "I had a right to her. Ten years. You stole that from me."

"No! No it wasn't like that. Jason, please! You have to listen!"

"The hell with you." He said it calmly, so calmly she stepped back as though she'd been slapped. The anger she could argue with, even reason with. Quiet rage left her helpless.

"Please, let me try to explain."

"There's nothing you can say that could make up for it. Nothing." He yanked his coat from the wall and stormed out.

"You're a damn fool, Jason Law." The Widow Marchant sat in her kitchen rocker and scowled.

"She lied to me. She's been lying for years."

"Hogwash." She fiddled with the tinsel on the little tree on the stand by the window. Cheerful strains from the Nutcracker floated in from the living room. "She did what she had to do, nothing more, nothing less."

He prowled around the room. He still wasn't sure why he'd come there instead of heading for Clancy's Bar. He'd walked in the snow for an hour, maybe more, then found himself standing on the widow's doorstep. "You knew, didn't you? You knew I was Clara's father."

"I had my ideas." The rocker squeaked gently as she moved. "She had the look of you."

That brought a peculiar thrill, one he didn't know what to do with. "She's the image of Faith."

"True enough if you don't look hard. The eyebrows are you, and the mouth. The sweet Lord knows the temperament is. Jason, if you'd known you were to be a father ten years back, what would you have done?"

"I'd have come back for her." He turned, dragging a hand through his hair. "I'd have panicked," he said more calmly. "But I'd have come back."

"I always thought so. But it—well, it's Faith's story to tell. You'd best go on back and hear it."

"It doesn't matter."

"Can't stand a martyr," she muttered.

He started to snap, then sighed instead. "It hurts. It really hurts."

"That's life for you," she said not unsympathetically. "Want to lose them both again?"

"No. God, no. But I don't know how much I can forgive."

The old woman raised both brows. "Fair enough. Give Faith the same courtesy."

Before he could speak again, the kitchen door burst open. In the doorway stood Faith, covered with snow, face washed with tears. Ignoring the wet she brought in with her, she ran to Jason. "Clara," she managed to stammer.

When he took her arms he felt the shudders. Terror flowed from her into him. "What's happened?"

"She's missing."

Chapter 9

"They're going to find her." Jason held her arm as they both stumbled through the snow to her car. "They probably have already."

"One of the kids said he thought she and Marcie went behind this farmhouse to look at the horses in the barn. But when they went back, they weren't there. It's dark." Faith fumbled with her keys.

"Let me drive."

She gave him no argument as she climbed in the passenger side. "Lorna and Bill called the sheriff from the farmhouse. Half the town's out there looking for them. But there's so much snow, and they're just little girls. Jason—"

He took her face in his hands, firmly. "We're going to find them."

"Yes." She wiped away tears with the heels of her hands. "Let's hurry."

He couldn't risk more than thirty miles an hour. They

crept down the snow-covered road, searching the landscape for any sign. The hills and fields lay pristine and undisturbed. To Faith they looked unrelenting. But while fear still overwhelmed her, she'd conquered the tears.

Ten miles out of town the fields were lit up like noonday. Groups of cars crisscrossed the road and men and women tramped through the snow calling. Jason had barely stopped when Faith was out and running toward the sheriff.

"We haven't found them yet, Faith, but we will. They won't have gone far."

"You've searched the barn and the outbuildings?"

The sheriff nodded at Jason. "Every inch."

"How about in the other direction?"

"I'm going to send some men that way."

"We'll go now."

The snow was blinding as he weaved through the other cars. He slackened his speed even more and started to pray. He'd been on a search party once in the Rockies. He hadn't forgotten what a few hours in the wind and snow could do.

"I should have made her wear another sweater." Faith gripped her hands together in her lap as she strained to see out the window. In her hurry she'd forgotten her gloves but didn't notice her numb fingers. "She hates it so when I fuss and I didn't want to spoil the evening for her. Christmas is so special for Clara. She's been so excited." Her voice broke as a ripple of fear became a wave. "I should have made her wear another sweater. She'll be— *Stop!*"

The car fishtailed as he hit the brakes. It took every ounce of control for him to deal with the swerve. Faith pushed open the door and stumbled out. "Over there, it's—"

"It's a dog." He had her by the arms before she could run across the empty field. "It's a dog, Faith."

"Oh, God." Beyond control, she collapsed against him. "She's just a little girl. Where could she be? Oh, Jason, where is she? I should have gone with her. If I'd been there she—"

"Stop it!"

"She's cold and she must be frightened."

"And she needs you." He gave her a quick shake. "She needs you."

Struggling for control, she pressed a hand to her mouth. "Yes. Yes, I'm all right. Let's go. Let's go a little further."

"You wait in the car. I'm going to walk across this field for a bit and see if I spot something."

"I'll go with you."

"I can move faster alone. I'll only be a few minutes." He started to urge her toward the car when a flash of red caught his eye. "Over there."

He gripped her arm as he tried to see through the snow. Just at the edge of the field, he saw it again.

"It's Clara." Faith was already struggling away. "She has a red coat." Snow kicked up around her as she ran. It fell cold and wet to mix with the tears that blinded her vision. With all the breath she had she called out. Arms spread wide, she caught both girls to her. "Oh, God, Clara, I've been so scared. Here, here now, you're frozen, both of you. We'll get to the car. Everything's going to be fine. Everything's all right now."

"Is my mom mad?" Shivering, Marcie wept against her shoulder.

"No, no, she's just worried. Everyone is."

"Up you go." Jason hauled Clara up in his arms. For one brief minute he gave himself the luxury of nuzzling his daughter. Looking back, he saw Faith gathering up Marcie. "Can you manage?"

She smiled, holding the still-weeping girl close. "No problem."

"Then let's go home."

"We didn't mean to get lost." Clara's tears ran down his collar.

"Of course you didn't."

"We just went to look at the horses and we got all turned around. We couldn't find anybody. I wasn't scared." Her breath hitched as she pressed against him. "Just Marcie."

His child. He felt his own vision blur as he wrapped his arms tighter around her. "You're both safe now."

"Mom was crying."

"She's okay, too." He stopped at the car. "Can you handle them both on your lap in the front? They'll be warmer."

"Absolutely." After Faith had settled in with Marcie, Jason handed her Clara. For one long moment, their gazes held over her head.

"We couldn't find the lights of the house with all the snow," Clara murmured as she held on to her mother. "Then we couldn't find the road for the longest time. It was so cold. I didn't lose my hat."

"I know, baby. Here, get your wet mittens off. You, too, Marcie. Jason has the heater turned all the way up. You'll be cooked before you know it." She ran kisses over two cold faces and fought the need to break down. "What Christmas carols did you sing?"

"'Jingle Bells,'" Marcie said with a sniffle.

"Ah, one of my favorites."

"And 'Joy to the World,'" Clara put in. The heater was pumping warm air over her hands and face. "You like that one better."

"So I do but I can't remember just how it starts. How does it start, Marcie?" She smiled at Clara and snuggled her closer.

In a thin, piping voice still wavery with tears Marcie started to sing. She was nearly through the first verse when they came to the rest of the search party.

"It's my dad!" Bouncing on Faith's lap, Marcie started to wave. "He doesn't look mad."

With a half laugh, Faith kissed the top of her head. "Merry Christmas, Marcie."

"Merry Christmas, Mrs. Monroe. See you tomorrow, Clara." Marcie barely had time to open the door before she was scooped up.

"What a night." There were waves and cheers as the car weaved through the crowd.

"It's Christmas Eve," Clara reminded her mother. The world was safe and warm again. "Maybe I should open that one big present tonight."

"Not a chance," Jason told her and tugged at her hair.

Faith turned Clara in her arms and squeezed tight.

"Don't cry, Mom."

"I have to, for just a minute." True to her word, her eyes were dry when they arrived home. An exhausted Clara dozed on Jason's shoulder as he carried her inside. "I'll take her up, Jason."

"We'll take her up."

She let her arms fall back to her sides and nodded.

They pulled off boots and socks and sweaters and wrapped Clara in warm flannel. She murmured a bit and tried to stay awake but the adventures of the evening took their toll. "It's Christmas Eve," she mumbled. "I'm going to get up real early in the morning."

"As early as you like," Faith told her as she pressed a kiss to her cheek.

"Can I have cookies for breakfast?"

"Half a dozen," Faith agreed recklessly. Clara smiled and was asleep before Faith pulled the blankets around her.

"I was afraid..." She let her hand linger on her daughter's cheek. "I was afraid I'd never see her like this again. Safe, warm. Jason, I don't know how to thank you for just being there. If I'd been alone—" She broke off and shook her head.

"I think we should go downstairs, Faith."

The tone made her press her lips together. She'd be ready, she promised herself, to handle the accusations, the bitterness, the resentment. "I think I'd like a drink," she said as they walked downstairs. "Some brandy. It looks like the fire's gone out."

"I'll take care of it. You get the brandy. There are some things I have to say."

"All right." She left him to go to the little cabinet in the dining room. When she came back, the fire was just catching. He straightened from it and took a snifter.

"Do you want to sit down?"

"No, I can't." She sipped, but it would have taken more than brandy to steady her nerves. "Whatever you have to say, Jason, you should say it."

Chapter 10

She stood looking at him, her back straight, her eyes burning with emotion, her hands clasping the snifter tightly. Part of him wanted to go to her, gather her close and just hold on. He'd found a child and nearly lost her in the same night. Did anything else matter? But inside was a void that had to be filled. Questions, demands, accusations had to be answered. There had to be an accounting before there could be understanding, and understanding before there could be forgiveness. But where did he start?

He walked to the tree. There was a star on top that shed silver light over all the other colors. "I'm not sure I know what to say. It isn't every day a man turns around and finds himself with a half-grown daughter. I feel cheated out of watching her learn to walk, hearing her talk, Faith. Nothing you can do or say can ever give that back to me, can it?"

"No."

He turned to see her holding the brandy at waist level.

Her face was very pale and calm. Whatever emotions she was feeling she managed to restrain. Yes, this was a different Faith than the one he'd left. The girl would never have been able to exert the self-control the woman did. "No excuses, Faith?"

"I guess I thought I had them, then tonight when I thought I'd lost her…" Her voice trailed off and she shook her head. "No excuses, Jason."

"She thinks Tom's her father."

"No!" Her eyes weren't calm now but brilliant. "Do you think I'd let her believe her father had deserted her, that he didn't care enough even to write? What she knows is basically the truth. I never lied to her."

"What is the truth?"

She took a steadying breath. When she looked at him her face was still pale but her voice was calm again. "That I loved her father, and he loved me, but he had to go away before he even knew about her and he wasn't able to come back."

"He would have."

Something rushed into her eyes but she turned away. "I told her that, too."

"Why?" The fury came back and he fought against it. "I have to know why you did what you did. I lost all those years."

"You?" Her temper was less easily controlled than her grief. Years of holding back bubbled inside her and burst out. "*You* lost?" she repeated as she whirled around. "You were gone and I was eighteen years old, pregnant and alone."

Guilt flared. He hadn't expected it. "I wouldn't have left if you'd told me."

"I didn't know." She put the brandy down and pushed back her hair with both hands. "It was just a week after you'd gone that I found out I was carrying our baby. I was thrilled." With a laugh, she wrapped her arms around her chest. For a moment she looked heartbreakingly young and innocent. "I was so happy. I waited every day, every night for you to call so I could tell you." Her eyes sobered. The smile faded. "But you never called, Jason."

"I needed time to set things up—a steady job, a place I could ask you to live in."

"You never understood it didn't matter where I lived, as long as it was with you." She shook her head before he could speak. "It doesn't matter now. That part's over. A week passed, then two, then a month. I got ill, just tension, morning sickness, but I began to realize you weren't going to call. You weren't coming back. I was angry for a while, acknowledging you just hadn't wanted me enough. Small-town girl."

"That's not true. That was never true."

She studied him a moment, almost dispassionately. The lights of the tree fell over his dark blond hair, glimmered in the deep, deep eyes that had always held their own secrets. Restlessness. "Wasn't it?" she murmured. "It was certainly true that you wanted out. I was part of Quiet Valley and you wanted out."

"I wanted you with me."

"But not enough to let me go with you." She shook her head when he started to speak. "Not enough to let me come to you until you'd proved the things you needed to prove. I didn't always understand that, Jason, but I began to when you came back."

"You weren't ever going to tell me about Clara, were you?"

She heard the bitterness again and closed her eyes against it. "I don't know. I honestly don't."

He drank, hoping it would warm the ice in his veins. "Tell me the rest."

"I wanted the baby, but I was scared, too scared even to tell my mother."

She picked up the brandy again but merely warmed her hands with it. "I should have of course, but I wasn't thinking clearly."

"Why did you marry Tom?" But even as he asked, he realized the old jealousies were fading. He only wanted to understand.

"Tom would come by almost every night. We'd talk. He didn't seem to mind me talking about you and God knows I needed to. Then one night we were sitting on the porch and I just broke down. I was three months pregnant and my body was changing. That morning I hadn't been able to snap my jeans." With a shaky laugh, she ran a hand over her face. "It sounds so silly, but I hadn't been able to snap my jeans and it was terrifying. It made me realize there was no going back. Everything just poured out while we sat there. He said he'd marry me. Of course I said no, but he began to reason it all out. You weren't coming back and I was pregnant. He loved me and wanted to marry me. The baby would have a name, a home, a family. It sounded so right the way he said it and I wanted the baby to be safe. I wanted to be safe."

She drank now because her throat ached. "It was wrong, right from the beginning. He knew I didn't love him, but he just wanted me, or thought he did. The first few months he tried, we both really tried. But after Clara came, he couldn't handle it. I could see every time he looked at her he thought of you. There was nothing I could do to change the fact that she was yours." She paused and found it easier to say it all. "There was nothing I would have done to change that. As long as I had her, I had part of you. Tom knew it, no matter how much I tried to be what he wanted. He started drinking, picking fights, staying out. It was as though he wanted me to ask for a divorce."

"But you didn't."

"I didn't because I…well, I felt I owed him. Then one day I came home from taking Clara out and he was gone. Divorce papers came in the mail, and that was that."

"Why didn't you ever try to contact me, Faith, through one of the magazines or newspapers?"

"And say what? Jason, remember me? By the way, you have a daughter back here in Quiet Valley. Drop in some time."

"One word—one word from you and I'd have left everything and come back. I never stopped loving you."

She closed her eyes. "I watched you walk away from me. I watched you get on the bus and leave me without a trace. I stood there for hours, half believing you'd get off at the next stop and come back. I was the one who had to stay behind, Jason."

"I called. Damn it, Faith, it only took me six months to get something started."

She smiled. "And when you called I was seven months pregnant. My mother didn't tell me for a long time, not until after Tom had left. She said you made her promise."

"I needed my pride."

"I know."

That she didn't question. He saw the way she smiled as she said it, as if she'd always understood. "You must have been terrified."

Her smile softened. "There were moments."

"You must have hated me."

"Never. How could I? You went away but you left me with the most beautiful thing in my life. Maybe you were right, maybe I was. Maybe we were both wrong, but there was Clara. Every time I looked at her, I could remember how much I loved you."

"How do you feel now?"

"Shaky." She laughed a little, then folded her hands, determined to do what was right. "Clara should be told. I'd prefer doing it myself."

The idea made him reach for the brandy again. "How do you think she'll take it?"

"She's learned to get along without a father. It doesn't mean she hasn't needed one." She sat up straight and raised her chin. "You have a right, of course, to see her whenever you like, but I won't have her bounced around. I also realize you can't be here for her all the time because of your work, but don't think you can just pop into her life and out again. You'll have to make an effort, to keep in touch with her, Jason."

So this was another fear she'd lived with, he realized. Maybe he deserved it. "You don't trust me, do you?"

"Clara's too important." She let out a little sigh. "So are you."

"If I told you I fell for her before I knew, would it make a difference?"

She thought of the toboggan, of the way he'd looked when Clara had thrown her arms around his neck. "She needs all the love she can get. We all do. She's so much like you, I—" She broke off when her eyes filled. "Damn, I don't want to do this." Impatient, she brushed tears away. "I'll tell her tomorrow, Jason. On Christmas. You and I can work out the arrangements. I know you're leaving soon, but if you could stay a few more days, give her some time, it would make it easier for all of us."

He rubbed at the tension at the back of his neck. "You never asked me for much of anything, did you?"

She smiled. "I asked you for everything. We were both too young to realize it."

"You always believed in magic, Faith." He pulled a box out of his pocket. "It's nearly midnight. Open it now."

"Jason." She pushed her hands through her hair. How could he think of presents now? "I don't think this is the time."

"It's ten years past time."

When he thrust the box at her she found herself gripping it with both hands. "I don't have anything to give you."

He touched her face, almost hesitantly. "You've just given me a daughter."

Relief poured through her. Instead of bitterness, she heard gratitude. Love, never dimmed, shimmered in her eyes. "Jason—"

"Please, open it."

She pulled off the glossy red paper and revealed the black velvet box beneath. With fingers not quite steady she opened it. The ring was a teardrop, frozen in place, glorious with the reflected lights from the tree.

"Paul told me it was the best he had."

"You bought this before you knew—"

"Yeah, before I knew I was going to ask the mother of my child to marry me. We'll be legal, the three of us." He took her hand and waited. "How about a second chance? I won't let you down, Faith."

"You never did." Close to tears again, she reached out her hand to his cheek. "It wasn't you, it wasn't me, it was life. Oh, Jason, I want this. Understand, all I've ever really wanted was to be married to you, have a family with you."

"Then let me put the ring on."

"Jason, it's not just me. If it were I'd leave with you this instant. We'd go to Hong Kong, Siberia, Peking. Anywhere. But it's not just me. I have to stay."

"It's not just you," he repeated. He took the ring and tossed the box aside. "And *I* have to stay. Do you think I'd leave you again? Do you think I could leave what's upstairs or the chance to have more that I can watch grow up? I'm not going anywhere."

"But you said—Hong Kong."

"I quit." When he grinned he felt the pressure of years melt away. "Today. That was one of the things I took care of this afternoon. I'm going to write a book." He took her by the shoulders. "I'm out of a job, I'm living in a room at the inn and asking you to marry me."

The breath backed up in her lungs. Her heart was pounding. Yes, she'd always believed in magic. It was standing in front of her. "Ten years ago, I thought I loved you as much as it was possible to love. You were a boy. In the last few days I've learned that loving a man is something quite different." She paused and saw the ring in his hand explode with the joyful lights on the tree. "If you'd asked me ten years ago I'd have said yes."

"Faith—"

With a laugh, she threw her arms around his neck. "You're going to get the same answer now. Oh, I love you, Jason, more than ever."

"We've got years to make up for."

"Yes." She met his mouth with equal hunger, equal hope. "We will. The three of us."

"The three of us." He let his forehead rest against hers. "I want more."

"We've more than enough time to give Clara a baby brother or sister for next Christmas." Her lips sought his again. "We've got more than enough time for everything."

They both heard the bells peal out from the town hall. Midnight.

"Merry Christmas, Faith."

She felt the ring slide onto her finger. All wishes were granted. "Welcome home, Jason."

* * * * *

ALL I WANT FOR CHRISTMAS

To Tom and Ky and Larry,
for having the good sense to marry well.

Prologue

Zeke and Zack huddled in the tree house. Important business, any plots or plans, and all punishments for infractions of the rules, were discussed in the sturdy wooden hideaway tucked in the branches of the dignified old sycamore.

Today, a light rain tapped on the tin roof and dampened the dark green leaves. It was still warm enough in the first days of September that the boys wore T-shirts. Red for Zeke, blue for Zack.

They were twins, as identical as the sides of a two-headed coin. Their father had used the color code since their birth to avoid confusion.

When they switched colors—as they often did—they could fool anyone in Taylor's Grove. Except their father.

He was on their minds at the moment. They had already discussed, at length, the anticipated delights and terrors of their first day in real school. The first day in first grade.

They would ride the bus, as they had done the year before,

in kindergarten. But this time they would stay in Taylor's Grove Elementary for a full day, just like the big kids. Their cousin Kim had told them that *real* school wasn't a playground.

Zack, the more introspective of the two, had thought over, worried about and dissected this problem for weeks. There were terrible, daunting terms like *homework* and *class participation,* that Kim tossed around. They knew that she, a sophomore in high school, was often loaded down with books. Big, thick books with no pictures.

And sometimes, when she was babysitting for them, she had her nose stuck in them for hours. For as long a time as she would have the telephone stuck to her ear, and that was long.

It was pretty scary stuff for Zack, the champion worrier.

Their father would help them, of course. This was something Zeke, the eternal optimist, had pointed out. Didn't they both know how to read stuff like *Green Eggs and Ham* and *The Cat in the Hat* because their dad helped them sound out the words? And they both knew how to write the whole alphabet, and their names and short things, because he showed them.

The trouble was, he had to work and take care of the house and them, as well as Commander Zark, the big yellow dog they'd saved from the animal shelter two years before. Their dad had, as Zack pointed out, an awful lot to do. And now that they were going to go to school, and have assignments and projects and real report cards, he was going to need help.

"He's got Mrs. Hollis to come in once a week and

do stuff." Zeke ran his miniature Corvette around the imaginary racetrack on the tree-house floor.

"It's not enough." A frown puckered Zack's forehead and clouded his lake-blue eyes. He exhaled with a long-suffering sigh, ruffling the dark hair that fell over his forehead. "He needs the companionship of a good woman, and we need a mother's love. I heard Mrs. Hollis say so to Mr. Perkins at the post office."

"He hangs around with Aunt Mira sometimes. She's a good woman."

"But she doesn't live with us. And she doesn't have time to help us with science projects." Science projects were a particular terror for Zack. "We need to find a mom." When Zeke only snorted, Zack narrowed his eyes. "We're going to have to spell in first grade."

Zeke caught his lower lip between his teeth. Spelling was his personal nightmare. "How're we going to find one?"

Now Zack smiled. He had, in his slow, careful way, figured it all out. "We're going to ask Santa Claus."

"He doesn't bring moms," Zeke said with the deep disdain that can only be felt by one sibling for another. "He brings toys and stuff. And it's forever until Christmas, anyway."

"No, it's not. Mrs. Hollis was bragging to Mr. Perkins how she already had half her Christmas shopping done. She said how looking ahead meant you could enjoy the holiday."

"Everybody enjoys Christmas. It's the best."

"Uh-uh. Lots of people get mad. Remember how we went to the mall last year with Aunt Mira and she complained and complained about the crowds and the prices and how there weren't any parking spaces?"

Zeke merely shrugged. He didn't look back as often, or as clearly, as his twin, but he took Zack at his word. "I guess."

"So, if we ask now, Santa'll have plenty of time to find the right mom."

"I still say he doesn't bring moms."

"Why not? If we really need one, and we don't ask for too much else?"

"We were going to ask for two-wheelers," Zeke reminded him.

"We could still ask for them," Zack decided. "But not a bunch of other things. Just a mom and the bikes."

It was Zeke's turn to sigh. He didn't care for the idea of giving up his big, long list. But the idea of a mother was beginning to appeal. They'd never had one, and the mystery of it attracted. "So what kind do we ask for?"

"We got to write it down."

Zack took a notebook and a stubby pencil from the table pushed against the wall. They sat on the floor and, with much argument and discussion, composed.

Dear Santa,
We have been good.

Zeke wanted to put in *very good,* but Zack, the conscience, rejected the idea.

We feed Zark and help Dad. We want a mom for Crissmas. A nice one who smells good and is not meen. She can smile a lot and have yello hair. She has to like little boys and big dogs. She wont mind dirt and bakes cookys. We want a pretty one who is smart and helps us with homework. We will take good care of her. We want biks a red one and a bloo one. You have lots of time to find the mom and make the biks so you can enjoi the hollidays. Thank you. Love, Zeke and Zack.

Chapter 1

Taylor's Grove, population two thousand three hundred and forty. No, forty-one, Nell thought smugly, as she strolled into the high school auditorium. She'd only been in town for two months, but already she was feeling territorial. She loved the slow pace, the tidy yards and little shops. She loved the easy gossip of neighbors, the front-porch swings, the frost-heaved sidewalks.

If anyone had told her, even a year before, that she would be trading in Manhattan for a dot on the map in western Maryland, she would have thought them mad. But here she was, Taylor's Grove High's new music teacher, as snug and settled in as an old hound in front of a fire.

She'd needed the change, that was certain. In the past year she'd lost her roommate to marriage and inherited a staggering rent she simply wasn't able to manage on her own. The replacement roommate, whom Nell had carefully interviewed, had moved out, as well. Taking everything of value out of the apartment. That nasty little adventure had led to the final, even nastier showdown with her almost-fiancé. When Bob berated her, called her stupid, naive and careless, Nell had decided it was time to cut her losses.

She'd hardly given Bob his walking papers when she received her own. The school where she had taught for three years was downsizing, as they had euphemistically put it. The position of music teacher had been eliminated, and so had Nell.

An apartment she could no longer afford, all but empty, a fiancé who had considered her optimistic nature a liability and the prospect of the unemployment line had taken the sheen off New York.

Once Nell decided to move, she'd decided to move big. The idea of teaching in a small town had sprung up fully rooted. An inspiration, she thought now, for she already felt as if she'd lived here for years.

Her rent was low enough that she could live alone and like it. Her apartment, the entire top floor of a remodeled old house, was a short, enjoyable walk from a campus that included elementary, middle and high schools.

Only two weeks after that first nervous day of school, she was feeling proprietary about her students and was looking forward to her first after-school session with her chorus.

She was determined to create a holiday program that would knock the town's socks off.

The battered piano was center stage. She walked to it and sat. Her students would be filing in shortly, but she had a moment.

She limbered up her mind and her fingers with the blues,

an old Muddy Waters tune. Old, scarred pianos were meant to play the blues, she thought, and enjoyed herself.

"Man, she's so cool," Holly Linstrom murmured to Kim as they slipped into the rear of the auditorium.

"Yeah." Kim had a hand on the shoulder of each of her twin cousins, a firm grip that ordered quiet and promised reprisals. "Old Mr. Striker never played anything like that."

"And her clothes are so, like, now." Admiration and envy mixed as Holly scanned the pipe-stem pants, long overshirt and short striped vest Nell wore. "I don't know why anybody from New York would come here. Did you see her earrings today? I bet she got them at some hot place on Fifth Avenue."

Nell's jewelry had already become legendary among the female students. She wore the unique and the unusual. Her taste in clothes, her dark gold hair, which fell just short of her shoulders and always seemed miraculously and expertly tousled, her quick, throaty laugh and her lack of formality had already gone a long way toward endearing her to her students.

"She's got style, all right." But, just then, Kim was more intrigued by the music than by the musician's wardrobe. "Man, I wish I could play like that."

"Man, I wish I could look like that," Holly returned, and giggled.

Sensing an audience, Nell glanced back and grinned. "Come on in, girls. Free concert."

"It sounds great, Miss Davis." With her grip firm on her two charges, Kim started down the sloping aisle toward the stage. "What is it?"

"Muddy Waters. We'll have to shoehorn a little blues

education into the curriculum." Sitting back, she studied the two sweet-faced boys on either side of Kim. There was a quick, odd surge of recognition that she didn't understand. "Well, hi, guys."

When they smiled back, identical dimples popped out on the left side of their mouths. "Can you play 'Chopsticks'?" Zeke wanted to know.

Before Kim could express her humiliation at the question, Nell spun into a rousing rendition.

"How's that?" she asked when she'd finished.

"That's neat."

"I'm sorry, Miss Davis. I'm kind of stuck with them for an hour. They're my cousins. Zeke and Zack Taylor."

"The Taylors of Taylor's Grove." Nell swiveled away from the piano. "I bet you're brothers. I see a slight family resemblance."

Both boys grinned and giggled. "We're twins," Zack informed her.

"Really? Now I bet I'm supposed to guess who's who." She came to the edge of the stage, sat and eyed the boys narrowly. They grinned back. Each had recently lost a left front tooth. "Zeke," she said, pointing a finger. "And Zack."

Pleased and impressed, they nodded. "How'd you know?"

It was pointless, and hardly fun, to mention that she'd had a fifty-fifty shot. "Magic. Do you guys like to sing?"

"Sort of. A little."

"Well, today you can listen. You can sit right in the front row and be our test audience."

"Thanks, Miss Davis," Kim murmured, and gave the boys a friendly shove toward the seats. "They're pretty good most of the time. Stay," she ordered, with an older cousin's absolute authority.

Nell winked at the boys as she stood, then gestured to the other students filing in. "Come on up. Let's get started."

A lot of the business onstage seemed boring to the twins. There was just talking at first, and confusion as sheet music was passed out and boys and girls were assigned positions.

But Zack was watching Nell. She had pretty hair and nice big brown eyes. Like Zark's, he thought with deep affection. Her voice was kind of funny, sort of scratchy and deep, but nice. Now and again she looked back toward him and smiled. When she did, his heart acted strange, kind of beating hard, like he'd been running.

She turned to a group of girls and sang. It was a Christmas song, which made Zack's eyes widen. He wasn't sure of the name, something about a midnight clear, but he recognized it from the records his dad played around the holiday.

A Christmas song. A Christmas wish.

"It's her." He hissed it to his brother, rapping Zeke hard in the ribs.

"Who?"

"It's the mom."

Zeke stopped playing with the action figure he'd had stuck in his pocket and looked up onstage, where Nell was now directing the alto section. "Kim's teacher is the mom?"

"She has to be." Deadly excited, Zeke kept his voice in a conspiratorial whisper. "Santa's had enough time to get the letter. She was singing a Christmas song, and she's got yellow hair and a nice smile. She likes little boys, too. I can tell."

"Maybe." Not quite convinced, Zeke studied Nell. She

was pretty, he thought. And she laughed a lot, even when some of the big kids made mistakes. But that didn't mean she liked dogs or baked cookies. "We can't know for sure yet."

Zack huffed out an impatient breath. "She knew us. She knew which was which. Magic." His eyes were solemn as he looked at his brother. "It's the mom."

"Magic," Zeke repeated, and stared, goggle-eyed, at Nell. "Do we have to wait till Christmas to get her?"

"I guess so. Probably." That was a puzzle Zack would have to work on.

When Mac Taylor pulled his pickup truck in front of the high school, his mind was on a dozen varied problems. What to fix the kids for dinner. How to deal with the flooring on his Meadow Street project. When to find a couple hours to drive to the mall and pick up new underwear for the boys. The last time he folded laundry, he'd noticed that most of what they had was doomed for the rag pile. He had to deal with a lumber delivery first thing in the morning and a pile of paperwork that night.

And Zeke was nervous about his first spelling test, which was coming up in a few days.

Pocketing his keys, Mac rolled his shoulders. He'd been swinging a hammer for the better part of eight hours. He didn't mind the aches. It was a good kind of fatigue, a kind that meant he'd accomplished something. His renovation of the house on Meadow Street was on schedule and on budget. Once it was done, he would have to decide whether to put it on the market or rent it.

His accountant would try to decide for him, but Mac

knew the final choice would remain in his own hands. That was the way he preferred it.

As he strode from the parking lot to the high school, he looked around. His great-great-grandfather had founded the town—hardly more than a village back then, settled along Taylor's Creek and stretching over the rolling hills to Taylor's Meadow.

There'd been no lack of ego in old Macauley Taylor.

But Mac had lived in D.C. for more than twelve years. It had been six years since he returned to Taylor's Grove, but he hadn't lost his pleasure or his pride in it, the simple appreciation for the hills and the trees and the shadows of mountains in the distance.

He didn't think he ever would.

There was the faintest of chills in the air now, and a good strong breeze from the west. But they had yet to have a frost, and the leaves were still a deep summer green. The good weather made his life easier on a couple of levels. As long as it held, he'd be able to finish the outside work on his project in comfort. And the boys could enjoy the afternoons and evenings in the yard.

There was a quick twinge of guilt as he pulled open the heavy doors and stepped into the school. His work had kept them stuck inside this afternoon. The coming of fall meant that his sister was diving headfirst into several of her community projects. He couldn't impose on her by asking her to watch the twins. Kim's after-school schedule was filling up, and he simply couldn't accept the idea of having his children becoming latchkey kids.

Still, the solution had suited everyone. Kim would take

the kids to her rehearsals, and he would save his sister a trip to school by picking them all up and driving them home.

Kim would have a driver's license in a few more months. A fact she was reminding everyone about constantly. But he doubted he'd plunk his boys down in the car with his sixteen-year-old niece at the wheel, no matter how much he loved and trusted her.

You coddle them. Mac rolled his eyes as his sister's voice played in his head. *You can't always be mother and father to them, Mac. If you're not interested in finding a wife, then you'll have to learn to let go a little.*

Like hell he would, Mac thought.

As he neared the auditorium, he heard the sound of young voices raised in song. Subtle harmony. A good, emotional sound that made him smile even before he recognized the tune. A Christmas hymn. It was odd to hear it now, with the sweat from his day just drying on his back.

He pulled open the auditorium doors, and was flooded with it. Charmed, he stood at the back and looked out on the singers. One of the students played the piano. A pretty little thing, Mac mused, who looked up now and then, gesturing, as if to urge her classmates to give more.

He wondered where the music teacher was, then spotted his boys sitting in the front row. He walked quietly down the aisle, raising a hand when he saw Kim's eyes shift to his. He settled behind the boys and leaned forward.

"Pretty good show, huh?"

"Dad!" Zack nearly squealed, then remembered just in time to speak in a hissing whisper. "It's Christmas."

"Sure sounds like it. How's Kim doing?"

"She's real good." Zeke now considered himself an expert on choral arrangements. "She's going to have a solo."

"No kidding?"

"She got red in the face when Miss Davis asked her to sing by herself, but she did okay." Zeke was much more interested in Nell right then. "She's pretty, isn't she?"

A little amazed at this announcement—the twins were fond of Kim, but rarely complimentary—he nodded. "Yeah. The prettiest girl in school."

"We could have her over for dinner sometime," Zack said slyly. "Couldn't we?"

Baffled now, Mac ruffled his son's hair. "You know Kim can come over whenever she wants."

"Not her." In a gesture that mimicked his father, Zack rolled his eyes. "Jeez, Dad. Miss Davis."

"Who's Miss Davis?"

"The m—" Zeke's announcement was cut off by his twin's elbow.

"The teacher," Zack finished with a snarling look at his brother. "The pretty one." He pointed, and his father followed the direction to the piano.

"She's the teacher?" Before Mac could reevaluate, the music flowed to a stop and Nell rose.

"That was great, really. A very solid first run-through." She pushed her tousled hair back. "But we need a lot of work. I'd like to schedule the next rehearsal for Monday after school. Three forty-five."

There was already a great deal of movement and mumbling, so Nell pitched her voice to carry the rest of her instructions over the noise. Satisfied, she turned to smile at the twins and found herself grinning at an older, and much more disturbing version, of the Taylor twins.

No doubt he was the father, Nell thought. The same thick dark hair curled down over the collar of a grimy T-shirt. The same lake-water eyes framed in long, dark lashes stared back at her. His face might lack the soft, slightly rounded appeal of his sons', but the more rugged version was just as attractive. He was long, rangy, with the kind of arms that looked tough without being obviously muscled. He was tanned and more than a little dirty. She wondered if he had a dimple at the left corner of his mouth when he smiled.

"Mr. Taylor." Rather than bother with the stairs, she hopped off the stage, as agile as any of her students. She held out a hand decorated with rings.

"Miss Davis." He covered her hand with his callused one, remembering too late that it was far from clean. "I appreciate you letting the kids hang out while Kim rehearsed."

"No problem. I work better with an audience." Tilting her head, she looked down at the twins. "Well, guys, how'd we do?"

"It was really neat." This from Zeke. "We like Christmas songs the best."

"Me, too."

Still flustered and flattered by the idea of having a solo, Kim joined them. "Hi, Uncle Mac. I guess you met Miss Davis."

"Yeah." There wasn't much more to say. He still thought she looked too young to be a teacher. Not the teenager he'd taken her for, he realized. But that creamy, flawless skin and that tidy little frame were deceiving. And very attractive.

"Your niece is very talented." In a natural movement,

Nell wrapped an arm around Kim's shoulders. "She has a wonderful voice and a quick understanding of what the music means. I'm delighted to have her."

"We like her, too," Mac said as Kim flushed.

Zack shifted from foot to foot. They weren't supposed to be talking about dumb old Kim. "Maybe you could come visit us sometime, Miss Davis," he piped up. "We live in the big brown house out on Mountain View Road."

"That'd be nice." But Nell noted that Zack's father didn't second the invitation, or look particularly pleased by it. "And you guys are welcome to be our audience anytime. You work on that solo, Kim."

"I will, Miss Davis. Thanks."

"Nice to have met you, Mr. Taylor." As he mumbled a response, Nell hopped back onstage to gather her sheet music.

It was too bad, she thought, that the father lacked the outgoing charm and friendliness of his sons.

Chapter 2

It didn't get much better than a drive in the country on a balmy fall afternoon. Nell remembered how she used to spend a free Saturday in New York. A little shopping—she supposed if she missed anything about Manhattan, it was the shopping—maybe a walk in the park. Never a jog. Nell didn't believe in running if walking would get you to the same place.

And driving, well, that was even better. She hadn't realized what a pleasure it was to not only own a car but be able to zip it along winding country roads with the windows open and the radio blaring.

The leaves were beginning to turn now as September hit its stride. Blushes of color competed with the green. On one particular road that she turned down out of impulse, the big trees arched over the asphalt, a spectacular canopy that let light flicker and flit through as the road followed the snaking trail of a rushing creek.

It wasn't until she glanced up at a road sign that she realized she was on Mountain View.

The big brown house, Zack had said, she remembered. There weren't a lot of houses here, two miles outside of town, but she caught glimpses of some through the shading trees. Brown ones, white ones, blue ones—some close to the creek bed, others high atop narrow, pitted lanes that served as driveways.

A lovely place to live, she thought. And to raise children. However taciturn and stiff Mac Taylor might have been, he'd done a wonderful job with his sons.

She already knew he'd done the job alone. It hadn't taken long for Nell to understand the rhythm of small towns. A comment here, a casual question there, and she'd had what amounted to a full biography of the Taylor men.

Mac had lived in Washington, D.C., since his family moved out of town when he was a young teenager. Six years ago, twin infants in tow, he'd moved back. His older sister had gone to a local college and married a town boy and settled in Taylor's Grove years before. It was she, the consensus was, who had urged him to come back and raise his children there when his wife took off.

Left the poor little infants high and dry, Mrs. Hollis had told Nell over the bread rack at the general store. Run off with barely a word, and hadn't said a peep since. And young Macauley Taylor had been mother and father both to his twins ever since.

Maybe, Nell thought cynically, just maybe, if he'd actually talked to his wife now and again, she'd have stayed with him.

Not fair, she thought. There was no decent excuse she

could think of for a mother deserting her infant children, then not contacting them for six years. Whatever kind of husband Mac Taylor had been, the children deserved better.

She thought of them now, those impish mirror images. She'd always been fond of children, and the Taylor twins were a double dose of enjoyment. She'd gotten quite a kick out of having them in the audience once or twice a week during rehearsals. Zeke had even shown her his very first spelling test—with its big silver star. If he hadn't missed just one word, he'd told her, he'd have gotten a gold one.

Nor had she missed the shy looks Zack sent her, or the quick smiles before he flushed and lowered his eyes. It was very sweet to be responsible for his first case of puppy love.

She sighed with pleasure as the car burst out from under the canopy of trees and into the light. Here were the mountains that gave the road its name, streaking suddenly into the vivid blue sky. The road curved and snaked, but they were always there, dark, distant and dramatic.

The land rose on either side of the road, in rolling hills and rocky outcroppings. She slowed when she spotted a house on the crest of a hill. Brown. Probably cedar, she thought, with a stone foundation and what seemed like acres of sparkling glass. There was a deck stretched across the second story, and there were trees that shaded and sheltered. A tire swing hung from one.

She wondered if this was indeed the Taylor house. She hoped her new little friends lived in such a solid, well-planned home. Then she passed the mailbox planted at the side of the road just at the edge of the long lane.

M. Taylor and sons.

It made her smile. Pleased, she punched the gas pedal and was baffled when the car bucked and stuttered.

"What's the problem here?" she muttered, easing off on the pedal and punching it again. This time the car shuddered and stopped dead. "For heaven's sake." Only mildly annoyed, she started to turn the key to start it again, and glanced at the dash. The little gas pump beside the gauge was brightly lit.

"Stupid," she said aloud, berating herself. "Stupid, stupid. Weren't you supposed to get gas *before* you left town?" She sat back, sighed. She'd meant to, really. Just as she'd meant to stop and fill up the day before, right after class.

Now she was two miles out of town without even fumes to ride on. Blowing the hair out of her eyes, she looked out at the home of M. Taylor and sons. A quarter-mile hike, she estimated. Which made it a lot better than two miles. And she had, more or less, been invited.

She grabbed her keys and started up the lane.

She was no more than halfway when the boys spotted her. They came racing down the rocky, pitted lane at a speed that stopped her heart. Surefooted as young goats, they streaked toward her. Coming up behind was a huge yellow dog.

"Miss Davis! Hi, Miss Davis! Did you come to see us?"

"Sort of." Laughing, she crouched down to give them both a hug and caught the faint scent of chocolate. Before she could comment, the dog decided he wanted in on the action. He was restrained enough to plant his huge paws on her thighs, rather than her shoulders.

Zack held his breath, then let it out when she chuckled

and bent down to rub Zark on head and shoulders. "You're a big one, aren't you? A big beauty."

Zark lapped her hand in perfect agreement. Nell caught a look exchanged quickly between the twins. One that seemed both smug and excited.

"You like dogs?" Zeke asked.

"Sure I do. Maybe I'll get one now. I never had the heart to lock one up in a New York apartment." She only laughed again when Zark sat and politely lifted a paw. "Too late for formalities now, buddy," she told him, but shook it anyway. "I was out driving, and I ran out of gas right smack at the bottom of your lane. Isn't that funny?"

Zack's grin nearly split his face. She liked dogs. She'd stopped right at their house. It was more magic, he was sure of it. "Dad'll fix it. He can fix anything." Confident now that he had her on his own ground, Zack took her hand. Not to be outdone, Zeke clasped the other.

"Dad's out back in the shop, building a 'rondak chair."

"A rocking chair?" Nell suggested.

"Nuh-uh. A 'rondak chair. Come see."

They hauled her around the house, passed a curving sunroom that caught the southern light. There was another deck in the back, with steps leading down to a flagstone patio. The shop in the backyard—the same cedar as the house— looked big enough to hold a family of four. Nell heard the thwack of a hammer on wood.

Bursting with excitement, Zeke raced through the shop door. "Dad! Dad! Guess what?"

"I guess you've taken another five years off my life."

Nell heard Mac's voice, deep and amused and tolerant, and found herself hesitating. "I hate to bother him when he's busy," she said to Zeke. "Maybe I can just call the station in town."

"It's okay, come on." Zack dragged her a few more feet into the doorway.

"See?" Zeke said importantly. "She came!"

"Yeah, I see." Caught off balance by the unexpected visit, Mac set his hammer down on his workbench. He pushed up the brim of his cap and frowned without really meaning to. "Miss Davis."

"I'm sorry to bother you, Mr. Taylor," she began, then saw the project he was working on. "An Adirondack chair," she murmured, and grinned. "A 'rondak chair. It's nice."

"Will be." Was he supposed to offer her coffee? he wondered. A tour of the house? What? She shouldn't be pretty, he thought irrelevantly. There was nothing particularly striking about her. Well, maybe the eyes. They were so big and brown. But the rest really was ordinary. It must be the way it was put together, he decided, that made it extraordinary.

Not certain whether she was amused or uncomfortable at the way he was staring at her, Nell launched into her explanation. "I was out driving. Partly for the pleasure of it, and partly to try to familiarize myself with the area. I've only lived here a couple months."

"Is that right?"

"Miss Davis is from New York City, Dad," Zack reminded him. "Kim told you."

"Yeah, she did." He picked up his hammer again, set it down. "Nice day for a drive."

"I thought so. So nice I forgot to get gas before I left town. I ran out at the bottom of your lane."

A flicker of suspicion darkened his eyes. "That's handy."

"Not especially." Her voice, though still friendly, had cooled. "If I could use your phone to call the station in town, I'd appreciate it."

"I've got gas," he muttered.

"See, I told you Dad could fix it," Zack said proudly. "We've got brownies," he added, struggling madly for a way to get her to stay longer. "Dad made them. You can have one."

"I thought I smelled chocolate." She scooped Zack up and sniffed at his face. "I've got a real nose for it."

Moving on instinct, Mac plucked Zack out of her arms. "You guys go get some brownies. We'll get the gas."

"Okay!" They raced off together.

"I wasn't going to abduct him, Mr. Taylor."

"Didn't say you were." He walked to the doorway, glanced back. "The gas is in the shed."

Lips pursed, she followed him out. "Were you traumatized by a teacher at an impressionable age, Mr. Taylor?"

"Mac. Just Mac. No, why?"

"I wondered if we have a personal or a professional problem here."

"I don't have a problem." He stopped at the small shed where he kept his lawn mower and garden tools, then said, "Funny how the kids told you where we lived, and you ran out of gas right here."

She took a long breath, studying him as he bent over to pick up a can, straighten and turn. "Look, I'm no happier about it than you, and after this reception, probably a lot less happy. It happens that this is the first car I've ever owned, and I'm still a little rough on the finer points. I ran out of gas last month in front of the general store. You're welcome to check."

He shrugged, feeling stupid and unnecessarily prickly. "Sorry."

"Forget it. If you'll give me the can, I'll use what I need to get back to town, then I'll have it filled and returned."

"I'll take care of it," he muttered.

"I don't want to put you out." She reached for the can and that started a quick tug-of-war. After a moment, the dimple at the corner of his mouth winked.

"I'm bigger than you."

She stepped back and blew the hair out of her eyes. "Fine. Go be a man, then." Scowling, she followed him around the house, then tried to fight off her foul mood as the twins came racing up. They each held a paper towel loaded with brownies.

"Dad makes the best brownies in the whole world," Zack told her, holding up his offering.

Nell took one and bit in. "You may be right," she was forced to admit, her mouth full. "And I know my brownies."

"Can you make cookies?" Zeke wanted to know.

"I happened to be known far and wide for my chocolate-chip." Her smile became puzzled as the boys eyed each other and nodded. "You come visit me sometime, and we'll whip some up."

"Where do you live?" Since his father wasn't paying close attention, Zeke stuffed an entire brownie in his mouth.

"On Market Street, right off the square. The old brick house with the three porches. I rent the top floor."

"Dad owns that," Zack told her. "He bought it and fixed it all up and now he rents it out. We're in real estate."

"Oh." She let out a long breath. "Really." Her rent checks were mailed to Taylor Management...on Mountain View Road.

"So you live in our house," Zack finished up.

"In a manner of speaking."

"The place okay with you?" Mac asked.

"Yes, it's fine. I'm very comfortable there. It's convenient to school."

"Dad buys houses and fixes them up all the time." Zeke wondered if he could get away with another brownie. "He likes to fix stuff."

It was obvious from the tidy and thoughtful renovation of the old house she now lived in that their father fixed them very well. "You're a carpenter, then?" she asked, reluctantly addressing Mac.

"Sometimes." They'd reached her car. Mac merely jerked his thumb to signal the boys and dog to keep off the road. He unscrewed the gas cap and spoke without looking around. "If you eat another one of those, Zeke, I'm going to have to have your stomach pumped."

Sheepishly Zeke replaced the brownie on the paper towel.

"Excellent radar," Nell commented, leaning on the car as Mac added the gas.

"Goes with the territory." He looked at her then. Her hair was windblown and gilded by the sun. Her face was rosy from the walk and the breeze. He didn't like what looking at her did to his pulse rate. "Why Taylor's Grove? It's a long way from New York."

"That's why. I wanted a change." She breathed deep as she looked around, at rock and tree and hill. "I got one."

"Pretty slow, compared to what you'd be used to."

"Slow's something I do very well."

He only shrugged. He suspected she'd be bored senseless in six months and heading out. "Kim's pretty excited about your class. She talks about it almost as much as she does getting her driver's license."

"That's quite a compliment. It's a good school. Not all of my students are as cooperative as Kim, but I like a challenge. I'm going to recommend her for all-state."

Mac tipped the can farther up. "She's really that good?"

"You sound surprised."

He shrugged again. "She always sounded good to me, but the old music teacher never singled her out."

"Rumor is he never took much interest in any of his students individually, or in extra work."

"You got that right. Striker was an old—" He caught himself, glanced back at his kids, who were standing close by, all ears. "He was old," Mac repeated. "And set in his ways. Always the same Christmas program, the same spring program."

"Yes, I've looked over his class notes. I'd say everyone should be in for a surprise this year. I'm told no student from Taylor's Grove ever went to all-state."

"Not that I heard."

"Well, we're going to change that." Satisfied now that they had managed a reasonable conversation, she tossed back her hair. "Do you sing?"

"In the shower." His dimple flickered again as his sons giggled. "No comments from the brats."

"He sings really, really loud," Zeke said, without fear of reprisal. "And he gets Zark howling."

"I'm sure that would be quite a show." Nell scratched the grinning dog between the ears. He thumped his tail, and then some internal clock struck and had him pivoting and racing up the hill.

"Here you go, Miss Davis. Here." Both boys stuffed the loaded paper towels into her hands and barreled off after the dog.

"I guess they don't keep still very long," she murmured, watching them chase the dog up the rise.

"That was nearly a record. They like you."

"I'm a likable person." She smiled, glancing back at him, only to find him staring at her again with that not-quite-pleased look in his eyes. "At least in most cases. If you'd just put that on the backseat, I'll have it filled up for you."

"It's not a problem." Mac replaced her gas cap and kept the empty can. "We're friendly in Taylor's Grove. In most cases."

"Let me know when I'm off probation." She leaned into her car to set the brownies on the passenger seat. Mac had a tantalizing and uncomfortable view of her jean-clad bottom. He could smell her, too, something light and spicy that spun in his head a lot more potently than the gas fumes.

"I didn't mean it like that."

Her head popped back out of the car. She licked a smear of brownie from her finger as she straightened. "Maybe not. In any case, I appreciate the help." Her grin flashed as she opened the car door. "And the chocolate."

"Anytime," he heard himself say, and wanted to regret it.

She settled behind the steering wheel, tossed him a quick,

saucy smile. "Like hell." Then she laughed and turned the ignition, revving the engine in a way that made Mac wince. "You should drop in on rehearsals now and again, Mac, instead of waiting out in the parking lot. You might learn something."

He wasn't certain he wanted to. "Put on your seat belt," he ordered.

"Oh, yeah." Obligingly, she buckled up. "Just not used to it yet. Say bye to the twins." She zoomed off at a speed just this side of reckless, waving a careless and glittering hand out the window.

Mac watched her until she rounded the bend, then slowly rubbed his stomach where the muscles were knotted. Something about that woman, he thought. Something about the way she was put together made him feel like he was defrosting after a very long freeze.

Chapter 3

Another half hour, Mac figured, and he could finish taping the drywall in the master bedroom. Maybe get the first coat of mud on. He glanced at his watch, calculated that the kids were home from school. But it was Mrs. Hollis's day, and she'd stay until five. That would give him plenty of time to hit the drywall, clean up and get home.

Maybe he'd give himself and the kids a treat and pick up pizza.

He'd learned not to mind cooking, but he still resented the time it took—the thinking, the preparation, the cleaning up afterward. Six years as a single parent had given him a whole new perspective on how hard his mother—that rare and old-fashioned homemaker—had worked.

Pausing a moment, he took a look around the master suite. He'd taken walls out, built others, replaced the old single-pane windows with double glazed. Twin skylights let in the fading sunlight of early October.

Now there were three spacious bedrooms on the second floor of the old house, rather than the four choppy rooms and oversize hallway he'd started with. The master suite would boast a bathroom large enough for tub and separate shower stall. He was toying with using glass block for that. He'd been wanting to work with it for some time.

If he stayed on schedule, the place would be put together by Christmas, and on the sale or rental market by the first of the year.

He really should sell it, Mac thought, running a hand over the drywall he'd nailed up that afternoon. He had to get over this sense of possession whenever he worked on a house.

In the blood, he supposed. His father had made a good living buying up damaged or depressed property, rehabing and renting. Mac had discovered just how satisfying it was to own something you'd made fine with your own hands.

Like the old brick house Nell lived in now. He wondered if she knew it was more than a hundred and fifty years old, that she was living in a piece of history.

He wondered if she'd run out of gas again.

He wondered quite a bit about Nell Davis.

And he shouldn't, Mac reminded himself, and turned away for his tools and tape. Women were trouble. One way or the other, they were trouble. One look at Nell and a smart man could see she was no exception.

He hadn't taken her up on her suggestion that he drop by the auditorium and catch part of a rehearsal. He'd started to a couple of times, but good sense had stopped him. She was the first woman in a very, very long time who had stirred him up. He didn't want to be stirred up, Mac thought with a scowl as he taped a seam. Couldn't afford to be, he reminded himself. He had too many obligations, too little free time, and, most important, two sons who were the focus of his life.

Daydreaming about a woman was bad enough. It made a man sloppy in his work, forgetful and...itchy. But doing something about it was worse. Doing something meant you had to find conversation and ways to entertain. A woman expected to be taken places, and pampered. And once you started to fall for her—really fall for her—she had the power to cut out your heart.

Mac wasn't willing to risk his heart again, and he certainly wasn't willing to risk his sons.

He didn't subscribe to that nonsense about children needing a woman's touch, a mother's love. The twins' mother had felt less connection with the children she'd borne than a cat felt toward a litter of kittens. Being female didn't give you a leg up on maternal feelings. It meant you were physically able to carry a child inside you, but it didn't mean that you'd care once that child was in your arms.

Mac stopped taping and swore. He hadn't thought about Angie in years. Not deeply. When he did, he realized the spot was still sore, like an old wound that had healed poorly. That was what he got, he supposed, for letting some little blonde stir him up.

Annoyed with himself, he stripped the last piece of tape off the roll. He needed to concentrate on his work, not on a woman. Determined to finish what he'd started, he marched down the stairs. He had more drywall tape in his truck.

The light outside was softening with the approach of dusk. Shorter days, he thought. Less time.

He was down the steps and onto the walk before he saw her. She was standing just at the edge of the yard, looking up at the house, smiling a little. She wore a suede jacket in a deep burnished orange over faded jeans. Some glittery stones dangled from her ears. Over her shoulder hung a soft-sided briefcase that looked well used.

"Oh. Hi." Surprise lit her eyes when she glanced over, and that immediately made him suspicious. "Is this one of your places?"

"That's right." He moved past her toward the truck and wished he'd held his breath. That scent she wore was subtle and sneaky.

"I was just admiring it. Beautiful stonework. It looks so sturdy and safe, tucked in with all the trees." She took a deep breath. There was the slap of fall in the air. "It's going to be a beautiful night."

"I guess." He found his tape, then stood, running the roll around in his hands. "Did you run out of gas again?"

"No." She laughed, obviously amused at herself. "I like walking around town this time of day. As a matter of fact, I was heading down to your sister's. She's a few doors down, right?"

His eyes narrowed. He didn't like the idea of the woman he was spending too much time thinking about hanging out with his sister. "Yeah, that's right. Why?"

"Why?" Her attention had been focused on his hands. There was something about them. Hard, callused. Big. She felt a quick and very pleasant flutter in the pit of her stomach. "Why what?"

"Why are you going to Mira's?"

"Oh. I have some sheet music I thought Kim would like."

"Is that right?" He leaned on the truck, measuring her. Her smile was entirely too friendly, he decided. Entirely too attractive. "Is it part of your job description to make house calls with sheet music?"

"It's part of the fun." Her hair ruffled in the light breeze. She scooped it back. "No job's worth the effort or the headaches if you don't have some fun." She looked back at the house. "You have fun, don't you? Taking something and making it yours?"

He started to say something snide, then realized she'd put her finger right on the heart of it. "Yeah. It doesn't always seem like fun when you're tearing out ceilings and having insulation raining down on your head." He smiled a little. "But it is."

"Are you going to let me see?" She tilted her head. "Or are you like a temperamental artist, not willing to show his work until the final brushstroke?"

"There's not much to see." Then he shrugged. "Sure, you can come in if you want."

"Thanks." She started up the walk, glanced over her shoulder when he stayed by the truck. "Aren't you going to give me a tour?"

He moved his shoulders again, and joined her.

"Did you do the trim on my apartment?"

"Yeah."

"It's beautiful work. Looks like cherry."

He frowned, surprised. "It is cherry."

"I like the rounded edges. They soften everything. Do you get a decorator in for the colors or pick them out yourself?"

"I pick them." He opened the door for her. "Is there a problem?"

"No. I really love the color scheme in the kitchen, the slate blue counters, the mauve floor. Oh, what fabulous stairs." She hurried across the unfinished living area to the staircase.

Mac had worked hard and long on it, tearing out the old and replacing it with dark chestnut, curving and widening the landing at the bottom so that it flowed out into the living space.

It was, undeniably, his current pride and joy.

"Did you build these?" she murmured, running a hand over the curve of the railing.

"The old ones were broken, dry-rotted. Had to go."

"I have to try them." She dashed up, turning back at the top to grin at him. "No creaks. Good workmanship, but not very sentimental."

"Sentimental?"

"You know, the way you look back on home, how you snuck downstairs as a kid and knew just which steps to avoid because they'd creak and wake up Mom."

All at once he was having trouble with his breathing. "They're chestnut," he said, because he could think of nothing else.

"Whatever, they're beautiful. Whoever lives here has to have kids."

His mouth was dry, unbearably. "Why?"

"Because." On impulse, she planted her butt on the railing and pushed off. Mac's arms came out of their own volition to catch her as she flew off the end. "It was made for sliding," she said breathlessly. She was laughing as she tilted her head up to his.

Something clicked inside her when their eyes met. And the fluttering, not so pleasant this time, came again.

Disconcerted, she cleared her throat and searched for something to say.

"You keep popping up," Mac muttered. He had yet to release her, couldn't seem to make his hands obey his head.

"It's a small town."

He only shook his head. His hands were at her waist now, and they seemed determined to slide around and stroke up her back. He thought he felt her tremble—but it might have been him.

"I don't have time for women," he told her, trying to convince himself.

"Well." She tried to swallow, but there was something hard and hot lodged in her throat. "I'm pretty busy myself." She let out a slow breath. Those hands stroking up and down her back were making her weak. "And I'm not really interested. I had a really bad year, as far as relationships go. I think…"

It was very hard to think. His eyes were such a beautiful shade of blue, and so intensely focused on hers. She wasn't sure what he saw, or what he was looking for, but she knew her knees were about to give out.

"I think," she began again, "we'd both be better off if you decide fairly quickly if you're going to kiss me or not. I can't handle this much longer."

Neither could he. Still, he took his time. He was, in all things, a thorough and thoughtful man. His eyes were open and on hers as he lowered his head, as his mouth hovered a breath from hers, as a small, whimpering moan sounded in her throat.

Her vision dimmed as his lips brushed hers. His were soft, firm, terrifyingly patient. The whisper of contact slammed a punch into her stomach. He lingered over her like a gourmet sampling delicacies, deepening the kiss degree by staggering degree until she was clinging to him.

No one had ever kissed her like this. She hadn't known anyone could. Slow and deep and dreamy. The floor seemed to tilt under her feet as he gently sucked her lower lip into his mouth.

She shuddered, groaned, and let herself drown.

She was very potent. The scent and feel and taste of her was overwhelming. He knew he could lose himself here, for a moment, for a lifetime. Her small, tight body was all but plastered to his. Her hands clutched his hair. In contrast to that aggressive gesture, her head fell limply back in a kind of sighing surrender that had his blood bubbling.

He wanted to touch her. His hands were aching with the need to peel off layer after layer and find the pale, smooth skin beneath. To test himself, and her, he slipped his fingers under her sweater, along the soft, hot flesh of her back, while his mouth continued its long, lazy assault on hers.

He imagined laying her down on the floor, on a tarp, on the grass. He imagined watching her face as he pleasured them both, of feeling her arch toward him, open, accepting.

It had been too long, he told himself as his muscles began to coil and his lungs to labor. It had just been too long.

But he didn't believe it. And it frightened him.

Unsteady, he lifted his head, drew back. Even as he began the retreat, she leaned against him, letting her head fall onto his chest. Unable to resist, he combed his fingers through her hair and cradled her there.

"My head's spinning," she murmured. "What was that?"

"It was a kiss, that's all." He needed to believe that.

It would help to ease the tightness around his heart and his loins.

"I think I saw stars." Still staggered, she shifted so that she could look up at him. Her lips curved, but her eyes didn't echo the smile. "That's a first for me."

If he didn't do something fast, he was going to kiss her again. He set her firmly on her feet. "It doesn't change anything."

"Was there something to change?"

The light was nearly gone now. It helped that he couldn't see her clearly in the gloom. "I don't have time for women. And I'm just not interested in starting anything."

"Oh." Where had that pain come from? she wondered, and had to fight to keep from rubbing a hand over her heart. "That was quite a kiss, for a disinterested man." Reaching down, she scooped up the briefcase she'd dropped before she'd run up the stairs. "I'll get out of your way. I wouldn't want to waste any more of your valuable time."

"You don't have to get huffy about it."

"Huffy." Her teeth snapped together. She jabbed a finger into his chest. "I'm well beyond huffy, pal, and working my way past steamed. You've got some ego, Mac. What, do you think I came around here to seduce you?"

"I don't know why you came around."

"Well, I won't be around again." She settled her briefcase strap on her shoulder, jerked her chin up. "Nobody twisted your arm."

He was dealing with an uncomfortable combination of desire and guilt. "Yours, either."

"I'm not the one making excuses. You know, I can't figure

out how such an insensitive clod could raise two charming and adorable kids."

"Leave my boys out of this."

The edge to the order had her eyes narrowing to slits. "Oh, so I have designs on them now, too? You idiot!" She stormed for the door, whirling at the last moment for a parting shot. "I hope they don't inherit your warped view of the female species!"

She slammed the door hard enough to have the bad-tempered sound echoing through the house. Mac scowled and jammed his hands in his pockets. He didn't have a warped view, damn it. And his kids were his business.

Chapter 4

Nell stood center stage and lifted her hands. She waited until she was sure every student's eyes were on her, then let it rip.

There was very little that delighted her more than the sound of young voices raised in song. She let the sound fill her, keeping her ears and eyes sharp as she moved around the stage directing. She couldn't hold back the grin. The kids were into this one. Doing Bruce Springsteen and the E Street Band's version of "Santa Claus is Coming to Town" was a departure from the standard carols and hymns their former choral director had arranged year after year.

She could see their eyes light up as they got into the rhythm. *Now punch it,* she thought, pulling more from the bass section as they hit the chorus. *Have fun with it.* Now the soprano section, high and bright... And the altos... Tenors... Bass...

She flashed a smile to signal her approval as the chorus flowered again.

"Good job," she announced. "Tenors, a little more next time. You guys don't want the bass section drowning you out. Holly, you're dropping your chin again. Now we have time for one more run-through of 'I'll Be Home for Christmas.' Kim?"

Kim tried to ignore the little flutter around her heart and the elbow nudge from Holly. She stepped down from her position in the second row and stood in front of the solo mike as though she were facing a firing squad.

"It's okay to smile, you know," Nell told her gently. "And remember your breathing. Sing to the last row, and don't forget to feel the words. Tracy." She held out a finger toward the pianist she'd dragooned from her second-period music class.

The intro started quietly. Using her hands, her face, her eyes, Nell signaled the beginning of the soft, harmonious, background humming. Then Kim began to sing. Too tentatively at first. Nell knew they would have to work on those initial nerves.

But the girl had talent, and emotion. Three bars in, Kim was too caught up in the song to be nervous. She was pacing it well, Nell thought, pleased. Kim had learned quite a bit in the past few weeks about style. The sentimental song suited her, her range, her looks.

Nell brought the chorus in, holding them back. They were background now for Kim's rich, romantic voice. Feeling her own eyes stinging, Nell thought that if they did it this well on the night of the concert, there wouldn't be a dry eye in the house.

"Lovely," Nell said when the last notes had died away. "Really lovely. You guys have come a long way in a very short time. I'm awfully proud of you. Now scram, and have a great weekend."

While Nell moved to the piano to gather up music, the chatter began behind her.

"You sounded really good," Holly told Kim.

"Honest?"

"Honest. Brad thought so, too." Holly shifted her eyes cagily to the school heartthrob, who was shrugging into his school jacket.

"He doesn't even know I'm alive."

"He does now. He was watching you the whole time. I know, because I was watching him." Holly sighed. "If I looked like Miss Davis, *he'd* be watching *me*."

Kim laughed, but shot a quick glance toward Brad under her lashes. "She's really fabulous. Just the way she talks to us and stuff. Mr. Striker always crabbed."

"Mr. Striker *was* a crab. See you later, huh?"

"Yeah." It was all Kim could manage, because it looked, it really looked, as though Brad were coming toward her. And he *was* looking at her.

"Hi." He flashed a grin, all white teeth, with a crooked incisor that made her heart flop around in her chest. "You did real good."

"Thanks." Her tongue tied itself into knots. This was Brad, she kept thinking. A senior. Captain of the football team. Student council president. All blond hair and green eyes.

"Miss Davis sure is cool, isn't she?"

"Yeah." *Say something*, she ordered herself. "She's

coming to a party at my house tonight. My mom's having some people over."

"Adults only, huh?"

"No, Holly's coming by and a couple other people." Her heart thundered in her ears as she screwed up her courage. "You could drop by if you wanted."

"That'd be cool. What time?"

She managed to close her mouth and swallow. "Oh, about eight," she said, struggling for the casual touch. "I live on—"

"I know where you live." He grinned at her again, and all but stopped her thundering heart. "Hey, you're not going with Chuck anymore, are you?"

"Chuck?" Who was Chuck? "Oh, no. We hung out for a while, but we sort of broke up over the summer."

"Great. See you later."

He strolled off to join a group of boys who were trooping offstage.

"That's a very cute guy," Nell commented from behind Kim.

"Yeah." The word was a sigh. Kim had stars in her eyes.

"Kimmy has a boyfriend," Zeke sang, in the high-pitched, annoying voice that was reserved for addressing younger siblings—or female cousins.

"Shut up, brat."

He only giggled and began to dance around the stage, singsonging the refrain. Nell saw murder shoot into Kim's eyes and created a diversion.

"Well, I guess you guys don't want to practice 'Jingle Bells' today."

"Yes, we do." Zack stopped twirling around the stage with his brother and dashed to the piano. "I know which one it is," he said, attacking Nell's neat pile of sheet music. "I can find it."

"I'll find it," Zeke said, but his brother was already holding the music up triumphantly.

"Good going." Nell settled on the bench with a boy on either side of her. She played a dramatic opening chord that made them both giggle. "Please, music is a serious business. And one, and two, and..."

They actually sang it now, instead of screaming it, as they had the first time she invited them to try. What they lacked in style, they made up for in enthusiasm. In spades.

Even Kim was grinning by the time they'd finished.

"Now you do one, Miss Davis." Zack gave her his soulful look. "Please."

"Your dad's probably waiting."

"Just one."

"Just one," Zeke echoed.

In a few short weeks, it had become impossible for her to resist them. "Just one," Nell agreed, and reached into the now-messy pile of music. "I picked up something you might like at the mall. I bet you've seen *The Little Mermaid*."

"Lots of times," Zeke boasted. "We've got the tape and everything."

"Then you'll recognize this." She played the opening of "Part of Your World."

Mac hunched his shoulders against the wind as he headed into the school. He was damn sick and tired of waiting out in the parking lot. He'd seen the other kids filing out more than ten minutes before.

He had things to do, damn it. Especially since he was stuck going over to Mira's for a party.

He hated parties.

He stomped down the hall. And he heard her. Not the words. He couldn't make out the words, because they were muffled by the auditorium doors. But the sound of her voice, rich and deep. A Scotch-and-soda voice, he'd thought more than once. Sensual, seductive. Sexy.

He opened the door. He had to. And the lush flow of it rolled over him.

A kid's song. He recognized it now from the mermaid movie the boys were still crazy about. He told himself no sane man would get tied up in knots when a woman sang a kid's song.

But he wasn't feeling very sane. Hadn't been since he made the enormous mistake of kissing her.

And he knew that if she'd been alone he would have marched right over to the piano and kissed her again.

But she wasn't alone. Kim was standing behind her, and his children flanked her. Now and again she glanced down at them as she sang, and smiled. Zack was leaning toward her, his head tilting in the way it did just before he climbed into your lap.

Something shifted inside him as he watched. Something painful and frightening. And very, very sweet.

Shaken, Mac stuffed his hands into his pockets, curled those hands into fists. It had to stop. Whatever was happening to him had to stop.

He took a long breath when the music ended. He thought—foolishly, he was sure—that there was something magical humming in the instant of silence that followed.

"We're running late," he called out, determined to break the spell.

Four heads turned his way. The twins began to bounce on the bench.

"Dad! Hey, Dad! We can sing 'Jingle Bells' really good! Want to hear us?"

"I can't." He tried to smile, softening the blow, when Zack's lip poked out. "I'm really running late, kids."

"Sorry, Uncle Mac." Kim scooped up her coat. "We kind of lost track."

While Mac shifted uncomfortably, Nell leaned over and murmured something to his sons. Something, Mac noted, that put a smile back on Zack's face and took the mutinous look off Zeke's. Then both of them threw arms around her and kissed her before they raced offstage for their coats.

"Bye, Miss Davis! Bye!"

"Thanks, Miss Davis," Kim added. "See you later."

Nell made a humming sound and rose to straighten her music.

Mac felt the punch of her cold shoulder all the way in the back of the auditorium. "Ah, thanks for entertaining them," he called out.

Nell lifted her head. He could see her clearly in the stage lights. Clearly enough that he caught the lift of her brow, the coolness of her unsmiling mouth, before she lowered her head again.

Fine, he told himself as he caught both boys on the fly. He didn't want to talk to her anyway.

Chapter 5

She didn't have to ignore him so completely. Mac sipped the cup of hard cider his brother-in-law had pressed on him and resentfully studied Nell's back.

She'd had it turned in his direction for an hour.

A hell of a back, too, he thought, half listening as the mayor rattled on in his ear. Smooth and straight, topped off by the fluid curve of her shoulders. It looked very seductive in the thin plum-colored jacket she wore over a short matching dress.

She had terrific legs. He didn't think he'd ever actually seen them before. He would have remembered. Every other time he'd run into her she'd had them covered up.

She'd probably worn a dress tonight to torment him.

Mac cut the mayor off in midstream and strode over to her. "Look, this is stupid."

Nell glanced up. She'd been having a pleasant conversation with a group of Mira's friends—and thoroughly enjoying the simple act of ignoring Mira's brother.

"Excuse me?"

"It's just stupid," he repeated.

"The need to raise more money for the arts in public school is stupid?" she asked, well aware he wasn't referring to the topic she'd been discussing.

"What? No. Damn it, you know what I mean."

"I'm sorry." She started to turn back to the circle of very interested faces, but he took her arm and pulled her aside. "Do you want me to cause a scene in your sister's house?" Nell said between her teeth.

"No." He weaved his way through the minglers, around the dining room table and through the kitchen door. His sister was busy replenishing a tray of canapés. "Give us a minute," he ordered Mira.

"Mac, I'm busy here." Distracted, Mira smoothed a hand over her short brunette hair. "Would you find Dave and tell him we're running low on cider?" She sent Nell a frazzled smile. "I thought I was organized."

"Give us a minute," Mac repeated.

Mira let out an impatient breath, but then her eyebrows shot up, drew in. "Well, well," she murmured, amused and clearly delighted. "I'll just get out of your way. I want a closer look at that boy Kim's so excited about." She picked up the tray of finger food and swung through the kitchen door.

Silence fell like a hammer.

"So." Casually, Nell plucked a carrot stick from a bowl. "Something on your mind, Macauley?"

"I don't see why you have to be so..."

"So?" She crunched into the carrot. "What?"

"You're making a point of not talking to me."

She smiled. "Yes, I am."

"It's stupid."

She located an open bottle of white wine, poured some into a glass. After a sip, she smiled again. "I don't think so. It seems to me that, for no discernible reason, I annoy you. Since I'm quite fond of your family, it seems logical and courteous to stay as far out of your way as I possibly can." She sipped again. "Now, is that all? I've been enjoying myself so far this evening."

"You don't annoy me. Exactly." He couldn't find anything to do with his hands, so he settled on taking a carrot stick and breaking it in half. "I'm sorry...for before."

"You're sorry for kissing me, or for behaving like a jerk afterward?"

He tossed the pieces of carrot down. "You're a hard one, Nell."

"Wait." Eyes wide, she pressed a hand to her ear. "I think something's wrong with my hearing. I thought, for just a minute, you actually said my name."

"Cut it out," he said. Then, deliberately: "Nell."

"This is a moment," she declared, and toasted him. "Macauley Taylor has actually initiated a conversation with me, *and* used my name. I'm all aflutter."

"Look." Temper had him rounding the counter. He'd nearly grabbed her before he pushed his anger back. "I just want to clear the air."

Fascinated, she studied his now-impassive face. "That's quite a control button you've got there, Mac. It's admirable.

Still, I wonder what would happen if you didn't push it so often."

"A man raising two kids on his own needs control."

"I suppose," she murmured. "Now, if that's all—"

"I'm sorry," he said again.

This time she softened. She was simply no good at holding a grudge. "Okay. Let's just forget it. Friends," she offered, and held out a hand.

He took it. It was so soft, so small, he couldn't make himself give it up again. Her eyes were soft, too, just now. Big, liquid eyes you'd have expected to see on a fawn. "You... look nice."

"Thanks. You, too."

"You like the party?"

"I like the people." Her pulse was starting to jump. Damn him. "Your sister's wonderful. So full of energy and ideas."

"You have to watch her." His lips curved slowly. "She'll rope you into one of her projects."

"Too late. She's got me on the arts committee already. And I've been volunteered to help with the recycling campaign."

"The trick is to duck."

"I don't mind, really. I think I'm going to enjoy it." His thumb was brushing over her wrist now, lightly. "Mac, don't start something you don't intend to finish."

Brow creased, he looked down at their joined hands. "I think about you. I don't have time to think about you. I don't want to have time."

It was happening again. The flutters and quivers she seemed to have no control over. "What do you want?"

His gaze lifted, locked with hers. "I'm having some trouble with that."

The kitchen door burst open, and a horde of teenagers piled in, only to be brought up short as Kim, in the lead, stopped on a dime.

Her eyes widened as she watched her uncle drop her teacher's hand, and the two of them jumped apart like a couple of teenagers caught necking on the living room sofa.

"Sorry. Ah, sorry," she repeated, goggling. "We were just..." She turned on her heel and shoved back at her friends. They scooted out, chuckling.

"That ought to add some juice to the grapevine," Nell said wryly. She'd been in town long enough to know that everyone would be speculating about Mac Taylor and Nell Davis by morning. Steadier now, she turned back to him. "Listen, why don't we try this in nice easy stages? You want to go out to dinner tomorrow? See a movie or something?"

Now it was his turn to stare. "A date? Are you asking me out on a date?"

Impatience flickered back. "Yes, a date. It doesn't mean I'm asking to bear you more children. On second thought, let's just quit while we're ahead."

"I want to get my hands on you." Mac heard himself say the words, knew it was too late to take them back.

Nell reached for her wine in self-defense. "Well, that's simple."

"No, it's not."

She braced herself and looked up at him again. "No," she agreed quietly. Just how many times, she wondered, had his face popped into her mind in the past few weeks? She couldn't count them. "It's not simple."

But something had to be done, he decided. A move forward, a move back. Take a step, he ordered himself. See what happens. "I haven't been to a movie without the kids... I can't remember. I could probably line up a sitter."

"All right." She was watching him now almost as carefully as he watched her. "Give me a call if it works out. I'll be home most of tomorrow, correcting papers."

It wasn't the easiest thing, stepping back into the dating pool—however small the pool and however warm the water. It irritated him that he was nervous, almost as much as his niece's grins and questions had irritated when she agreed to babysit.

Now, as he climbed the sturdy outside steps to Nell's third-floor apartment, Mac wondered if it would be better all around if they forgot the whole thing.

As he stepped onto her deck, he noted that she'd flanked the door with pots of mums. It was a nice touch, he thought. He always appreciated it when someone who rented one of his homes cared enough to bother with those nice touches.

It was just a movie, he reminded himself, and rapped on the door. When she opened it, he was relieved that she'd dressed casually—a hip-grazing sweater over a pair of those snug leggings Kim liked so much.

Then she smiled and had his mouth going dry.

"Hi. You're right on time. Do you want to come in and see what I've done to your place?"

"It's your place—as long as you pay the rent," he told her, but she was reaching out, taking his hand, drawing him in.

Mac had dispensed with the walls that had made stingy little rooms and had created one flowing space of living, dining and kitchen area. And she'd known what to do with it.

There was a huge L-shaped couch in a bold floral print that should have been shocking, but was, instead, perfect. A small table under the window held a pot of dried autumn leaves. Shelves along one wall held books, a stereo and a small TV, and the sort of knickknacks he knew women liked.

She'd turned the dining area into a combination music room and office, with her desk and a small spinet. A flute lay on a music stand.

"I didn't bring a lot with me from New York," she said as she shrugged into her jacket. "Only what I really cared about. I'm filling in with things from antique shops and flea markets.

"We got a million of them," he murmured. "It looks good." And it did—the old, faded rug on the floor, the fussy priscillas at the windows. "Comfortable."

"Comfortable's very important to me. Ready?"

"Sure."

And it wasn't so hard after all.

He'd asked her to pick the movie, and she'd gone for comedy. It was surprisingly relaxing to sit in the darkened theater and share popcorn and laughter.

He only thought about her as a woman, a very attractive woman, a couple of dozen times.

Going for pizza afterward seemed such a natural progression, he suggested it himself. They competed for a table in the crowded pizzeria with teenagers out on date night.

"So…" Nell stretched out in the booth. "How's Zeke's career in spelling coming along?"

"It's a struggle. He really works at it. It's funny, Zack can spell almost anything you toss at him first time around, but Zeke has to study the word like a scholar with the Dead Sea Scrolls."

"He's good at his arithmetic."

"Yeah." Mac wasn't sure how he felt about her knowing so much about his kids. "They're both taken with you."

"It's mutual." She skimmed a hand through her hair. "It's going to sound odd, but…" She hesitated, not quite sure how to word it. "But that first day at rehearsal, when I looked around and saw them? I had this feeling, this— I don't know, it was like, 'Oh, there you are. I was wondering when you'd show up.' It sounds strange, but it was as if I was expecting them. Now, when Kim comes without them, I feel let down."

"I guess they kind of grow on you."

It was more than that, but she didn't know how to explain. And she wasn't entirely sure Mac would accept the fact that she'd very simply fallen for them. "I get a kick out of them telling me about their school day, showing me their papers."

"First report cards are almost here." His grin flashed. "I'm more nervous than they are."

"People put too much emphasis on grades."

His brows shot up at the comment. "This from a teacher?"

"Individual ability, application, effort, retention. Those things are a lot more important than *A, B* or *C.* But I can tell you, in confidence, that Kim's aceing advanced chorus and music history."

"No kidding?" He felt a quick surge of pride. "She never did that well before. *B*s mostly."

"Mr. Striker and I have markedly different approaches."

"You're telling me. Word around town is that the chorus is dynamite this year. How'd you pull it off?"

"The kids pull it off," she told him, sitting up when their pizza was served. "My job is to make them think and sing like a team. Not to slam Mr. Striker," she added, taking a generous bite. "But I get the impression he was just putting in time, counting the days until he could retire. If you're going to teach kids, you have to like them, and respect them. There's a lot of talent there, some of it extremely rough." When she laughed, the roses in her cheek bloomed deeper. "And some of those kids will do nothing more than sing in the shower for the rest of their lives—for which the world can be grateful."

"Got some clinkers, huh?"

"Well…" She laughed again. "Yes, I have a few. But they're enjoying themselves. That's what counts. And there are a few, like Kim, who are really something special. I'm sending her and two others for auditions to all-state next week. And after the holiday concert I'm going to hold auditions for the spring musical."

"We haven't had a musical at the high school in three years."

"We're going to have one this year, Buster. And it's going to be terrific."

"It's a lot of work for you."

"I like it. And it's what I'm paid for."

Mac toyed with a second slice. "You really do like it, don't you? The school, the town, the whole bit?"

"Why shouldn't I? It's a fine school, a fine town."

"It ain't Manhattan."

"Exactly."

"Why'd you leave?" He winced. "Sorry, none of my business."

"It's all right. I had a bad year. I guess I was getting restless before that, but the last year was just the pits. They eliminated my job at the school. Economic cutbacks. Downsizing. The arts are always the first to suffer." She shrugged. "Anyway, my roommate got married. I couldn't afford the rent on my own—not if I wanted to eat with any regularity—so I advertised for another one. Took references, gauged personalities." With a sigh, she propped her chin on her elbow. "I thought I was careful. But about three weeks after she moved in, I came home and found that she'd cleaned me out."

Mac stopped eating. "She robbed you?"

"She skinned me. TV, stereo, whatever good jewelry I had, cash, the collection of Limoges boxes I'd started in college. I was really steamed, and then I was shaken. I just wasn't comfortable living there after it happened. Then the guy I'd been seeing for about a year started giving me lectures on my stupidity, my naïveté. As far as he was concerned, I'd gotten exactly what I'd deserved."

"Nice guy," Mac muttered. "Very supportive."

"You bet. In any case, I took a good look at him and our relationship and figured he was right on one level. As long as I was in that rut, with him, I was getting what I deserved. So I decided to climb out of the rut, and leave him in it."

"Good choice."

"I thought so." And so was he, she thought, studying Mac's face. A very good choice. "Why don't you tell me what your plans are with the house you're renovating."

"I don't guess you'd know a lot about plumbing."

She only smiled. "I'm a quick learner."

It was nearly midnight when he pulled up in front of her apartment. He hadn't intended to stay out so late. He certainly hadn't expected to spend more than an hour talking to her about wiring and plumbing and load-bearing walls. Or drawing little blueprints on napkins.

But somehow he'd managed to get through the evening without feeling foolish, or pinned down or out of step. Only one thing worried him. He wanted to see her again.

"I think this was a good first step." She laid a hand over his, kissed his cheek. "Thanks."

"I'll walk you up."

Her hand was already on the door handle. Safer, she'd decided for both of them, if she just hurried along. "You don't have to. I know the way."

"I'll walk you up," he repeated. He stepped out, rounded the hood. They started up the stairs together. The tenant on the first floor was still awake. The mutter of a television, and its ghost gray light, filtered through the window.

Since the breeze had died, it was the only sound. And overhead countless stars wheeled in a clear black sky.

"If we do this again," Mac began, "people in town are going to start talking about us, making out that we're..." He wasn't quite sure of the right phrase.

"An item?" Nell supplied. "That bothers you."

"I don't want the kids to get any ideas, or worry, or… whatever." As they reached the landing, he looked down at her and was caught again. "It must be the way you look," he murmured.

"What must?"

"That makes me think about you." It was a reasonable explanation, he decided. Physical attraction. After all, he wasn't a dead man. He was just a careful one. "That makes me think about doing this."

He cupped her face in his hands—a gesture so sweet, so tender, it had every muscle in her body going lax. It was just as slow, as stunning, as sumptuous, as the first time. The touch of his mouth on hers, the shuddering patience, the simple wonder of it.

Could it be this? she wondered. Could it be this that she'd been waiting for? Could it be him?

He heard her soft, breathy sigh as he eased his mouth from hers. Lingering, he knew, would be a mistake, and he let his hands fall away before they could reach for more.

As if to capture one final taste, Nell ran her tongue over her lips. "You're awfully good at that, Macauley. Awfully good."

"You could say I've been saving up." But he didn't think it was that at all. He was very much worried it wasn't that. "I'll see you."

She nodded weakly as he headed down the steps. She was still leaning dreamily against the door when she heard his car start and drive away.

For a moment, she would have sworn the air rang with the distant music of sleigh bells.

Chapter 6

The end of October meant parent-teacher conferences, and a much-anticipated holiday for students. It also meant a headache for Mac. He had to juggle the twins from his sister to Kim to Mrs. Hollis, fitting in a trip to order materials and an electrical inspection.

When he turned his truck into the educational complex, he was jumpy with nerves. Lord knew what he was about to be told about his children, how they behaved when they were out of his sight and his control. He worried that he hadn't made enough time to help them with their schoolwork and somehow missed a parental step in preparing them for the social, educational and emotional demands of first grade.

Because of his failure, his boys would become antisocial, illiterate neurotics.

He knew he was being ridiculous, but he couldn't stop his fears from playing over and over like an endless loop in his brain.

"Mac!" The car horn and the sound of his name had him turning and focusing, finally, on his sister's car. She leaned out the window, shaking her head at him. "Where were you? I called you three times."

"Bailing my kids out of jail," he muttered, and changed course to walk to her car. "I've got a conference in a minute."

"I know. I've just come from a meeting at the high school. Remember, we compared schedules."

"Right. I shouldn't be late."

"You don't get demerits. My meeting was about raising funds for new chorus uniforms. Those kids have been wearing the same old choir robes for twelve years. We're hoping to raise enough to put them in something a little snazzier."

"Fine, I'll give you a donation, but I shouldn't be late." Already he was imagining the young, fresh-faced first grade teacher marking him tardy, just another item on a growing list of negatives about Taylor males.

"I just wanted to say that Nell seemed upset about something."

"What?"

"Upset," Mira repeated, pleased that she finally had his full attention. "She came up with a couple of nice ideas for fundraisers, but she was obviously distracted." Mira lifted a brow, eyeing her brother slyly. "You haven't done anything to annoy her, have you?"

"No." Mac caught himself before he shifted guiltily from foot to foot. "Why should I?"

"Couldn't say. But since you've been seeing her—"

"We went to the movies."

"And for pizza," Mira added. "A couple of Kim's friends spotted you."

The curse of small towns, Mac thought, and stuffed his hands in his pockets. "So?"

"So nothing. Good for you. I like her a lot. Kim's crazy about her. I suppose I'm feeling a bit protective. She was definitely upset, Mac, and trying not to show it. Maybe she'd talk to you about it."

"I'm not going to go poking around in her personal life."

"The way I see it, you're part of her personal life. See you later." She pulled off without giving him a chance for a parting shot.

Muttering to himself, Mac marched up to the elementary school. When he marched out twenty minutes later, he was in a much lighter mood. His children had not been declared social misfits with homicidal tendencies after all. In fact, their teacher had praised them.

Of course, he'd known all along.

Maybe Zeke forgot the rules now and then and talked to his neighbor. And maybe Zack was a little shy about raising his hand when he knew an answer. But they were settling in.

With the weight of first grade off his shoulders, Mac headed out. Impulse had him swinging toward the high school. He knew his conference had been one of the last of the day. He wasn't sure how teachers' meetings worked at the high school, but the lot was nearly empty. He spotted Nell's car, however, and decided it wouldn't hurt just to drop in.

It wasn't until he was inside that he realized he didn't have a clue as to where to find her.

Mac poked his head into the auditorium, but it was empty. Since he'd come that far, he backtracked to the main office and caught one of the secretaries as she was leaving for the day. Following her directions, he turned down a corridor, headed up a ramp and turned right.

Nell's classroom door was open. Not like any classroom he'd done time in, he thought. This one had a piano, music stands, instruments, a tape recorder. There was the usual blackboard, wiped clean, and a desk where Nell was currently working.

He watched her for a long moment, the way her hair fell, the way her fingers held the pen, the way her sweater draped at the neck. It occurred to him that if he'd ever had a teacher who looked like that, he would have been a great deal more interested in music.

"Hi."

Her head snapped up. There was a martial light in her eyes that surprised him, a stubborn set to her jaw. Even as he watched, she took a long breath and worked up a smile.

"Hello, Mac. Welcome to bedlam."

"Looks like a lot of work." He stepped inside, up to the desk. It was covered with papers, books, computer printouts and sheet music, all in what appeared to be ordered piles.

"Finishing up the first marking period, grades, class planning, fundraising strategy, fine-tuning the holiday concert—and trying to make the budget stretch to producing the spring musical." Trying to keep her foul mood to herself, she sat back. "So, how was your day?"

"Pretty good. I just had a conference with the twins' teacher. They're doing fine. I can stop sweating report cards."

"They're great kids. You've got nothing to worry about."

"Worry comes with the territory. What are you worried about?" he asked before he could remind himself he wasn't going to pry.

"How much time have you got?" she shot back.

"Enough." Curious, he eased a hip onto the edge of her desk. He wanted to soothe, he discovered, to stroke away that faint line between her brows. "Rough day?"

She jerked her shoulders, then pushed away from her desk. Temper always forced her to move. "I've had better. Do you know how much school and community support the football team gets? All the sports teams." She began to slap cassette tapes into a box—anything to keep her hands busy. "Even the band. But the chorus, we have to go begging for every dollar."

"You're ticked off about the budget?"

"Why shouldn't I be?" She whirled back, eyes hot. "No problem getting equipment for the football team so a bunch of boys can go out on the field and tackle each other, but I have to spend an hour on my knees if I want eighty bucks to get a piano tuned." She caught herself, sighed. "I don't have anything against football. I like it. High school sports are important."

"I know a guy who tunes pianos," Mac said. "He'd probably donate his time."

Nell rubbed a hand over her face, slid it around to soothe the tension at the back of her neck. *Dad can fix anything,* she thought, just as the twins had claimed. Have a problem? Call Mac.

"That would be great," she said, and managed a real smile. "If I can beat my way through the paperwork and get approval. You can't even take freebies without going through the board." It irritated her, as always. "One of the worst aspects of teaching is the bureaucracy. Maybe I should have stuck with performing in clubs."

"You performed in clubs?"

"In another life," she muttered, waving it away. "A little singing to pay my way through college. It was better than waiting tables. Anyway, it's not the budget, not really. Or even the lack of interest from the community. I'm used to that."

"Do you want to tell me what it is, or do you want to stew about it?"

"I was having a pretty good time stewing about it." She sighed again, and looked up at him. He seemed so solid, so dependable. "Maybe I'm too much of an urbanite after all. I've had my first run-in with old-fashioned rural attitude, and I'm stumped. Do you know Hank Rohrer?"

"Sure. He has a dairy farm out on Old Oak Road. I think his oldest kid is in the same class as Kim."

"Hank, Jr. Yes. Junior's one of my students—a very strong baritone. He has a real interest in music. He even writes it."

"No kidding? That's great."

"You'd think so, wouldn't you?" Nell tossed her hair back and went to her desk again to tidy her already tidy papers. "Well, I asked Mr. and Mrs. Rohrer to come in this morning because Junior backed out of going to all-state auditions this weekend. I knew he had a very good chance of making it, and I wanted to discuss the possibility with his parents of a music scholarship. When I told them how talented Junior was and how I hoped they'd encourage him to change his mind about the auditions, Hank Senior acted as though I'd just insulted him. He was appalled." There was bitterness in her voice now, as well as anger. "'No son of his was going to waste his time on singing and writing music like some...'"

She trailed off, too furious to repeat the man's opinion of musicians. "They didn't even know Junior was in my class. Thought he was taking shop as his elective this year. I tried to smooth it over, said that Junior needed a fine-art credit to graduate. I didn't do much good. Mr. Rohrer could barely swallow the idea of Junior staying in my class. He went on about how Junior didn't need singing lessons to run a farm. And he certainly wasn't going to allow him to take a Saturday and go audition when the boy had chores. And I'm to stop putting any fancy ideas about college in the boy's head."

"They've got four kids," Mac said slowly. "Tuition might be a problem."

"If that were the only obstacle, they should be grateful for the possibility of scholarship." She slapped her grade book closed. "What we have is a bright, talented boy who has dreams, dreams he'll never be able to explore because his parents won't permit it. Or his father won't," she added. "His mother didn't say two words the entire time they were here."

"Could be she'll work on Hank once she has him alone."

"Could be he'll take out his annoyance with me on both of them."

"Hank's not like that. He's set in his ways and thinks he knows all the answers, but he isn't mean."

"It's a little tough for me to see his virtues after he called me—" she had to take a deep breath "—a slick-handed flat-lander who's wasting his hard-earned tax dollars. I could have made a difference with that boy," Nell murmured as she sat again. "I know it."

"So maybe you won't be able to make a difference with Junior. You'll make a difference with someone else. You've already made one with Kim."

"Thanks." Nell's smile was brief. "That helps a little."

"I mean it." He hated to see her this way, all that brilliant energy and optimism dimmed. "She's gained a lot of confidence in herself. She's always been shy about her singing, about a lot of things. Now she's really opening up."

It did help to hear it. This time Nell's smile came easier. "So I should stop brooding."

"It doesn't suit you." He surprised himself, and her, by reaching down to run his knuckles over her cheek. "Smiling does."

"I've never been able to hold on to temperament for long. Bob used to say it was because I was shallow."

"Who the hell's Bob?"

"The one who's still in the rut."

"Clearly where he belongs."

She laughed. "I'm glad you dropped by. I'd have probably sat here for another hour clenching my jaw."

"It's a pretty jaw," Mac murmured, then shifted away. "I've got to get going. I've got Halloween costumes to put together."

"Need any help?"

"I..." It was tempting, too tempting, and far too dangerous, he thought, to start sharing family traditions with her. "No, I've got it covered."

Nell accepted the disappointment, nearly masked it. "You'll bring them by Saturday night, won't you? To trick-or-treat?"

"Sure. I'll see you." He started out but stopped at the doorway and turned back. "Nell?"

"Yes?"

"Some things take a while to change. Change makes some people nervous."

She tilted her head. "Are you talking about the Rohrers, Mac?"

"Among others. I'll see you Saturday night."

Nell studied the empty doorway as his footsteps echoed away. Did he think she was trying to change him? Was she? She sat back, pushing away from the paperwork. She'd never be able to concentrate on it now.

Whenever she was around Macauley Taylor, it was hard to concentrate. When had she become so susceptible to the slow, thorough, quiet type? From the moment he'd walked into the auditorium to pick up Kim and the twins, she admitted.

Love at first sight? Surely she was too sophisticated, too smart, to believe in such a thing. And surely, she added, she was too smart to put herself in the vulnerable position of falling in love with a man who didn't return her feelings.

Or didn't want to, she thought. And that was even worse.

It couldn't matter that he was sweet and kind and devoted to his children. It shouldn't matter that he was handsome and strong and sexy. She wouldn't let it matter that being with him, thinking of him, had her longing for things. For home, for family, for laughter in the kitchen and passion in bed.

She let out a long breath, because it did matter. It mattered very much when a woman was teetering right on the edge of falling in love.

Chapter 7

Mid-November had stripped the leaves from the trees. There was a beauty even in this, Nell had decided. Beauty in the dark, denuded branches, in the papery rustle of dried leaves along the curbs, in the frost that shimmered like diamond dust on the grass in the mornings.

She caught herself staring out of the window too often, wishing for snow like a child hoping for a school holiday.

It felt wonderful. Wonderful to anticipate the winter, to remember the fall. She often thought about Halloween night, and all the children who had come knocking on her door dressed as pirates and princesses. She remembered the way Zeke and Zack had giggled when she pretended not to recognize them in the elaborate astronaut costumes Mac had fashioned for them.

She found herself reminiscing about the bluegrass concert Mac had taken her to. Or the fun they'd had when she ran into him and the boys at the mall just last week, all of them on a mission to complete their Christmas lists early.

Now, strolling past the house Mac was remodeling, she thought of him again. It had been so sweet, the way he'd struggled over choosing just the right outfit for Kim's present. No thoughtless gifts from Macauley Taylor for those he cared about. It had to be the right color, the right style.

She'd come to believe everything about him was right.

She passed the house, drawing in the chilly air of evening, her mood buoyant. That afternoon she'd been proud to announce that two of her students would participate in all-state chorus.

She had made a difference, Nell thought, shutting her eyes on the pleasure of it. Not just the prestige, certainly not simply the delight of having the principal congratulate her. The difference, the important one, had been the look on her students' faces. The pride, not just on Kim's face and that of the tenor who would go to all-state with her. But on the faces of the entire chorus. They all shared in the triumph, because over the past few weeks they had become a team.

Her team. Her kids.

"It's cold for walking."

Nell jolted, tensed, then laughed at herself when she saw Mac step away from the shadow of a tree in his sister's yard. "Lord, you gave me a start. I nearly went into my repel-the-mugger stance."

"Taylor's Grove's a little sparse when it comes to muggers. Are you going to see Mira?"

"No, actually, I was just out walking. Too much energy to stay in." The smile lit her face. "You've heard the good news?"

"Congratulations."

"It's not me—"

"Yeah, it is. A lot of it." It was the only way he knew to tell her how proud he was of what she'd done. He glanced back toward the house, where lights gleamed. "Mira and Kim are in there crying."

"Crying? But—"

"Not that kind of crying." Female tears always embarrassed him. He shrugged. "You know, the other kind."

"Oh." In response, Nell felt her own eyes sting. "That's nice."

"Dave's going around with a big fat grin on his face. He was talking to his parents when I ducked out. Mira's already called ours, as well as every other friend and relative in the country."

"Well, it's a big deal."

"I know it is." His teeth flashed. "I've made a few calls myself. You must be feeling pretty pleased with yourself."

"You bet I am. Seeing the kids today when I made the announcement…well, it was the best. And it's a hell of a kickoff for our fundraiser." She shivered as the wind shuddered through the trees.

"You're getting cold. I'll drive you home."

"That'd be nice. I keep waiting for snow."

In the way of every countryman since Adam, he sniffed the air, checked out the sky. "You won't have to wait much longer." He opened the truck door for her. "The kids have already gotten their sleds out."

"I might buy one for myself." She settled back, relaxed. "Where are the boys?"

"There's a sleepover at one of their friends'." He gestured

toward the house across the street from Mira's. "I just dropped them off."

"They must be thinking a lot about Christmas now, with snow in the air."

"It's funny. Usually right after Halloween they start barraging me with lists and pictures of toys from catalogs, stuff they see on TV." He turned the truck and headed for the square. "This year they told me Santa's taking care of it. I know they want bikes." His brow creased. "That's all I've heard. They've been whispering together about something else, but they clam up when I come around."

"That's Christmas," Nell said easily. "It's the best time for whispers and secrets. What about you?" She turned to smile at him. "What do you want for Christmas?"

"More than the two hours' sleep I usually get."

"You can do better than that."

"When the kids come downstairs in the morning, and their faces light up, I've got all I want." He stopped in front of her apartment. "Are you going back to New York for the holiday?"

"No, there's nothing there."

"Your family?"

"I'm an only child. My parents usually spend the holiday in the Caribbean. Do you want to come in, have some coffee?"

It was a much more appealing idea than going home to an empty house. "Yeah, thanks." When they started up the stairs, he tried to swing tactfully back to the holidays and her family. "Is that where you spent Christmas as a kid? In the Caribbean?"

"No. We had a fairly traditional setting in Philadelphia.

Then I went to school in New York, and they moved to Florida." She opened the door and took off her coat. "We aren't very close, really. They weren't terribly happy with my decision to study music."

"Oh." He tossed his jacket over hers while she moved into the kitchen to put on the coffee. "I guess that's why you got so steamed about Junior."

"Maybe. They didn't really disapprove so much as they were baffled. We get along much better long-distance." She glanced over her shoulder. "I think that's why I admire you."

He stopped studying the rosewood music box on a table and stared at her. "Me?"

"Your interest and involvement with your children, your whole family. It's so solid, so natural." Tossing back her hair, she reached into the cookie jar and began to spread cookies on a plate. "Not everyone is as willing, or as able, to put in so much time and attention. Not everyone loves as well, or as thoroughly." She smiled. "Now I've embarrassed you."

"No. Yes," he admitted, and took one of the cookies. "You haven't asked about their mother." When she said nothing, Mac found himself talking. "I was just out of college when I met her. She was a secretary in my father's real estate office. She was beautiful. I mean eye-popping beautiful, the kind that bowls you over. We went out a couple of times, we went to bed, she got pregnant."

The flat-voiced recitation had Nell looking up. Mac bit into the cookie, tasting bitterness. "I know that sounds like she did it on her own. I was young, but I was old enough to know what I was doing, old enough to be responsible."

He had always taken his responsibilities seriously, Nell

thought, and he always would. You only had to look at him to see the dependability.

"You didn't say anything about love."

"No, I didn't." It was something he didn't take lightly. "I was attracted, so was she. Or I thought she was. What I didn't know was that she'd lied about using birth control. It wasn't until after I'd married her that I found out she'd set out to 'snag the boss's son.' Her words," he added. "Angie saw an opportunity to improve her standard of living."

It surprised him that even now, after all this time, it hurt both pride and heart to know he'd been so carelessly used.

"To make a long story short," he continued, in that same expressionless tone, "she hadn't counted on twins, or the hassle of motherhood. So, about a month after the boys were born, she cleaned out my bank account and split."

"I'm so sorry, Mac," Nell murmured. She wished she knew the words, the gesture, that would erase that cool dispassion from his eyes. "It must have been horrible for you."

"It could have been worse." His eyes met Nell's briefly before he shrugged it off. "I could have loved her. She contacted me once, telling me she wanted me to foot the bill for the divorce. In exchange for that, I could have the kids free and clear. Free and clear," he repeated. "As if they were stocks and bonds instead of children. I took her up on it. End of story."

"Is it?" Nell moved to him, took his hands in hers. "Even if you didn't love her, she hurt you."

She rose on her toes to kiss his cheek, to soothe, to comfort. She saw the change in his eyes—and, yes, the hurt in them. It explained a great deal, she thought, to hear him tell the story. To see his face as he did. He'd been disillusioned, devastated. Instead of giving in to it, or leaning on his parents for help with the burden, he'd taken his sons and started a life with them. A life for them.

"She didn't deserve you, or the boys."

"It wasn't a hardship." He couldn't take his eyes off hers now. It wasn't the sympathy so much as the simple, unquestioning understanding that pulled at him. "They're the best part of me. I didn't mean it to sound like it was a sacrifice."

"You didn't. You don't." Her heart melted as she slid her arms around him. She'd meant that, too, as a comfort. But something more, something deeper, was stirring inside her. "You made it sound as if you love them. It's very appealing to hear a man say that he thinks of his children as a gift. And to know he means it."

He was holding her, and he wasn't quite sure how it had happened. It seemed so easy, so natural, to have her settled in his arms. "When you're given a gift, an important one, you have to be careful with it." His voice thickened with a mix of emotions. His children. Her. Something about the way she was looking up at him, the way her lips curved. He lifted a hand to stroke her hair, lingered over it a moment before he remembered to back away. "I should go."

"Stay." It was so easy, she discovered, to ask him. So easy, after all, to need him. "You know I want you to stay. You know I want you."

He couldn't take his eyes off her face, and the need was so much bigger, so much sweeter, than he'd ever imagined. "It could complicate things, Nell. I've got a lot of baggage. Most of it's in storage, but—"

"I don't care." Her breath trembled out. "I don't even have

any pride at the moment. Make love with me, Mac." On a sigh, she pulled his head down and pressed her lips to his. "Just love me tonight."

He couldn't resist. It was a fantasy that had begun to wind through him, body and mind, the moment he first met her. She was all softness, all warmth. He'd done without both of those miraculous female gifts for so long.

Now, with her mouth on his and her arms twined around him, she was all he could want.

He'd never considered himself romantic. He wondered if a woman like Nell would prefer candlelight, soft music, perfumed air. But the scene was already set. He could do nothing more than lift her into his arms and carry her to the bedroom.

He turned on a lamp, surprised at how suddenly his nerves vanished when he saw hers reflected in her eyes.

"I've thought about this a long time," he told her. "I want to see you, every minute I'm touching you. I want to see you."

"Good." She looked up at him and his smile soothed away some of her tension. "I want to see you."

He carried her to the bed and lay down beside her, stroking a hand through her hair, over her shoulders. Then he dipped his head to kiss her.

It was so easy, as if they had shared nights and intimacy for years. It was so thrilling, as if each of them had come to the bed as innocent as a babe.

A touch, a taste, patient and lingering. A murmur, a sigh, soft and quiet. His hands never rushed, only pleasured, stroking over her, unfastening buttons, pausing to explore.

Her skin quivered under his caress even as it heated. A

hundred pulse points thrummed, speeding at the brush of a fingertip, the flick of a tongue. Her own hands trembled, pulling a laughing groan from her that ended on a broken whimper when she at last found flesh.

Making love. The phrase had never been truer to her. For here was an exquisite tenderness mixed with a lustful curiosity that overpowered the senses, tangled in the system like silken knots. Each time his mouth returned to hers, it went deeper, wider, higher, so that he was all that existed for her. All that needed to.

She gave with a depthless generosity that staggered him. She fit, body to body, with him, with a perfection that thrilled. Each time he thought his control would slip, he found himself sliding easily back into the rhythm they set.

Slow, subtle, savoring.

She was small, delicately built. The fragility he sensed made his hands all the more tender. Even as she arched and cried out the first time, he didn't hurry. It was gloriously arousing for him simply to watch her face, that incredibly expressive face, as every emotion played over it.

He fought back the need to bury himself inside her, clung to control long enough to protect them both. Their eyes locked when at last he slipped into her. Her breath caught and released, and then her lips curved.

Outside, the wind played against the windows, making a music like sleigh bells. And the first snow of the season began to fall as quietly as a wish.

Chapter 8

He couldn't get enough of her. Mac figured at worst it was a kind of insanity, at best a temporary obsession. No matter how many demands there were on his time, his brain, his emotions, he still found odd moments, day and night, to think about Nell.

Though he knew it was cynical, he wished it could have been just sex. If it was only sex, he could put it down to hormones and get back to business. But he didn't just imagine her in bed, or fantasize about finding an hour to lose himself in that trim little body.

Sometimes, when she slipped into his head, she was standing in front of a group of children, directing their voices with her hands, her arms, her whole self. Or she'd be seated at the piano, with his boys on either side of her, laughing with them. Or she'd just be walking through town, with her hands in her pockets and her face lifted toward the sky.

She scared him right down to the bone.

And she, he thought as he measured his baseboard trim, she was so easy about the whole thing. That was a woman for you, he decided. They didn't have to worry about making the right moves, saying the right thing. They just had to… to be, he thought. That was enough to drive a man crazy.

He couldn't afford to be crazy. He had kids to raise, a business to run. Hell, he had laundry to do if he ever got home. And damn it, he'd forgotten to take the chicken out of the freezer again.

They'd catch burgers on the way to the concert, he told himself. He had enough on his mind without having to fix dinner. Christmas was barreling toward him, and the kids were acting strange.

Just the bikes, Dad, they told him. *Santa's making them, and he's taking care of the big present.*

What big present? Mac wondered. No interrogation, no tricks, had pulled out that particular answer. For once his kids were closed up tight. That was an idea that disturbed him. He knew that in another year, two if he was lucky, they'd begin to question and doubt the existence of Santa and magic. The end of innocence. Whatever it was they were counting on for Christmas morning, he wanted to see that they found it under the tree.

But they just grinned at him when he prodded and told him it was a surprise for all three of them.

He'd have to work on it. Mac hammered the trim into place. At least they'd gotten the tree up and baked some cookies, strung the popcorn. He felt a little twinge of guilt over the fact that he'd evaded Nell's offer to help with the decorating. And ignored the kids when they asked if she could come over and trim the tree with them.

Was he the only one who could see what a mistake it would be to have his children become too attached? She'd only been in town for a few months. She could leave at any time. Nell might find them cute, attractive kids, but she didn't have any investment in them.

Damn it, now *he* was making them sound like stocks and bonds.

It wasn't what he meant, Mac assured himself. He simply wasn't going to allow anyone to walk out on his sons again.

He wouldn't risk it, not for anything in heaven or on earth.

After nailing the last piece of baseboard in place, he nodded in approval. The house was coming together just fine. He knew what he was doing there. Just as he knew what he was doing with the boys.

He only wished he had a better idea of what to do with Nell.

"Maybe it'll happen tonight." Zeke watched his breath puff out like smoke as he and his twin sat in the tree house, wrapped against the December chill in coats and scarves.

"It's not Christmas yet."

"But it's the Christmas concert," Zeke said stubbornly. He was tired of waiting for the mom. "That's where we saw her first. And they'll have the music and the tree and stuff, so it'll be like Christmas."

"I don't know." Zack liked the idea, a lot, but was more cautious. "Maybe, but we don't get any presents until Christmas."

"We do, too. When Mr. Perkins pretends to be Santa

at the party at the firehouse. That's whole weeks before Christmas, and he gives all the kids presents."

"Not *real* presents. Not stuff you ask for." But Zack set his mind to it. "Maybe if we wish real hard. Dad likes her a lot. Aunt Mira was telling Uncle Dave that Dad's found the right woman even if he doesn't know it." Zack's brow creased. "How could he not know it if he found her?"

"Aunt Mira's always saying stuff that doesn't make sense," Zeke said, with the easy disdain of the young. "Dad's going to marry her, and she's going to come live with us and be the mom. She has to be. We've been good, haven't we?"

"Uh-huh." Zack played with the toe of his boot. "Do you think she'll love us and all that?"

"Probably." Zeke shot his twin a look. "I love her already."

"Me, too." Zack smiled in relief. Everything was going to be okay after all.

"All right, people." Nell pitched her voice above the din in the chorus room. It doubled as backstage on concert nights, and students were swarming around, checking clothes, makeup and hair and working off preperformance jitters by talking at the top of their lungs. "Settle down."

One of her students had his head between his knees, fighting off acute stage fright. Nell sent him a sympathetic smile as her group began to quiet.

"You've all worked really hard for tonight. I know a lot of you are jumpy because you have friends and family out in the audience. Use the nerves to sharpen your performance. Please try to remember to go out onstage in the organized, dignified manner we've practiced."

There were some snickers at that. Nell merely lifted a brow. "I should have said remember to be more dignified and more orderly than you've managed at practice. Diaphragms," she said. "Projection. Posture. Smiles." She paused, lifted a hand. "And above all, I expect you to remember the most vital ingredient in tonight's performance. Enjoy it," she said, and grinned. "It's Christmas. Now let's go knock 'em dead."

Her heart was doing some pretty fancy pumping of its own as she directed the children onstage, watched them take their positions on the risers as the murmurs from the audience rose and ebbed. For many, Nell knew, this concert would be her first test. Decisions from the community would be made tonight as to whether the school board had made a good or a bad choice in their new music teacher.

She took a deep breath, tugged at the hem of her velvet jacket and stepped onstage.

There was polite applause as she approached the solo mike.

"Welcome to Taylor's Grove High School's holiday concert," she began.

"Gosh, Dad, doesn't Miss Davis look pretty?"

"Yeah, Zack, she does." *Lovely* was more the word, he thought, in that soft-looking deep forest-green suit, with holly berries in her hair and a quick, nervous smile on her face.

She looked terrific in the spotlight. He wondered if she knew it.

At the moment, all Nell knew was nerves. She wished she could see faces clearly. She'd always preferred seeing her audience when she was performing. It made it more intimate, more fun. After her announcement, she turned, saw every student's eyes on hers, then smiled in reassurance.

"Okay, kids," she murmured, in an undertone only they could hear. "Let's rock."

She started them off with a bang, the Springsteen number, and it had eyes popping wide in the audience. This was not the usual yawn-inspiring program most had been expecting.

When the applause hit, Nell felt the tension dissolve. They'd crossed the first hurdle. She segued from the fun to the traditional, thrilled when the auditorium filled with the harmony on "Cantate Domine," delighted when her sopranos soared on "Adeste Fideles," grinning when they bounced into "Jingle Bell Rock," complete with the little stage business of swaying and hand clapping they'd worked on.

And her heart swelled when Kim approached the mike and the first pure notes of her solo flowed into the air.

"Oh, Dave." Sniffling, Mira clutched her husband's hand, then Mac's. "Our baby."

Nell's prediction had been on target. When Kim stepped back in position, there were damp eyes in every row. They closed the concert with "Silent Night," only voices, no piano. The way it was meant to be sung, Nell had told her students. The way it was written to be sung.

When the last note died and she turned to gesture to her chorus, the audience was already on its feet. The kick of it jolted through her as she turned her head, saw the slack jaws, wide eyes and foolish grins of her students.

Nell swallowed tears, waiting until the noise abated slightly before crossing to the mike again. She knew how to play it.

"They were terrific, weren't they?"

As she'd hoped, that started the cheers and applause all over again. She waited it out.

"I'd like to thank you all for coming, for supporting the chorus. I owe a special thanks to the parents of the singers onstage tonight for their patience, their understanding and their willingness to let me share their children for a few hours every day. Every student onstage has worked tremendously hard for tonight, and I'm delighted that you appreciate their talent, and their effort. I'd like to add that the poinsettias you see onstage were donated by Hill Florists and are for sale at three dollars a pot. Proceeds to go to the fund for new choir uniforms. Merry Christmas, and come back."

Before she could step away from the mike, Kim and Brad were standing on either side of her.

"There's just one more thing." Brad cleared his throat until the rustling in the audience died down. "The chorus would like to present a token of appreciation to Miss Davis for all her work and encouragement. Ah..." Kim had written the speech out, but Brad had been designated to say it. He fumbled a little, grinned self-consciously at Kim. "This is Miss Davis's first concert at Taylor High. Ah..." He just couldn't remember all the nice words Kim had written, so he said what he felt. "She's the best. Thanks, Miss Davis."

"We hope you like it," Kim murmured under the applause as she handed Nell a brightly wrapped box. "All the kids chipped in."

"I'm..." She didn't know what to say, was afraid to try. When she opened the box, she stared, misty-eyed, down at a pin shaped like a treble clef.

"We know you like jewelry," Kim began. "So we thought—"

"It's beautiful. It's perfect." Taking a steadying breath, she turned to the chorus. "Thanks. It means almost as much to me as you do. Merry Christmas."

"She got a present," Zack pointed out. They were waiting in the crowded corridor outside the auditorium to congratulate Kim. "That means we could get one tonight. We could get her."

"Not if she goes home right after." Zack had already worked this out. He was waiting for his moment. When he saw her, he pounced. "Miss Davis! Over here, Miss Davis!"

Mac didn't move. Couldn't. Something had happened while he sat three rows back, watching her on the stage. Seeing her smile, seeing tears in her eyes. Just seeing her.

He was in love with her. It was nothing he'd ever experienced. Nothing he knew how to handle. Running seemed the smartest solution, but he didn't think he could move.

"Hi!" She crouched down for hugs, squeezing the boys tight, kissing each cheek. "Did you like the concert?"

"It was real good. Kim was the best."

Nell leaned close to Zeke's ear. "I think so, too, but it has to be a secret."

"We're good at keeping secrets." He smiled smugly at his brother. "We've had one for weeks and weeks."

"Can you come to our house now, Miss Davis?" Zack clung to her hand and put all his charm into his eyes. "Please? Come see our tree and the lights. We put lights everywhere so you can see them from all the way down on the road."

"I'd like that." Testing the water, she glanced up at Mac. "But your dad might be tired."

He wasn't tired, he was flattened. Her lashes were still damp, and the little pin the kids had given her glinted against her velvet jacket. "You're welcome to come out, if you don't mind the drive."

"I'd like it. I'm still wired up." She straightened, searching for some sign of welcome or rebuff in Mac's face. "If you're sure it isn't a bad time."

"No." His tongue was thick, he realized. As if he'd been drinking. "I want to talk to you."

"I'll head out as soon as I'm finished here, then." She winked at the boys and melted back into the crowd.

"She's done wonders with those kids." Mrs. Hollis nodded to Mac. "It'll be a shame to lose her."

"Lose her?" Mac glanced down at his boys, but they were already in a huddle, exchanging whispers. "What do you mean?"

"I heard from Mr. Perkins, who got it from Addie McVie at the high school office, that Nell Davis was offered her old position back at that New York school starting next fall. Nell and the principal had themselves a conference just this morning." Mrs. Hollis babbled on as Mac stared blankly over her head. "Hate to think about her leaving us. Made a difference with these kids." She spied one of her gossip buddies and elbowed her way through the crowd.

Chapter 9

Control came easily to Mac—or at least it had for the past seven years. He used all the control at his disposal to keep his foul mood and bubbling temper from the boys.

They were so excited about her coming, he thought bitterly. Wanted to make certain all the lights were lit, the cookies were out, the decorative bell was hung on Zark's collar.

They were in love with her, too, he realized. And that made it a hell of a mess.

He should have known better. He *had* known better. Somehow he'd let it happen anyway. Let himself slip, let himself fall. And he'd dragged his kids along with him.

Well, he'd have to fix it, wouldn't he? Mac got himself a beer, tipped the bottle back. He was good at fixing things.

"Ladies like wine," Zack informed him. "Like Aunt Mira does."

He remembered Nell had sipped white wine at Mira's party. "I don't have any," he muttered.

Because his father looked unhappy, Zack hugged Mac's leg. "You can buy some before she comes over next time."

Reaching down, Mac cupped his son's upturned face. The love was so strong, so vital, Mac could all but feel it grip him by the throat. "Always got an answer, don't you, pal?"

"You like her, don't you, Dad?"

"Yeah, she's nice."

"And she likes us, too, right?"

"Hey, who wouldn't like the Taylor guys?" He sat at the kitchen table, pulled Zack into his lap. He'd discovered when his sons were infants that there was nothing more magical than holding your own child. "Most of the time *I* even like you."

That made Zack giggle and cuddle closer. "She has to live all by herself, though." Zack began to play with the buttons of his father's shirt. A sure sign, Mac knew, that he was leading up to something.

"Lots of people live alone."

"We've got a big house, and two whole rooms nobody sleeps in except when Grandma and Pop come to visit."

His radar was humming. Mac tugged on his son's ear. "Zack, what are you getting at?"

"Nothing." Lip poked out, Zack toyed with another button. "I was just wondering what it would be like if she came and lived here." He peeked up under his lashes. "So she wouldn't be lonely."

"Nobody said she was lonely," Mac pointed out. "And I think you should—"

The doorbell rang, sending the dog into a fit of excited barking and jingling. Zeke flew into the kitchen, dancing from foot to foot. "She's here! She's here!"

"I got the picture." Mac ruffled Zack's hair, set him on his feet. "Well, let her in. It's cold out."

"I'll do it!"

"*I'll* do it!"

The twins had a fierce race through the house to the front door. They hit it together, fought over the knob, then all but dragged Nell over the threshold once they'd yanked the door open.

"You took so long," Zeke complained. "We've been waiting forever. I put on Christmas music. Hear? And we've got the tree lit and everything."

"So I see." It was a lovely room, one she tried not to resent having only now been invited into.

She knew Mac had built most of the house himself. He'd told her that much. He'd created an open, homey space, with lots of wood, a glass-fronted fireplace where stockings were already hung. The tree, a six-foot blue spruce, was wildly decorated and placed with pride in front of the wide front window.

"It's terrific." Letting the boys pull her along, Nell crossed over to give the tree a closer look. "Really wonderful. It makes the little one in my apartment look scrawny."

"You can share ours." Zack looked up at her, his heart in his eyes. "We can get you a stocking and everything, and have your name put on it."

"They do it at the mall," Zeke told her. "We'll get you a big one."

Now they were pulling at her heart, as well as her hands. Filled with the emotion of the moment, she crouched down to hug them to her. "You guys are the best." She laughed as Zark pushed in for attention. "You, too." Her arms full of kids and dog, she looked up to smile at Mac as he stepped in from the kitchen. "Hi. Sorry I took so long. Some of the kids hung around, wanting to go over every mistake and triumph of the concert."

She shouldn't look so right, so perfect, snuggling his boys under the tree. "I didn't hear any mistakes."

"They were there. But we'll work on them."

She scooted back, sitting on a hassock and taking both boys with her. As if, Mac thought, she meant to keep them.

"We don't have any wine," Zack informed her solemnly. "But we have milk and juice and sodas and beer. Lots of other things. Or..." He cast a crafty look in his father's direction. "Somebody could make hot cocoa."

"One of my specialties." Nell stood to shrug out of her coat. "Where's the kitchen?"

"I'll make it," Mac muttered.

"I'll help." Baffled by his sudden distance, she walked to him. "Or don't you like women in your kitchen?"

"We don't get many around here. You looked good up onstage."

"Thanks. It felt good being there."

He looked past her, into the wide, anticipation-filled eyes of his children. "Why don't you two go change into your pajamas? The cocoa'll be finished by the time you are."

"We'll be faster," Zeke vowed, and shot toward the stairs.

"Only if you throw your clothes on the floor. And don't." He turned back into the kitchen.

"Will they hang them up, or push them under the bed?" Nell asked.

"Zack'll hang them up and they'll fall on the floor. Zeke'll push them under the bed."

She laughed, watching him get out milk and cocoa. "I meant to tell you, a few days ago they came in with Kim to rehearsal. They'd switched sweaters—you know, the color code. I really impressed them when I knew who was who anyway."

He paused in the act of measuring cocoa into a pan. "How did you?"

"I guess I didn't think about it. They're each their own person. Facial expressions. You know how Zeke's eyes narrow and Zack looks under his lashes when they're pleased about something. Inflections in the voice." She opened a cupboard at random, looking for mugs. "Posture. There are all sorts of little clues if you pay attention and look closely enough. Ah, found them." Pleased with herself, she took out four mugs and set them on the counter. She tilted her head when she saw him studying her. Analytically, she thought. As if she were something to be measured and fit into place. "Is something wrong?"

"I wanted to talk to you." He busied himself with heating the cocoa.

"So you said." She found she needed to steady herself with a hand on the counter. "Mac, am I misreading something, or are you pulling back?"

"I don't know that I'd call it that."

Something was going to hurt. Nell braced for it. "What would you call it?" she said, as calmly as she could.

"I'm a little concerned about the boys. About the fallout when you move on. They're getting too involved." Why did that sound so stupid? he wondered. Why did he feel so stupid?

"*They* are?"

"I think we've been sending the wrong signals, and it

would be best for them if we backed off." He concentrated on the cocoa as if it were a nuclear experiment. "We've gone out a few times, and we've..."

"Slept together," she finished, cool now. It was the last defense.

He looked around, sharply. But he could still hear the stomping of little feet in the room overhead. "Yeah. We've slept together, and it was great. The thing is, kids pick up on more things than most people think. And they get ideas. They get attached."

"And you don't want them to get attached to me." Yes, she realized. It was going to hurt. "You don't want to get attached."

"I just think it would be a mistake to take it any further."

"Clear enough. The No Trespassing signs are back up, and I'm out."

"It's not like that, Nell." He set the spoon down, took a step toward her. But there was a line he couldn't quite cross. A line he'd created himself. If he didn't make certain they both stayed on their own sides of it, the life he'd so carefully built could crumble. "I've got things under control here, and I need to keep them that way. I'm all they've got. They're all I've got. I can't mess that up."

"No explanations necessary." Her voice had thickened. In a moment, she knew, it would begin to shake. "You made it clear from the beginning. Crystal clear. Funny, the first time you invite me into your home, it's to toss me out."

"I'm not tossing you out, I'm trying to realign things."

"Oh, go to hell, and keep your realignments for your houses." She sprinted out of the kitchen.

"Nell, don't go like this." But by the time he reached the

living room, she was grabbing her coat, and his boys were racing down the stairs.

"Where are you going, Miss Davis? You haven't—" Both boys stopped, shocked by the tears streaming down her face.

"I'm sorry." It was too late to hide them, so she kept heading for the door. "I have to do something. I'm sorry."

And she was gone, with Mac standing impotently in the living room and both boys staring at him. A dozen excuses spun around in his head. Even as he tried to grab one, Zack burst into tears.

"She went away. You made her cry, and she went away."

"I didn't mean to. She—" He moved to gather his sons up and was met with a solid wall of resistance.

"You ruined everything." A tear spilled out of Zeke's eyes, heated by temper. "We did everything we were supposed to, and you ruined it."

"She'll never come back." Zack sat on the bottom step and sobbed. "She'll never be the mom now."

"What?" At his wits' end, Mac dragged his hand through his hair. "What are you two talking about?"

"You ruined it," Zeke said again.

"Look, Miss Davis and I had a…disagreement. People have disagreements. It's not the end of the world." He wished it didn't feel like the end of his world.

"Santa sent her." Zack rubbed his eyes with his fists. "He sent her, just like we asked him. And now she's gone."

"What do you mean, Santa sent her?" Determined, Mac sat on the steps. He pulled a reluctant Zack into his lap and tugged Zeke down to join them. "Miss Davis came from New York to teach music, not from the North Pole."

"We know that." Temper set aside, Zeke sought comfort,

turning his face into his father's chest. "She came because we sent Santa a letter, months and months ago, so we'd be early and he'd have time."

"Have time for what?"

"To pick out the mom." On a shuddering sigh, Zack sniffed and looked up at his father. "We wanted someone nice, who smelled good and liked dogs and had yellow hair. And we asked, and she came. And you were supposed to marry her and make her the mom."

Mac let out a long breath and prayed for wisdom. "Why didn't you tell me you were thinking about having a mother?"

"Not *a* mom," Zeke told him. "*The* mom. Miss Davis is the mom, but she's gone now. We love her, and she won't like us anymore because you made her cry."

"Of course she'll still like you." She'd hate him, but she wouldn't take it out on the boys. "But you two are old enough to know you don't get moms from Santa."

"He sent her, just like we asked him. We didn't ask for anything else but the bikes." Zack burrowed into his lap. "We didn't ask for any toys or any games. Just the mom. Make her come back, Dad. Fix it. You always fix it."

"It doesn't work like that, pal. People aren't broken toys or old houses. Santa didn't send her, she moved here for a job."

"He did, too, send her." With surprising dignity, Zack pushed off his father's lap. "Maybe you don't want her, but we do."

His sons walked up the stairs, a united front that closed him out. Mac was left with emptiness in the pit of his stomach and the smell of burned cocoa.

Chapter 10

She should get out of town for a few days, Nell thought. Go somewhere. Go anywhere. There was nothing more pathetic than sitting alone on Christmas Eve and watching other people bustle along the street outside your window.

She'd turned down every holiday party invitation, made excuses that sounded hollow even to her. She was brooding, she admitted, and it was entirely unlike her. But then again, she'd never had a broken heart to nurse before.

With Bob it had been wounded pride. And that had healed itself with embarrassing speed.

Now she was left with bleeding emotions at the time of year when love was most important.

She missed him. Oh, she hated to know that she missed him. That slow, hesitant smile, the quiet voice, the gentleness of him. In New York, at least, she could have lost herself in the crowds, in the rush. But here, everywhere she looked was another reminder.

Go somewhere, Nell. Just get in the car and drive.

She ached to see the children. Wondered if they'd taken their sleds out in the fresh snow that had fallen yesterday. Were they counting the hours until Christmas, plotting to stay awake until they heard reindeer on the roof?

She had presents for them, wrapped and under her tree. She'd send them via Kim or Mira, she thought, and was miserable all over again because she wouldn't see their faces as they tore off the wrappings.

They're not your children, she reminded herself. On that point Mac had always been clear. Sharing himself had been difficult enough. Sharing his children had stopped him dead.

She would go away, she decided, and forced herself to move. She would pack a bag, toss it in the car and drive until she felt like stopping. She'd take a couple of days. Hell, she'd take a week. She couldn't bear to stay here alone through the holidays.

For the next ten minutes, she tossed things into a suitcase without any plan or sense of order. Now that the decision was made, she only wanted to move quickly. She closed the lid on the suitcase, carried it into the living room and started for her coat.

The knock on her door had her clenching her teeth. If one more well-meaning neighbor stopped by to wish her Merry Christmas and invite her to dinner, she was going to scream.

She opened the door and felt the fresh wound stab through her. "Well, Macauley... Out wishing your tenants happy holidays?"

"Can I come in?"

"Why?"

"Nell." There was a wealth of patience in the word. "Please, let me come in."

"Fine, you own the place." She turned her back on him. "Sorry, I haven't any wassail, and I'm very low on good cheer."

"I need to talk to you." He'd been trying to find the right way and the right words for days.

"Really? Excuse me if I don't welcome it. The last time you needed to talk to me is still firmly etched in my mind."

"I didn't mean to make you cry."

"I cry easily. You should see me after a greeting-card commercial on TV." She couldn't keep up the snide comments, and she gave in, asking the question that was uppermost in her mind. "How are the kids?"

"Barely speaking to me." At her blank look, he gestured toward the couch. "Will you sit down? This is kind of a complicated story."

"I'll stand. I don't have a lot of time, actually. I was just leaving."

His gaze followed hers and landed on the suitcase. His mouth tightened. "Well, it didn't take long."

"What didn't?"

"I guess you took them up on that offer to teach back in New York."

"Word does travel. No, I didn't take them up. I like my job here, I like the people here, and I intend to stay. I'm just going on a holiday."

"You're going on a holiday at five o'clock on Christmas Eve?"

"I can come and go as I please. No, don't take off your coat," she snapped. Tears were threatening. "Just say your piece and get out. I still pay the rent here. On second thought, just leave now. Damn it, you're not going to make me cry again."

"The boys think Santa sent you."

"Excuse me?"

As the first tear spilled over, he moved to her, brushed it away with his thumb. "Don't cry, Nell. I hate knowing I made you cry."

"Don't touch me." She whirled away and fumbled a tissue out of the box.

He was discovering exactly how it felt to be sliced in two. "I'm sorry." Slowly he lowered his hand to his side. "I know how you must feel about me now."

"You don't know the half of it." She blew her nose, struggled for control. "What's this about the boys and Santa?"

"They wrote a letter back in the fall, not long before they met you. They decided they wanted a mom for Christmas. Not *a* mom," Mac explained as she turned back to stare at him. "*The* mom. They keep correcting me on that one. They had pretty specific ideas about what they wanted. She was supposed to have yellow hair and smile a lot, like kids and dogs and bake cookies. They wanted bikes, too, but that was sort of an afterthought. All they really wanted was the mom."

"Oh." She did sit now, lowering herself onto the arm of the sofa. "That explains a couple of things." Steadying herself, she looked back at him. "Put you in quite a spot, didn't it? I know you love them, Mac, but starting a relationship with me to try to please your children takes things beyond parental devotion."

"I didn't know. Damn it, do you think I'd play with their feelings, or yours, that way?"

"Not theirs," she said hollowly. "Certainly not theirs."

He remembered how delicate she had seemed when they made love. There was more fragility now. No roses in her cheeks, he saw with a pang of distress. No light in her eyes. "I know what it's like to be hurt, Nell. I never would have hurt you deliberately. They didn't tell me about the letter until the night... You weren't the only one I made cry that night. I tried to explain that Santa doesn't work that way, but they've got it fixed in their heads that he sent you."

"I'll talk to them if you want me to."

"I don't deserve—"

"Not for you," she said. "For them."

He nodded, accepting. "I wondered how it would make you feel to know they wished for you."

"Don't push me, Mac."

He couldn't help it, and he kept his eyes on hers as he moved closer. "They wished for you for me, too. That's why they didn't tell me. You were our Christmas present." He reached down, touched her hair. "How does that make you feel?"

"How do you think I feel?" She batted his hand away and rose to face the window. "It hurts. I fell in love with the three of you almost from the first glance, and it hurts. Go away, leave me alone."

Somehow a fist had crept into his chest and was squeezing at his heart. "I thought you'd go away. I thought you'd leave us alone. I wouldn't let myself believe you cared enough to stay."

"Then you were an idiot," she mumbled.

"I was clumsy." He watched the tiny lights on her tree shining in her hair and gave up any thought of saving himself. "All right, I was an idiot. The worst kind, because I kept hiding from what you might feel, from what I felt. I didn't fall in love with you right away. At least I didn't know it. Not until the night of the concert. I wanted to tell you. I didn't know how to tell you. Then I heard something about the New York offer and it was the perfect excuse to push you out. I thought I was protecting the kids from getting hurt." No, he wouldn't use them, he thought in disgust. Not even to get her back. "That was only part of it. I was protecting myself. I couldn't control the way I felt about you. It scared me."

"Now's no different from then, Mac."

"It could be different." He took a chance and laid his hands on her shoulders, turned her to face him. "It took my own sons to show me that sometimes you've just got to wish. Don't leave me, Nell. Don't leave us."

"I was never going anywhere."

"Forgive me." She started to turn her head away, but he cupped her cheek, held it gently. "Please. Maybe I can't fix this, but give me a chance to try. I need you in my life. We need you."

There was such patience in his voice, such quiet strength in the hand on her face. Even as she looked at him, her heart began to heal. "I love you. All of you. I can't help it."

Relief and gratitude flavored the kiss as he touched his lips to hers. "I love you. I don't want to help it." Drawing her close, he cradled her head on his shoulder. "It's just been the three of us for so long, I didn't know how to make room.

I think I'm figuring it out." He eased her away again and reached into his coat pocket. "I bought you a present."

"Mac." Still staggered from the roller-coaster emotions, she rubbed her hands over her damp cheeks. "It isn't Christmas yet."

"Close enough. I think if you'd open it now, I'd stop having all this tightness in my chest."

"All right." She dashed another tear aside. "We'll consider it a peace offering, then. I may even decide to…" She trailed off when the box was open in her hand. A ring, the traditional single diamond crowning a gold band.

"Marry me, Nell," he said quietly. "Be the mom."

She raised dazzled eyes to his. "You move awfully quickly for someone who always seems to take his time."

"Christmas Eve." He watched her face as he took the ring out of the box. "It seemed like the night to push my luck."

"It was a good choice." Smiling, she held out her hand. "A very good choice." When the ring was on her finger, she lifted her hand to his cheek. "When?"

He should have known it would be simple. With her, it would always be simple. "New Year's Eve's only a week away. It would be a good start to a new year. A new life."

"Yes."

"Will you come home with me tonight? I left the kids at Mira's. We could pick them up, and you'd spend Christmas where you belong." Before she could answer, he smiled and kissed her hand. "You're already packed."

"So I am. It must be magic."

"I'm beginning to believe it." He framed her face with his hands, lowered his mouth for a long, lingering kiss. "Maybe

I didn't wish for you, but you're all I want for Christmas, Nell."

He rubbed his cheek over her hair, looked out at the colored lights gleaming on the houses below. "Did you hear something?" he murmured.

"Mmm..." She held him close, smiled. "Sleigh bells."

* * * * *

GABRIEL'S ANGEL

Chapter 1

Damn snow. Gabe downshifted to second gear, slowed the Jeep to fifteen miles an hour, swore and strained his eyes. Through the frantic swing of the wipers on the windshield all that could be seen was a wall of white. No winter wonderland. Snow pelted down in flakes that looked as big and as mean as a man's fist.

There would be no waiting out this storm, he thought as he took the next curve at a crawl. He considered himself lucky that after six months he knew the narrow, winding road from town so well. He could drive almost by feel, but a newcomer wouldn't stand a chance. Even with that advantage, his shoulders and the back of his neck were tight with tension. Colorado snows could be as vicious in spring as they were in the dead of winter, and they could last for an hour or a day. Apparently this one had been a surprise to everyone—residents, tourists and the National Weather Service.

He had only five miles to go. Then he could unload his supplies, stoke his fire and enjoy the April blizzard from the comfort of his cabin, with a hot cup of coffee or an ice-cold beer.

The Jeep chugged up the incline like a tank, and he was grateful for its sturdy perseverance. The unexpected snowfall might force him to take three times as long to make the twenty-mile trip from town to home, but at least he'd get there.

The wipers worked furiously to clear the windshield. There were seconds of white vision followed by seconds of white blindness. At this rate there would be better than two feet by nightfall. Gabe comforted himself with the thought that he'd be home long before that, even as the air in the Jeep turned blue from his cursing. If he hadn't lost track of the time the day before, he'd have had his supplies and been able to laugh at the weather.

The road went into a lazy S and Gabe took it cautiously. It was difficult for him to move slowly under any circumstances, but over the winter he had gained a healthy respect for the mountains and the roads that had been blasted through them. The guardrail was sturdy enough, but beneath it the cliffs were unforgiving. He wasn't worried so much about making a mistake himself—the Jeep was solid as a rock—but he thought of others who might be traveling north or south on the pass, pulling over to the side or stopping dead in the middle of the road.

He wanted a cigarette. His hands gripping the wheel hard, he all but lusted for a cigarette. But it was a luxury that would have to wait. Three miles to go.

The tension in his shoulders began to ease. He hadn't seen

another car in more than twenty minutes, and he wasn't likely to now. Anyone with any sense would have taken shelter. From this point on he could almost feel his way home. A good thing. Beside him the radio was squawking about roads closed and activities canceled. It always amazed Gabe that people planned so many meetings, luncheons, recitals and rehearsals on any given day.

But that was human nature, he supposed. Always planning on drawing together, if only to sell a bunch of cakes and cookies. He preferred to be alone. At least for now. Otherwise he wouldn't have bought the cabin and buried himself in it for the past six months.

The solitude gave him freedom, to think, to work, to heal. He'd done some of all three.

He nearly sighed when he saw—or rather felt—the road slant upward again. This was the final rise before his turnoff. Only a mile now. His face, which had been hard and tight with concentration, relaxed. It wasn't a smooth or particularly handsome face. It was too thin and angular to be merely pleasant, and the nose was out of alignment due to a heated disagreement with his younger brother during their teens. Gabe hadn't held it against him.

Because he'd forgotten to wear a hat, his dark blond hair fell untidily around his face. It was long and a bit shaggy over the collar of his parka and had been styled hastily with his fingers hours before. His eyes, a dark, clear green, were starting to burn from staring at the snow.

While his tires swished over the cushioned asphalt he glanced down at his odometer, saw that there was only a quarter mile left, then looked back to the road. That was when he saw a car coming at him out of control.

He didn't even have time to swear. He jerked the Jeep to the right just as the oncoming car seemed to come out of its spin. The Jeep skimmed over the snow piled on the shoulder, swaying dangerously before the tires chewed down to the road surface for traction. He had a bad moment when he thought the Jeep was going to roll over like a turtle. Then all he could do was sit and watch and hope the other driver was as lucky.

The oncoming car was barreling down the road sideways. Though only seconds had passed, Gabe had time to think of how nasty the impact would be when the car slammed into him. Then the driver managed to straighten out. With only feet between them the car fishtailed and swerved to avoid the collision, then began to slide helplessly toward the guardrail. Gabe set his emergency brake and was out of the Jeep when the car rammed into the metal.

He nearly fell on his face, but his boots held as he raced across the road. It was a compact—a bit more compact now, with its right side shoved in and its hood sprung like an accordion, also on the passenger side. He had another moment to think, and he grimaced at the thought of what would have happened if the car had hit on the driver's side.

Fighting his way through the snow, he managed to make it to the wrecked car. He saw a figure slumped over the wheel, and he yanked at the door. It was locked. With his heart in his throat, he began to pound against the window.

The figure moved. A woman, he saw from the thick wave of wheat-blond hair that spilled onto the shoulders of a dark coat. He watched her reach up and drag a ski cap from her head. Then she turned her face to the window and stared at him.

She was white, marble-white. Even her lips were colorless.

Her eyes were huge and dark, the irises almost black with shock. And she was beautiful, stunningly, breathtakingly beautiful. The artist in him saw the possibilities in the diamond-shaped face, the prominent cheekbones, the full lower lip. The man in him rejected them and banged on the glass again.

She blinked and shook her head as if to clear it. As the shock passed out of them, he saw that her eyes were blue, a midnight-blue. They filled now with a rush of concern. In a quick movement she rolled down the window.

"Are you hurt?" she demanded before he could speak. "Did I hit you?"

"No, you hit the guardrail."

"Thank God." She let her head slump back on the seat for a moment. Her mouth was as dry as dust. And her heart, though she was already fighting to control it, was thudding in her throat. "I started to skid coming down the incline. I thought—I hoped—I might be able to ride it out. Then I saw you and I was sure I was going to hit you."

"You would have if you hadn't swerved away toward the rail." He glanced at the front of her car again. The damage could have been worse, much worse. If she'd been going any faster... There was no use speculating. He turned to her again, studying her face for signs of shock or concussion. "Are you all right?"

"Yes. I think so." She opened her eyes again and tried to smile at him. "I'm sorry. I must have given you quite a scare."

"At least." But the scare was over now. He was less than a quarter of a mile from hearth and home, and stuck in the snow with a strange woman whose car wasn't going anywhere for several days. "What the hell are you doing out here?"

She took the furiously bitten-off words in stride as she unhooked her seat belt. The long, deep breaths she'd been taking had gone a long way toward steadying her. "I must have gotten turned around in the storm. I was trying to get down to Lonesome Ridge to wait it out, find a place for the night. That's the closest town, according to the map, and I was afraid to pull over on the shoulder." She glanced over at the guardrail and shuddered. "What there is of it. I don't suppose there's any way I'm going to get my car out of here."

"Not tonight."

Frowning, Gabe stuck his hands in his pockets. The snow was still falling, and the road was deserted. If he turned around and walked back to his Jeep, leaving her to fend for herself, she might very well freeze to death before an emergency vehicle or a snowplow came along. However much he'd have liked to shrug off the obligation, he couldn't leave a woman stranded in this storm.

"The best I can do is take you with me." There wasn't an ounce of graciousness in his tone. She hadn't expected any. If he was angry and impatient about nearly being plowed into, and inconvenienced on top of it, he was entitled.

"I'm sorry."

He moved his shoulders, aware that he'd been rude. "The turnoff for my cabin's at the top of the hill. You'll have to leave your car and ride in the Jeep."

"I'd appreciate it." With the engine off and the window open, the cold was beginning to seep through her clothes. "I'm sorry for the imposition, Mr.—?"

"Bradley. Gabe Bradley."

"I'm Laura." She slipped out of the safety harness that had

undoubtedly saved her from injury. "I have a suitcase in the trunk, if you wouldn't mind giving me a hand with it."

Gabe took the keys and stomped back toward the trunk, thinking that if he'd only left an hour earlier that afternoon he'd be home—alone—at this moment.

The case wasn't large, and it was far from new. The lady with only one name traveled light, he thought. He muttered to himself as he hefted it out of the trunk. There was no use being angry with her, or being snotty. If she hadn't managed to skid quite so well, if she hadn't avoided him, they might have been needing a doctor now instead of a cup of coffee and dry feet.

Deciding to be more civil, Gabe turned to tell her to go across to the Jeep. She was standing, watching him, with the snow falling on her uncovered hair. That was when he saw she was not only beautiful, she was very, very pregnant.

"Oh, God" was all he could manage.

"I'm really sorry to be so much trouble," Laura began. "And I want to thank you in advance for the lift. If I could call from your cabin and find a tow truck, maybe we could clear this whole thing up quickly."

He hadn't heard a word she'd said. Not one. All he could do was stare at the ripe slope beneath her dark coat. "Are you sure you're all right? You didn't tell me you were— Are you going to need a doctor?"

"I'm fine." This time she smiled, fully. The cold had brought the color back into her face. "Really. The baby wasn't hurt. He's annoyed a bit, I'd say from the way he's kicking me, but we hardly felt the impact. We didn't ram the guardrail, we sort of slid into it."

"You might have…" What? he wondered. "Jarred something."

"I'm fine," she said again. "I was strapped in, and the snow, though it started it all, cushioned the hit." Noting that he still seemed unconvinced, she tossed back her snow-covered hair. Her fingers, though they were tucked into subtle, silk-lined leather, were going numb. "I promise, I'm not going to give birth in the middle of the road—unless you plan on standing here for a few more weeks."

She was all right…he hoped. And the way she was smiling at him made him feel like an idiot. Deciding to take her word for it, he offered her a hand. "Let me help you."

The words, such simple words, went straight to her heart. She could have counted on her hands the number of times she had heard them.

He didn't know how to deal with pregnant women. Were they fragile? It had always seemed to him that the opposite must be true, given what they had to go through, but now, faced with one, he was afraid she'd shatter at a touch.

Mindful of the slippery road, Laura took a firm grip on his arm as they started across. "It's beautiful here," she said when they reached the Jeep. "But I have to admit, I'm going to appreciate the snow more from inside." She glanced at the high step below the door of the Jeep. "I think you're going to have to give me a bit of a boost. I'm not as agile as I used to be."

Gabe stowed her case, wondering exactly where to grab her. Mumbling, he put a hand under her elbow and another on her hip. Laura slid into the seat with less fuss than he'd expected.

"Thanks."

He grunted a response as he slammed the door. He skirted the hood, then took his place behind the wheel. It took a little maneuvering, but with a minimum of effort they inched back onto the road.

The dependable Jeep started up the hill. Laura uncurled her hands as they moved along at a steady pace. They'd finally stopped shaking. "I wasn't sure anyone lived along here. If I'd known, I'd have begged a roof long before this. I wasn't expecting a snowstorm in April."

"We get them later than this." He said nothing for a moment. He respected other people's privacy as zealously as his own. But these were unusual circumstances. "You're traveling alone?"

"Yes."

"Isn't that a little risky in your condition?"

"I'd planned on being in Denver in a couple of days." She laid a hand lightly on her belly. "I'm not due for six weeks." Laura took a deep breath. It was a risk to trust him, but she really had no other option. "Do you live alone, Mr. Bradley?"

"Yes."

She shifted her gaze just enough to study him as he turned down a narrow, snow-covered lane. At least she assumed a lane was buried somewhere under all the white. There was something tough and hard about his face. Not rugged, she thought. It was too lean and fine-boned for that. It was coldly sculpted, as she imagined a mythic warrior chief's might be.

But she remembered the stunned male helplessness in his eyes when he'd seen she was pregnant. She believed she'd be safe with him. She had to believe that.

He felt her gaze and read her thoughts easily enough. "I'm not a maniac," he said mildly.

"I appreciate that." She smiled a little, then turned to look out the windshield again.

The cabin could barely be seen through the snow, even when he stopped in front of it. But what Laura could see, she loved. It was a squat rectangle of wood with a covered porch and square-paned windows. Smoke puffed from the chimney.

Though it was buried under snow, there was a path of flat rocks leading from the lane to the front steps. Evergreens mantled with white trooped around the corners. Nothing had ever looked as safe and warm as this snow-decked little cabin in the mountains.

"It's lovely. You must be happy here."

"It does the job." Gabe came around to help her down. She smelled like the snow, he thought, or perhaps more like water, the pure, virginal water that poured down the mountain in the spring. "I'll take you in," he told her, knowing both his reaction and his comparison were ridiculous. "You can warm up by the fire." Gabe opened the front door and waved her in. "Go ahead. I'll bring in the rest."

He left her alone, snow dripping wet from her coat onto the woven mat inside the door.

The paintings. Laura stood just where she was and stared openmouthed at the paintings. They covered the walls, they were stacked in corners, they were piled on tables. Only a few were framed. They didn't need the ornamentation. Some were half finished, as though the artist had lost interest or motivation. There were oils, in colors vivid and harsh, and watercolors in soft, misty hues that might have sprung from dreams. Shrugging out of her coat, Laura moved in for a closer look.

There was a scene from Paris, the Bois de Boulogne. She remembered it from her honeymoon. Looking at it made her eyes swim and her muscles tense. Breathing deeply, she forced herself to look at it until her emotions settled.

An easel was set near the window, where the light would come in and fall on the canvas. She resisted the temptation to go over and steal a look. She already had the sensation that she was trespassing.

What was she going to do? Laura gripped her hands together tightly as she let the despair come. She was stranded, her car wrecked, her money dwindling. And the baby— The baby wasn't going to wait until she made things right.

If they found her now...

They weren't going to find her. Deliberately she unlaced her hands. She'd come this far. No one was going to take her baby, now or ever.

She turned as the door to the cabin opened. Gabe shifted the bags he'd carried inside, leaving them jumbled together in a pile. He, too, shrugged out of his coat and hung it on a hook by the door.

He was as lean as his face had indicated. Though he might have been a bit under six feet, the spare toughness of his build gave the illusion of more height, more power. More like a boxer than an artist, Laura thought as she watched him kick the clinging snow from his boots. More like a man of the outdoors than one who came from graceful mansions and gentle blood.

Despite what she knew of his aristocratic background, he wore flannel and corduroy and looked perfectly suited to the rustic cabin. Laura, who came from humbler stock, felt fussy and out of place in her bulky Irish knit sweater and tailored wool.

"Gabriel Bradley," she said, and gestured widely toward the walls. "My brain must have been scrambled before. I didn't put it together. I love your work."

"Thanks." Bending, he hefted two of the bags.

"Let me help—"

"No." He strode off into the kitchen, leaving Laura biting her lip.

He wasn't thrilled to have her company, she thought. Then she shrugged. It couldn't be helped. As soon as it was reasonably safe for her to leave, she would leave. Until then... Until then Gabriel Bradley, artist of the decade, would have to make do.

It was tempting just to take a seat and passively stay out of his way. Once she would have done just that, but circumstances had changed her. She followed him into the adjoining kitchen. Counting the baby she carried, there were three of them in the little room, and it was filled to capacity.

"At least let me make you something hot to drink." The ancient two-burner stove looked tricky, but she was determined.

He turned, brushed against her belly and was amazed at the wave of discomfort he felt. And the tug of fascination. "Here's the coffee," he mumbled, handing her a fresh can.

"Got a pot?"

It was in the sink, which was filled with water that had once been sudsy. He had been trying to soak out the stains from the last time he'd used it. He moved to get it, bumped her again and stepped back.

"Why don't you let me take care of it?" she suggested. "I'll put this stuff away and start the coffee, and you can call a tow truck."

"Fine. There's milk. Fresh."

She smiled. "I don't suppose you have any tea."

"No."

"Milk's fine, then. Thank you."

When he left, Laura busied herself in the kitchen. It was too small for it to be complicated. She used her own system in storing the goods since it appeared Gabe had none. She'd only emptied the first bag when he reappeared in the doorway.

"Phone's out."

"Out?"

"Dead. We lose service a lot when there's a storm."

"Oh." Laura stood holding a can of soup. "Is it usually out for long?"

"Depends. Sometimes a couple hours, sometimes a week."

She lifted a brow. Then she realized that he was perfectly serious. "I guess that puts me in your hands, Mr. Bradley."

He hooked his thumbs in his front pockets. "In that case, you'd better call me Gabe."

Laura frowned down at the can in her hand. When things got bad, you made the best of them. "Want some soup?"

"Yeah. I'll, ah...put your things in the bedroom."

Laura simply nodded, then began to search for a can opener.

She was a piece of work, all right, Gabe decided as he carried Laura's suitcase into his room. Not that he was an expert when it came to women, but he wasn't what anyone would have called a novice, either. She hadn't batted an eye when he'd told her that the phone was dead and they were effectively cut off from the outside world. Or, to put it more precisely, that she was cut off from everyone but him.

Gabe glanced into the streaked mirror over his battered dresser. As far as he knew, no one had ever considered him harmless before. A quick, cocky smile flashed over his face. He hadn't always been harmless, when it came right down to it.

This, of course, was an entirely different situation.

Under other circumstances he might have entertained some healthy fantasies about his unexpected guest. That face. There was something haunting, something indefinable, about that kind of beauty. When a man looked at it, he automatically began to wonder and imagine. Even if she hadn't been carrying a child, the fantasies would have remained only that. Fantasies. He'd never been enthusiastic about flings and one-night stands, and he certainly wasn't in any shape for a relationship. Celibacy had been the order of the day for the past few months. The desire to paint had finally seduced him again. Gabe needed no other love affair.

But as for more practical matters, he did have a guest, a lone woman who was very pregnant—and very secretive. He hadn't missed the fact that she'd told him only her first name and hadn't volunteered any information about who she was and where and why she was traveling. Since it was unlikely that she'd robbed a bank or stolen secrets for terrorists, he wouldn't press too hard right now.

But, given the strength of the storm and the seclusion of the cabin, they were likely to be together for a few days. He was going to find out more about the calm and mysterious Laura.

What was she going to do? Laura stared at the empty plate in her hand and saw a hint of her reflection. How could she get to Denver or Los Angeles or Seattle—or any huge, swallowing city that was far enough away from Boston—when she was trapped here? If only she hadn't felt that urgent need to move on this morning. If she'd stayed in that quiet little motel room another day she might still have had some control over what was happening.

Instead, she was here with a stranger. Not just any stranger, Laura reminded herself. Gabriel Bradley, artist— wealthy, respected artist from a wealthy, respected family. But he hadn't recognized her. Laura was certain of that. At least he had yet to recognize her. What would happen when he did, when he found out who she was running from? For all she knew, the Eagletons might be close family friends of the Bradleys. The gesture of her hand over the mound of her stomach was automatic and protective.

They wouldn't take her baby. No matter how much money and how much power they wielded, they wouldn't take her baby. And if she could manage it they would never find her or the child.

Setting down the plate, she turned her attention to the window. How odd it was to look out and see nothing. It gave her a nice, settled feeling to know that no one could see in, either. She was effectively curtained off from everyone. Or nearly everyone, she corrected, thinking again of Gabe.

Perhaps the storm had been a blessing. When there was no choice, she found it best to look on the bright side. No one could follow her trail in this kind of weather. And who would think of looking for her in some tiny, out-of-the-way cabin in the mountains? It felt safe. She would cling to that.

She heard him moving around in the next room, heard the sound of his boots on the hardwood, the thud of a log being added to the fire. After so many months alone she found even the sound of another human being a comfort.

"Mr. Bradley...Gabe?" She stepped through the doorway to see him adjusting the screen in front of the fire. "Could you clear off a table?"

"Clear off a table?"

"So we could eat...sitting down."

"Yeah."

She disappeared again while he tried to figure out what to do with the paints, brushes, canvas stretchers and general disorder on the picnic table that had once served as a dining area. Annoyed at having his space compromised, he spread his equipment throughout the room.

"I made some sandwiches, too." Using a bent cookie sheet as a makeshift tray, she carried in bowls and plates and cups. Embarrassed and edgy, Gabe snatched it from her.

"You shouldn't be carrying heavy things."

Her brows lifted. Surprise came first. No one had ever pampered her. And certainly her life, which had rarely been easy, had been hardest over the past seven months. Then gratitude came, and she smiled. "Thanks, but I'm careful."

"If you were careful, you'd be in your own bed with your feet up and not snowbound with me."

"Exercise is important." But she sat and let him set out the dishes. "And so's food." With her eyes closed, she breathed in the scents. Hot, simple, fortifying. "I hope I didn't put too much of a dent in your supplies, but once I got started I couldn't stop."

Gabe picked up half a sandwich that was thick with

cheese, crisp bacon and sliced hothouse tomatoes. "I'm not complaining." The truth was, he'd gotten into the habit of eating right out of the pan over the kitchen sink. Hot food made with more care than hurry tasted one hell of a lot better from a plate.

"I'd like to pay you back, for the bed and the food."

"Don't worry about it." He scooped up clam chowder while he studied her. She had a way of sticking out her chin that made him think of pride and will. It made an interesting contrast with the creamy skin and the slender neck.

"That's kind of you, but I prefer paying my own way."

"This isn't the Hilton." She wore no jewelry, he noted, not even a plain gold band on her finger. "You cooked the meal, so we'll call it even."

She wanted to argue—her pride wanted to argue—but the simple truth was, she had very little cash, except for the baby fund she'd scrupulously set aside in the lining of her suitcase. "I'm very grateful." She sipped at the milk, though she detested it. The scent of his coffee was rich and forbidden. "Have you been here long, in Colorado?"

"Six months, seven, I guess."

That gave her hope. The timing was good, almost too good. From the looks of the cabin, he didn't spend much time poring over the newspapers, and she hadn't noticed a television. "It must be a wonderful place to paint."

"So far."

"I couldn't believe it when I walked in. I recognized your work right away. I've always admired it. In fact, my— someone I knew bought a couple of your pieces. One of them was a painting of a huge, deep forest. It seemed as though you could step right into it and be completely alone."

He knew the work, and, oddly enough, he'd had the same feeling about it. He couldn't be sure, but he thought it had been sold back east. New York, Boston, perhaps Washington, D.C. If his curiosity about her persisted, it would only take a phone call to his agent to refresh his memory.

"You didn't say where you were traveling from."

"No." She continued to eat, though her appetite had fled. How could she have been foolish enough to describe the painting? Tony had bought it, or rather had snapped his fingers and arranged for his lawyers to buy it on his behalf because Laura had admired it. "I've been in Dallas for a while."

She'd been there almost two months before she'd discovered that the Eagletons' detectives were making discreet inquiries about her.

"You don't sound like a Texan."

"No, I suppose I don't. That's probably because I've lived all over the country." That was true enough, and she was able to smile again. "You're not from Colorado."

"San Francisco."

"Yes, I remember reading that in an article about you and your work." She would talk about him. From her experience men were easily distracted when the conversation centered on themselves. "I've always wanted to see San Francisco. It seems like a lovely place, the hills, the bay, the beautiful old houses." She gave a quick gasp and pressed a hand to her stomach.

"What is it?"

"The baby's just restless." She smiled, but he noted that her eyes were shadowed with fatigue and her complexion was pale again.

"Look, I don't know anything about what you're going through, but common sense tells me you should be lying down."

"Actually, I am tired. If you wouldn't mind, I'd like to rest for a few minutes."

"The bed's through here." He rose and, not certain she could get up and down on her own, offered her a hand.

"I'll take care of the dishes later if…" Her words trailed off as her knees buckled.

"Hold on." Gabe put his arms around her and had the odd, rather humbling sensation of having the baby move against him.

"I'm sorry. It's been a long day, and I guess I pushed it further than I should have." She knew she should move away, pull back on her own, but there was something exquisite about leaning against the hard, sturdy body of a man. "I'll be fine after a nap."

She didn't shatter as he'd once thought she might, but now she seemed so soft, so delicate, that he imagined her dissolving in his hands. He would have liked to comfort her, would have liked to go on holding her like that while she leaned into him, trusting, depending. Needing him. Calling himself a fool, he picked her up.

Laura started to protest, but it felt so good to be off her feet. "I must weigh a ton."

"That's what I was expecting, but you don't."

She found she could laugh, even though the fatigue was smothering her. "You're a real charmer, Gabe."

His own awkwardness began to fade as he moved through the door to the bedroom. "I haven't had many opportunities to flirt with pregnant ladies."

"That's all right. You redeemed yourself by rescuing this one from a snowstorm." With her eyes half-closed, she felt herself being lowered onto a bed. It might be nothing more than a mattress and a rumpled sheet, but it felt like heaven. "I want to thank you."

"You've been doing that on an average of every five minutes." He pulled a slightly ragged comforter over her. "If you really want to thank me, get some sleep and don't go into labor."

"Fair enough. Gabe?"

"Yeah."

"Will you keep trying the phone?"

"All right." She was nearly asleep. He had a moment's attack of guilt for wanting to press her while she was vulnerable. Right now, she didn't look as though she had the strength to brush away a fly. "Do you want me to call anyone for you? Your husband?"

She opened her eyes at that. Though they were clouded with fatigue, they met his levelly, and he saw that she wasn't down for the count yet.

"I'm not married," she said, very clearly. "There's no one to call."

Chapter 2

In the dream she was alone. That didn't frighten her. Laura had spent a large portion of her life alone, so she was more comfortable in solitude than in a crowd. There was a soft, misty quality to the dream—like the seascape she had seen on the wall of Gabe's cabin.

Oddly, she could even hear the ocean, purring and lapping off in the distance, though a part of her knew she was in the mountains. She walked through a pearl-colored fog, listening to the waves. Under her feet sand shifted, warm and soft. She felt safe and strong and strangely unencumbered. It had been a long, long time since she had felt so free, so at ease.

She knew she was dreaming. That was the best part. If she could have managed it, she would have stayed there, in the soft-focused fantasy of it, forever. It would be so easy to keep her eyes closed and cling to the utter peace of the dream.

Then the baby was crying. Screaming. A pulse began to beat in her temple as she listened to the high, keening wails.

She started to sweat, and the clean white fog changed to a dark, threatening gray. No longer warm, the air took on a chill that whipped straight to the bone.

The cries seemed to come from everywhere and nowhere, echoing and rebounding as she searched. Sobbing for breath, she fought her way through the mist as it circled and thickened. The cries became louder, more urgent. Her heart was beating in her throat, and her breath rasped and her hands shook.

Then she saw the bassinet, with its pretty white skirt and its lacy pink-and-blue ruffles. The relief was so great that her knees sagged.

"It's all right," she murmured as she gathered the child in her arms. "It's all right. I'm here now." She could feel the baby's warm breath against her cheek, could feel the weight in her arms as she rocked and soothed. The fine scent of powder surrounded her. Gently she cradled the child, murmuring and comforting as she began to lift the concealing blanket from its face.

And there was nothing, nothing in her arms but an empty blanket.

Gabe was sitting at the picnic table, sketching her face, thinking of her, when he heard her cry out. The moan was so long, so desperate, that he snapped the pencil in two before he jumped up and raced to the bedroom.

"Hey, come on." Feeling awkward, he took her by the shoulders. She jerked so hard that he had to fight back his own panic, as well as hers, to hold on to her. "Laura, take it easy. Are you in pain? Is it the baby? Laura, tell me what's going on."

"They took my baby!" There was hysteria in her voice, but

it was a hysteria that was laced with fury. "Help me! They took my baby!"

"No one took your baby." She was still fighting him, with a strength that awed him. Moving on instinct, he wrapped his arms around her. "You're having a dream. No one took your baby. Here." He clamped a hand around her wrist, where her pulse was beating like a jackhammer, and dragged her hand to her belly. "You're safe, both of you. Relax before you hurt yourself."

When she felt the life beneath her palms, she slumped against him. Her baby was safe, still inside her, where no one could touch him. "I'm sorry. It was a dream."

"It's okay." Without being aware of it, he was stroking her hair, cradling her as she had cradled the baby of her imagination, rocking her gently in an age-old comforting motion. "Do us both a favor and relax."

She nodded, feeling protected and sheltered. Those were two sensations she had experienced very rarely in her twenty-five years. "I'm all right, really. It must have been the shock from the accident catching up with me."

He drew her away, angry with himself because he wanted to go on holding her, shielding her. When she had asked him for help, he had known, without understanding why, that he would do anything to protect her. It was almost as though he had been dreaming himself, or had been caught up in her dream.

The snow was still falling in sheets outside the window and the only light was what came slanting through the bed-room door from the main cabin. It was dim and slightly yellow, but he could see her clearly, and he wanted to be certain that she saw him, as well. He wanted answers, and he wanted them now.

"Don't lie to me. Under normal circumstances you'd be entitled to your privacy, but right now you're under my roof for God knows how long."

"I'm not lying to you." Her voice was so calm, so even, that he nearly believed her. "I'm sorry if I upset you."

"Who are you running from, Laura?"

She said nothing, just stared at him with those dark blue eyes. He swore at her, but she didn't flinch. He sprang up to pace the room, but she didn't shudder. Abruptly he dropped down on the bed again and caught her chin in his hand. She went absolutely still. Gabe would have sworn that for an instant she stopped breathing. Though it was ridiculous, he had the odd sensation that she was bracing for a blow.

"I know you're in trouble. What I want to know is how big. Who's after you, and why?"

Again she said nothing, but her hand moved instinctively to protect the child she carried.

Since the baby was obviously the core of the problem, they would begin there. "The baby's got a father," he said slowly. "You running from him?"

She shook her head.

"Then who?"

"It's complicated."

He lifted a brow as he jerked his head toward the window. "We've got nothing but time here. This keeps up, it could be a week before the main roads are open."

"When they do, I'll go. The less you know, the better off we'll both be."

"That won't wash." He was silent a moment, trying to

organize his thoughts. "It seems to me that the baby is very important to you."

"Nothing is or can be more important."

"Do you figure the strain you're carrying around is good for it?"

He saw the regret in her eyes instantly, saw the concern, the almost imperceptible folding into herself. "There are some things that can't be changed." She took a long breath. "You have a right to ask questions."

"But you don't intend to answer them."

"I don't know you. I have to trust you, to a point, because I have no choice. I can only ask you to do the same."

He moved his hand away from her face. "Why should I?"

She pressed her lips together. She knew he was right. But sometimes right wasn't enough. "I haven't committed a crime, I'm not wanted by the law. I have no family, no husband looking for me. Is that enough?"

"No. I'll take that much tonight because you need to sleep, but we'll talk in the morning."

It was a reprieve—a short one, but she'd learned to be grateful for small things. With a nod, she waited for him to walk to the door. When it shut and the darkness was full again, she lay down. But it was a long, long time before she slept.

It was silent, absolutely silent, when Laura woke. She opened her eyes and waited for memory to return. There had been so many rooms, so many places where she'd slept, that she was used to this confusion upon waking.

She remembered it all…Gabriel Bradley, the storm, the cabin, the nightmare. And the sensation of waking in fear to find herself safe, in his arms. Of course, the safety was only temporary, and his arms weren't for her. Sighing, she turned her head to look out the window.

The snow was still falling. It was almost impossible to believe, but she lay and watched it, thinner now, slower, but still steady. There would be no leaving today.

Tucking her hand under her cheek, she continued to watch. It was easy to wish that the snow would never stop and that time would. She could stay here, cocooned, isolated, safe. But time, as the child she carried attested, never stopped. Rising, she opened her suitcase. She would put herself in order before she faced Gabe.

The cabin was empty. She should have felt relieved at that. Instead, the cozy fire and polished wood made her feel lonely. She wanted him there, even if it was just the sound of his movements in another room. Wherever he had gone, she reminded herself, he would be back. She started to walk into the kitchen to see what could be done about breakfast.

She saw the sketches, a half dozen of them, spread out on the picnic table. His talent, though raw in pencil or charcoal drawing, was undeniable. Still, it made her both uneasy and curious to see how someone else—no, how Gabriel Bradley— perceived her.

Her eyes seemed too big, too haunted. Her mouth was too soft, too vulnerable. She rubbed a finger over it as she frowned at the drawing. She'd seen her face countless times, in glossy photographs, posed for the best angle. She'd been draped in silks and furs, drenched in jewels. Her face and form had sold gallons of perfume, hawked fortunes in clothes and gems.

Laura Malone. She'd nearly forgotten that woman, the

woman they'd said would be the face of the decade. The woman who had, briefly, held her own destiny in her hands. She was gone, erased.

The woman in the sketches was softer, rounder and infinitely more fragile. And yet she seemed stronger. Laura lifted a sketch and studied it. Or did she just want to see the strength, need to see it?

When the front door opened, she turned, still holding the pencil sketch. Gabe, covered with snow, kicked the door shut again. His arms were loaded with wood.

"Good morning. Been busy?"

He grunted and stomped the worst of the snow from his boots, then walked, leaving a wet trail, to the firebox to dump his wood. "I thought you might sleep longer."

"I would have." She patted her belly. "He wouldn't. Can I fix you some breakfast?"

Drawing off his gloves, he tossed them down on the hearth. "Already had some. You go ahead."

Laura waited until he'd stripped off his coat. Apparently they were back on friendly terms again. Cautiously friendly. "It seems to be letting up a little."

He sat on the hearth to drag his boots off. Snow was caked in the laces. "We've got three feet now, and I wouldn't look for it to stop before afternoon." He drew out a cigarette. "Might as well make yourself at home."

"I seem to be." She held up the sketch. "I'm flattered."

"You're beautiful," he said offhandedly as he set his boots on the hearth to dry. "I can rarely resist drawing beautiful things."

"You're fortunate." She dropped the sketch back on the table. "It's so much more rewarding to be able to depict beauty than it is to be beautiful." Gabe lifted a brow. There was a trace, only a trace, of bitterness in her tone. "Things," she explained. "It's strange, but once people see you as beautiful, they almost always see you as a thing."

Turning, she slipped into the kitchen, leaving him frowning after her.

She brewed him fresh coffee, then idled away the morning tidying the kitchen. Gabe gave her room. Before night fell again, he would have some answers, but for now he was content to have her puttering around while he worked.

She seemed to need to be busy. He had thought a woman in her condition would be content to sleep or rest or simply sit and knit for most of the day. He decided it was either nervous energy or her way of avoiding the confrontation he'd promised her the night before.

She didn't ask questions or stand over his shoulder, so they rubbed along through the morning without incident. Once, he glanced over to see her tucked into a corner of the sagging sofa reading a book on childbirth. Later she threw some things together in the kitchen and produced a thick, aromatic stew.

She said little. He knew she was waiting, biding her time until he pushed open the door he'd unlocked the night before. He, too, was waiting, biding his time. By midafternoon he decided she looked rested. Taking up his sketch pad and a piece of charcoal, he began to work while she sat across from him peeling apples.

"Why Denver?"

The only sign of her surprise was a quick jerk of the paring knife. She didn't look up or stop peeling. "Because I've never been there."

"Under the circumstances, wouldn't you be better off in some place that's familiar?"

"No."

"Why did you leave Dallas?"

She set the apple down and picked up another. "Because it was time."

"Where's the baby's father, Laura?"

"Dead." There wasn't even a shadow of emotion in her voice.

"Look at me."

Her hands stilled as she lifted her gaze, and he saw that that much, at least, was true.

"You don't have any family who could help you?"

"No."

"Didn't he?"

Her hand jerked again. This time the blade nicked her finger. The blood welled up as Gabe dropped his pad to take her hand. Once again she saw her face in the sweeping charcoal lines.

"I'll get you a bandage."

"It's only a scratch," she began, but he was already up and gone. When he returned he dabbed at the wound with antiseptic. Again Laura was baffled by the care he displayed. The sting came and went; his touch remained gentle.

He was kneeling in front of her, his brows drawn together as he studied the thin slice in her finger. "Keep this up and I'll think you're accident-prone."

"And I'll think you're the original Good Samaritan." She smiled when he looked up. "We'd both be wrong."

Gabe merely slipped a bandage over the cut and took his seat again. "Turn your head a little, to the left." When she complied, he picked up his pad and turned over a fresh sheet. "Why do they want the baby?"

Her head jerked around, but he continued to sketch.

"I'd like the profile, Laura." His voice was mild, but the demand in it was very clear. "Turn your head again, and try to keep your chin up. Yes, like that." He was silent as he formed her mouth with the charcoal. "The father's family wants the baby. I want to know why."

"I never said that."

"Yes, you did." He had to hurry if he was going to capture that flare of anger in her eyes. "Let's not beat that point into the ground. Just tell me why."

Her hands were gripped tightly together, but there was as much fear as fury in her voice. "I don't have to tell you anything."

"No." He felt a thrill of excitement—and, incredibly, one of desire—as he stroked the charcoal over the pad. The desire puzzled him. More, it worried him. Pushing it aside, he concentrated on prying answers from her. "But since I'm not going to let it drop, you may as well."

Because he knew how to look, and to see, he caught the subtle play of emotions over her face. Fear, fury, frustration. It was the fear that continued to pull him over the line.

"Do you think I'd bundle you and your baby off to them, whoever the hell they are? Use your head. I haven't got any reason to."

He'd thought he would shout at her. He'd have sworn he was on the verge of doing so. Then, in a move that surprised them both, he reached out to take her hand. He was more surprised than she to feel her fingers curl instinctively into his. When she looked at him, emotions he'd thought unavailable to him turned over in his chest.

"You asked me to help you last night."

Her eyes softened with gratitude, but her voice was firm. "You can't."

"Maybe I can't, and maybe I won't." But as much as it went against the grain of what he considered his character, he wanted to. "I'm not a Samaritan, Laura, good or otherwise, and I don't like to add someone else's problems to my own. But the fact is, you're here, and I don't like playing in the dark."

She was tired, tired of running, tired of hiding, tired of trying to cope entirely on her own. She needed someone. When his hand was covering hers and his eyes were calm and steady on hers, she could almost believe it was him she needed.

"The baby's father is dead," she began, picking her way carefully. She would tell him enough to satisfy him, she hoped, but not all. "His parents want the baby. They want…I don't know, to replace, to take back, something that they've lost. To…to ensure the lineage. I'm sorry for them, but the baby isn't their child." There was that look again, fierce, protective. A mother tiger shielding her cub. "The baby's mine."

"No one would argue with that. Why should you have to run?"

"They have a lot of money, a lot of power."

"So?"

"So?" Angry again, she pushed away. The contact that had been so soothing for both of them was broken. "It's easy to say that when you come from the same world. You've always had. You've never had to want and to wonder. No one takes from people like you, Gabe. They wouldn't dare. You don't know what it's like to have your life depend on the whims of others."

That she had was becoming painfully obvious. "Having money doesn't mean you can take whatever you want."

"Doesn't it?" She turned to him, her face set and cold. "You wanted a place to paint, somewhere you could be alone and be left alone. Did you have to think twice about how to arrange it? Did you have to plan or save or make compromises, or did you just write a check and move in?"

His eyes were narrowed as he rose to face her. "Buying a cabin is a far cry from taking a baby from its mother."

"Not to some. Property is property, after all."

"You're being ridiculous."

"And you're being naive."

His temper wavered, vying with amusement. "That's a first. Sit down, Laura, you make me nervous when you swing around."

"I'm not going to break," she muttered, but she eased into a chair. "I'm strong, I take care of myself. I had an examination just before I left Dallas, and the baby and I are fine. Better than fine. In a few weeks I'm going to check into a hospital in Denver and have my baby. Then we're going to disappear."

He thought about it. He almost believed the woman sitting across from him could accomplish it. Then he remembered how lost and frightened she'd been the night before. There was no use pointing out the strain she'd been under and its consequences for her. But he knew now what button to push.

"Do you think it's fair to the baby to keep running?"

"No, it's horribly, horribly unfair. But it would be worse to stop and let them take him."

"Why are you so damn sure they would, or could?"

"Because they told me. They explained what they thought was best for me and the child, and they offered to pay me." The venom came into her voice at that, black and bitter. "They offered to give me money for my baby, and when I refused they threatened to simply take him." She didn't want to relive that dreadful, terrifying scene. With an effort she cleared it from her mind.

He felt a swift and dark disgust for these people he didn't even know. He buried it with a shake of his head and tried to reason with her. "Laura, whatever they want, or intend, they couldn't just take what isn't theirs. No court would just take an infant from its mother without good cause."

"I can't win on my own." She closed her eyes for a moment because she wanted badly to lay her head down and weep out all the fear and anguish. "I can't fight them on their own ground, Gabe, and I won't put my child through the misery of custody suits and court battles, the publicity, the gossip and speculation. A child needs a home, and love and security. I'm going to see to it that mine has all of those things. Whatever I have to do, wherever I have to go."

"I won't argue with you about what's right for you and the baby, but sooner or later you're going to have to face this."

"When the time comes, I will."

He rose and paced over to the fire to light another cigarette. He should drop it, just leave it—her—alone and let her follow her own path. It was none of his business. Not his problem. He swore, because somehow, the moment she'd taken his arm to cross the road, she'd become his business.

"Got any money?"

"Some. Enough to pay a doctor, and a bit more."

He was asking for trouble. He knew it. But for the first time in almost a year he felt as though something really mattered. Sitting on the edge of the hearth, he blew out smoke and studied her.

"I want to paint you," he said abruptly. "I'll pay you the standard model's fee, plus room and board."

"I can't take your money."

"Why not? You seem to think I have too much for my own good, anyway."

Shame brought color flooding into her cheeks. "I didn't mean it—not like that."

He brushed her words aside. "Whatever you meant, the fact remains that I want to paint you. I work at my own pace, so you'll have to be patient. I'm not good at compromise, but owing to your condition I'm willing to make some concessions and stop when you're tired or uncomfortable."

It was tempting, very tempting. She tried to forget that she'd traded on her looks before and concentrate on what the extra money would mean to the baby. "I'd like to agree, but the fact is, your work is well-known. If the portrait was shown, they'd recognize me."

"True enough, but that doesn't mean I'd be obliged to tell anyone where we'd met or when. You have my word that no one will ever trace you through me."

She was silent for a moment, warring with herself. "Would you come here?"

Hesitating only a moment, he tossed his cigarette into the fire. He rose, walked over, then crouched in front of her chair. She, too, had learned how to read a face. "Your word?"

"Yes."

Some risks were worth taking. She held both hands out to his, putting her trust into them.

With the continuing fall of snow, it was a day without a sunrise, a sunset, a twilight. The day stayed dim from morning on, and then night closed in without fanfare. And the snow stopped.

Laura might not have noticed if she hadn't been standing by the window. The flakes didn't appear to have tapered off, but to have stopped as if someone had thrown a switch. There was a vague sense of disappointment, the same she remembered feeling as a young girl when a storm had ended. On impulse, she bundled herself in her boots and coat and stepped out onto the porch.

Though Gabe had shoveled it off twice during the day, the snow came almost to her knees. Her boots sank in and disappeared. She had the sensation of being swallowed up by a soft, benign cloud. She wrapped her arms around her chest and breathed in the thin, cold air.

There were no stars. There was no moon. The porch light tossed its glow only a few feet. All she could see was white. All she could hear was silence. To some the high blanket of snow might have been a prison, something to chafe against. To Laura it was a fortress.

She'd decided to trust someone other than herself again. Standing there, soaking up the pure dark, the pure quiet, she knew that the decision had been the right one.

He wasn't a gentle man, or even a contented man, but he

was a kind one, and, she was certain, a man of his word. If they were using each other, her for sanctuary, him for art, it was a fair exchange. She needed to rest. God knew she needed whatever time she could steal to rest and recover.

She hadn't told him how tired she was, how much effort it took for her just to keep on her feet for most of the day. Physically the pregnancy had been an easy one. She was strong, she was healthy. Otherwise she would have crumpled long before this. But the past few months had drained every ounce of her emotional and mental reserves. The cabin, the mountains, the man, were going to give her time to build those reserves back up again.

She was going to need them.

He didn't understand what the Eagletons could do, what they could accomplish with their money and their power. She'd already seen what they were capable of. Hadn't they paid and maneuvered to have their son's mistakes glossed over? Hadn't they managed, with a few phone calls and a few favors called in, to have his death, and the death of the woman with him, turned from the grisly waste it had been into a tragic accident?

There had never been any mention in the press about alcohol and adultery. As far as the public was concerned, Anthony Eagleton, heir to the Eagleton fortune, had died as a result of a slippery road and faulty steering, and not his criminally careless drunk driving. The woman who had died with him had been turned from his mistress into his secretary.

The divorce proceedings that Laura had started had been erased, shredded, negated. No shadow of scandal would fall over the memory of Anthony Eagleton or over the family name. She'd been pressured into playing the shocked and grieving widow.

She had been shocked. She had grieved. Not for what had been lost—not on a lonely stretch of road outside of Boston—but for what had been lost so soon after her wedding night.

There was no use looking back, Laura reminded herself. Now, especially now, she had to look forward. Whatever had happened between her and Tony, they had created a life. And that life was hers to protect and to cherish.

With the spring snow glistening and untouched as far as she could see, she could believe that everything would work out for the best.

"What are you thinking?"

Startled, she turned toward Gabe with a little laugh. "I didn't hear you."

"You weren't listening." He pulled the door closed behind him. "It's cold out here."

"It feels wonderful. How much is there, do you think?"

"Three and a half, maybe four feet."

"I've never seen so much snow before. I can't imagine it ever melting and letting the grass grow."

His hands were bare. He tucked them in the pockets of his jacket. "I came here in November and there was already snow. I've never seen it any other way."

She tried to imagine that, living in a place where the snow never melted. No, she thought, she would need the spring, the buds, the green, the promise. "How long will you stay?"

"I don't know. I haven't thought about it."

She turned to smile at him, though she felt a touch of envy

at his being so unfettered. "All those paintings. You'll need to have a show."

"Sooner or later." He moved his shoulders, suddenly restless. San Francisco, his family, his memories, seemed very far away. "No hurry."

"Art needs to be seen and appreciated," she murmured, thinking out loud. "It shouldn't be hidden up here."

"And people should?"

"Do you mean me, or is that what you're doing, too? Hiding?"

"I'm working," he said evenly.

"A man like you could work anywhere, I think. You'd just elbow people aside and go to it."

He had to grin. "Maybe, but now and again I like to have some space. Once you make a name, people tend to look over your shoulder."

"Well, I, for one, am glad you came here, for whatever reason." She brushed the hair away from her face. "I should go back in, but I don't want to." She was smiling as she leaned back against the post.

His eyes narrowed. When he cupped her face in his hands, his fingers were cold and firm. "There's something about your eyes," he murmured, turning her face fully into the light. "They say everything a man wants a woman to say, and a great deal he doesn't. You have old eyes, Laura. Old, sad eyes."

She said nothing, not because her mind was empty, but because it was suddenly filled with so many things, so many thoughts, so many wishes. She hadn't thought she could feel anything like this again, and certainly not this longing for a man. Her skin warmed with it, even though his touch was cool, almost disinterested.

The sexual tug surprised her, even embarrassed her a little. But it was the emotional pull, the slow, hard drag of it, that kept her silent.

"I wonder what you've seen in your life."

As if of their own volition, his fingers stroked her cheek. They were long, slender, artistic, but hard and strong. Even so, he might merely have been familiarizing himself with the shape of her face, with the texture of her skin. An artist with his subject.

The longing leaped inside her, the foolish, impossible longing to be loved, held, desired, not for her face, not for the image a man could see, but for the woman inside.

"I'm getting tired," she said, managing to keep her voice steady. "I think I'll go to bed now."

He didn't move out of her way immediately. And his hand lingered. He couldn't have said what kept him there, staring at her, searching the eyes he found so fascinating. Then he stepped back quickly and shoved the door open for her.

"Good night, Gabe."

"Good night."

He stayed out in the cold, wondering what was wrong with him. For a moment, damn it, for a great deal longer than a moment, he'd found himself wanting her. Filled with self-disgust, he pulled out a cigarette. A man had to be sinking low to think about making love to a woman who was more than seven months along with another man's child.

But it was a long time before he could convince himself he'd imagined it.

Chapter 3

He wondered what she was thinking. She looked so serene, so quietly content. The pale pink sweater she wore fell into a soft cowl at her throat. Her hair shimmered to her shoulders. Again she wore no jewelry, nothing to draw attention away from her, nothing to draw attention to her.

Gabe rarely used models in his work, because even if they managed to hold the pose for as long as he demanded they began to look bored and restless. Laura, on the other hand, looked as though she could sit endlessly with that same soft smile on her face.

That was part of what he wanted to capture in the portrait. That inner patience, that...well, he supposed he could call it a gracious acceptance of time—what had come before, and what was up ahead. He'd never had much patience, not with people, not with his work, not with himself. It was a trait he could admire in her without having the urge to develop it himself.

Yet there was something more, something beyond the utterly feminine beauty and the Madonna-like calm. From time to time he saw a fierceness in her, a warriorlike determination. He could see that she was a woman who would do whatever was necessary to protect what was hers. Judging from her story, all that was hers was the child she carried.

She had more to tell, he mused as he ran the pencil over the pad. The bits and pieces she'd offered had only been given to keep him from asking more. He hadn't asked for more. It wasn't his usual style, once he'd decided an explanation was called for, to accept a partial one. He couldn't quite make himself push for the whole when even the portion she'd given him had plainly cost her so much.

There was still time. The radio continued to squawk about the roads that were closed and the snow that was yet to come. The Rockies could be treacherous in the spring. Gabe estimated it would be two weeks, perhaps three, before a trip could be managed with real safety.

It was odd, but he would have thought the enforced company would annoy him. Instead, he found himself pleased to have had his self-imposed solitude broken. It had been a long time since he'd done a portrait. Maybe too long. But he hadn't been able to face flesh and blood, not since Michael.

In the cabin, cut off from memories and reminders, he'd begun the healing process. In San Francisco he hadn't been able to pick up a brush. Grief had done more than make him weak. For a time it had made him...blank.

But here, secluded, solitary, he'd painted landscapes, still lifes, half-remembered dreams and seascapes from old sketches. It had been enough. Not until Laura had he felt the need to paint the human face again.

Once he'd believed in destiny, in a pattern of life that was meant to be even before birth. Michael's death had changed that. From that point, Gabe had had to blame something, someone. It had been easiest, and most painful, to blame himself. Now, sketching Laura, thinking over the odd set of circumstances that had brought her into his life, he began to wonder again.

And what, he asked himself yet again, was she thinking?

"Are you tired?"

"No." She answered, but she didn't move. He'd stationed a chair by the window, angling it so that she was facing him but still able to look out. The light fell over her, bringing no shadows. "I like to look at the snow. There are tracks in it now, and I wonder what animals might have passed by without us seeing. And I can see the mountains. They look so old and angry. Back east they're more tame, more good-natured."

He absently murmured his agreement as he studied his sketch. It was good, but it wasn't right, and he wanted to begin working on canvas soon. He set the pad aside and frowned at her. She stared back, patient and—if he wasn't reading her incorrectly—amused. "Do you have anything else to wear? Something off-the-shoulder, maybe?"

The amusement was even more evident now. "Sorry, my wardrobe's a bit limited at the moment."

He rose and began to pace, to the fire, to the window, back to the table. When he strode over to take her face in his hand and turn it this way and that, she sat obligingly. After three days of posing, she was used to it. She might have been an arrangement of flowers, Laura thought, or a bowl of fruit. It was as if that one moment of awareness on the snow-covered porch had never happened. She'd already convinced herself that she'd imagined that look in his eyes—and, more, her response to it.

He was the artist. She was the clay. And she'd been there before.

"You have a completely feminine face," he began, talking more to himself than to her. "Alluring and yet composed, and soft, even with the angular shape and those cheekbones. It's not threatening, and yet, it's utterly distracting. This—" his thumb brushed casually over her full lower lip "—says sex, even while your eyes promise love and devotion. And the fact that you're ripe—"

"Ripe?" She laughed, and the hands that had clenched in her lap relaxed again.

"Isn't that what pregnancy is? It only adds to the fascination. There's a promise and a fulfillment and—despite education and progress—a compelling mystery to a woman with child. Like an angel."

"How?"

As he spoke, he began to fuss with her hair, drawing it back, piling it up, letting it fall again. "We see angels as ethereal creatures, mystic, above human desires and flaws, but the fact is, they were human once."

His words appealed to her, made her smile. "Do you believe in angels?"

His hand was still in her hair, but he'd forgotten, totally forgotten, the practical reason for it. "Life wouldn't be worth much if you didn't." She had the hair of an angel, shimmery-blond, cloud-soft. Feeling suddenly awkward, he drew his hand away and tucked it in the pocket of his baggy corduroys.

"Would you like to take a break?" she asked him. Her hands were balled in her lap again.

"Yeah. Rest for an hour. I need to think this through." He stepped back automatically when she rose. When he wasn't working, he took great care not to come into physical contact with her. It was disturbing how much he wanted to touch her. "Put your feet up." When she lifted a brow at that, he shifted uncomfortably. "It recommended it in that book you leave lying around. I figured it wouldn't hurt for me to glance through it, under the circumstances."

"You're very kind."

"Self-preservation." Things happened to him when she smiled like that. Things he recognized but didn't want to acknowledge. "The more I make sure you take care of yourself, the less chance there is of you going into labor before the roads are clear."

"I've got more than a month," she reminded him. "But I appreciate you worrying about me—about us."

"Put your feet up," he repeated. "I'll get you some milk."

"But I—"

"You've only had one glass today." With an impatient gesture, he motioned her to the sofa before he walked into the kitchen.

With a little sigh of relief, Laura settled back against the cushions. Putting her feet up wasn't as easy as it once had been, but she managed to prop them on the edge of the coffee table. The heat from the fire radiated toward her, making her wish she could curl up in front of it. If she did, she thought wryly, it would take a crane to haul her back up again.

He was being so kind, Laura thought as she turned her head toward the sound of Gabe rummaging in the kitchen.

He didn't like her to remind him of it, but he was. No one had ever treated her quite like this—as an equal, yet as someone to be protected. As a friend, she thought, without tallying a list of obligations, a list of debts that had to be paid. Whether he listed them or not, someday, when she was able, she'd find a way to pay him back. Someday.

She could see the future if she closed her eyes and thought calm thoughts. She'd have a little apartment somewhere in the city. Any city. There would be a room for the baby, something in sunny yellows and glossy whites, with fairy-tale prints on the walls. She'd have a rocking chair she could sit in with the baby during the long, quiet nights, when the rest of the world was asleep.

And she wouldn't be alone anymore.

Opening her eyes, she saw Gabe standing over her. She wanted, badly, to reach up, to take his hands and draw in some of the strength and confidence she felt radiating from him. She wanted, more, for him to run his thumb along her lip again, slowly, gently, as though she were a woman, rather than a thing to be painted.

Instead, she reached up to take the glass of milk he held. "After the baby's born and I finish nursing, I'm never going to drink a drop of milk again."

"This is the last of the fresh," he told her. "Tomorrow you go on powdered and canned."

"Oh, joy." Grimacing, she downed half the contents of the glass. "I pretend it's coffee, you know. Strong, black coffee." She sipped again. "Or, if I'm feeling reckless, champagne. French, in fluted crystal."

"It's too bad I don't have any wineglasses handy. It would help the illusion. Are you hungry?"

"It's a myth about eating for two, and if I gain much more weight I'll begin to moo." Content, she settled back again. "That painting of Paris...did you do it here?"

He glanced over at the work. So she'd been there, he thought. It was a moody, almost surreal study of the Bois de Boulogne. "Yes, from old sketches and memory. When were you there?"

"I didn't say I'd been to Paris."

"You wouldn't have recognized it otherwise." He took the empty glass out of her hand and set it aside. "The more secretive you are, Laura, the more it makes me want to dig."

"A year ago," she said stiffly. "I spent two weeks there."

"How did you like it?"

"Paris?" She ordered herself to relax. It had been a lifetime ago, almost long enough that she could imagine it had all happened to someone else. "It's a beautiful city, like an old, old woman who still knows how to flirt. The flowers were blooming, and the smells were incredible. It rained and rained, for three days, and you could sit and watch the black umbrellas hurrying by and the blossoms opening up."

Instinctively he put a hand over hers to calm the agitated movement of her fingers. "You weren't happy there."

"Paris in the spring?" She concentrated on making her hands go limp. "Only a fool wouldn't be happy there."

"The baby's father...was he with you there?"

"Why does it matter?"

It shouldn't have mattered. But now, whenever he looked at the painting, he would think of her. And he had to know. "Did you love him?"

Had she? Laura looked back at the fire, but the only answers were within herself. Had she loved Tony? Her lips curved a little. Yes, she had, she had loved the Tony she'd imagined him to be. "Very much. I loved him very much."

"How long have you been alone?"

"I'm not." She laid a hand on her stomach. When she felt the answering movement, her smile widened. Taking Gabe's hand, she pressed it against her. "Feel that? Incredible, isn't it? Someone's in there."

He felt the stirring beneath his hand, gentle at first, then with a punch that surprised him. Without thinking, he moved closer. "That felt like a left jab. Makes you feel as though it's fighting to get out." He knew the feeling, the impatience, the frustration at being trapped in one world while you longed for another. "How does it feel from the other side?"

"Alive." Laughing, she left her hand over his. "In Dallas they put a monitor on, and I could hear the baby's heartbeat. It was so fast, so impatient. Nothing in the world ever sounded so wonderful. And I think…"

But he was looking at her now, deeply, intently. Their hands were still joined, their bodies just brushing. Even as the life inside her quickened, so did her pulse. The warmth, the intimacy, of the moment washed over her, leaving her breathless and full of needs.

He wanted to hold her, badly. The urge to gather her close and just hold on was so sharp, so intense that he hurt. He dreamed of her every night when he struggled for sleep on the floor of the spare room. In his dreams they were curled in bed together, with her breath warm on his cheek and her hair tangled in his hands. And when he woke from the dreams he told himself he was mad. He told himself that again now and moved aside.

Though they were no longer touching, he could feel, as well as hear, her long, quiet sigh.

"I'd like to work some more, if you're up to it."

"Of course." She wanted to weep. That was natural, she told herself. Pregnant women wept easily. Their emotions ran on the surface, to be bruised and battered without effort, and often without cause.

"I've got something in mind. Hold on a minute."

She waited, still sitting, while he went into the spare room. Moments later he came back holding a navy blue shirt.

"Put this on. I think the contrast between the man's shirt and your face might be the answer."

"All right." Laura went into the bedroom and stripped off the big pink sweater. She started to draw an arm through the sleeve and then she caught his scent. It was there, clinging to the heavy cotton. Tough, and unapologetically sexual. Man. Unable to resist, she rubbed her cheek over it. The material was soft. The scent was not, but somehow even the scent of him made her feel safe. And yet, foolish as it seemed, it made her feel a dull, deep tremor of desire.

Wasn't it wrong to want as a woman, to want Gabe as a man, when she carried such a responsibility? But it didn't seem wrong when she felt so close to him. He had sorrows, too. She could see them, sense them. Perhaps it was that common ground, and their isolation, that made her feel as though she'd known him, cared about him, for so long.

With a sigh, she slipped into the shirt. What did she know about her own feelings? The first, the only, time she'd trusted them completely had brought misery. Whatever emotions Gabe stirred in her, she would be wise to keep gratitude in the forefront.

When she stepped back into the main cabin, he was going through his sketches, rejecting, considering, accepting. He glanced up and realized that his conception of Laura fell far, far short of the mark.

She looked like the angel he'd spoken of, illusory, golden, yet tied now to the earth. He preferred to think of her as an illusion rather than as a woman, one who stirred him.

"That's more of the look I want," he said, managing to keep his voice steady. "The color's good on you, and the straight-line masculine style is a nice contrast."

"You may not get it back anytime soon. It's wonderfully comfortable."

"Consider it a loan."

He walked over to the chair as she sat and shifted into the precise pose she'd been in before the break. Not for the first time, Gabe wondered if she'd modeled before. That was another question, for another time.

"Let's try something else." He shifted her, mere inches, muttering to himself. Laura nearly smiled. She was back to being a bowl of fruit.

"Damn, I wish we had some flowers. A rose. Just one rose."

"You could imagine one."

"I may." He tilted her head a fraction to the left before he stood back. "This feels right, so I'm going to draw it on canvas. I've wasted enough time on rough sketches."

"Three whole days."

"I've completed paintings in half that time when things clicked."

She could see it, him sitting on a tall stool at an easel, working feverishly, brows lowered, eyes narrowed, those long, narrow hands creating. "There are some in here you haven't finished at all."

"Mood changed." He was already making broad strokes on canvas with his pencil. "Do you finish everything you start?"

She thought about that. "I suppose not, but people are always saying you should."

"When something's not right, why drag it out to the bitter end?"

"Sometimes you promise," she murmured, thinking of her marriage vows.

Because he was watching her closely, he saw the swift look of regret. As always, though he tried to block it, her emotions touched a chord in him. "Sometimes promises can't be kept."

"No. But they should be," she said quietly. Then she fell silent.

He worked for nearly an hour, defining, refining, perfecting. She was giving him the mood he wanted. Pensive, patient, sensuous. He already knew, even before the first brush stroke, that this would be one of his best. Perhaps his very best. And he knew he would have to paint her again, in other moods, in other poses.

But that was for tomorrow. Today, now, he needed to capture the tone of her, the feel, the simplicity. That was pencil lines and curves. Black against white, and a few shades of gray. Tomorrow he would begin filling in, adding the color, the complexities. When he had finished he would have the whole of her on canvas, and he would know her fully, as no one had ever before or would ever again.

"Will you let me see it as you go along?"

"What?"

"The painting." Laura kept her head still but shifted her eyes from the window to him. "I know artists are supposed to be temperamental about showing their work before it's finished."

"I'm not temperamental." He lifted his gaze to hers, as if inviting her to disagree.

"Anyone could see that." Though she kept her expression sober, he could hear the amusement in her voice. "So will you let me see it?"

"Doesn't matter to me. As long as you realize that if you see something you don't like I won't change it."

This time she did laugh, more freely, more richly than before. His fingers tightened on the pencil. "You mean if I see something that wounds my vanity? You don't have to worry about that. I'm not vain."

"All beautiful women are vain. They're entitled."

"People are only vain if their looks matter to them."

This time he laughed, but cynically. He set down his pencil. "And yours don't matter to you?"

"I didn't do anything to earn them, did I? An accident of fate, or a stroke of luck. If I were terribly smart or talented somehow I'd probably be annoyed with my looks, because people look at them and nothing else." She shrugged, then settled with perfect ease into the pose again. "But since I'm neither of those, I've learned to accept that looking a certain way is...I don't know, a gift that makes up for a lack of other things."

"What would you trade your beauty for?"

"Any number of things. But then, a trade isn't earning, either, so it wouldn't count. Will you tell me something?"

"Probably." He took a rag out of his back pocket and dusted off his hands.

"Which are you more vain about, your looks or your work?"

He tossed the rag aside. It was odd that she could look so sad, so serious, and still make him laugh. "No one's ever accused me of being beautiful, so there's no contest." He started to turn the easel. When she began to rise, he motioned her back. "No, relax. Look from there and tell me what you think."

Laura settled back and studied. It was only a sketch, less detailed than many of the others he'd done. It was her face and torso, her right hand resting lightly just below her left shoulder. For some reason it seemed a protective pose, not defensive, but cautious.

He'd been right about the shirt, she realized. It made her seem more of a woman than any amount of lace or silks could have. Her hair was long and loose, falling in heavy, disordered curls that contradicted the pose. She hadn't expected to find any surprises in her face, but as she studied his conception of it, she shifted uncomfortably in her chair.

"I'm not as sad as you make me look."

"I've already warned you I wouldn't change anything."

"You're free to paint as you please. I'm simply telling you that you have a misconception."

There was a huffiness in her voice that amused him. He turned the easel around again but didn't bother to look at his work. "I don't think so."

"I'm hardly tragic."

"Tragic?" He rocked back on his heels as he studied her.

"There's nothing tragic about the woman in the painting. *Valiant* is the word."

She smiled at that and pushed herself out of the chair. "I'm not valiant, either, but it's your painting."

"We agree on that."

"Gabe!"

She flung out a hand. The urgency in her voice had him crossing to her quickly and gripping her hand. "What is it?"

"Look, look out there." She turned to him, using her free hand to point.

Not urgency, Gabe realized. He was tempted to strangle her. Excitement. The excitement of seeing a solitary buck less than two yards from the window. It stood deep in snow, its head lifted, scenting the air. Arrogantly, and without a trace of fear, it stared at them through the glass.

"Oh, he's wonderful. I've never seen one so big before, or so close."

It was easy to share the pleasure. A deer, a fox, a hawk circling overhead…those were some of the things that had helped him over his own grief.

"A few weeks ago I hiked down to a stream about a mile south of here. I came across a whole family. I was downwind, and I managed three sketches before the doe spotted me."

"This whole place belongs to him. Can you imagine it? Acres and acres. He must know it, even enjoy it, or else he wouldn't look so sure of himself." She laughed again, and pressed her free hand to the frosted glass. "You know, it's as if we were exhibits and he'd come to take a quick look around the zoo."

The deer nosed down in the snow, perhaps looking for the grass that was buried far beneath, perhaps scenting another animal. He moved slowly, confident in his solitude. Around him the trees dripped with ice and snow.

Abruptly he raised his head, his crown of antlers plunging high in the air. In bounds and leaps he raced across the snow and disappeared into the woods beyond.

Laughing, Laura turned, then instantly forgot everything.

She hadn't realized they had moved so close together. Nor had he. Their hands were still linked. Beside them the sun streamed in, losing power as the afternoon moved toward evening. And the cabin, like the woods beyond, was absolutely silent.

He touched her. He hadn't known he would, but the moment his fingers grazed her cheek he knew he needed to. She didn't move away. Perhaps he would have accepted it if she had. He wanted to believe he would have accepted it. But she didn't move.

There were nerves. He felt them in the hand that trembled in his. He had them, too. Another new experience. How did he approach her, when he knew he had no business approaching her? How did he resist what common sense told him he had to resist?

Yet her skin was warm under his touch. Real. Not a portrait, but a woman. Whatever had happened in her life, whatever had made her into the woman she was, that was yesterday. This was now. Her eyes, wide and more than a little frightened, were on his. She didn't move. She waited.

He swore at himself even as he slowly, ever so slowly, lowered his lips to hers.

It was madness to allow it. It was more than madness to want it. But even before his lips touched hers she felt herself give in to him. As she gave, she braced herself, not knowing what to expect for herself, or for him.

It might have been the first. That was her one and only thought as his mouth closed over hers. Not just the first with him but the first with anyone. No one had ever kissed her like this. She had known passion, the quick, almost painful desire that came from heat and frenzy. She had known demands, some that she could answer, some that she could not. She had known the anger and the hunger a man could have for a woman, but she had never known, had never imagined, this kind of reverence.

And yet, even with that, there were hints of darker needs, needs held down by chains, that made the embrace more exciting, more involving, than any other. His hands were in her hair, searching, exploring, while his lips moved endlessly over hers. She felt the world tip and knew instinctively that he would be there to right it again.

He had to stop. He couldn't stop. One taste, just one taste, and he craved more. It seemed he'd been empty, without knowing it, and now—incredibly, swiftly, terrifyingly—he was filled.

Her hands, hesitant, somehow innocent, slipped over his arms to his shoulders. When she parted her lips, there was that same curious shyness in the invitation. He could smell the spring, though it was still buried beneath the snow, could smell it in her hair, on her skin. Even the wood smoke that always tinted the air in the cabin couldn't overwhelm it. Logs shifted in the grate, and the wind that came up with evening began to moan against the window. And Laura, her mouth warm and giving under his, sighed.

He wanted to play out the fantasy, to draw her up into

his arms and take her to bed. To lie with her, to slip his shirt from her and feel her skin against his own. To have her touch him, hold on to him. Trust him.

The war inside him raged on. She wasn't merely a woman, she was a woman who was carrying a child. And growing inside her was not merely a child, but the child of another man, one she had loved.

She wasn't his to love. He wasn't hers to trust. Still, she pulled at him, her secrets, her eyes, eyes that said much, much more than her words, and her beauty, which she didn't seem to understand went far beyond the shape and texture of her face.

So he had to stop, until he resolved within himself exactly what he wanted—and until she trusted him enough to tell him the whole truth.

He would have drawn her away from him, but she pressed her face into his shoulder. "Please don't say anything, just for a minute."

There were tears in her voice, and they left him more shaken than the kiss had. The tug-of-war increased, and finally he lifted a hand to stroke her hair. The baby turned, moving inside her, against him, and he wondered what in God's name he was going to do.

"I'm sorry." Her voice was under control again, but she didn't let go. How could she have known how badly she needed to be held, when there had been so few times in her life when anyone had bothered? "I don't mean to cling."

"You're not."

"Well." Drawing herself up straight, she stepped back. There were no tears, but her eyes glimmered with the effort it took to hold them in. "You were going to say that you didn't mean for that to happen, but it's all right."

"I didn't mean for that to happen," he said evenly. "But that's not an apology."

"Oh." A little nonplussed, she braced a hand on the back of the chair. "I suppose what I meant is that I don't want you to feel— I don't want you to think that I— Hell." With that, she gave in and sat. "I'm trying to say that I'm not upset that you kissed me and that I understand."

"Good." He felt better, much better than he'd thought he would. Casually he dragged over another chair and straddled it. "What do you understand, Laura?"

She'd thought he would let it go at that, take the easy way out. She struggled to say what she felt without saying too much. "That you felt a little sorry for me, and involved a bit, because of the situation, and the painting, too." Why couldn't she relax again? And why was he looking at her that way? "I don't want you to think that I misunderstood. I would hardly expect you to be…" The ground was getting shakier by the minute. She was ready to shut up entirely, but he quirked a brow and gestured with his hands, inviting her, almost challenging her, to finish.

"I realize you wouldn't be attracted to me—physically, that is—under the circumstances. And I don't want to think that I interpreted what just happened as anything other than a—a sort of kindness."

"That's funny." As if he were considering the idea, Gabe reached up and scratched his chin. "You don't look stupid. I'm attracted to you, Laura, and there's a part of that attraction that's very, very physical. Making love with you may not be possible under the circumstances, but that doesn't mean that the desire to do so isn't there."

She opened her mouth as if to speak, but ended up just lifting her hands and then letting them fall again.

"The fact that you're carrying a child is only part of the reason I can't make love with you. The other, though not as obvious, is just as important. I need the story, Laura, your story. All of it."

"I can't."

"Afraid?"

She shook her head. Her eyes glimmered, but her chin lifted. "Ashamed."

He would have expected almost any other reason than that. "Why? Because you weren't married to the baby's father?"

"No. Please don't ask me."

He wanted to argue, but he bit the words back. She was looking pale and tired and just too fragile. "All right, for now. But think about this. I have feelings for you, and they're growing much faster than either of us might like. Right now I'm damned if I know what to do about it."

When he rose, she reached up and touched his arm. "Gabe, there's nothing to do. I can't tell you how much I wish it were otherwise."

"Life's what you make it, angel." He touched her hair then stepped away. "We need more wood."

Laura sat in the empty cabin and wished more than she had ever wished for anything that she had made a better job of hers.

Chapter 4

More snow had fallen during the night. It was, compared to what had come before, hardly more than a dusting. The fresh inches lay in mounds and drifts over the rest, where the wind had blown them. In places the snow was as high as a man. Miniature mountains of it lay cozily against the windowpanes, shifting constantly in the wind.

Already the sun was melting the fresh fall, and if Laura listened she could hear the water sliding down the gutters from the roof like rain. It was a friendly sound, and it made her think of hot tea by a sizzling fire, a good book read on a lazy afternoon, a nap on the sofa in early evening.

But this was morning, only an hour or two past dawn. As usual, she had the cabin to herself.

Gabe was chopping wood. From the kitchen, where she was optimistically heating milk and a chocolate bar in a pan, she could hear the steady thud of the ax. She knew the woodbox was full, and the stack of logs outside the rear door was still high. Even if the snow lasted into June, they would still have an ample supply. Artist or not, he was a physical man, and she understood his need to do something manual and tiring.

It seemed so…normal, she thought. Her cooking in the kitchen, Gabe splitting logs, icicles growing long and shiny on the eaves outside the window. Their little world was so well tuned, so self-contained. It was like this every morning. She would rise to find him already outdoors, shoveling, chopping, hauling. She would make fresh coffee or warm what he'd left in the pot. The portable radio would bring her news from the outside, but it never seemed terribly important. After a little while he would come in, shake and stomp the snow off, then accept the cup of coffee she offered him. The routine would continue with him taking his place in behind the easel and Laura taking hers by the window.

Sometimes they would talk. Sometimes they would not.

Beneath the routine, she sensed some kind of hurry in him that she couldn't understand. Though he might paint for hours, his movements controlled and measured, he still seemed impatient to finish. The fact was, the portrait was coming along faster than she could ever have imagined. She was taking shape on canvas—or rather the woman he saw when he looked at her was taking shape. Laura couldn't understand why he had chosen to make her look so otherworldly, so dreamy. She was very much a part of the world. The child she carried grounded her to it.

But she'd learned not to complain, because he didn't listen.

He'd done other sketches, as well, some full-length, some just of her face. She told herself he was entitled, particularly if that was all the payment she could give him for the roof over her head. A few of the sketches made her uneasy, like the one he'd drawn when she'd fallen asleep on the sofa late one afternoon. She'd looked so…defenseless. And she'd felt defenseless when she'd realized that he'd watched her and drawn her while she was unaware of it.

Not that she was afraid of him. Laura poked halfheartedly at the mixture of powdered milk, water and chocolate. He'd been kinder to her than she'd had any right to expect. And, though he could be terse and brusque, he was the gentlest man she'd ever known.

Perhaps he was attracted to her. Men had often been attracted to her face. But whether he was or not he treated her with respect and care. She'd learned not to expect those things when there was attraction.

With a shrug, she poured the liquid into a mug. Now wasn't the time to focus on the feeling Gabe might or might not have. She was on her own. Fixing a mental image of creamy hot chocolate in her mind, Laura downed half the contents of the mug. She made a face, sighed, then lifted the mug again. In a matter of days she would be on her way to Denver again.

A sudden pain had her gripping the side of the counter for support. She held on, fighting back the instinctive need to call for Gabe. It was nothing, she told herself as it began to ease. Moving carefully, she started into the living room. Gabe's chopping stopped. It was in that silence that she heard the other sound. An engine? The panic came instantly, and almost as quickly was pushed down. They hadn't found her. It was ridiculous to even think it. But she walked quickly, quietly, to the front window to look out.

A snowmobile. The sight of it, shiny and toylike, might

have amused and pleased her if she hadn't seen the uniformed state trooper on it. Preparing to stand her ground if it came to that, Laura moved to the door and opened it a crack.

Gabe had worked up a warm, healthy sweat. He appreciated being outdoors, appreciated the crisp air, the rhythm of his work. He couldn't say that it kept his mind off Laura. Nothing did. But it helped him put the situation into perspective.

She needed help. He was going to help her.

There were some who knew him who would have been more than a little surprised by his decision. It wasn't that anyone would have accused him of being unfeeling. The sensitivity in his paintings was proof of his capacity for emotion, passion, compassion. But few would have thought him capable of unconditional generosity.

It was Michael who had been generous.

Gabe had always been self-absorbed—or, more accurately, absorbed in his art, driven to depict life, with all its joys and pains. Michael had simply embraced life.

Now he was gone. Gabe brought the ax down, his breath whistling through his teeth and puffing white in the thin air. And Michael's leaving had left a hole so big, so great, that Gabe wasn't certain it could ever be filled.

He heard the engine when his ax was at the apex of his swing. Distracted, he let it fall so that the blade was buried in wood. Splinters popped out to join others on the trampled snow. With a quick glance toward the kitchen window, Gabe started around the cabin to meet the visitor.

He didn't make a conscious decision to protect the woman inside. He didn't have to. It was the most natural thing in the world.

"How ya doing?" The cop, his full cheeks reddened by wind and cold, shut off the engine and he nodded to Gabe.

"Well enough." He judged the trooper to be about twenty-five and half frozen. "How's the road?"

Giving a short laugh, the trooper stepped off the snowmobile. "Let's just say I hope you've got no appointments to keep."

"Nothing pressing."

"Good thing." He offered a gloved hand. "Scott Beecham."

"Gabe Bradley."

"I heard somebody bought the old McCampbell place." With his hands on his hips, Beecham studied the cabin. "A hell of a winter to pick for moving in. We're swinging by to check on everybody on the ridge, seeing if they need supplies or if anyone's sick."

"I stocked up the day of the storm."

"Good for you." He gestured toward the Jeep. "At least you've got a fighting chance in a four-wheel drive. Could've filled a used car lot with some of the vehicles towed in. We're checking around on a compact, an '84 Chevy that took a spin into the guardrail about a quarter mile from here. Abandoned. Driver might have wandered out and got lost in the blizzard."

"My wife," Gabe said. In the doorway, Laura opened her eyes wide. "She was worried that something had happened to me and got the idea of driving into town." Gabe grinned and drew out a cigarette. "Damn near ran into me. At the rate things were going, I figured it was best to leave the car where it was and get us back here. Haven't been able to get back out to check on the damage."

"Not as bad as some I've seen the last few days. Was she hurt?"

"No. Scared ten years off both of us, though."

"I'll bet. Afraid we're going to have to tow the vehicle in, Mr. Bradley." He glanced toward the house. His voice was casual, but Gabe sensed that he was alert. "Your wife, you say?"

"That's right."

"Name on the registration was Malone, Laura Malone."

"My wife's maiden name," Gabe said easily.

On impulse, Laura pushed open the door. "Gabe?"

Both men turned to look at her. The trooper pulled off his hat. Gabe merely scowled.

"I'm sorry to interrupt—" she smiled "—but I thought the officer might like some hot coffee."

The trooper replaced his hat. "That's mighty tempting, ma'am, and I appreciate it, but I have to get along. Sorry about your car."

"My own fault. Can you tell us when the road will be open?"

"Your husband ought to be able to manage a trip into town in a day or two," Beecham said. "I wouldn't recommend the drive for you, ma'am, for the time being."

"No." She smiled at him and hugged her elbows. "I don't think I'll be going anywhere for a little while yet."

"I'll just be on my way." Beecham straddled the snowmobile again. "You got a shortwave, Mr. Bradley?"

"No."

"Might not be a bad idea to pick one up next time you're in town. More dependable than the phones. When's your baby due?"

Gabe just stared for a moment. The pronoun had stunned him. "Four or five weeks."

"You got yourself plenty of time, then." With a grin, Beecham started the engine. "This your first?"

"Yes," Gabe murmured. "It is."

"Nothing quite like it. Got myself two girls. Last one decided to be born on Thanksgiving. Hardly had two bites of pumpkin pie when I had to drive to the hospital. My wife still says it was my mother's sausage stuffing that started her off." He raised a hand and his voice. "Take care, Mrs. Bradley."

They watched, Gabe from the yard, Laura from the doorway, as the snowmobile scooted up the lane. And then they were alone.

Clearing his throat, Gabe started up the stairs. Laura said nothing, but she stepped out of the way and closed the door behind him. She waited until he was sitting on the low stone hearth, unlacing his boots.

"Thank you."

"For what?"

"You told the trooper that I was your wife."

Still frowning, he pried off a boot. "It seemed less complicated that way."

"For me," Laura agreed. "Not for you."

He shrugged his shoulders and then rose to go into the kitchen. "Any coffee?"

"Yes." She heard the glass pot chink against the mug, heard the liquid pour into the stoneware. He'd lied for her, protected her, and all she had done was take from him. "Gabe." Praying that her instincts and her conscience were right, she walked to the doorway.

"What the hell is this?" He had the pan she'd used to heat the milk in his hand.

For a moment the tension fled. "If you're desperate enough, it's hot chocolate."

"It looks like... Well, never mind what it looks like." He set it back on the stove. "That powdered stuff tastes filthy, doesn't it?"

"It's hard to argue with the truth."

"I'll try to make it into town tomorrow."

"If you do, could you..." Embarrassed, she let her words trail off.

"What do you want?"

"Nothing. It's stupid. Listen, could we sit down a minute?" He took her hand before she could back away. "What do you want from town, Laura?"

"Marshmallows, to toast in the fireplace. I told you it was stupid," she murmured, and tried to tug her hand away.

He wanted, God, he wanted just to fold her into his arms. "Is that a craving or just a whim?"

"I don't know. It's just that I look at the fireplace and think about marshmallows." Because he wasn't laughing at her, it was easy to smile. "Sometimes I can almost smell them."

"Marshmallows. You don't want anything to go with them? Like horseradish?"

She made a face at him. "Another myth."

"You're spoiling all my preconceptions." He wasn't sure when he'd lifted her hand to his lips, but after the faintest taste of her skin he dropped it again. "And you're not wearing the shirt."

Though he was no longer touching it, her hand felt warm,

warm and impossibly soft. "Oh." She took a long breath. He was thinking of the painting, not of her. He was the artist with his subject again. "I'll change."

"Fine." More than a little shaken by the extent of his desire for her, he turned back to the counter and his coffee.

The decision came quickly, or perhaps it had been made the moment she'd heard him lie for her, protect her. "Gabe, I know you want to work right away, but I'd like... I feel like I should... I want to tell you everything, if you still want to hear it."

He turned back, his eyes were utterly clear and intent. "Why?"

"Because it's wrong not to trust you." Again the breath seemed to sigh out of her. "And because I need someone. We need someone."

"Sit down," he said simply, leading her to the couch.

"I don't know where to start."

It would probably be easier for her to start further back, he thought as he tossed another log in the fire. "Where do you come from?" he asked when he joined her on the couch.

"I've lived a lot of places. New York, Pennsylvania, Maryland. My aunt had a little farm on the Eastern Shore. I lived with her the longest."

"Your parents?"

"My mother was very young when I was born. Unmarried. She... I went to live with my aunt until...until things became difficult for her, financially. There were foster homes after that. That isn't really the point."

"Isn't it?"

She took a steadying breath. "I don't want you to feel

sorry for me. I'm not telling you this so that you'll feel sorry for me."

The pride was evident in the tilt of her head, in the tone of her voice—the same quiet pride he was trying to capture on canvas. His fingers itched for his sketch pad, even as they itched to touch her face. "All right, I won't."

With a nod, she continued. "From what I can gather, things were very hard on my mother. Even without the little I was told, it's easy enough to imagine. She was only a child. It's possible that she wanted to keep me, but it didn't work out. My aunt was older, but she had children of her own. I was essentially another mouth to feed, and when it became difficult to do so, I went into foster care."

"How old were you?"

"Six the first time. For some reason it just never seemed to work out. I would stay in one place for a year, in another for two. I hated not belonging, never being a real part of what everyone else had. When I was about twelve I went back with my aunt for a short time, but her husband had problems of his own, and it didn't last."

He caught something in her voice, something that made him tense. "What sort of problems?"

"They don't matter." She shook her head and started to rise, but Gabe put his hand firmly on hers.

"You started this, Laura, now finish it."

"He drank," she said quickly. "When he drank he got mean."

"Mean? Do you mean violent?"

"Yes. When he was sober, he was discontented and critical. Drunk, he was—could be—vicious." She rubbed a hand over her shoulder, as if she were soothing an old wound.

"My aunt was his usual target, but he often went after the children."

"Did he hit you?"

"Unless I was quick enough to get out of his way." She managed a ghost of a smile. "And I learned to be quick. It sounds worse than it was."

He doubted it. "Go on."

"The social services took me away again and placed me in another home. It was like being put on hold. I remember when I was sixteen, counting the days until I'd be of age and able to at least fend for myself. Make...I don't know, make some of my own decisions. Then I was. I moved to Pennsylvania and got a job. I was working as a clerk in a department store in Philadelphia. I had a customer, a woman, who used to come in regularly. We got friendly, and one day she came in with a man. He was short and balding—looked like a bulldog. He nodded to the woman and told her she'd been absolutely right. Then he handed me a business card and told me to come to his studio the next day. Of course, I had no intention of going. I thought... That is, I'd gotten used to men..."

"I imagine you did," Gabe said dryly.

It still embarrassed her, but since he seemed to take it in stride she didn't dwell on it. "In any case, I set the card aside and would have forgotten about it, but one of the girls who worked with me picked it up later and went wild. She told me who he was. You might know the name. Geoffrey Wright."

Gabe lifted a brow. Wright was one of the most respected fashion photographers in the business—no, *the* most. Gabe might not know much about the fashion business, but a name like Geoffrey Wright's crossed boundaries. "It rings a bell."

"When I found out he was a professional, a well-known photographer, I decided to take a chance and go to see him. Everything happened at once. He was very gruff and had me in makeup and under the lights before I could babble an excuse. I was terribly embarrassed, but he didn't seem to notice. He barked out orders, telling me to stand, sit, lean, turn. He had a fur in his vault—a full-length sable. He took it out and tossed it around my shoulders. I thought I was dreaming. I must have said so aloud, because while he was shooting he laughed and told me that in a year I could wear sable to breakfast."

Saying nothing, Gabe settled back. With his eyes narrowed, he could see her, enveloped in furs. There was a twist in his stomach as he thought about her becoming one of Wright's young and casually disposable mistresses.

"Within a month I had done a layout for *Mode* magazine. Then I did another for *Her,* and one for *Charm.* It was incredible. One day I was selling linens and the next I was having dinner with designers."

"And Wright?"

"No one in my life had ever been as good to me as Geoffrey. Oh, I knew he saw me as a commodity half the time, but he set himself up as, I don't know, a watchdog. He had plans, he'd tell me. Not too much exposure too quickly. Then, in another two years, there wouldn't be a person in the Western world who wouldn't recognize my face. It sounded exciting. Most of my life I'd been essentially anonymous. He liked that, the fact that I'd come from nothing, from nowhere. I know some of his other models saw him as cold. He often was. But he was the closest thing I'd ever had to a father."

"Is that how you saw him?"

"I suppose. And then, after all he'd done for me, after all the time he'd invested, I let him down." She started to rise again, and again Gabe stopped her.

"Where are you going?"

"I need some water."

"Sit. I'll get it."

She used the time to compose herself. Her story was only half done, and the worst part, the most painful part, was yet to come. He brought her a clear glass with ice swimming in it. Laura took two long sips, then continued.

"We went to Paris. It was like being Cinderella and being told midnight never had to come. We were scheduled to be there for a month, and because Geoffrey wanted a very French flavor to the pictures we went all over Paris for the shoot. We went to a party one night. It was one of those gorgeous spring nights when all the women are beautiful and the men handsome. And I met Tony."

He caught the slight break in her voice, the shadow of pain in her eyes, and knew without being told that she was speaking now of her baby's father.

"He was so gallant, so charming. The prince to my Cinderella. For the next two weeks, whenever I wasn't working, I was with Tony. We went dancing, we ate in little cafés and walked in the parks. He was everything I'd thought I'd wanted and knew I could never have. He treated me as though I were something rare and valuable, like a diamond necklace. There was a time when I thought that was love."

She fell silent for a moment, brooding. That had been her mistake, her sin, her vanity. Even now, a year later, it cut at her.

"Geoffrey grumbled and talked about rich young pups

sowing wild oats, but I wouldn't listen. I wanted to be loved, I wanted so terribly for someone to care, to want me. When Tony asked me to marry him, I didn't think twice."

"You married him?"

"Yes." She looked at him again. "I know I led you to believe that I hadn't married the baby's father. It seemed easiest."

"You don't wear a ring."

Color washed into her face. The shame of it. "I sold them."

"I see." There was no condemnation in the two words, but she felt it nonetheless.

"We stayed in Paris for our honeymoon. I wanted to go back to the States and meet his family, but he said we should stay where we were happy. It seemed right. Geoffrey was furious with me, lectured and shouted about me wasting myself. At the time I thought he meant my career, and I ignored him. It was only later that I realized he meant my life."

She jumped when a log fell apart in the fire. It was easier to continue if she looked at the flames, she discovered. "I thought I'd found everything I'd ever wanted. When I look back I realize that those weeks we spent in Paris were like a kind of magic, something that's not quite real but that you believe because you aren't clever enough to see the illusion. Then it was time to come home."

She linked her hands together and began to fidget. He had come to recognize it as a sign of inner turmoil. Though the urge was there, he didn't take them in his to calm her. "The night before we were to leave, Tony went out. He said he had some business to tie up. I waited for him, feeling a little sorry for myself that my new husband would leave me alone on our last night in Paris. Then, as it got later and later, I stopped feeling sorry for myself and started feeling frightened. By the time he got back, it was after three and I was angry and upset."

She fell silent again. Gabe pulled the afghan from the back of the couch and spread it over her lap. "You had a fight."

"Yes. He was very drunk and belligerent. I'd never seen him like that before, but I was to see him like that again. I asked him where he'd been and he said—essentially he told me it was none of my business. We started shouting at each other, and he told me he'd been with another woman. At first I thought he said that just to hurt me, but then I saw that it was true. I started to cry."

That was the worst of it, Laura thought, looking back on the way she'd crumbled and wept. "That only made him angrier. He tossed things around the suite, like a little boy having a tantrum. He said things, but the gist of it was that I'd have to get used to the way he lived, and that I hardly had a right to be upset when I'd been Geoffrey's whore."

Her voice broke on the last word, so she lifted the glass and cooled her throat with the water. "That hurt the most," she managed. "Geoffrey was almost like a father to me, never, never anything else. And Tony knew, he knew that I'd never been with anyone before our wedding night. I was so angry then, I stood up and began to shout at him. I don't even know what I said, but he went into a rage. And he—"

Gabe saw her fingers tighten like wires on the soft folds of the afghan. Then he saw how she deliberately, and with great care, relaxed them again. With an effort, he kept his voice calm. "Did he hit you, Laura?"

She didn't answer, couldn't seem to push the next words

out. Then he touched a hand to her cheek and turned her face to his. Her eyes were brimming over.

"It was so much worse than with my uncle, because I couldn't get away. He was so much stronger and faster. With my uncle, he'd simply struck out at anyone who didn't get out of the way in time. With Tony, there was something viciously deliberate in the way he tried to hurt me. Then he—" But she couldn't bring herself to speak of what had happened next.

It was a moment before she went on, and Gabe sat in silence as the rage built and built inside him until he thought he'd explode. He understood temper, he had a hair-trigger one of his own, but he could never understand, never forgive, anyone who inflicted pain on someone smaller, weaker.

"When it was over," she continued, calmer now, "he just went to sleep. I lay there, not knowing what to do. It's funny, but later, when I talked with other women who had had some of the same experiences, I found out that it's fairly common to believe you had it coming somehow.

"The next morning, he wept and he apologized, promised that it would never happen again. That became the pattern for the time we were together."

"You stayed with him?"

The color came and went in her face, and part of that, too, was shame. "We were married, and I thought I could make it work. Then we went back to his parents' home. They hated me right from the start. Their son, the heir to the throne, had gone behind their back and married a commoner. We lived with them, and though there was talk about getting our own house, nothing was ever done about it. You could sit at the same table, hold a conversation with them, and be totally ignored. They were amazing. Tony got worse. He began to see other women, almost flaunting them. They knew what he was doing, and they knew what was happening to me. The cycle got uglier and uglier, until I knew I had to get out. I told him I wanted a divorce.

"That seemed to snap him out of it for a while. He made promises, swore he'd go into therapy, see a marriage counselor, anything I wanted. We even began to look at houses. I have to admit that I'd stopped loving him by this time, and that it was wrong, very wrong, for me to stay with him, to make promises myself. What I didn't realize was that his parents were pulling on the other end. They held the financial strings and were making it difficult for him to move out. Then I discovered I was pregnant."

She laid a hand over her belly, her fingers spread. "Tony was, well, at best ambivalent about the idea of having a child. His parents were thrilled. His mother immediately started redecorating a nursery. She bought antique cribs and cradles, silver spoons, Irish linen. Though it made me nervous, the way she was taking over, I thought that the baby might be the way to help us come together. But they weren't looking at me as the baby's mother, any more than they'd looked at me as Tony's wife. It was *their* grandchild, *their* legacy, *their* immortality. We stopped looking for houses, and Tony began to drink again. I left the night he came home drunk and hit me."

She drew a careful breath and continued to stare at the fire. "It wasn't just me he was hitting now, but the child. That made all the difference. In fact, it made it incredibly easy to walk out. I called Geoffrey, buried my pride and asked for a loan. He wired me two thousand dollars. I got an apartment of my own, found a job and started divorce proceedings. Ten days later, Tony was dead."

The pain came, dull and low. Laura shut her eyes and rode it out. "His mother came to see me, begged me to bury the divorce papers, to come to the funeral as Tony's widow. His reputation, his memory, were all that was important now. I did what she asked, because—because I could still remember those first days in Paris. After the funeral I went back to their house. They'd told me there were things we needed to talk about. That was when they told me what they wanted, what they intended to have. They said they would pay all my medical expenses, that I would have the best possible care. And that after the baby was born they would give me a hundred thousand dollars to step aside. When I refused, when I had the nerve to be angry at what they were suggesting, they explained that if I didn't cooperate they would simply take the baby. Tony's baby. They made it very clear that they had enough money and influence to win a custody suit. They would bring out the 'fact' that I had been Geoffrey's mistress, that I had taken money from him. They'd checked my background and would show that due to my upbringing I would be an unstable influence on a child. That they, as the child's grandparents, could provide a better environment. They gave me twenty-four hours to think it over. And I ran."

He didn't speak for several minutes. What she had told him had left a bitter taste in his mouth. He had asked for her story, had all but demanded it. Now that he had it, he wasn't at all sure he could handle it.

"Laura, no matter what you were told, how you were threatened, I don't believe they could take the child."

"That isn't enough? Don't you see? As long as there's a

chance, I can't risk it. I'd never be able to fight them on their terms. I don't have the money, the connections."

"Who are they?" When she hesitated, he took her hand again. "You've trusted me with this much."

"Their name is Eagleton," she said. "Thomas and Lorraine Eagleton of Boston."

His brows drew together. He knew the name. Who didn't? But because of his family's position, it was more than a name, more than an image. "You were married to Anthony Eagleton?"

"Yes." She turned to him then. "You knew him, didn't you?"

"Not well. Barely. He was more—" More Michael's age, he'd started to say. "He was younger. I met him once or twice when he came to the Coast." And what he had seen hadn't impressed him enough to have him form any opinion. "I read that he had been killed in a car accident, and I suppose a wife was mentioned, but this past year has been a little difficult, and I didn't pay attention. My family has socialized with the Eagletons occasionally, but they aren't well acquainted."

"Then you know they're an old, well-established family with old, well-established money. They consider this child a part of their…holdings. They've had me followed all across the country. Every time I would settle in a place and begin to relax I'd discover that detectives were making inquiries about me. I can't—I won't—let them find me."

He rose, to pace, to light a cigarette, to try to organize his thoughts and, more, his feelings. "I'd like to ask you something."

She sighed tiredly. "All right."

"Once before, when I asked you if you were afraid, you said no, that you were ashamed. I want to know why."

"I didn't fight back, and I didn't try hard enough to fix what was wrong. I just let it happen to me. You have no idea how difficult it is to sit here and admit that I let myself be used, that I let myself be beaten, that I let myself be driven down so low that I accepted it all."

"Do you still feel that way?"

"No." Her chin lifted. "No one's ever going to take control of my life again."

"Good." He sat on the hearth. The smoke from his cigarette disappeared up the draft. "I think you've had a hell of a time, angel, worse than anyone deserves. Whether you brought some of it on yourself, as you choose to think, or if it was just a matter of circumstances, doesn't really matter at this point. It's over."

"It's not as easy as that, Gabe. I don't just have myself to worry about now."

"How far are you willing to go to fight them?"

"I've told you I can't—"

He interrupted her with a wave of his hand. "If you had the means. How far?"

"All the way. As far and as long as it takes. But that isn't the point, because I don't have the means."

He drew on his cigarette, studied it with apparent interest, then tossed it into the fire. "You would, if you were married to me."

Chapter 5

She said nothing, could say nothing. He sat on the hearth, his legs folded up, his eyes very cool, very calm, on her face. Part of the enormity of his talent was his ability to focus on an expression and draw the underlying emotions out of it. Perhaps because he did it so well, he also knew how to mask emotions when they were his own.

She could hear the logs sizzling behind him. The midmorning sunlight sparkled through the frost on the windowpanes and landed at his feet. He seemed totally at ease, as though he'd just suggested that they have soup for lunch. If her life had depended upon it, Laura couldn't have said whether it meant any more to him than that.

Using the table for leverage, she rose.

"I'm tired. I'm going in to lie down."

"All right. We can talk about this later."

She whirled around, and it wasn't anguish or fear he saw on her face now, it was fury, livid and clear. "How could you sit there and say something like that to me after everything I've told you?"

"You might consider that I said it because of everything you've told me."

"Oh, the Good Samaritan again." She detested the bitterness in her voice, but she could do nothing to stop it. "The white knight, riding in full of chivalry and good intentions to save the bumbling, inept female. Do you think I should fall on my knees and be grateful? That I would blindly let myself be taken over again, fall back into the same pitiful, destructive pattern a second time, because a man offers me a way out?"

He thought about controlling his temper, then rose, deciding to let her see it. "I have no desire to control you, and I'll be damned if you're going to stand there and compare me with some weak-minded alcoholic wife-beater."

"What then—the knight on a white charger, selflessly rescuing damsels in distress?"

He laughed at that, but his anger was still on the edge. "No one's ever accused me of that. I'm very selfish, which is another reason for my suggestion. I'm moody—you've been around me long enough to know that. I have a temper and I can get angry. But I don't hit women, and I don't use them."

With an effort, she pulled her emotions back in and forced them to settle. "I didn't mean to imply that you did, or to compare you with someone else. It's the situation that's comparable."

"One has nothing to do with the other. The fact that I have money only works to your advantage."

"I didn't marry Tony for his money."

"No." His tone softened. "No, I'm sure you didn't. But in this case I'm willing to accept that you marry me for mine."

"Why?"

Something flickered in his eyes and was gone before she could read it. "That might have been the wisest question to ask first."

"Maybe you're right." She already regretted the outburst of temper and harsh words, as she invariably did. "I'm asking it now."

With a nod, he roamed the room, stopping before the nearly completed portrait. He stared at it, as he had stared at it countless times before, trying to understand, to define, not only Laura, but himself.

"I feel something for you. I'm not sure what it is, but it's very strong. Stronger than anything I've felt before." He lifted a finger to the face on canvas. He wished he could explain himself completely, to himself, to her, but he'd always expressed himself best through painting. "I'm attracted to you, Laura, and I've discovered recently that I've been alone long enough."

"That might be enough, almost enough, for marriage, but not for me, not to me. Not with what you'd be taking on."

"I have some debts to pay," he murmured, then turned to her again. "Helping you, and the child, might just clear the slate."

Whatever anger she'd felt evaporated. It only took the kindness and the grief in his eyes. "You've already helped us, more than I can ever repay."

"I don't want payment." The impatience, the edge, was back in his voice. "What I want is you. How many ways do you want me to say it?"

"I don't think I want you to say it." The nerves began to eat at her again, and she twisted her fingers together. He meant it. She had no doubt that he meant what he said. The prospect of being wanted by him both thrilled and terrified her. "Don't you see, I've already made one terrible mistake."

He crossed to her, gently drawing her hands apart and into his. "You're not indifferent to me?"

"No, but—"

"You're not afraid of me?"

Some of the tension seeped out of her. "No."

"Then let me help you."

"I'm going to have another man's child."

"No." He took her face in his hands because he wanted her eyes on his. "Marry me, and the child is ours. Privately, publicly, totally."

The tears came back. "They'll come."

"Let them. They won't touch you again, and they won't take the baby."

Safety. Could what had always eluded her really be only a promise away? She opened her mouth, knowing that agreement was on her tongue. Then her heart turned over in her chest and she lifted a hand to his cheek. "How could I do this to you?"

For an answer, he put his lips to hers. The need was there, she couldn't deny it, couldn't pretend it away. She tasted it as his mouth drew from hers. She felt it when his hand skimmed through her hair to brace, both possessive and supportive, at the back of her neck. Instinctively, wanting to give, she lifted her other hand to his face. They rested there, comforting.

She wasn't the only one who had demons, Laura thought. She wasn't the only one who needed love and understanding.

Because he was strong, it was easy to forget that he, too, might have pain. Seeking to soothe, she drew him closer into her arms.

He could have sunk into her, into the softness, the generosity. This was what he wanted to capture on canvas, her warmth, her spirit. And this was what he was forced to admit he would never have the skill to translate. This part of her beauty, this most essential part, could never be painted. But it could be cherished.

"You need me," he murmured as he drew her away. "And I need you."

She nodded, then rested her head on his shoulder, because that seemed to say it all.

Due to fresh flurries, it was three days before Gabe risked a trip into town. Laura watched him as he downed a final cup of coffee before pulling on his coat.

"I'll be as quick as I can."

"I'd rather you took your time and paid attention to the roads."

"The Jeep drives like a tank." He accepted the gloves she held out to him but didn't put them on. "I don't like leaving you alone."

"Gabe, I've been taking care of myself for a long time."

"Things have changed. My lawyers have probably sent the marriage license."

Immediately she began to fuss with the breakfast dishes. "That would be quick work."

"They get paid to work fast, and it's been three days since I contacted them. If I can arrange it, I'd like to bring a justice of the peace back here with me."

A cup slipped out of her hand and plopped into the soapy water. "Today?"

"You haven't changed your mind?"

"No, but—"

"I want my name on the birth certificate." He had a moment of panic, vague and disturbing, at her hesitation. "It would be less complicated if we were married before the baby's born."

"Yes, that makes sense." It seemed so rushed. She plunged her hands into the water and began to wash. Her first wedding had been rushed, too, a whirlwind of flowers and champagne and white silk.

"I realize you might prefer something a little more festive, but under the circumstances—"

"No." She turned and managed a smile. "No, I don't care about that. If you can arrange it for today, here, that's fine."

"All right, then. Laura, I'd feel better if you rested until I got back. You didn't sleep well."

She turned back again. No, she hadn't slept well. The nightmare had come back, and she hadn't rested until Gabe had come in and finally slipped into bed with her. "I won't overdo."

"I don't think it would tax your strength for you to kiss me goodbye."

That made her smile. She turned, her hands still dripping, to lift her lips to his.

"Not even married yet and you're already kissing me as though we've been together twenty years." He changed the mood simply by nipping her lip. In seconds she was clinging to him, and there was nothing casual about the embrace.

"Better," he murmured. "Now go lie down. I'll be back in less than two hours."

"Be careful."

He closed the door. In moments she heard the sound of the Jeep's engine chugging to life. Moving into the living room, she watched Gabe drive away.

Strangely enough, even as the quiet settled over the cabin, she didn't feel alone. She felt nervous, she admitted with a little laugh. Brides were entitled to nerves. If Gabe had his way—and she'd come to believe that he nearly always did—they would be married that afternoon.

And her life, Laura realized, would change yet again.

This time it would be better. She would make it better.

As the ache in her lower back grew worse, she pressed her hand against it. Blaming the discomfort she'd been feeling all morning on the mattress and a restless night, she walked over to the portrait.

He'd finished it the day before. She knew, because he'd explained it to her, that the paint would take a few days to set and dry completely, so she didn't touch it. She sat on the stool Gabe sometimes used and studied her own face.

So this was how he saw her, she thought. Her skin was pale, with only a faint shadow of color along her cheekbones. It was partly that whiteness, that translucence, that made her appear like the angel he sometimes called her. She looked as though she were caught in a daydream, one of the many she'd indulged in during the hours Gabe had painted. As she had told him—as she had complained—there was too much vulnerability. It was in her eyes, around her mouth. There was something strong and independent about the pose, about the way her head was tilted, but that lost, sad look in her eyes seemed to negate the strength.

She was reading too much into it, Laura decided as the pain dug, deep and dull, into her back. Rubbing at it, she rose to look around the cabin.

She would be married here, in a matter of hours. There would be no crowd of well-wishers, no pianist playing romantic songs, no trail of rose petals. Yet, with or without the trimmings, she would be a bride. She might not be able to make it look festive, but at least she could tidy up.

The pain in her back drove her to lie down. Two hours later she heard the Jeep coming down the lane. For a moment longer she lay there, working to block out the discomfort. Later, she told herself, she would soak the ache away in a hot tub. She walked into the living room just as Gabe ushered an elderly couple into the cabin.

"Laura, this is Mr. and Mrs. Witherby. Mr. Witherby is a justice of the peace."

"Hello. It's so nice of you to come all this way."

"Part of the job," Mr. Witherby said, adjusting his fogging glasses. "'Sides that, your young man here wasn't going to take no for an answer."

"Don't you worry about this old man here." Mrs. Witherby patted her husband's arm and studied Laura. "He loves to complain."

"Can I get you something, some coffee?"

"Don't you fuss. Mr. Bradley's got a carload of supplies. You just sit down and let him take care of it." She had already walked over to lead Laura to the couch with her frail hands. "Man's nervous as a goose at Christmas," she confided. "Let him keep busy for a spell."

Though she couldn't imagine Gabe being nervous about anything, she thought the Witherbys would expect such emotion from a man about to marry. Laura listened to Gabe rattling bags and cans in the kitchen. "Maybe I should help him."

"Now, you sit right here." Mrs. Witherby motioned to her husband to sit, as well. "A woman's entitled to be waited on when she's carrying. The good Lord knows you won't have much time to sit once that baby's born."

Grateful, Laura shifted to ease the throbbing in her back. "You have children?"

"Had six of them. Now we've got twenty-two grandchildren and five great-grandchildren."

"And another on the way," Mr. Witherby stated, pulling out a pipe.

"You can just put that smelly thing away," his wife told him. "You aren't smoking up this room with this lady expecting."

"I wasn't going to light it," he said, and began to chew on the stem.

Satisfied that her husband had been put in his place, Mrs. Witherby turned back to Laura. "That's a pretty picture there." She indicated a sprawling landscape that might very well sell for an amount in six figures. "Your man's an artist fellow?"

Her man. Laura experienced a twinge of panic and a glow of pleasure at the phrase. "Yes, Gabe's an artist."

"I like pictures," she said comfortably. "Got me one of the seashore over my sofa."

Gabe walked back in carrying an armful of flowers. Feeling awkward, he cleared his throat. "They sold them at the market."

"And he bought them out, too," Mrs. Witherby cackled. Then, with a few wheezes, she heaved herself off the couch. "You got a vase? She can't be carrying all of them."

"No, at least...I don't know."

"Men." She sighed and then winked at Laura. "Give them to me and let me take care of it. You can do something useful, like putting more wood on that fire. Wouldn't want your lady to catch a chill."

"Yes, ma'am."

If he'd ever felt more of a fool, he couldn't remember when. Wanting to keep his hands busy, he moved to the fire.

"Don't let her browbeat you, boy," Mr. Witherby advised him from the comfort of his chair. "She's already spent fifty-two years nagging me."

"Somebody had to," Mrs. Witherby called out from the kitchen, and he chuckled.

"Sure you two know what you're getting into?"

Gabe dusted his hands on the thighs of his jeans and grinned. "No."

"That's the spirit." Witherby laughed and rested his head against the back of the chair. "Essie, get that bag of bones you call a body moving, will you? These two people want to get married while they're still young."

"Keep your tongue in your mouth," she muttered. "Already lost his teeth." She came in carrying a watering can filled with flowers. She set it in the middle of the coffee table, nodded her approval, then handed Laura a single white carnation.

"Thank you. They're lovely." She started to rise and nearly

winced at the stab of pain in her back. Then Gabe was there to take her hand and draw her to his side.

They stood in front of the fire with wood crackling and the scent of the flowers merging with that of the smoke. The words were simple and very old. Despite the countless weddings she'd been to, Mrs. Witherby dabbed at her eyes.

To love. To honor. To cherish.

For richer. For poorer.

Forsaking all others.

The ring he slipped onto her finger was very plain, just a gold band that was a size too large. Looking at it, Laura felt something grow inside her. It was warm and sweet and tremulous. Curling her hand into his, she repeated the words, and meant them, from her heart.

Let no man put asunder.

"You may kiss the bride," Witherby told him, but Gabe didn't hear.

It was done. It was irrevocable. And until that moment he hadn't been completely aware of how much it would mean to him.

With her hand still caught in his, he kissed her and sealed the promise.

"Congratulations." Mrs. Witherby brushed her dry lips over Gabe's cheek, then Laura's. "Now you sit down, Mrs. Bradley, and I'm going to fix you a nice cup of tea before we drag your husband off again."

"Thank you, but we don't have any tea."

"I bought some," Gabe put in.

"That and everything else he could lay his hands on. Come on, Ethan, give me a hand."

"You ought to be able to fix a cup of tea by yourself."

Mrs. Witherby rolled her eyes. "You'd think the old goat would have a little more romance, seeing as he's married more'n five hundred couples in his time. In the kitchen, Ethan, and give these young people five minutes alone."

He grumbled about wanting his supper, but he followed her.

"They're wonderful," Laura murmured.

"I don't think I'd have gotten him away from his TV if she hadn't shoved him out the door."

Silence followed, awkward. "It was nice of you to think of flowers...and the ring."

He lifted her hand and studied it. "They don't have a jewelry store in Lonesome Ridge. They sell these at the hardware in a little case next to sixpenny nails. It may just turn your finger green."

She laughed and knew she'd treasure it even more now. "You may not believe it, but you may have saved my life by buying that tea."

"I got some marshmallows, too."

She hated it, despised herself for not being able to control it, but she started to cry. "I'm sorry. I can't seem to do anything about this."

Discomfort surged through him. He was feeling edgy himself, and tears did nothing to help matters. "Look, I know it wasn't exactly the wedding of the century. We can have some sort of party or reception back in San Francisco."

"No, no, that's not it." Though she urged her hands over her face, the tears kept coming. "It was lovely and sweet and I don't know how to thank you."

"Not crying would be a good start." He had a bandanna in his pocket, one that he used more often than not as a paint rag. He drew it out and offered it to her. "Laura, we're legally married. That means you don't have to be grateful for every bunch of daisies I hand you."

She sniffled into the cloth and tried to smile. "I think it was the marshmallows that did it."

"Keep this up and you won't get any more."

"I want you to know…" She dried her face and managed to compose herself. "I want you to know that I'm going to do everything I can to make you happy, to make you comfortable, so that you never regret what you did today."

"I'm going to regret it," he said suddenly impatient, "if you keep making it sound as though I gave someone else the last life jacket as the ship was sinking. I married you because I wanted to, not to be noble."

"Yes, but I—"

"Shut up, Laura." To make certain she did, he closed his mouth over hers. And for the first time she felt the true strength of his passion and need and desire. With a little murmur of surprise, she drew him closer.

This was what he had needed, all he had needed, to settle him. Yet even as the first layer of tension dissolved, a new layer, one built on desire, formed.

"Before too much longer," he said against her mouth, "we're going to finish this. I want to make love with you, Laura. And after I do you won't have the strength to thank me."

Before she could think of a response, Mrs. Witherby came in with her tea. "Now let the poor thing rest and drink this while it's hot." She set the cup on the table in front of Laura. "I hate to drag you out on your wedding day, Mr. Bradley, but the sooner you drive us back to town, the sooner you

can get back and fix your wife that nice steak you bought
for supper."

She moved over to gather up her coat. On impulse, Laura
drew one of the flowers from the watering can and took it
to her. "I'm never going to forget you, Mrs. Witherby."

"There now." Touched, she sniffed at the flower. "You
just take care of yourself and that baby of yours. Shake a
leg, Ethan."

"I should only be an hour," Gabe told her. "The roads
aren't too bad. I really think you should rest, Laura. You
look exhausted."

"I'm supposed to look glowing, but I promise I won't lift
anything heavier than a teacup until you get back."

This time she watched the Jeep drive away, running her
finger over and over her wedding ring. It took so little, she
thought, to change so much. She bent, trying to ease the ache
in her back, then she crossed the room to finish her tea.

Her back had never ached like this, not even after she'd
worked a full day on her aunt's farm. The pain was constant
and deep. She tried stretching out, then curling up, then
stretching out again. Impatient with herself, she tried to ignore it, concentrating instead on roasting marshmallows and
warming tea.

She'd been alone less than ten minutes when the first contraction hit.

It wasn't the vague warning pain she'd read about. It was
sharp and long. Caught off guard, she had no time to breathe
her way over it. Instead, she tensed, fought against it, then
collapsed against the cushions when it faded.

It couldn't be labor. Her forehead broke out in sweat as
she tried to dismiss the idea. It was too early, a month too

early, and it had come on so suddenly. False labor, she assured herself. Brought on by nerves and by the excitement of the day.

But the back pain. Struggling to keep calm, she pushed herself into a sitting position. Was it possible she'd been having back labor all morning?

No, it had to be false labor. It had to be.

But when the second contraction hit she began to time them.

She was in bed when Gabe returned, but she couldn't call out to him, because she was riding out the latest contraction. The fear that had gripped her in a stranglehold for the past hour faded a bit. He was here, and somehow that meant that everything would be all right. She heard him toss a log on the fire, took a last cleansing breath as the pain passed and called out.

The urgency in her voice had him across the room in three strides. At the bedroom door he paused, and his heart jumped into his throat.

She was propped against the pillows, half lying, half sitting. Her face was bathed in sweat. Her eyes, always dark, were sheened with moisture and nearly black.

"I have to go back on our deal," she managed, struggling with a smile because she saw the same blank fear she felt reflected on his face. "The baby's decided to come a little early."

He didn't ask if she was sure or fumble with reasons why it wasn't a good idea. He wanted to, but he found himself beside the bed, with her hand gripped in his. "Take it easy. Just hold on and I'll phone for a doctor."

"Gabe, the phone's out." Nerves skipped in and out of her voice. "I tried it when I realized this was happening so fast."

"Okay." Fighting for calm, he brushed the damp hair away from her face. "There was an accident on the way into town. Lines must have gone down. I'll get some extra blankets and I'll take you in."

She pressed her lips together. "Gabe, it's too late. I couldn't make the trip." She tried to swallow, but fear had dried up the moisture in her mouth and throat. "I've been in labor for hours, all morning, and I didn't know it. It was back labor, and I didn't pay attention. With everything that was going on, I thought it was nerves and the restless night I'd had."

"Hours," he murmured, and eased himself down on the edge of the bed. His mind went blank, but then her fingers tightened on his. "How far apart are the pains?"

"Five minutes. I've been—" She let her head fall back and began to breathe in short, deep gasps. Gabe slipped his hand over her and felt the hardening of her abdomen.

He'd glanced through the birth and baby books she'd brought with her. To pass the time, he'd told himself, but there had been something deep inside him that had been compelled to understand what she was going through. Perhaps it was instinct that had had him absorbing the advice, the details, the instructions. Now, seeing her in pain, everything he'd read seemed to slip away from him.

When the contraction passed, her face was shiny with fresh sweat. "Getting closer," she whispered. "There's not much time." Though she bit down on her lips, a sob escaped her. "I can't lose the baby."

"The baby's going to be fine, and so are you." He squeezed her hand once reassuringly. They would need towels, lots of them. String and scissors had to be sterilized. It was really very simple when you thought about it. He only hoped it was as simple when you put it into practice.

"Just hang on. I have to get some things." He saw the doubt flash in her eyes, and he leaned over her. "I'm not going to leave you. I'm going to take care of you, Laura. Trust me."

She nodded, and with her head slumped back on the pillow, she closed her eyes.

When he came back, her eyes were focused on the ceiling and she was panting. After setting fresh towels on the foot of the bed, he spread another blanket over her. "Are you cold?"

She shook her head. "The baby will need to be kept warm. He's not full-term."

"I've built up the fire, and there are plenty of blankets." Gently he wiped her face with a cool, damp cloth. "You've talked to doctors, you've read the books. You know what to expect."

She looked up at him, trying to swallow past a dry throat. Yes, she knew what to expect, but reading about it, imagining it, was a far cry from the experience.

"They lied." Her mouth moved into a weak smile when his brows drew together. "They try to tell you it doesn't hurt so much if you ride out the pain."

He brought her hand to his lips and held it there. "Yell all you want. Scream the roof down. Nobody's going to hear."

"I'm not screaming this baby into the world." Then she gasped, and her fingers dug into his. "I can't—"

"Yes, you can. Pant. Pant, Laura. Squeeze my hand. Harder. Concentrate on that." He kept his eyes locked on hers while she pushed air out. "You're doing fine, better than fine." When her body went lax, he moved to the foot of the bed. "The pains are closer?" As he spoke, he knelt on the mattress and shifted the blanket.

"Almost on top of each other."

"That means it's almost over. Hold on to that."

She tried to moisten her dry lips, but her tongue was thick. "If anything happens to me, promise you'll—"

"Nothing's going to happen." He bit off the words. Their eyes met again, hers glazed with pain, his dark with purpose. "Damn it, I'm not going to lose either of you now, understand? The three of us are going to pull this off. Now, you've got work to do, angel."

Each time the pains hit her, he shuddered with it. Time seemed to drag as she struggled through them, then race again as she rested. Gabe moved back and forth, to arrange her pillows, to wipe her face, then knelt again to check the progress of birth.

He could hear the fire roaring in the next room, but he still worried that the cabin would be too cold. Then he worried about the heat, because Laura's laboring body was like a furnace.

He hadn't known birth could be so hard on a woman. He knew she was close to total exhaustion, but she managed to pull herself through time after time, recharging somehow during the all-too-brief moments between contractions. Pain seemed to tear through her, impossibly hard, impossibly ruthless. His own shirt was soaked with sweat, and he swore constantly, silently, as he urged her to breathe, to pant, to concentrate. All his ambitions, his joys, his griefs, whittled down to focus on that one room, that one moment, that one woman.

It seemed to him that she should weaken, with her body being battered by the new life fighting to be born. But as the moments passed she seemed to draw on new reserves of strength. There was something fierce and valiant about her face as she pushed herself forward and braced for whatever happened next.

"Do you have a name picked out?" he asked, hoping to distract her.

"I made lists. Sometimes at night I'd try to imagine what the baby would look like and try to— Oh, God."

"Hold on. Breathe, angel. Breathe through it."

"I can't. I have to push."

"Not yet, not yet. Soon." From his position at the foot of the bed, he ran his hands over her. "Pant, Laura."

Her concentration kept slipping in and out. If she stared into his eyes, if she pulled the strength from them, she would make it. "I can't hold off much longer."

"You don't have to. I can see the head." There was wonder in his voice when he looked back at her. "I can see it. Push with the next one."

Giddy, straining with the effort, she bore down. She heard the long, deep-throated moan, but she didn't know it was her own voice. Gabe shouted at her, and in response she automatically began to pant again.

"That's good, that's wonderful." He barely recognized his own voice, or his own hands. Both were shaking. "I have the head. Your baby's beautiful. The shoulders come next."

She braced herself, desperate to see. "Oh, God." Tears mixed with sweat as she steepled her hands over her mouth. "It's so little."

"And strong as an ox. You have to push the shoulders

out." Sweat dripped off his forehead as he cupped the baby's head in his hand and leaned over it. "Come on, Laura, let's have a look at the rest of it."

Her fingers dug into the blankets, and her head fell back. And she gave birth. Over her own gasping breaths she heard the first cry.

"A boy." Gabe's eyes were wet as he held the squirming new life in his hands. "You have a son."

As the tears rolled, she began to laugh. The pain and the terror were forgotten. "A boy. A little boy."

"With a loud mouth, ten fingers and ten toes." He reached for her hand and gripped it hard. "He's perfect, angel."

Their fingers linked over the baby, and the cabin echoed with the high, indignant wails of the newborn.

She couldn't rest. Laura knew Gabe wanted her to sleep, but she couldn't shut her eyes. The baby, nearly an hour old now, was wrapped in blankets and tucked in the curve of her arm. He was sleeping, she thought, but she couldn't stop herself from tracing a fingertip over his face.

So tiny. Five pounds, seven ounces, on the vegetable scale that Gabe had unearthed and scrubbed down. Seventeen and a half inches tall, and with only a bit of pale blond peach fuzz covering his head. She couldn't stop looking at him.

"He's not going to disappear, you know."

Laura glanced up at the doorway and smiled. Fatigue had left her skin almost pale enough to see through. Triumph had given her eyes a rich glow. "I know." She held out a hand in invitation. "I'm glad you came in," she said as he sat on the bed. "I know you must be exhausted, but I'd like you to stay a minute."

"You did all the work," he murmured, running a finger down the baby's cheek.

"That's not true, and that's the first thing I want to say. We wouldn't have made it without you."

"Of course you would have. I was basically a cheerleader."

"No." Her hand tightened on his, demanding that he look at her. "You were as responsible for his life as I was. I know what you said about having your name on the birth certificate, about helping us, but I want you to know it's more than that. You brought him into the world. There's nothing I can ever do or say that could be enough. Don't look like that." She gave a quiet laugh and settled back among the pillows. "I know you hate to be thanked, and that's not what I'm doing."

"Isn't it?"

"No." She shifted the baby from her arm to his. It was a gesture that said more, much more, than the words that followed it. "I'm telling you that you got more than a wife today."

The baby went on sleeping peacefully, cupped between them.

He didn't know what to say. He touched the tiny hand and watched it curl reflexively. As an artist he'd thought he understood the full range of beauty. Until today.

"I've been reading about preemies," he began. "His weight is good, and from what the book says a baby born after the thirty-fourth week is in pretty good shape, but I want to get you both into a hospital. Will you be strong enough to travel into Colorado Springs tomorrow?"

"Yes. We'll both be strong enough."

"We'll leave in the morning, then. Do you think you could eat now?"

"Only a horse."

He grinned, but he couldn't quite bring himself to give her back the baby. "You may have to settle for beefsteak. Isn't he hungry?"

"I imagine he'll let us know."

Just as Laura had been, he was compelled to trace the shape of the child's face. "What about that name? We can't keep calling him *he*."

"No, we can't." Laura stroked the soft down on his head. "I was wondering if you'd like to pick his name."

"Me?"

"Yes, you must have a favorite, or a name of someone who's important to you. I'd like you to choose."

"Michael," he murmured, looking down at the sleeping infant.

Chapter 6

San Francisco. It was true that Laura had always wanted to see it, but she had never expected to arrive there with a two-week-old son and a husband. And she had never expected to be shown into a tall, gracious house near the Bay.

Gabe's house. Hers, too, she thought as she rubbed her thumb nervously over her wedding ring. It was foolish to be jumpy because the house was beautiful and big. It was ridiculous to feel small and insecure because you could taste the wealth and the prominence just by breathing the air.

But she did.

She stepped into the tiled foyer and wished desperately for the comfort of the tiny cabin. It had begun to snow again the day they'd left Colorado, and though the mild spring breeze and the tiny buds here were wonderful, she found herself wishing for the cold and ferocity of the mountains.

"It's lovely," she managed, glancing up at the gentle curve of the stairs.

"It was my grandmother's." Gabe set down the luggage and took in the familiar surroundings. It was a house he'd always appreciated for its beauty and its balance. "She held on to it after her marriage. Shall I show you around, or would you rather rest?"

She nearly winced. It was as though he were talking to a guest. "If I rested as much as you'd like, I'd sleep my way through the rest of the year."

"Then why don't I show you the upstairs." He knew he sounded polite, overly polite, but he'd been edgy ever since they'd stepped off the plane. The farther away from Colorado they'd gotten, the further Laura had withdrawn from him. It was nothing he could put his finger on, but it was there.

Hefting two cases, he started up the stairs. He was bringing his wife, and his son, home. And he didn't know quite what to say to either of them. "I've used this bedroom." He strode in and set the cases at the foot of a big oak bed. "If there's another you'd prefer, we can arrange it."

She nodded, thinking that though they'd shared a motel room while the baby had been in the hospital they had only shared a bed in the cabin, the night before Michael had been born. It would be different here. Everything would be different here.

"It's a beautiful room."

Her voice was a little stiff, but she smiled, trying to soften it. The room was lovely, with its high ceilings and the glossy antiques. There was a terrace, and through the glass doors she could see a garden below, with green leaves already formed. The floors were dark with age and gleaming, just as the Oriental rug was faded with age and rich with heritage.

"The bath's through there," Gabe told her as she ran a

finger down the carving in an old chifforobe. "My studio's at the end of the hall. The light's best there, but there's a room next to this that might do as a nursery."

When they spoke of the baby, things always relaxed between them. "I'd love to see it. After all those days in the incubator, Michael deserves a room of his own."

She followed Gabe out and into the next room. It was decorated in blues and grays with a stately four-poster and a many-cushioned window seat. As with the other rooms she'd seen, paintings hung on the wall, some of them Gabe's, others by artists he respected.

"It's beautiful, but what would you do with all these things?"

"They can be stored." He dismissed the furnishings with a shrug. "Michael can stay in our room until his is finished."

"You don't mind? He's bound to wake during the night for weeks yet."

"I could stick the pair of you in a hotel until it's convenient."

She started to speak, but then she recognized the look in his eyes. "Sorry. I can't get used to it."

"Get used to it." He moved over to cup her face in his hand. Whenever he did that, she was almost ready to believe that dreams came true. "I may not have the equipment to feed him, but I figure I can learn to change a diaper." He stroked a thumb under her jawline. "I've been told I'm clever with my hands."

The heat rushed into her face. She was torn between stepping into his arms and backing away. The baby woke and decided for her. "Speaking of feeding…"

"Why don't you use the bedroom, where you can be comfortable? I have some calls to make."

She knew what was coming. "Your family?"

"They're going to want to meet you. Are you up to it this evening?"

She wanted to snap that she wasn't an invalid, but she knew he wasn't speaking of her physical health. "Yes, of course."

"Fine. I'll make arrangements about the nursery. Did you have any colors in mind?"

"Well, I..." She expected to paint the room herself. She'd wanted to. Things were different now, she reminded herself. The cabin had easily become theirs, but the house was his. "I'd like yellow," she told him. "With white trim."

She sat in a chair by the window while Michael suckled hungrily. It was so good to have him with her all the time instead of having to go to the hospital to feed him, touch him, watch him. It had been so hard to leave him there and go back to a hotel room and wait until she could go back and see him again.

Smiling, she looked down at him. His eyes were closed, and his hand was pressed against her breast.

He was already gaining weight. Healthy, the doctor in Colorado Springs had said. Sound as a dollar. And the tag on his little wristband had read Michael Monroe Bradley.

Who was Michael? she wondered. Gabe's Michael. She hadn't asked, but knew that the name, the person, was important.

"You're Michael now," she murmured as the baby began to doze at her breast.

Later she laid him on the bed, surrounding him with

pillows though she knew he couldn't roll yet. Going to her suitcase, she took out her hairbrush. It was silly, of course, to feel compelled to leave some mark of herself on the room. But she set the brush on Gabe's bureau before she left.

She found him downstairs, in a dark-paneled library with soft gray carpet. Because he was on the phone, she started to back out, but he waved her in and continued to talk.

"The paintings should be here by the end of the week. Yes, I'm back in harness again. I haven't decided. You take a look first. No, I'm going to be tied up here for a few days, thanks anyway. I'll let you know." He hung up, then glanced at Laura. "Michael?"

"He's asleep. I know there hasn't been time, but he's going to need his own bed. I thought I could run out and buy something if you could watch him for a little while."

"Don't worry about it. My parents are coming over soon."

"Oh."

He sat on the edge of the desk and frowned at her. "They're not monsters, Laura."

"Of course not, it's just that... It seems we're so out in the open," she blurted out. "The more people who know about Michael, the more dangerous it is."

"You can't keep him in a glass bubble. I thought you trusted me."

"I did. I do," she amended quickly, but not quickly enough.

"Did," Gabe repeated. It wasn't anger he felt so much as pressing regret. "You made a decision, Laura. On the day he was born, you gave him to me. Are you taking him back?"

"No. But things are different here. The cabin was—"

"An excellent place to hide. For both of us. Now it's time to deal with what happens next."

"What does happen?"

He picked up a paperweight, an amber ball with darker gold streaks in the center. He set it down again, then crossed to her. She'd shed weight quickly. Her stomach was close to flat, her breasts were high and full, her hips were impossibly narrow. He wondered how it would feel to hold her now, now that the waiting was over.

"We might start with this."

He kissed her, gently at first, until he felt her first nerves fade into warmth. That was what he'd been desperate for, that promise, that comfort. When he gathered her close, she fitted against him as he'd once imagined she would. Her hair, bound up, was easily set free with a sweep of his hand. She made a small sound—a murmur of surprise or acceptance— and then her arms went around him.

And the kiss was no longer gentle.

Passion, barely restrained, and hunger, far from sated, rippled from him into her. An ache, long buried, grew in her until she was straining against him, whispering his name.

Then his lips were roaming over her face, raking over her throat, searing her skin, then cooling it, then searing it again, while his hands stroked and explored with a new freedom.

Too soon. Some sane part of him knew it was too soon for anything more than a touch, a taste. But the more he indulged in her, the more his impatience grew. Taking her by the shoulders, he drew her away and fought to catch his breath.

"You may not trust me as you once did, angel, but trust this. I want you."

Giving in to the need, she held on to him, pressing her face into his shoulder. "Gabe, is it so wrong of me to wish it was just the three of us?"

"Not wrong." He stared over the top of her head as he stroked her hair. "Just not possible, and less than fair to Michael."

"You're right." Drawing a breath, she stepped back. "I want to go check on him."

Shaken by the emotions he pulled out of her, she started back up the stairs. Halfway up, she stopped, stunned.

She was in love with him. It wasn't the love she'd come to accept, the kind that came from gratitude and dependence. It wasn't even the strong, beautiful bond that had been forged when they'd brought Michael into the world. It was more basic than that, the most elemental love of woman for man. And it was terrifying.

She had loved once before, briefly, painfully. That love had kept her chained down. All her life she'd been a victim, and her marriage had both accented that and ultimately freed her. She'd learned through necessity how to be strong, how to take the right steps.

She couldn't be that woman again, she thought as her fingers gripped the banister. She wouldn't. That was what had bothered her most about the house, about the things in it. She had stepped into a house like this before, a house in which she had been out of place and continually helpless.

Not again, she told herself, and shut her eyes. Never again.

Whatever she felt for Gabe, she wouldn't allow it to change her back into that kind of woman. She had a child to protect.

The doorbell rang. Laura sent one swift look over her shoulder, then fled up the stairs.

When Gabe opened the door, he was immediately enveloped in soft fur and strong perfume. It was his mother, a woman of unwavering beauty and unwavering opinions. She didn't believe in brushing cheeks, she believed in squeezing, hard and long.

"I've missed you. I didn't know what it would take to drag you off that mountain, but I didn't think it would be a wife and a baby."

"Hello, Mother." He smiled at her, giving her a quick sweeping look that took in her stubbornly blond hair and her smooth cheeks. She had Michael's eyes. They were a darker green than his own, with touches of gray. Seeing them brought a pang and a pleasure. "You look wonderful."

"So do you, except for the fact that you've lost about ten pounds and can't afford to. Well, where are they?" With that, Amanda Bradley marched inside.

"Give the boy a chance, Mandy." Gabe exchanged bear hugs with his father, a tall, spare man with a hangdog expression and a razor-sharp mind. "Glad you're back. Now she'll take to rattling your cage instead of mine."

"I can handle you both." She was already slipping off her gloves with short, quick little motions. "We brought a bottle of champagne over. I thought since we missed the wedding, the birth and everything else, we should at least toast the homecoming. For heaven's sake, Gabe, don't just stand there, I'm dying to see them."

"Laura went up to check the baby. Why don't we go in and sit down?"

"This way, Mandy," Cliff Bradley said, taking his wife's arm when she started to object.

"Very well, then. You can hold me off for five minutes by telling me how your work's been going."

"Well." He watched his parents sit but couldn't relax enough to follow suit. "I've already called Marion. The paintings I finished in Colorado should be delivered to her gallery by the end of the week."

"That's wonderful. I can't wait to see them."

His hands were in his pockets as he moved around the room with a restlessness both of his parents recognized. "There's one piece in particular I'm fond of. I plan to hang it in here, over the fire."

Amanda lifted a brow and glanced at the empty space above the mantel. Gabe had always claimed that nothing suited that spot. "It must be very special."

"You'll have to judge for yourself." He drew out a cigarette, then set it down when Laura moved into the doorway.

She said nothing for a moment, just studied the couple on the couch. His parents. His mother was lovely, her smooth skin almost unlined, her hair swept back to accent her aristocratic features and fine bones. There were emeralds at her ears and at her throat. She wore a rose silk suit with a fox stole carelessly thrown over her shoulders.

His father was tall and lean, like Gabe. Laura saw a diamond wink at his pinky. He looked sad and quiet, but she saw his eyes sharpen as he studied her.

"This is my wife, Laura, and our son."

Braced for whatever was to come, holding the baby protectively against her breasts, she stepped into the room. Amanda rose first, only because she always seemed to move quicker than anyone else.

"It's so nice to meet you at last." Amanda had reservations, a chestful of them, but she offered a polite smile. "Gabe didn't mention how lovely you were."

"Thank you." She felt a little trip-hammer of fear in her throat. Laura knew formidable when she saw it. Instinctively she lifted her chin. "I'm glad you could come. Both of you."

Amanda noted the little gesture of pride and defiance and approved. "We wanted to meet you at the airport, but Gabe put us off."

"Rightly so," Cliff added in his soothing, take-your-time voice. "If I'd been able to, I'd have held Mandy off another day."

"Nonsense. I want to see my grandchild. May I?"

Laura's arms had tightened automatically. Then she looked at Gabe and relaxed her hold. "Of course." With care and caution, she shifted the slight weight into Amanda's arms.

"Oh, how beautiful." The cool, sophisticated voice wavered. "How precious." The scents, the baby scents of talc and mild soap and fragile skin, made her sigh. "Gabe said he was premature. No problems?"

"No, he's fine."

As if to prove it, Michael opened his eyes and stared out owlishly.

"There, he looked right at me." With emeralds glowing on her skin, Amanda grinned foolishly and cooed. "Looked right at your gran, didn't you?"

"He looked at me." Cliff leaned closer to chuck the baby under the chin.

"Nonsense. Why should he want to look at you? Do

something useful, Cliff, like opening the champagne." She clucked and cooed at the baby while Laura stood twisting her hands. "I hope you don't object to the wine. I didn't ask if you were nursing."

"Yes, I am, but I don't think a sip would hurt either of us."

Approving a second time, Amanda started for the couch. Laura took an instinctive step forward, then made herself stop. This wasn't Lorraine Eagleton, and she wasn't the same woman who had once cowered. But as hard as she tried to dispel the image, she saw herself standing just outside the family circle.

"I'd get glasses," she said lamely, "but I don't know where they are."

Saying nothing, Gabe went to a cabinet and drew out four champagne flutes.

Cliff took Laura's arm. "Why don't you sit down, dear? You must be tired after traveling."

"You sound like Gabe." Laura found herself smiling as she eased into a chair.

Glasses were passed. Amanda lifted hers. "We'll drink to— For goodness' sake, I don't know the child's name."

"It's Michael," Laura offered. She saw the grief flash into Amanda's eyes before she closed them. When she opened them again, they were wet and brilliant.

"To Michael," she murmured, and after a sip she leaned down to kiss the baby's cheek. Looking up, she smiled at Gabe. "Your father and I have something in the car for the baby. Would you get it?"

Though they didn't touch, and the glance lasted only a

moment, Laura saw something pass between them. "I'll just be a minute."

"We won't eat her, for heaven's sake," Amanda muttered as her son left the room.

With a laugh, Cliff rubbed her shoulder. There was something familiar about the gesture. It was Gabe's, Laura realized. The same casual intimacy.

"Have you been to San Francisco before?" he asked Laura, snapping her back to the present.

"No, I— No. I'd like to offer you something, but I don't know what we have." Or even where the kitchen is, she thought miserably.

"Don't worry about it." Cliff draped his arm comfortably over the back of the chair. "We don't deserve anything after barging in on your first day home."

"Families don't barge," Amanda put in.

"Ours does." Grinning, he leaned over and chucked the baby under the chin again. "Smiled at me."

"Grimaced, you mean." With a laugh of her own, Amanda kissed her husband's cheek. "Granddad."

"I take it the cradle's for Michael and the roses are for me." Gabe strode in, carrying a dark pine cradle heaped with frilly sheets and topped with a spray of pink roses.

"Oh, the flowers. I completely forgot. And no, they're certainly not for you, but for Laura." Amanda handed the baby to her husband and rose. Though she moved to rise, Laura saw Cliff tuck the baby easily in the crook of his arm. "We'll need some water for these," Amanda decided. "No, no, I'll get it myself."

No one argued with her as she marched out of the room, carrying the flowers.

"It's very lovely," Laura began, bending from the chair to run a finger along the smooth wood of the cradle. "We were just talking about the baby needing a bed of his own."

"The Bradley bed," Cliff stated. "Fix those sheets, Gabe, and let's see how he takes to it."

"This cradle's a family tradition." Obediently Gabe lifted out the extra sheets and smoothed on white linen. "My great-grandfather built it, and all the Bradley children have had their turn rocking in it." He took the baby from his father. "Let's see how you fit, old man."

Laura watched Gabe set the baby down and give the cradle a gentle push. Something seemed to break inside her. "Gabe, I can't."

Crouched at her feet beside the cradle, he looked up. There was a dare in his eyes, a challenge, and, she was certain, a buried anger. "Can't what?"

"It isn't right, it isn't fair." She drew the baby from the cradle into her arms. "They have to know." She might have fled right then and there, but Amanda came back into the room holding a crystal vase filled with roses. Sensing tension, and intrigued by it, she continued in.

"Where would you like these, Laura?"

"I don't know, I can't— Gabe, please."

"I think they'll look nice by the window," she said mildly, then moved over to arrange them to her satisfaction. "Now, then, don't you three gentlemen think you could find something to occupy yourselves while Laura and I have a little talk?"

Panic leaping within, Laura looked from one to the other, then back at her husband. "Gabe, you have to tell them."

He took the baby and settled him on his shoulder. His

eyes, very clear and still sparking with anger, met hers. "I already have." Then he left her alone with his mother.

Amanda settled herself on the sofa again. She crossed her legs and smoothed her skirts. "A pity there isn't a fire. It's still cool for this time of year."

"We haven't had a chance—"

"Oh, dear, don't mind me." She waved a hand vaguely at a chair. "Wouldn't you rather sit?" When Laura did so without a word, she lifted a brow. "Are you always so amenable? I should certainly hope not, as I liked you better when you stuck your chin out at me."

Laura folded her hands in her lap. "I don't know what to say. I hadn't realized Gabe had explained things to you. The way you were acting…" She let her words trail off. Then, when Amanda continued to wait patiently, she tried again. "I thought you believed that Michael was, well, biologically Gabe's."

"Should that make such a big difference?"

She was calm again, at least outwardly, and able to meet Amanda's eyes levelly. "I would have expected it to, especially with a family like yours."

Amanda drew her brows together as she thought that through. "Shall I tell you that I'm acquainted with Lorraine Eagleton?" She saw the instant, overwhelming fear and backed up. She wasn't often a tactful woman, but she wasn't cruel. "We'll save talk of her for another time. Right now, I think I should explain myself instead. I'm a pushy woman, Laura, but I don't mind being pushed back."

"I'm not very good at that."

"Then you'll have to learn, won't you? We may be friends, or we may not, I can't tell so soon, but I love my son. When he left all those months ago, I wasn't sure I'd ever have him back. You, for whatever reason, brought him back, and for that I'm grateful."

"He would have come when he was ready."

"But he might not have come back whole. Let's leave that." Again, the vague gesture. "And get to the point. Your son. Gabe considers the child his. Do you?"

"Yes."

"No hesitation there, I see." Amanda smiled at her, and Laura was reminded of Gabe. "If Gabe considers Michael his son, and you consider Michael his son, why should Cliff and I feel differently?"

"Bloodlines."

"Let's leave the Eagletons out of this for the time being," Amanda said. Laura merely stared, surprised that the mark had been hit so directly. "If Gabe had been unable to have children and had adopted one, I would love it and think of it as my grandchild. So, don't you think you should get past this nonsense and accept it?"

"You make it sound very simple."

"It sounds to me as though your life's been complicated enough." Amanda picked up the glass of champagne she'd discarded before. "Do you have any objections to our being Michael's grandparents?"

"I don't know."

"An honest woman." Amanda sipped.

"Do you have any objections to me being Gabe's wife?"

With the slightest of smiles, Amanda raised her glass to Laura. "I don't know. So I suppose we'll both have to wait and see. In the meantime, I'd hate to think that I'd be discouraged from seeing Gabe or Michael because we haven't made up our minds about each other."

"No, of course not. I wouldn't do that. Mrs. Bradley, no one's ever been as kind or as generous with me as Gabe. I swear to you I won't do anything to hurt him."

"Do you love him?"

Uneasy, Laura cast a look toward the doorway. "We haven't...Gabe and I haven't talked about that. I needed help, and I think he needed to give it."

Pursing her lips, Amanda studied her glass. "I don't believe that's what I asked you."

The chin came up again. "That's something I should discuss with Gabe before anyone else."

"You're tougher than you look. Thank God for that." Finishing off the sparkling beverage, she set down the empty glass. "I might just like you at that, Laura. Or, of course, we might end up detesting each other. But whatever is between the two of us doesn't change the fact that Gabe has committed himself to you and the child. You're family." She sat back, lifting both brows, but inside she felt a faint twist of sympathy. "From the look on your face, that doesn't thrill the life out of you."

"I'm sorry. I'm not used to being in a family."

"You've had a very rough time, haven't you?" There was compassion there, but not so much that it made Laura uncomfortable. Mentally Amanda made a note to do a little digging on the Eagletons.

"I'm trying to put that behind me."

"I hope you succeed. Some things in the past need to be remembered. Others are best forgotten."

"Mrs. Bradley, may I ask you something?"

"Yes. On the condition that after this question call me Amanda or Mandy or anything—except, please God, Mother Bradley."

"All right. Who was Michael named for?"

Amanda's gaze drifted to the empty cradle and lingered there. There was a softening, a saddening, in her face that compelled Laura to touch her hand. "My son, Gabe's younger brother. He died just over a year ago." With a long sigh, she rose. "It's time we left you to settle in."

"Thank you for coming." She hesitated because she was never quite sure what people expected. Then listening to her heart, she kissed Amanda's cheek. "Thank you for the cradle. It means a great deal to me."

"And to me." She brushed her hand over it before she left the room. "Clifton, aren't you the one who said we shouldn't stay more than a half hour?"

His voice carried, muffled, from upstairs. Clucking her tongue, Amanda pulled on her gloves. "Always poking around in Gabe's studio. The poor dear doesn't know a Monet from a Picasso, but he loves to look over Gabe's work."

"He did some beautiful things in Colorado. You must be so proud of him."

"More every day." She heard her husband coming and glanced upstairs. "Do let me know if you want any help setting up the nursery or finding a good pediatrician. I also expect you'll understand if I buy out the baby boutiques."

"I don't—"

"Not understand, then, but you'll have to tolerate. Kiss your new daughter-in-law goodbye, Cliff."

"You don't have to tell me that." Rather than the formal,

meaningless kiss she was expecting, Laura received a hearty hug that left her dazed and smiling. "Welcome to the Bradleys, Laura."

"Thank you." She had an urge to hug him back, to just throw her arms around his neck and breath in that nice, spicy aftershave she'd caught on his throat. Feeling foolish, she folded her hands instead. "I hope you'll come back, maybe next week for dinner, when I've had a chance to find things."

"Cooks, too?" He pinched Laura's cheek. "Nice work, Gabe."

When they were gone, she stood in the foyer, rubbing a finger over her cheek. "They're very nice."

"Yes, I've always thought so."

The sting was still in his voice, so she steadied herself and looked at him. "I owe you an apology."

"Forget it." He started to stride back into the library, then stopped and turned around. He'd be damned if he'd forget it. "Did you think I would lie to them about Michael? That I would have to?"

She accepted his anger without flinching. "Yes."

He opened his mouth, rage boiling on his tongue. Her answer had him shutting it again. "Well, you shoot straight from the hip."

"I did think so, and I'm glad I was wrong. Your mother was very kind to me, and your father…"

"What about my father?"

He hugged me, she wanted to say, but she didn't believe he could possibly understand how much that had affected her. "He's so much like you. I'll try not to disappoint them, or you."

"You'd do better not to disappoint yourself." Gabe dragged a hand through his hair. It fell in a tumble of dark blond disorder, the way she liked it best. "Damn it, Laura, you're not on trial here. You're my wife, this is your home, and for better or worse the Bradleys are your family."

She set her teeth. "You'll have to give me time to get used to it," she said evenly. "The only families I've ever known barely tolerated me. I'm through with that." She swung away to start up the stairs, then called over her shoulder, "And I'm painting Michael's nursery myself."

Not certain whether to laugh or swear, Gabe stood at the foot of the stairs and stared after her.

Chapter 7

Laura brushed the glossy white enamel paint over the baseboard. In her other hand she held a stiff piece of cardboard as a guard against smearing any of the white over the yellow walls she'd already finished.

On the floor in the far corner was a portable radio that was tuned to a station that played bouncy rock. She'd kept the volume low so that she could hear Michael when he woke. It was the same radio Gabe had kept on the kitchen counter in the cabin.

She wasn't sure which pleased her more, the way the nursery was progressing or the ease with which she could bend and crouch. She'd even been able to use part of her hospital fund to buy a couple of pairs of slacks in her old size. They might still be a tad snug in the waist, but she was optimistic.

She wished the rest of her life would fall into order as easily.

He was still angry with her. With a shrug, Laura dipped

her brush into the paint can again. Gabe had a temper, he had moods. He had certainly never attempted to deny or hide that. And the truth was, she'd been wrong not to trust him to do the right thing. So she'd apologized. She couldn't let his continuing coolness bother her. But, of course, it did.

They were strangers here, in a way that they had never been strangers in the little cabin in Colorado. It wasn't the house, though a part of her still blamed the size and the glamour of it. Before, the simple mechanics of space had required them to share, to grow close, to depend on each other. Being depended on had become important to Laura, even if it had only been to provide a cup of coffee at the right time. Now, beyond her responsibilities to Michael, there was little for her to do. She and Gabe could spend hours under the same roof and hardly know each other existed.

But it wasn't walls and floors and windows that made the difference. It was quite simply the difference—the difference between them. She was still Laura Malone, from the wrong side of the tracks, the same person who had been moved and shuffled from house to house, without ever being given the chance to really live there. The same person who had been handed from family to family without ever being given the chance to really belong.

And he was... Her laugh was a bit wistful. He was Gabriel Bradley, a man who had known his place from the moment he'd been born. A man who would never wonder if he'd have the same place tomorrow.

That was what she wanted for Michael, only that. The money, the name, the big, sprawling house with the stained-glass windows and the graceful terraces, didn't matter. Belonging did. Because she wanted it, was determined to have it for her son, she was willing to wait to belong herself. To Gabe.

The only time they were able to pull together was when Michael was involved. Her lips curved then. He loved the baby. There could be no doubt about that. It wasn't pity or obligation that had him crouching beside the cradle or walking the floor at three in the morning. He was a man capable of great love, and he had given it unhesitatingly to Michael. Gabe was attentive, interested, gentle and involved. When it came to Michael.

It was only with her, when they had to deal with each other one on one, that things became strained.

They didn't touch. Though they lived in the same house, slept in the same bed, they didn't touch, except in the most casual and impersonal of ways. As a family they had gone out to choose all the things Michael would need—the crib and other nursery furniture, blankets, a windup swing that played a lullaby, soft stuffed animals that Michael would undoubtedly ignore for months. It had been easy, even delightful, to discuss high chairs and playpens and decide together what would suit. Laura had never expected to be able to give her son so much or to be able to share in that giving.

But when they'd come home the strain had returned.

She was being a fool, Laura told herself. She'd been given a home, protection and care, and, most of all, a kind and loving father for her son. Wishing for more was what had always led her to disappointment before.

But she wished he would smile at her again—at her, not at Michael's mother, not at the subject of his painting.

Perhaps it was best that they remained as they were, polite friends with a common interest. She wasn't entirely sure how she would manage when the time came for him to turn to her as a woman. The time would come, his desire was there, and he was too physical a man to share the bed with her without fully sharing it much longer.

Her experience with lovemaking had taught her that man demanded and woman submitted. He wouldn't have to love her, or even hold her in affection, to need her. God, no one knew better how little affection, how little caring, there could be in a marriage bed. A man like Gabe would have many demands, and loving him as she did she would give. And the cycle she'd finally managed to break would begin again.

Gabe watched her from the doorway. Something was wrong, very wrong. He could see the turmoil on her face, could see it in the set of her shoulders. It seemed that the longer they were here the less she relaxed. She pretended well, but it was only pretense.

It infuriated him, and the harder he held on to his temper the more infuriated he became. He hadn't so much as raised his voice to her since their first day in the house, and yet she seemed continually braced for an outburst.

He'd given her as much room as was humanly possible, and it was killing him. Sleeping with her, having her turn to him during the night, her skin separated from his only by the fragile cotton of a nightgown, had given new meaning to insomnia.

He'd taken to working during the middle of the night and spending his free time in the studio or at the gallery, anywhere he wouldn't be tempted to take what was his only legally.

How could he take when she was still so delicate,

physically, emotionally? However selfish he'd always been, or considered himself, he couldn't justify gratifying himself at her expense—or frightening her by letting her see just how desperately, how violently, he wanted her.

Yet there was passion in her, the dark, explosive kind. He'd seen that, and other things, in her eyes. She needed him, as much as he needed her. He wasn't sure either of them understood where their need might take them.

He could be patient. He was aware that her body needed time to heal, and he could give her that. But he wasn't sure he could give her the time it might take for her mind to heal.

He wanted to cross to her, to sit down beside her and stroke his hand over her hair. He wanted to reassure her. But he had no idea what words to use. Instead, he tucked his hands into his pockets.

"Still at it?"

Laura started, splattering paint on her hand. She sat back on her heels. "I didn't hear you come in."

"Don't get up," he told her. "You make quite a picture." He stepped into the room, glancing at the sunny walls before looking down at her. She wore an old pair of jeans, obviously his. He could see the clothesline she'd used to secure the waist. One of his shirts was tented over her, its hem torn at her hip.

"Mine?"

"I thought it would be all right." She picked up a rag to wipe the paint from her hand. "I could tell from the splatters on them they'd already been worked in."

"Perhaps you don't know the difference between painting and—" he gestured toward the wall "—painting."

She'd nearly fumbled out an apology before she realized he was joking. So the mood had passed. Perhaps they were friends again. "Not at all. I thought your pants would give me artistic inspiration."

"You could have come to the source."

She set the brush on top of the open paint can. Relief poured through her. Though he didn't know, Gabe had found exactly the right words to reassure her. "I would never have suggested that the celebrated Gabriel Bradley turn his genius to a lowly baseboard."

It seemed so easy when she was like this, relaxed, with a hint of amusement in her eyes. "Obviously afraid I'd show you up."

She smiled, a bit hesitantly. He hadn't looked at her in quite that way for days. Then she was scrambling back up on her knees as he joined her on the floor. "Oh, Gabe, don't. You'll get paint all over you, and you look so nice."

He had the brush in his hand. "Do I?"

"Yes." She tried to take it away from him, but he didn't give way. "You always look so dashing when you go to the gallery."

"Oh, God." The instant disgust on his face made her laugh.

"Well, you do." She checked the urge to brush at the hair on his forehead. "It's quite different from the rugged-outdoorsman look you had in Colorado, though that was nice, too."

He wasn't certain whether to smile or sneer. "Rugged outdoorsman?"

"That's right. The cords and the flannel, the untidy hair

and the carelessly unshaven face. I think Geoffrey would have loved to photograph you with an ax...." She was staring at him, seeing him as he'd been and as he was. Abruptly she became aware that her hand was still covering his on the handle of the brush. Drawing it away, she struggled to remember her point. "You're not dressed for work now, and I was in the fashion business long enough to recognize quality. Those pants are linen, and you'll ruin them."

He was well aware of the sudden tension in her fingers and the look that had come into her eyes, but he only lifted a brow. "Are you saying I'm sloppy?"

"Only when you paint."

"Pot calling the kettle," he murmured, ignoring the way she jumped when he ran a finger down her cheek. He held it up to prove his point.

Laura wrinkled her nose at the smear of white paint on his fingertip—and tried to ignore the heat on her skin where his finger had brushed. "I'm not an artist." With a rag in one hand, she took his wrist in the other to clean the paint from his fingertip.

Such beautiful hands, she thought. She could imagine how it would feel to have them move over her, slowly, gently. To have them stroke and caress the way a man's might if he cared deeply about the woman beneath the skin he was touching. Her imagination had her moistening her lips as she lifted her gaze to his.

They knelt knee to knee on the drop cloth, with his hand caught in hers. It amazed her when she felt his pulse begin to thud. In his eyes she saw what he hadn't allowed her to see for days. Desire, pure and simple. Unnerved by it, drawn to it, she leaned toward him. The rag slipped out of her hand.

And the baby cried out.

They both jerked, like children caught raiding the cookie jar.

"He'll be hungry, and wet, too, I imagine," she said as she started to rise. Gabe shifted his hand until it captured hers.

"I'd like you to come back here after you've tended to him."

Longing and anxiety tangled, confusing her. "All right. Don't worry about the mess. I'll finish up later."

She was more than an hour with Michael, and she was a bit disappointed that Gabe didn't come in, as he often did, to hold the baby or play with him before he slept again. Those were the best times, those simple family times. Tucking the blankets around her son, she reminded herself that she couldn't expect Gabe to devote every free minute to her and the child.

Satisfied that the baby was dry and content, she left him to go into the adjoining bath and freshen up. After she'd washed the paint from her face, she studied herself in the mirrored wall across from the step-down tub. She didn't look seductive in baggy, masculine clothes, with her hair tugged back in a ponytail. Regardless of that, for an instant in the nursery, Gabe had been seduced.

Was that what she wanted?

How could she know what she wanted? She pressed her fingers to her eyes and tried to sort out her feelings. Confusion, and little else. One moment she imagined what it would be like, being with Gabe, making love with him. The next moment she was remembering the way it had been before, when love had had little to do with it.

It was wrong to continually let memories intrude. She told herself she was too sensible for that. Or wanted to be. She'd been in therapy, she'd talked to counselors and other women who had been in situations all too similar to her own. Because she'd had to stay on the move, she hadn't been able to remain with any one group for long, but they had helped her. Just learning that she wasn't alone in what had happened to her, seeing and talking with others who had turned their lives around again, had given her the strength to go on.

She knew—intellectually she knew—that what had happened to her was the result of a man's illness and her own insecurity. But it was one thing to know it and another to accept it and go on, to risk another relationship.

She wanted to be normal, was determined to be. That had been the communal cry from all the sessions in all the towns. Along with the fear and the anger and the self-disgust, there had been a desperate mutual need to be normal women again.

But that step, that enormous, frightening step from past to future, was so difficult to take. Only she could do it, Laura told herself as she continued to stare into her own eyes. With Gabe, and her feelings for him, she had a chance. If she was willing to take it.

How could she know how close they could be, how much they could mean to each other, if she didn't allow herself to want the intimacy?

Catching her lower lip between her teeth, she turned to study the lush bath. It was nearly as large as many of the rooms she'd lived in during her life. White on white on white, it gleamed and glistened and invited indulgence. She could sink into hot, deep water in the tub and soak until her skin was soft and pink. She still had most of a bottle of perfume, French and suggestive, that Geoffrey had bought her in Paris. She could dab it on her damp skin so that the scent seeped into her pores. Then she could...what?

She had nothing lovely or feminine to wear. The only clothes she hadn't taken to thrift shops or secondhand stores during her cross-country flight were maternity clothes. The two pairs of slacks and the cotton blouses didn't count.

In any case, what would it matter if she had a closetful of lace negligees? She wouldn't know what to do or say. It had been so long since she'd thought of herself strictly as a woman. Perhaps she never had. And surely it was better to try to reestablish that early friendship with Gabe before they attempted intimacy.

If that was what he wanted. What she wanted.

Turning away from the mirror, she went to find him.

She couldn't have been more surprised when she walked into the nursery and found the painting finished, the cans sealed and the brushes cleaned. As she stared, Gabe folded the drop cloth.

"You finished it," she managed.

"I seem to have struggled through without doing any damage."

"It's beautiful. The way I'd always imagined." She stepped into the empty room and began arranging furniture in her head. "There should be curtains, white ones, though I suppose dotted swiss is too feminine for a boy."

"I couldn't say, but it sounds like it. It's warm enough, so I've left the windows open." He tossed the drop cloth over a stepladder. "I don't want to put Michael in here until the smell of the paint's gone."

"No," she agreed absently, wondering if the crib should go between the two windows.

"Now that this is out of the way, I have something for you. A belated Mother's Day present."

"Oh, but you gave me the flowers already."

He took a small box out of his pocket. "There wasn't the time or the opportunity for much else then. We were living out of a suitcase and spending all of our time at the hospital. Besides, the flowers were from Michael. This is from me."

That made it different. Intimate. Again she found herself drawn to him, and again she found herself pulled away. "You don't have to give me anything."

The familiar impatience shimmered. He barely suppressed it. "You're going to have to learn how to take a gift more graciously."

He was right. And it was wrong of her to continue to compare, but Tony had been so casual, so lavish, in his gifts. And they had meant so little. "Thank you." She took the box, opened it and stared.

The ring looked like a circle of fire, with its channel-linked diamonds flashing against its gold band and nestled in velvet. Instinctively she ran a fingertip over it and was foolishly amazed that it was cool to the touch.

"It's beautiful. Absolutely beautiful. But—"

"There had to be one."

"It's just that it's a wedding ring, and I already have one."

He took her left hand to examine it. "I'm surprised your finger hasn't fallen off from wearing this thing."

"There's nothing wrong with it," she said, and nearly snatched her hand away.

"So sentimental, angel?" Though his voice had gentled,

his hand was firm on hers. Now, perhaps, he would be able to dig a bit deeper into what she was feeling for him, about him. "Are you so attached to a little circle of metal?"

"It was good enough for us before. I don't need anything else."

"It was a temporary measure. I'm not asking you to toss it out the window, but be a little practical. If you weren't always curling your finger up, it would fall right off."

"I could have it sized."

"Suit yourself." He slipped it from her finger, then replaced it with the diamond circle. "Just consider that you have two wedding rings." When he offered her the plain band, Laura curled it into her fist. "The new one holds the same intentions."

"It is beautiful." Still, she pushed the old ring onto the index finger of her right hand, where it fit more snugly. "Thank you, Gabe."

"We did better than that before."

She didn't have to be reminded. Yet the memories flooded back when he slipped his arms around her. Emotions poured through with those memories the moment his mouth was on hers. His lips were firm and warm and hinted, just hinted, at his impatience as they slanted across hers. Though his arms remained gentle around her, his touch light and testing, she sensed a volcano in him, simmering and smoking.

As if to soothe, she leaned into him and lifted a hand to his cheek. Understanding. Acceptance.

Her touch triggered the need crawling inside him, and his arms tightened and his mouth crushed down on hers. She responded with a moan that he barely heard, with a shudder that he barely felt. Tense, hungry, he fell victim to her as much as to his own demands.

He had wanted before, casually and desperately and all the degrees in between. Why, then, did this seem like a completely new experience? He had held women before, known their softness, tasted their sweetness. But he had never known a softness, never experienced a sweetness, like Laura's.

He took his mouth on a slow, seeking journey over her face, along her jawline, down her throat, drinking in, then devouring. His hands, long and limber, slipped under her full shirt, then roamed upward. At first the slender line of her back was enough, the smooth skin and the quick tremors all he required. Then the need to touch, to possess, grew sharper. As his mouth came back to hers, he slid his hand around to cup, then claim, her breast.

The first touch made her catch her breath, pulling air in quickly, then letting it out again in a long, unsteady sigh. How could she have known, even blinded by love and longings, how desperately she'd need to have his hands on her? This was what she wanted, to be his in every way, in all ways. The confusion, the doubts, the fears, drained away. No memories intruded when he held her like this. No whispers of the past taunted her. There was only him, and the promise of a new life and an enduring love.

Her knees were trembling so she braced her body against his, arching in an invitation so instinctive that only he recognized it.

The room smelled of paint and was bright with the sun that streamed through the uncurtained windows. It was empty and quiet. He could fantasize about pulling her to the floor, tugging at her clothes until they were skin-to-skin on the polished hardwood. He could imagine taking her in the sun-washed room until they were both exhausted and replete.

With another woman he might have done so without giving a thought to where or when, and little more to how. But not with Laura.

Churning, he drew her away from him. Her eyes were clouded. Her mouth was soft and full. With a restraint he hadn't known he possessed, Gabe swore only in his mind.

"I have work to do."

She was floating, drifting on a mist so fine it could only be felt, not seen. At his words, she began the quick, confused journey back to earth. "What?"

"I have work to do," he repeated, stepping carefully away from her. He detested himself for taking things so far when he knew she was physically unable to cope with his demands. "I'll be in the studio if you need me."

If she needed him? Laura thought dimly as his footsteps echoed down the hall. Hadn't she just shown him how much she needed him? It wasn't possible that he hadn't felt it, that he hadn't understood it. With an oath, she turned and walked to the window. There she huddled on the small, hard seat and stared down at the garden, which was just beginning to bloom.

What was there about her, she wondered, that made men look at her as a thing to be taken or rejected at will? Did she appear so weak, so malleable? She curled her hands into fists as frustration spread through her. She wasn't weak, not any longer, and a long time, in some ways a lifetime, had passed since she had been malleable. She wasn't a young girl caught up in fairy-tale lies now. She was a woman, a mother, with responsibilities and ambitions.

Perhaps she loved, and perhaps this time would be as unwise a love as before. But she wouldn't be used, she wouldn't be ignored, and she wouldn't be molded.

Talk was cheap, Laura thought as she propped her chin on her knees. Doing something about it was a little costlier. She should go in to Gabe now and make herself clear. She cast a look at the door, then turned back to the window. She didn't have the courage.

That had always been her problem. She could say what she would or would not do, but when it came down to acting on it she found passivity easier than action. There had been a time in her life when she'd believed that the passive way was best for her. That had been until her marriage to Tony had fallen viciously apart. She'd done something then, Laura reminded herself, or had begun to do something, then had allowed herself to be pressured and persuaded to erase it.

It had been like that all her life. As a child she hadn't had a choice. She'd been told to live here or live there, and she had. Each house had had its own sets of rules and values, and she'd had to conform. Like one of those rubber dolls, she thought now, that you could bend and twist into any position you liked.

Too much of the child had remained with the woman, until the woman had been with child.

The only positive action she felt she'd ever taken in her life had been to protect the baby. And she had done it, Laura reminded herself. It had been terrifying and hard, but she hadn't backed down. Didn't that mean that buried beneath years of quiet compliance was the strength she'd always wanted to have? She had to believe that and, if she did, to act on it.

Loving Gabe didn't mean, couldn't mean, that she would sit quietly by while he made decisions for her. It was time to take a stand.

Rising, she walked out of the empty nursery and started down the hall. With each step her resolve wavered and had to be shored up again. At the door to his studio, she hesitated again, rubbing the heel of her hand on her chest, where the ache of uncertainty lodged. Taking one last breath, she opened the door and walked in.

He was by the long bank of windows, a brush in his hand, working on one of the paintings that had been stacked half-finished against the wall of the cabin. She remembered it. It was a snow scene, very stark and lonely and somehow appealing. The whites and cold blues and silvers gave a sense of challenge.

Laura was glad of it. A sense of challenge was precisely what she needed.

He hadn't heard her come in, so intent was he on his work. There were no sweeping strokes or bold slashes now, only a delicacy. He was adding details so minute, so exact, that she could almost hear the winter wind.

"Gabe?" It was amazing how much courage it could take to say a name.

He stopped immediately, and when he turned the annoyance on his face was very apparent. Interruptions were never tolerated here. Living alone, he hadn't had to tolerate them.

"What is it?" He clipped the words off, and he didn't set down his brush or move from the painting. It was obvious that he intended to continue exactly where he'd left off the moment he'd nudged her out of his way.

"I need to talk to you."

"Can't it wait?"

She nearly said yes, but then she brought herself up short. "No." She left the door open in case the baby should cry out, and walked to the center of the room. Her stomach twisted, knotted. Her chin came up. "Or, if it can, I don't want it to."

He lifted a brow. He'd heard that tone in her voice only a handful of times in the weeks they'd been together. "All right, but make it fast, will you? I want to finish this."

Her temper flared too quickly to surprise her. "Fine, then, I'll sum it up in one sentence. If I'm going to be your wife, I want you to treat me like one."

"I beg your pardon?"

She was too angry to see that he was stunned, and too angry to recognize her own shock at her words. "No, you don't. You've never begged anyone's pardon in your life. You don't have to. You do exactly what suits you. If that means being kind, you can be the kindest man I've ever known. If it means being arrogant, you take that just as far."

With deliberate care, he set his brush down. "If there's a point to this, Laura, I'm missing it."

"Do you want me or don't you?"

He only stared at her. If she continued to stand in the pool of light, her eyes dark and defiant, her cheeks flushed with color, he might beg. "That's the point?" he said steadily.

"You tell me you want me, then you ignore me. You kiss me, then you walk away." She dragged a hand through her hair. When her fingers tangled with the ribbon that held it back, she tugged it out in annoyance. Pale and fragile, her hair fell around her shoulders. "I realize the main reason we're married is because of Michael, but I want to know where I stand. Am I to be a guest here who's alternately indulged and ignored, or am I to be your wife?"

"You are my wife." With his own temper rising, he pushed himself off his stool. "And it's not a matter of me ignoring you. I've simply got a lot of work to catch up on."

"You don't work twenty-four hours a day. At night—" Her courage began to fail. She thrust out the rest of the words. "Why won't you make love with me?"

It was fortunate that he'd set his brush down, or else he might have snapped it in half. "Do you expect performance on demand, Laura?"

Embarrassed color flooded her cheeks. That had once been expected of her, and it shamed her more than she could say to think she'd demanded it. "No. I didn't mean it to sound that way. I only thought it was best that you know how I felt." She took a step back, then turned to go. "I'll let you get back to work."

"Laura." He preferred, much preferred, her anger to the humiliation he'd seen. And caused. "Wait." He started after her when she whirled around.

"Don't apologize."

"All right." There was still fire in her, he saw, and he wasn't entirely sure he should be relieved. "I'll just give you a more honest explanation."

"It isn't necessary." She started toward the door again, but he grabbed her arm and yanked her around. He saw it and cursed at it—the instant fear that leaped into her eyes.

"Damn it, don't look at me like that. Don't ever look at me like that." Without his realizing it, his fingers had tightened on her arm. When she winced, he released her, dropping his hands to his side. "I can't make myself over for you, Laura. I'll yell when I need to yell and fight when I need to fight, but I told you once before, and I'll say it again. I don't hit women."

The fear had risen, a bitter bile in her throat. It was detestable. She waited for it to pass before she spoke. "I don't expect you to, but I can't make myself over for you, either. Even if I could, I don't know what you want. I know I should be grateful to you."

"The hell with that."

"I should be grateful," she continued, calm again. "And I am, but I've found out something about myself this past year. I'll never be anyone's doormat ever again. Not even yours."

"Do you think that's what I want?"

"I can't know what you want, Gabe, until you know yourself." She'd gone this far, Laura told herself, and she would finish. "Right from the beginning you expected me to trust you. But after everything we've been through you still haven't been able to make yourself trust me. If we're ever going to be able to make this marriage work you're going to have to stop looking at me as a good deed and start seeing me as a person."

"You have no idea how I see you."

"No, I probably don't." She managed a smile. "Maybe when I do it'll be easier for both of us." She heard the baby crying and glanced down the hall. "He doesn't seem to be able to settle today."

"I'll get him in a minute. He can't be hungry again. Wait." If she could be honest, he told himself, then so could he. He put a hand on her arm to hold her there. "It's easy enough to clear up one misunderstanding. I haven't made love with you, not because I haven't wanted to, but because it's too soon."

"Too soon?"

"For you."

She started to shake her head. Then his meaning became clear. "Gabe, Michael's over four weeks old."

"I know how old he is. I was there." He held up a hand before she could speak. "Damn it, Laura, I saw what you went through. How hard it was on you. However I feel, it simply isn't possible for me to act on it until I know you're fully recovered."

"I had a baby, not a terminal illness." She let out a huff of breath, but she found it wasn't annoyance or even amusement she felt. It was pleasure, the rare and wonderful pleasure of being cared for. "I feel fine. I am fine. In fact, I've probably never been better in my life."

"Regardless of how you feel, you've just had a baby. From what I've read—"

"You've read about this, too?"

That infuriated him—that wide-eyed wonder and the trace of humor in her eyes. "I don't intend to touch you," he said stiffly, "until I'm sure you're fully recovered."

"What do you want, a doctor's certificate?"

"More or less." He started to touch her cheek, then thought better of it. "I'll see to Michael."

He left her standing in the hall, unsure whether she was angry or amused or delighted. All that she was sure of was that she was feeling, and her feelings were all for Gabe.

Chapter 8

"I can't believe how fast he's growing." Feeling very grand-motherly but sporting a sleek new hairstyle, Amanda sat in the bentwood rocker in Michael's new nursery and cuddled the baby.

"He's making up for being premature." Still not quite certain how she felt about her mother-in-law, Laura continued to fold tiny clothes that were fresh from the laundry. "We had our checkup today, and the doctor said Michael was healthy as a horse." She pressed a sleeper to her cheek. It was soft, almost as soft as her son's skin. "I wanted to thank you for recommending Dr. Sloane. She's wonderful."

"Good. But I don't need a pediatrician to tell me this child's healthy. Look at this grip." Amanda chuckled as Michael curled his fingers around hers, but she stopped short of allowing him to suck on her sapphire ring. "He has your eyes, you know."

"Does he?" Delighted, Laura moved to stand over them.

The baby smelled of talc—Amanda of Paris. "It's too early to tell, I know, but I'd hoped he did."

"No doubt about it." Amanda continued to rock as she studied her daughter-in-law. "And what about *your* checkup? How are you?"

"I'm fine." Laura thought about the slip of paper she'd tucked into the top drawer of her dresser.

"Looking a bit tired to me." There wasn't any sympathy in the voice; it was brusque and matter-of-fact. "Haven't you done anything about getting some help?"

Laura's spine straightened automatically. "I don't need any help."

"That's absurd, of course. With a house this size, a demanding husband and a new baby, you can use all the help you can get, but suit yourself." Michael began to coo, pleasing Amanda. "Talk to Gran, sweetheart. Tell Gran just how it is." The baby responded with more gurgles. "Listen to that. Before long you'll have plenty to say for yourself. Just make sure 'My gran's beautiful' is one of the first. There's a sweet boy." She dropped a kiss on his brow before looking up at Laura. "I'd say a change is in order here, and I'm more than happy to leave that to you." With what she considered a grandmother's privilege, Amanda handed the wet baby to Laura. She continued to sit as Laura took Michael to the changing table.

There was a great deal she'd have liked to say. Amanda was accustomed to voicing her opinions loud and clear—and, if necessary, beating anyone within reach over the head with it. It chafed a bit to hold back, but she'd learned enough in the past few weeks about the Eagletons and about Laura's life with them. Treading carefully, she tried a new tactic.

"Gabe's spending a lot of time at the gallery."

"Yes. I think he's nearly decided to go ahead with a new showing." Almost drowning in love, Laura leaned over to nuzzle Michael's neck.

"Have you been there?"

"The gallery? No, I haven't."

Amanda tapped a rounded, coral-tipped nail on the arm of the rocker. "I'd think you'd be interested in Gabe's work."

"Of course I am." She held Michael over her head, and he began to bubble and smile. "I just haven't thought it wise to take Michael in and interrupt."

It was on the tip of Amanda's tongue to remind Laura that Michael had grandparents who would delight in having him to themselves for a few hours. Again she bit the words back. "I'm sure Gabe wouldn't mind. He's devoted to the boy."

"Yes, he is." Laura retied the ribbons on Michael's pale blue booties. "But I also know he needs some time to organize his work, his career." She handed her son a small cloth bunny, and he stuck it happily in his mouth. "Do you know why Gabe is hesitating about a showing?"

"Have you asked him?"

"No, I—I didn't want to pressure him about it."

"A little pressure might be just what he needs."

Frowning, Laura turned. "Why?"

"It has to do with Michael, my son Michael. I'd prefer it if you asked Gabe the rest."

"They were close?"

"Yes." She smiled. She'd learned it hurt less to remember than to try to forget. "They were very close, though they were very different. He was devastated when Michael was killed. I believe the time in the mountains helped Gabe get back his art. And I believe you and the baby helped him get back his heart."

"If that's true, I'm glad. He's helped me more than I can ever repay."

Amanda gave Laura an even look. "Payments aren't necessary between a husband and wife."

"Perhaps not."

"Are you happy?"

Stalling, Laura laid the baby in the crib and wound the musical mobile so that he could shake his fists and kick at it. "Of course I am. Why wouldn't I be?"

"That was my next question."

"I'm very happy." She went back to folding and storing baby clothes. "It was nice of you to visit, Amanda. I know how busy your schedule is."

"Don't think you can politely show me out the door before I'm ready to go."

Laura turned and saw the faint, amused smile on Amanda's lips. Bad manners were enough out of character for her to make her flush. "I'm sorry."

"Don't be. I don't expect for you to be comfortable with me yet. I'm not entirely sure I'm comfortable with you, either."

A bit more relaxed, Laura smiled back. "I'm sure you're always comfortable. I envy that about you. And I am sorry."

Amanda brushed aside the apology and rose to roam the room. She liked what her daughter-in-law had done here. It was a bright, cheerful place, not overly fussy, and just traditional enough to make her remember the nursery she had set up herself so many years before. There were the scents of powder and fresh linen.

A loving place, she thought. She knew she wouldn't have wanted any more for her son. It was very obvious to her that Laura had untapped stores of love.

"This is a charming room. I think so every time I step into it." Amanda patted the head of the four-foot lavender teddy bear. "But you can't hide here forever."

"I don't know what you mean." But she did.

"You said you'd never been to San Francisco, and now you're here. Have you gone to a museum, to the theater? Have you strolled down to Fisherman's Wharf, ridden a streetcar, explored Chinatown, any of the things a newcomer would surely do?"

Defensive now, Laura spoke coolly. "No, I haven't. But it's only been a few weeks."

It was time, Amanda decided, to stop circling and get to the point. "Let's deal woman-to-woman a moment, Laura. Forget the fact that I'm Gabe's mother. We're alone. Whatever is said here doesn't have to go any further."

Laura's palms were starting to sweat. She brushed them dry on the thighs of her slacks. "I don't know what you want me to say."

"Whatever needs to be said." When Laura remained silent, Amanda nodded. "All right, I'll begin. You've had some miserable spots in your life, some of them tragic. Gabe gave us the bare essentials, but I learned a good deal more by knowing who and what to ask." Amanda sat down again and crossed her legs. She didn't miss the flash in Laura's eyes. "Wait until I've finished. Then you can be as offended as you like."

"I'm not offended," Laura said stiffly. "But I don't see the purpose in discussing what used to be."

"Until you look what used to be square in the face, you won't be able to go on with what might be." She tried to keep her voice brisk, but even her solid composure wavered. "I know that Tony Eagleton abused you, and that his parents overlooked what was monstrous, even criminal, behavior. My heart breaks for you."

"Please." Her voice was strangled as she shook her head. "Don't."

"No sympathy allowed, Laura, even woman-to-woman?"

Again she shook her head, afraid to accept it and, more, to need it. "I can't bear to think back on it. And I can't stand pity."

"Sympathy and pity are entirely different things."

"All that's behind me. I'm a different person than I was then."

"I have no way of agreeing, as I didn't know you before. But I can say that anyone who stood on her own all these months must have great reserves of strength and determination. Isn't it time you used them, and fought back?"

"I have fought back."

"You've taken sanctuary, a much-needed one. I won't argue that running as you did took courage and stamina. But there comes a time to take a stand."

Hadn't she said that to herself time and time again? Hadn't she hated herself for only saying it? She looked at her son, who gurgled and reached for the colorful birds circling over his head.

"And what? Go to court, to the press, drag the whole ugly mess out for everyone to gawk at?"

"If necessary." Her voice took on a tone of pride that carried to all corners of the room. "The Bradleys aren't afraid of scandal."

"I'm not a—"

"But you are," Amanda told her. "You're a Bradley, and so is that child. It's Michael I'm thinking of in the long run, but I'm also thinking of you. What difference does it make what anyone thinks, what anyone knows? You have nothing to be ashamed of."

"I let it happen," Laura said, with a kind of dull fury. "I'll always be ashamed of that."

"My dear child." Unable to prevent herself, Amanda rose to put her arms around Laura. After the first shock, Laura felt herself being drawn in. Perhaps it was because the comfort came from a woman, but it broke down her defences as nothing else ever had.

Amanda let her weep, even wept with her. The fact that she did, that she could, was more soothing than any words could have been. Cheek-to-cheek, woman-to-woman, they held each other until the storm passed. The bond that Laura had never expected to know was forged in tears. With her arm still around Laura, Amanda led her to the gaily striped daybed.

"That's been coming on for a while, I'd say," Amanda murmured. She drew a lace-edged handkerchief out of her breast pocket and unashamedly wiped her eyes.

"I don't know." Laura used the back of her wrist to smear away already-drying tears. "I suppose. Crying isn't something I should need, not anymore. It's only when I look back and remember."

"Now listen to me," Amanda said. All the softness had been erased from her voice. "You were young and alone, and you have nothing, nothing, to be ashamed of. One day you'll realize that for yourself, but for now it might be enough to know you're not alone anymore."

"Sometimes I'm so angry, just so angry that I was used as a convenience, or a punching bag, or a status symbol." It was amazing to her that fury could bring calm and wipe out pain. "When I am I know that no matter what it costs I'll never go back to that."

"Then stay angry."

"But...the anger for me, that's personal." She looked across the room at the crib. "It's when I think of Michael and I know they're going to try to take him...then I'm afraid."

"They don't just have to go through you now, do they?"

Laura looked back. Amanda's face was set. Her eyes glittered. So this was where Gabe got his warrior look, Laura thought, and felt a new kind of love stir. It was the most natural thing in the world for Laura to reach out and take her hand. "No, they don't."

They both heard the door open and close on the first floor. Immediately Laura began to brush her hands over her face. "That must be Gabe, home from the gallery. I don't want him to see me like this."

"I'll go down and keep him occupied." On impulse, she glanced at her watch. "Do you have plans for this afternoon?"

"No. Just to—"

"Good. Come down when you're tidied up."

Ten minutes later, Laura came down to find Gabe cornered in the living room, scowling into a glass of club soda.

"Then it's all settled." Amanda fluffed a hand through her hair, well satisfied. "Laura. Good. Are you ready?"

"Ready?"

"Yes. I've explained to Gabe that we're going shopping. He's absolutely delighted with the reception I've planned for the two of you next week." The reception she'd only begun to plan on her way downstairs.

"Resigned," he corrected, but he had to smile at his mother. The smile faded when he glanced over at Laura. "What's wrong?"

"Nothing." It had been foolish to think that a quick wash and fresh makeup could hide anything from him. "Your mother and I were getting sentimental over Michael."

"What your wife needs is an afternoon out." Amanda rose, then leaned over to kiss Gabe. "I'd scold you for keeping her locked up this way, but I love you too much."

"I never—"

"Never once nudged her out of the house," his mother finished for him. "So it's up to me. Get your purse, dear. We have to find you something wonderful for the reception. Gabe, I imagine Laura needs your credit cards."

"My— Oh." Feeling like a tree blowing in a strong wind, he reached for his wallet.

"These should do." Amanda plucked two of them and handed them to Laura. "Ready?"

"Well, I... Yes," she said on impulse. "Michael's just been fed and changed. You shouldn't have any trouble."

"I can handle things," he told her, feeling more than a little put out. In the first place, he'd have taken her shopping himself if she'd asked. And in the second, though he didn't want to admit it, he wasn't totally sure of himself alone with the baby.

Reading her son perfectly, Amanda kissed him again. "Behave and we may bring you back a present."

He couldn't suppress the grin. "Out," he ordered. Then he caught Laura in turn and kissed her with the same light affection. It surprised him when she returned the embrace so ardently.

"Don't let her talk you into anything with bows," he murmured. "They wouldn't suit you. You should try to find something to match your eyes."

"If you don't let the girl go, we won't buy anything at all," Amanda said dryly, but she was pleased and a bit misty-eyed to see that her son was indeed in love with his wife.

It wasn't anyone's fault that Michael chose that particular afternoon to demand all the time and attention an infant could possibly demand. Gabe walked, rocked, changed, coddled and all but stood on his head. For his part, Michael gurgled, stared owlishly—and wept piteously whenever he was set down. He did everything but sleep.

In the end, Gabe gave up any idea of working for the rest of the day and carted Michael around with him. With the baby nestled in the crook of his arm, he ate a chicken leg and scanned the newspaper. Since no one was around to chuckle at him behind their hands, he discussed world politics and the major-league box scores with Michael while the baby shook a rattle and blew bubbles.

They took a walk in the garden once Gabe located one of the small knit hats Laura had bought to protect Michael from spring breezes. It gave him enormous pleasure to watch the baby's cheeks turn pink and his eyes look around, alert and interested.

He had Laura's eyes, Gabe thought as he studied them. The same shape, the same color, but without the shadows

that made hers both sad and fascinating. Michael's eyes were
clear and innocent of sorrow.

Michael whimpered at first, then decided to accept his
fate, when Gabe slipped him into the little baby swing. After
tucking his blankets in around him, Gabe sat cross-legged
in front of him and began to stretch.

The daffodils were up in a glory of white and yellow trumpets. Baby irises poked through, purple and exotic. Lilacs,
though still shy of their full bloom, offered their scent. For
the first time since his own tragedy, Gabe felt at peace. In
the mountains, all through the winter, he'd begun to heal.
But here, at home, with spring all around, he could finally
see and accept that life did go on.

The baby continued to rock, pink-cheeked and bright-
eyed, his hands lifting and falling to the rhythm. His little
face was already filling out, taking on his own personal look
and shape. Gone was the terrifying fragility of the newborn.
He was, Gabe supposed, already growing up.

"I love you, Michael."

And when he spoke he spoke both to the one who was
gone and to the one who rocked contentedly in front of him.

She hadn't meant to be gone so long, but the chaotic few
hours breezing through the shops had brought back the way
she had felt during that brief period when she'd been on her
own and eager to test life.

There had been a moment or two of guilt over using
Gabe's credit cards so freely. Then it had been almost too
easy, with Amanda lending support, to justify the purchases.
She was Laura Bradley now.

She had an eye for color and line that came naturally and

had been sharpened by her time as a model, so what she had chosen was neither extravagant nor fussy. It had given Laura a great deal of satisfaction to see Amanda nod with approval over her selections.

It was a step, Laura told herself as she carried her bags and boxes through the front door. It might be a step only a woman would understand, but it was definitely a step. She was taking her life in hand again, if only by acknowledging that she needed clothes—clothes that suited her own taste and style—to live it. She was humming when she walked upstairs.

It was there that she found them together, Gabe sprawled over the bed, with Michael snuggled in the curve of his arm. Her husband was sound asleep. Her son had kicked free of his light blanket and was shaking a rattle at the ceiling.

Quietly she set down her bags and crossed to them. It was a purely male scene, the man stretched across the bed, shoes still on, a spy thriller lying facedown on the coverlet, a glass of something that had once been cold leaving a ring on the antique nightstand.

The child, as if he understood that he was a part of this man's world, lay quietly and thought his own thoughts.

She wished she had even a portion of Gabe's skill. If she had, she would have drawn them together like this. Then the scene, the sweetness of it, would never be lost. For a while she sat on the edge of the bed and watched them.

It was so intimate, she thought, watching a man while he slept. She wanted to brush at the dark blond hair on his forehead, to trace the roughly hewn lines of his face, but she was afraid it would disturb him. Then the vulnerability would be gone, and this look at the private side of him would be over.

He was a beautiful man, though he didn't like to hear it. The compassion in him, which he often coated over with sarcasm or temper, ran deep. When she looked at him now, freely, without his being aware, she could see every reason why she'd fallen in love with him.

When Michael began to fret, she murmured and leaned over him, trying to pick him up without waking Gabe. At the first movement, Gabe's eyes opened. They were drowsy and very close to hers.

"I'm sorry. I didn't want to wake you."

He said nothing. Going with a dream she couldn't see but was very much a part of, he cupped a hand at the back of her head and drew her lips to his. There was a tenderness there that she hadn't felt for a very long time, an offering, a promise.

It was a promise she wanted, if only he would give it. It was a promise she would believe in.

Michael, scenting his mother, decided it was time to eat.

Unsettled and wishing they'd had just a moment more, Laura eased back. When Michael began to root at her breast, she undid two buttons and let him have his way.

"Did he wear you out?"

"We were taking a short break." It never failed to fascinate him how perfectly beautiful she looked when she was nursing the baby. He'd already sketched her like this, but that was for himself. "I didn't realize how much energy you need to handle someone so small."

"It gets worse. When we were shopping I saw a woman with a toddler. She never stopped running. Your mother tells me she used to collapse every afternoon when you'd finally worn down enough to take a nap."

"Lies." He shoved a couple of pillows behind his back and settled comfortably. "I was a perfectly behaved child."

"Then it was some other child who drew with crayon all over the silk wallpaper."

"Artistic expression. I was a prodigy."

"No doubt."

He just lifted a brow. Then he spotted her bags across the room. "I was going to ask if you had a good time with my mother, but the answer's obvious."

She caught herself on the verge of an apology. That had to stop, she reminded herself. "It was wonderful to buy shoes and actually see them when I stood up, and a dress that had a waist in it."

"I suppose that's difficult for a woman, losing her figure during pregnancy."

"I loved every minute of it. The first time I couldn't hook a pair of slacks I was ecstatic." She started to go on, then stopped. That was something he would never be a part of, she realized. The first joys and fears, the first movements. Looking down at Michael, she wished with all her heart that he was Gabe's child in every way. "Still, I'm happy now not to look like an aircraft carrier."

"It was more like a dirigible."

"You give the most charming compliments."

He waited until she shifted Michael to her other breast. There was an urge inside of him to trace his finger there, just above where the baby suckled. It wasn't sexual, or even romantic, it was more a wondering. Instead, he tucked his hands behind his head.

"I tossed some leftovers together. I've no idea if they're edible."

Again there was the urge to apologize. Determined, Laura merely smiled. "I'm hungry enough for marginally edible."

"Good." Now he did lean forward, but only to trace a fingertip over Michael's head. "Come on down when he's settled. After this afternoon, I have a feeling he'll go out like a light when his belly's full."

"I won't be long." She waited until she was alone, then closed her eyes, hoping she had the courage to carry out her plans for the rest of the evening.

She hadn't been just a woman in so long. Laura stood in front of the mirrored wall, fogged now from the steam of her bath. She looked like a woman. Her nightgown was the palest blue, nearly white. She'd chosen it because it had reminded her of the way the snow had looked on the mountains in Colorado. It fell down her body from thin straps and a lacy bodice. She ran her hand down it experimentally. The material was very thin and very soft.

Should she wear her hair up, or wear it down? Did it matter?

What would it be like to be Gabe's wife...really his wife? She pressed a hand to her stomach, waiting for the nerves to ebb. Memories threatened to surface, and she fought them back. Tonight she would take Amanda's advice. She would think not of what had been, but of what could be.

She loved him so much, but she didn't know how to tell him. Words were so difficult, so irrevocable. Worse, she was afraid that he would take her love with the same discomfort and disregard as he did her gratitude. But tonight…she hoped tonight she could begin to show him.

He was stripping off his shirt when she opened the door to the adjoining bedroom. For a moment the light coming from behind her fell over her hair and ran through the thin fabric of her gown. All movement stopped as though it were a play, just as the curtain rose. He felt the heat and the tightening in his stomach.

Then she switched off the bathroom light. He pulled off his shirt.

"I checked on Michael." Gabe was surprised he could speak at all, but the words sounded normal enough. "He's sleeping. I thought I might work for an hour or two."

"Oh." She caught herself before she could twist her hands together. She was a grown woman. A grown woman should know how to seduce her husband. "I know you lost time this afternoon when I went out."

"I liked taking care of him." She was so slim, so beautifully frail, with her milky white skin and that blue-white gown. The angel again, with a fall of blond curls instead of a halo.

"You're a wonderful father, Gabe." She took a step toward him. She was already beginning to tremble.

"Michael makes it easy."

Should she have known it would be so difficult to simply cross a room? "Do I make it hard, to be a husband?"

"No." He lifted the back of his hand to her cheek. Her eyes were shades upon shades darker than the flow of silk she wore. He drew back, surprised by his own nerves. "You must be tired."

She bit off a sigh as she turned away. "It's obvious I'm not very good at this. Since seducing you isn't working, we'll try the more practical approach."

"Is that what you were doing?" He wanted to be amused, but his muscles were tight with tension. "Seducing me?"

"Badly." Opening her drawer, she drew out a small slip of paper. "This is my doctor's report. It says that I'm a normal, healthy woman. Would you care to read it?"

This time his lips twitched. "Covered all the bases, did you?"

"You said you wanted me." The paper crumpled in her hand. "I thought you meant it."

He had her arms before she could retreat. Her eyes were dry, but he could see, just by looking, her fractured pride. The burden he already felt grew heavier. What they had was still so tenuous. If he made a mistake it might vanish completely.

"I meant it, Laura, started meaning it from the first day you were with me. It hasn't been easy, being with you, needing you, and not being able to touch."

Gingerly she laid a hand on his chest and felt his muscles tighten. "There's no reason you can't now."

He slid his hands up to her shoulders so that his fingers brushed over the thin straps of her gown. If it was a mistake, he had no choice but to make it. "No physical one any longer. When I take you to bed, there can only be the two of us. No ghosts. No memories." When she dropped her gaze, he drew her closer, challenging her to lift it again. "You won't think of anyone but me."

Whether it was a threat or a promise, he lowered his mouth to hers. Her hands fluttered, then were trapped between their bodies.

It was only the press of lips upon lips, but her blood began to pound. The stirring he could cause so easily started in her stomach and spread, long before his hands moved over her, long before her lips parted.

Her hands were imprisoned, but she didn't feel vulnerable. His mouth wasn't gentle, but she didn't feel afraid. As the kiss deepened, as the intimacy grew, she didn't think of anyone but him.

She tasted as she had the very first time, ripe and fresh. With his tongue he plundered her mouth, greedy for the flavor of her. There would be no turning back now, not when she was caught close in his arms and the lights were dim. He could hear her shuddering breath, and the steady ticking of the pendulum clock in the hallway. It was dark, it was quiet, they were alone. And tonight he would take a wife.

Her heart thudded against his bare chest, adding excitement. He ran his hands over her, feeling the smoothness of her skin, the slickness of her gown, feeling every tremble and every sigh his touch incited.

Greedy, he nipped his teeth into her lip as his hands moved lower. Passion sprung out, from him, from her, mixing together in a sudden, breath-stopping fury. Then he felt her body give against his in the ultimate gift of trust. The emotions that rose up in him tempered his desire. Tenderness, achingly sweet, more precious than diamonds, took its place.

Her hands were free. The paper still crumpled in her palm fluttered to the floor as she slipped her arms around him. Tentatively still. Her bones seemed to liquefy, degree by degree, until she wondered why she didn't simply slide out of his hands. Her mind, which had been swirling with needs, clouded with a pleasure that was softer, truer, than any she had ever imagined.

She stroked her hands over his back, feeling the muscle, the power. Wonder filled her at the discovery that anyone with such strength could be so gentle. His lips brushed over hers, testing, almost teasing, inviting her to set the pace. Or perhaps he was challenging her.

Hunger leaped inside her until she was locked against him, her mouth seeking, avid, impatient. Then she was swept up into his arms. In the dim light she saw his eyes, only his eyes, their clear green darkened by need. Hers remained open and on his as he lowered her onto the bed.

She expected speed, a frenzy of greed and a drive for gratification. She wouldn't have thought less of him for it. Her love wouldn't have diminished. Against hers, his body was taut and straining. Circling her arms around him, she prepared to give him whatever he required.

But it wasn't speed he sought. And the greed was not only to take, but also to give.

When he ranged kisses over her throat, lingering, nibbling, she, too, went taut. She could only whisper his name as he continued the slow journey over her shoulders and down to the curve of her breasts, then up again, in teasing circles. Instinctively she turned her head, seeking his mouth, his jaw, his temple, as her body turned hot and cold with pleasure.

He needed to take care, for her. At the first touch, he'd been terrified. She had been with another man, she had had a child, but he knew the extent of her innocence. He'd seen it, hour after hour, when he'd painted her. He'd felt it each and every time he'd drawn her against him. If he was going to take that innocence, he was going to give her beauty in return.

She was so...responsive. Her body seemed to ebb and

flow at the touch of his hands. Wherever he tasted, her skin grew warm. Yet even as she gave, and offered, there was a shyness about her, the slightest of hesitations. He wanted to take her beyond that.

Slowly, with movements that were little more than a whisper along her skin, he drew the gown downward, following the trail of lace with his lips. At her first moan, his blood swam. He hadn't known that a sound, only a sound, could be so alluring. With light, openmouthed kisses he sensitized her skin until she began to shiver beneath him. In the lamplight she was exquisite, her skin like marble, her hair like silver. Her eyes were full of needs and uncertainties.

As he had once used his skill, his insight, to draw her emotions on canvas, he used it now to set them free.

She had never known there could be such sensitivity between a man and a woman. Even through the clouds of pleasure and the steadily rising tide of desire, she sensed his patience. She had never been so driven to touch a man before. With her fingertips and her palms, with her lips and her tongue, she discovered him. The urge came, strong, just to hold him, to wrap tight around him and hold on.

Then, without warning, he was taking her up, making her arch and gasp in shock and indescribable delight. Her mind and body were drained of everything but sensation. For an instant there was a terror of being totally out of control. His name burst out of her as she was carried away by a climax so strong, so intense, that she was left limp and dazed in the aftermath.

"Please, I can't... I've never..."

"I know." Strangely humbled, he lowered his lips to hers. He had wanted to give, had been driven to, but he hadn't known that in giving, so much would be returned to him. "Just relax. There's no hurry."

"But you haven't—"

He laughed against her throat. "I intend to. There's time. I want to touch you," he murmured, and began the slow, seductive journey again.

It wasn't possible. She would have said it couldn't be possible for her body to leap back in response to so gentle, so light, a touch. Yet within moments she was trembling again, aching again, wanting again. His tongue skimmed over her stomach, dipped to the curve of her thigh, until she was writhing, a victim now of her own desire and of the taste of heaven he'd already given her.

Then, impossibly, incredibly, she was tossed up and over again. This time, when she gasped and faltered, he slid into her.

Her moan merged with his.

Damp flesh pressed against damp flesh as they moved together. She'd never felt so strong, so utterly free, as she did now, joined as closely as was conceivable with Gabe.

She was everything he'd ever wanted, everything he'd ever dreamed of. Indeed, it was like a dream now, with the bursts and shudders of pleasure ripping through him. With his face pressed against her throat, he could smell her lightly provocative fragrance, mixed with the pungent, earthy scent of passion. He would go to the grave remembering that dizzying combination.

Her breath was fast and frenzied in his ear. Her body was just as fast and frenzied beneath his. He could feel her nails as she dug heedlessly into his back.

He would remember all of it.

Then he remembered nothing, and he let himself go.

Chapter 9

There had been a time, a brief time, when Laura had dressed in elegant clothes and gone to elegant parties. She had met people whose names were printed in slick magazines and flashed in bold headlines in tabloids. She'd danced with celebrities and dined with princes of fashion. However much it had seemed like a dream, it had been real.

It was true enough that she had enjoyed her time modeling for Geoffrey. The work might have been hard, but she'd been young enough, untried enough, to have been dazzled by the glamour—even after ten hours on her feet.

He had taught her how to stand, how to walk, even how to look interested when fatigue was all but pouring out of her ears. He'd shown her how to use makeup to enhance subtly or strikingly, how to use her hair to express a mood.

All the things he'd taught her had helped her maintain an image during public events with the Eagletons. She'd been able to appear sophisticated and untroubled. At times, appearances were a great comfort.

She wasn't afraid she would embarrass herself or Gabe at the reception his parents were giving at their Nob Hill estate. But she wasn't certain she wanted to step back into that life again, either.

How might things have been if Gabe had been an ordinary man, a man of ordinary means? They might have found a little house with a little backyard and been swallowed up by anonymity. A part of her yearned for that, for the simplicity of it.

But that was wrong. Laura fastened the earrings she'd bought the week before, starbursts of blue stones. If Gabe had come from a different family and a different life, he wouldn't be the man she loved. The man she was almost ready to believe was beginning to love her.

There was nothing about him she wanted to change, not his looks, not his manner. She might wish occasionally that he would share with her a bit more of his thoughts and feelings, but she continued to hope that someday he would.

She wanted to be a full part of his life—lover, wife and partner. So far, she had come to be the first two.

When the door opened, she turned.

"If you're about ready, we'll—"

And he stopped and stared. This was the woman she'd only told him about, the one who had graced the covers of magazines and modeled silks and sables. Long-limbed and slender, she stood in front of the beveled mirror in a dress of midnight-blue. It was very simple, leaving her shoulders and throat bare, then caught like a wish at her breasts to fall ruler-straight to her feet.

She'd wound her hair up, swept it back, so that only a few wheat-colored curls escaped to tease her temples.

She was beautiful, gloriously so, yet even as he was drawn to her, he felt as though he were looking at a stranger.

"You look wonderful." But he kept his hand on the knob and the room between them. "I'll have to paint you like this." *Beauty on Ice,* he thought, cool, aloof and unapproachable.

"I took your advice on the color." She picked up her purse, then clasped and unclasped it as she wondered why he was looking at her as though he'd never seen her before. "And I avoided bows."

"So I see." She should have sapphires, a collar of them, around her throat. "It's still a bit cool. Do you have a wrap?"

"Yes." Irked by his tone, she walked to the bed and snatched up a wide silk scarf in a riot of jewel-like colors. It was then that he noticed that the back of the skirt was slit to the thigh.

"I imagine you'll create quite a stir in that little number."

She cringed inwardly, but, falling back on appearances, she managed to keep her face calm. "If you don't like the dress, why don't you just say so?" She swirled the scarf over her shoulders. "It's too late to change, but believe me, I won't wear it again."

"Just a minute." He grabbed her hand as she started through the doorway. He could feel the smooth gold of her plain wedding ring on the index finger of her right hand. She was still his Laura, he thought as he linked his fingers with hers. He'd only had to look in her eyes to see it.

"I have to get Michael ready," she mumbled, and tried again to move past him.

"Do you expect an apology because I'm human enough to be jealous?"

Her face went still, her eyes blank. "I'm not wearing it to

attract other men. I bought it because I liked it and I thought it suited me."

He brought a hand to her face and swore roundly when she jerked. "Look at me. No, damn it, not at him, at me." Her eyes lashed back up to him. "Remember who I am, Laura. And remember this—I won't tolerate having my every mood, my every word, compared with someone else's."

"I'm not trying to do that."

"Maybe you're not trying to, but you do."

"You expect me to turn my life around overnight. I can't."

"No." He ran his thumb over the ring again. "I don't suppose you can. But you can remember that I'm part of your new life, not your old one."

"You're nothing like him." It was becoming easier to let her hand relax in his. "I know that. I guess sometimes it's easier to expect the worst than to hope for the best."

"I can't promise you the best."

No, he wouldn't make promises he couldn't keep. That was the beauty of him. "You could hold me. That's as close as I need to get."

When his arms came around her, he pressed her cheek against the shoulder of his black evening jacket. It smelled of him, and that made the last twists of tension dissolve.

"I suppose I was jealous, too."

"Oh?"

She smiled as she drew back enough to look into his face. "You look so good tonight."

"Really?" There was both discomfort and amusement in his tone.

"I've never seen you in evening clothes." She ran her finger down the dark lapel, which rested against a crisp white shirt. "Sort of like Heathcliff in a tux."

He laughed and cupped her face in his hands. "What a mind you have, angel. There's no hero in here."

"You're wrong." Her eyes were very solemn, very serious. "You're mine." He shrugged, but she kept him close. "Please, just this once, let me say it without you brushing it aside."

He just flicked a finger down her nose. "Don't expect me to walk around in armor too long. Let's get the baby. My mother knows how to make you miserable if you're late."

He wasn't a hero. He certainly wasn't comfortable being seen as one. Gabe was much more at ease discussing his work or speculating on the Giants' chances during the rest of the baseball season. He preferred arguments to good deeds.

When someone saw you as heroic, you invariably let them down. They expected you to have the right answers, the key to the lock, the light in the dark.

Michael had seen him as a hero. And, of course, he had let his brother down.

Michael had loved parties like this, Gabe thought as he sipped at the champagne that seemed to flow endlessly. He had loved the laughter, the people and the gossip. Michael had been unashamedly fond of rumors and whispers.

People had loved him moments after meeting him. He had been outgoing, funny, and as warm with strangers as with friends. It was Michael who had been the hero, doing favors without tallying the score, always willing to help or simply to be enthusiastic about a project.

Yet he'd had that streak of temper and toughness that had balanced him, prevented him from being overly...overly good, Gabe supposed.

God, he missed him still, at times unbearably.

There were people here who had known Michael, who had raised a glass with him or swapped stories with him. Perhaps that was what made it seem worse tonight, being in their parents' home, where they had grown up and shared so much and knowing that Michael would never walk into that room again.

Somehow you went on. One part of your life closed up, and another opened. Gabe looked across the room to where Laura stood talking to his father.

Sometime between the moment she'd rolled down the window of a wrecked car and the moment she'd placed a newborn child in his arms he'd fallen in love with her. It had come not with trumpets and flares but with quiet, soothing murmurs.

If there were such things as angels, one had sent Laura to him when he'd needed her most.

She was grateful to him, and open enough to give him love and affection in return for what he had given her. There were days when he believed that would be enough, for today, and for the tomorrows they would have together.

Then there were the other times.

He wanted to grab her, to demand again and again that she look at him, see who he was, what he felt. That she forget what had happened before and trust in what was happening now. He wanted to erase, the way he might have blanked out a canvas, what had gone on before, all the things that had put shadows in her eyes, all the things that made her hesitate just that split second before she smiled.

But he knew better than most that when you painted over part of someone's life you stole something. Bad experience or good, what had happened to Laura had made her what she was, the woman he loved.

But loving as he did, and being a selfish man, he wanted to be loved back, completely, without the strings of gratitude or the shadows of vulnerability. Wanting wouldn't make it so, but time might. He could give her a little more of that.

Someone laughed across the room. Glasses chinked. There was a scent of wine, flowers and women's fragrances. The night had cooperated with a full moon, and its glow shimmered just outside the open terrace doors. The room was ablaze with lamplight. Wanting a few moments away from the crowd and the noise, he slipped upstairs to check on his son.

"The boy looks more like you every time I see him," Cliff was saying.

"Do you think so?" The thought had Laura lighting up. Perhaps she was vain after all.

"Absolutely. Though no one would believe you were a new mother, the way you're looking tonight." He patted her cheek in the way that always made her feel shy and delighted. "My Gabe has excellent taste."

"Shame on you, Cliff, flirting with a beautiful woman when your wife's not looking."

"Marion." Cliff bent down from his rangy height to give the newcomer a kiss. "Late as always."

"Amanda's already scolded me." She turned, sipping at her champagne, to give Laura a thorough study. "So this is the mysterious Laura."

"My new daughter." Cliff gave Laura a quick squeeze

around the shoulders. "An old friend, Marion Trussalt. The Trussalt Gallery handles Gabe's paintings."

"Yes, I know. It's nice to meet you." She wasn't a beautiful woman, Laura thought, but she was oddly striking, with her sleek cap of black hair and her dark eyes. She wore a flowing rainbow-colored sheath that managed to be both arty and sophisticated.

"Yes, it is, since we have Gabe in common." Marion tapped a finger on the rim of her glass and smiled, but her eyes didn't warm. Laura recognized carefully polished disdain when she saw it. "You have his heart, and I his soul, you might say."

"Then it would seem we both want the best for him."

"Oh." Marion raised her glass. "Absolutely. Cliff, Amanda told me to remind you that hosts are supposed to mingle."

He grimaced. "Slave driver. Laura, be sure to work your way over to the buffet. You're getting too thin already." With that he went to do his duty.

"Yes, you're amazingly slender for someone who had a child—what was it? A month ago?"

"Almost two." Laura shifted her glass of sparkling water to her other hand. She didn't deal well with subtle attacks.

"Time flies." Marion touched her tongue to her upper lip. "It's odd that in all that time you haven't stirred yourself to come down to the gallery."

"You're right. I'll have to come down and see Gabe's work in a proper setting." She steadied herself. Under no circumstances was she going to allow herself to be intimidated or to fall into the trap of reading between the lines. If Gabe had ever had any kind of romantic involvement with Marion, it had ended. "He relies on you, I know. And I hope you'll be able to persuade him to go through with a new showing."

"I haven't decided that's really a good idea for the time being." Marion turned to smile at someone across the room who had called her name.

"Why? The paintings are wonderful."

"That isn't the only issue." She turned back to give Laura a quick, glittering look. She hadn't been Gabe's lover, nor had there every been any urge on either side to make it so. Her feelings for Gabriel Bradley went far beyond the physical. Gabe was an artist, a great one, and she had been—and intended to go on being—the catalyst for his success.

If he had married within his circle, or chosen someone who could have enhanced or furthered his career, she would have been pleased. But for him to have wasted himself, and her ambitions, on a beautiful face and a smeared reputation was more than Marion could bear.

"Did I mention that I knew your first husband?"

If she had thrown her drink into Laura's face she would have been no less shocked. The cocoon that she had been able to draw around herself and Michael suffered its first crack.

"No. If you'll excuse me—"

"A fascinating man, I always thought. Certainly young, and a bit wild, but fascinating. A tragedy that he died so young, before he ever saw his child." She tilted her glass back until only a sheen of bubbles remained.

"Michael," Laura said evenly, "is Gabe's child."

"So I'm told." She smiled again. "There were the oddest rumors just before and just after Tony died. Some said that he was on the verge of divorcing you, that he'd already removed you from the family home because you were, well, indiscreet." With a shrug, Marion set her glass aside. "But that's all in the past now. Tell me, how are the Eagletons? I haven't spoke with Lorraine for ages."

She was going to be ill, violently and humiliatingly ill, unless she succeeded in fighting back her rolling nausea. "Why are you doing this?" she whispered. "Why should you care?"

"Oh, my dear, I care about anything that has to do with Gabe. I intend to see him reach the very top, and I don't intend to watch him be dragged down. That's a lovely dress," she added. Then she saw Amanda approaching and slipped away.

"Laura, are you all right? You're white as a sheet. Come, let me find you a chair."

"No, I need some air." Turning, she fled through the open glass doors and onto the smooth stone terrace beyond.

"Here, now." Coming up behind her, Amanda took her arm and steered her to a chair. "Sit a minute before Gabe comes along. He'll take one look at you and pounce on me for insisting you come out and socialize too soon."

"It's nothing to do with that."

"And something to do with Marion." Amanda took the water glass out of Laura's tightening grip. "If she led you to believe that there was something—personal—between herself and Gabe, I can only say its totally untrue."

"That wouldn't matter."

With a little laugh, Amanda cast a look back inside. "If you mean that, then you're a better woman than I. I've known one of my husband's former…interests for over thirty-five years. I'd still like to spit in her eye."

With a laugh of her own, Laura drew in the softly scented evening. "I know Gabe's faithful to me."

"And so you should. You should also know that Marion and Gabe were never lovers." She moved her shoulders a bit. "I can't say that I know about all of my son's affairs, but I do know that he and Marion only have art in common. Now, what did she say to upset you?"

"It was nothing." Laura brushed her fingers over her temples, as if to soothe away an ache. "Really, it was my own fault, overreacting. She only mentioned that she'd met my first husband."

"I see." Annoyed, Amanda turned her sharp-eyed glance into the drawing room again. "Well, I have to say I find it very insensitive to bring up the subject at your wedding reception. One would have thought a woman like Marion would have more taste."

"It's over and it's best forgotten." Straightening her shoulders, Laura prepared to go back in. "I'd appreciate it if you wouldn't mention any of this to Gabe. There's no reason to annoy him."

"No, I agree. I'll speak with Marion myself."

"No." Laura picked up her glass again and sipped slowly. "If there's anything that needs to be said, I'll say it myself."

Amanda's smile spread and she said easily, "If that's what you'd like."

"Yes. Amanda…" A decision made quickly, she thought, was sometimes the best. "Could I leave Michael with you one day next week? I'd like to go into the gallery and see Gabe's paintings."

* * *

Laura woke up out of breath and shivering. She struggled her way out of the nightmare to find herself in Gabe's arms.

"Just relax. You're all right."

She drew in a big gulp of air, then let it out slowly. "Sorry," she muttered, dragging a hand through her hair.

"Want anything? Some water?"

"No." As the fear passed, annoyance took its place. The glowing dial of the alarm clock read 4:15. They'd been in bed for only three hours, and now she was wide-awake and restless.

With his arm still around her, Gabe lay back on his pillow. "You haven't had a nightmare since Michael was born. Did something happen at the party tonight?"

She thought of Marion and gritted her teeth. "Why do you ask?"

"I noticed that you seemed upset, and my mother annoyed."

"Did you think that I had an argument with your mother?" That made her smile and settle more comfortably against him. "No, in fact we get along very well."

"You sound surprised."

"I didn't expect to make friends with her. I kept waiting for her to bring out her broom and pointed hat."

He laughed and kissed her shoulder. "Just try criticizing my work."

"I wouldn't dare." Unconsciously she began to stroke her fingers through his hair. When she was here, like this, she believed she could handle anything that threatened her new family. "She showed me the mural in the parlor. The one with all the mythical creatures."

"I was twenty, and romantic." And he'd asked his mother a dozen times to have it painted over.

"I like it."

"No wonder you get along with her."

"I did like it." She shifted so that she could rest her arms on his chest. There was only a little moonlight, but she could see him. She didn't realize that it was her first completely unstudied move toward him, but he did. "What's wrong with unicorns and centaurs and fairies?"

"They have their place, I suppose." But all he was currently interested in was making love with her.

"Good. Then don't you think the side wall in Michael's room is the perfect place for a mural?"

He tugged at a curl that fell over her cheek. "Are you offering me a commission?"

"Well, I've seen a few samples of your work, and it's not bad."

He tugged harder. "Not bad?"

"Shows promise." With a quick laugh, she ducked before he could pull her hair again. "Why don't you submit some sample sketches for consideration?"

"And my fee?"

He was smiling; her skin was warming. Laura began to think the nightmare had been a blessing in disguise. "Negotiable."

"Tell you what. I'll do the mural on one condition."

"Which is?"

"That you let me paint you again, nude."

Her eyes widened. Then she laughed, sure he was joking. "You should at least let me wear a beret."

"You've been watching too many old movies, but you can wear a beret if you like—just nothing else."

"I couldn't."

"All right, then, scratch the beret."

"Gabe, you're not serious."

"Of course I am." To prove it, and to please himself, he ran a hand over her. "You have a beautiful body...long dancer's limbs, smooth white skin, a narrow waist."

"Gabe." She spoke to stop not his roaming hands but his conversation. She stopped neither.

"I've wanted to paint you nude since the first time we made love. I can still see the way you looked when I drew the nightgown away. Capturing that femininity, that subtle sexuality, would be a triumph."

She laid her cheek on his heart. "I'd be embarrassed."

"Why? I know what you look like. Every inch of you." He cupped her breasts, scraping his thumbs lightly over her nipples. Her instant response rippled through him.

"No one else does." Her voice was husky now. Hardly realizing it, she began to run her hands over him. The journey was long, lazy, thorough.

There was something incredibly exciting about the idea. No one else knew the secrets of her body, the dips and curves. No one else knew how a touch here, a stroke there, could make her shyness melt into passion. He did want to capture that on canvas, the beauty of her, the sweetness of her inhibitions. The fire of passion just discovered. But he could wait.

"I suppose I could just hire a model."

Her head came up at that. "You—" The jealousy rose, so swift and powerful that it left her momentarily speechless.

"It's art, angel," he said, amused and not at all displeased. "Not a centerfold."

"You're trying to blackmail me."

"You're very sharp."

Her eyes narrowed. In deliberate seduction that surprised them both, she shifted so that her body rubbed tantalizingly over his. "Only if I get to choose the model."

His pulse was thudding. As she lowered her head to brush kisses over his chest, he closed his eyes. "Laura."

"No, Mrs. Drumberry. I met her tonight."

He opened his eyes. But when she used her teeth to tug on his nipple he arched beneath her. "Mabel Drumberry is a hundred and five."

"Exactly." She chuckled but continued her explorations, with a growing sense of power and discovery. "I wouldn't trust you closed up in your studio with some sexy young redhead with lush curves."

He started to laugh, but the sound became a moan as her hand ranged lower. "Don't you think I can resist a sexy young redhead?"

"Of course, but she wouldn't be able to resist you." She rubbed her cheek along his jawline, which was already roughened with morning stubble. "You're so beautiful, Gabe. If I could paint, I'd show you."

"What you're doing is driving me crazy."

"I hope so," she murmured, and lowered her mouth to his.

She'd never had the confidence to take charge, had never been sure enough of her skill or her appeal. Now it seemed right and wonderfully fulfilling to tease and taunt her man in passion.

His hands were in her hair, his fingers tangled and tense,

as she dipped her tongue into his mouth and explored. Her moves were instinctive rather than experienced, and all the more seductive for it.

The power came to her not in a wild burst but with quiet certainty. She could be his partner here, his full partner. It was easy to show love, almost as easy as it was to feel it.

As she discovered him, she discovered herself. She wasn't as patient as he, not here. Strangely, in the daylight, the opposite was true. She saw him as a man who needed to move quickly, decisively, and if mistakes were made because of hurry they could be corrected or just as easily ignored. She was more cautious, more prone to think through alternatives before acting.

But in bed, in the role of the seductress, she found little patience in herself.

She was wild and wanton. Gabe found himself reaching for her, then being rocked helplessly by the sensations she brought to him. It was like having a different woman in bed, one who felt like Laura, smelled like Laura, one he wanted as desperately as he wanted Laura.

When her mouth came down on his, it was Laura's taste, yet somehow darker, riper. And her body was like a furnace as she moved over him.

He tried to remember that this was his wife, his shy and still-innocent wife, who required infinite care and gentleness. He had yet to release his full range of passion with her. With Laura he had taken his time, used every drop of his sensitivity.

Now she was stripping him down to the nerve ends.

She could feel the power, and it was glorious. Despite her excitement, her mind was clear as a bell. She could make him weak, she could make him desperate. She could make him tremble. Breathlessly she pressed her lips to pulse points that she found by instinct. His heart was racing. For her. She could feel his body shudder at her touch. When he groaned, it was her own name she heard.

She heard herself laugh, and there was something sultry in the sound. A feminine triumph. The clock in the hallway struck five, and the echo went on and on in her head.

Then his arms were locked around her and the sound that was coming from his throat was long and primitive. His control snapped like a rubber band stretched too far. Needs only half satisfied, so long held in check, flooded free. His mouth covered hers, bruisingly. But it wasn't a skip of fear she felt. It was a leap of victory.

Trapped in madness, they rolled across the bed, seeking, taking, demanding, with a kind of greed that made the mouth go dry and the soul shudder. The modest gown she wore was torn aside, seams ripping, lace shredding. His hands were everywhere, and they were far from gentle.

There was no shame. There was no shyness. This was freedom, a different kind from what he had already shown her. As desperate as he, she opened for him. When he plunged into her, the shock vibrated, wave after wave.

Fast and furious, they locked into their own rhythm, each driving the other.

Endless pleasure, sharp and edgy. Insatiable need spreading like wildfire. As she gave herself to him, as she asked and received more, Laura realized that, for the lucky, time could indeed stop.

Chapter 10

When the sky darkened, Laura was in the garden. It had become her habit to spend her mornings there while the baby slept or sat rocking in his swing in the sunlight. Since her arrival in Gabe's home, she'd found little to do indoors. The house almost took care of itself and, as she had once told him, Gabe was only sloppy when he painted.

More than that, there were too many rooms, too much space that she didn't yet feel a part of. In the nursery, which she'd decorated herself and where, through necessity, she spent many hours during the day and night, she felt at home. The rest of the house, with its heirlooms and its beautiful old rugs, its polished wood and its faded wallpaper, remained aloof to her.

But as spring had taken hold she had discovered an affinity and a talent for gardening, as well as a need for space and air. She liked the sunlight and the smells and the feel of the earth under her hands. She devoured books on plants, much as she had on childbirth, so that she could become familiar with flowers and shrubs and the care they required.

The tulips were beginning to bloom, and the azaleas were already ripe with blossoms. Someone else had planted them, but Laura had no trouble taking them to heart as her own. They flowered afresh every year. Nor did she feel awkward adding her own touches with moss roses and snapdragons.

Already she was planning to plant new bulbs in the fall, daylilies, windflowers, poppies. Then, over the winter, she would root her own spring flowers from seed, starting them in little peat pots that she would set in the sunroom on the east side of the house.

"I'll teach you how to plant them next year," she told Michael. She could already imagine him toddling around the garden on short, sturdy legs, patting at the dirt, trying to snatch butterflies off blossoms.

He would laugh. There would be so much for him to laugh about. She would be able to catch him up in her arms and swing him around so that his eyes, which were still as stubbornly blue as hers, glowed and his laughter bounced on the air. Then Gabe would stick his head out of his studio window and demand to know what all the ruckus was about.

But he wouldn't really be annoyed. He'd come down, saying that if there was going to be so much noise he might as well forget about working for the morning. He'd sit on the ground with Michael in his lap and they'd laugh together about nothing anyone else would understand.

Sitting back on her heels, Laura wiped her brow with the back of a gloved hand. Dreaming had always been her escape, her defense, her survival. Now it didn't seem like any of those things, because she was beginning to believe dreams could come true.

"I love your daddy," she told Michael, as she told him at least once every day. "I love him so much that it makes me believe in happy endings."

When the shadow fell over her, Laura glanced up and saw the first dark clouds roll over the sun. She was tempted to ignore them, and she might have if she hadn't known it took more than a quick minute to gather up all her gardening tools, Michael's supplies and the baby himself.

"Well, the rain's good for the flowers, isn't it, sweetie?" She stored the tools and bags of peat moss and fertilizers in the small shed near the back door, then drew Michael out of the swing. With the acquired coordination of motherhood, she carried the baby, his little cache of toys and the folded swing indoors.

She'd barely started upstairs when the first crack of thunder had both her and Michael jumping. As he began to wail, she fought back her own longstanding fear of storms and soothed him.

He calmed down much more quickly than she as she walked and rocked and murmured reassurances. Though the rain held off, she could watch the fury raging in the sky through Michael's windows. Lightning slashed, turning the light from gray to mauve, then back to gray, in the blink of an eye.

Eventually he began to doze, but she continued to hold him, as much for her own comfort as his.

"Silly, isn't it?" she murmured. "A grown woman more afraid of thunder than a tiny baby." As the rain began to lash at the house, she made herself set the sleeping child in his crib so that she could close the windows.

At least that would keep her busy, Laura told herself as she moved from room to room to shut the windows against the pelting rain. Still, each time thunder boomed she jerked back. It wasn't until she started back into the nursery, telling herself she'd curl up on the daybed and read until the storm passed, that she remembered Gabe's studio. Thinking only of his work, she rushed down the hall.

She was grateful that the storm hadn't knocked out the power. The lights flared on at a touch. It seemed that her luck had held. The floor was wet by the ribbon of windows, but none of his paintings were stored there. Laura hurried down the line, shutting each one until the rain was muffled by the glass.

She started to do the practical thing and go for a mop, but then it struck her that this was the first time she had been in Gabe's studio alone. He'd never asked her not to go in, but the lack of privacy she'd lived with most of her life had made her fastidious about respecting that of others. Now, though, with the lights bright overhead and the thunder rolling in the distance, she felt comfortable there, as she did in the nursery. As she had in the cabin in the mountains.

The room smelled of him, she realized. It held that mixture of paint and turpentine, with the powdery addition of chalk, that often clung to his clothes and his hands. It was a scent that invariably put her at ease, even though it was also a scent that invariably aroused her. Like the man, she thought, the scent drew her emotions. She could love him and be comforted by him, just as she could be excited and confused by him.

What did he want from her? she wondered. And why? She thought she understood part of it. He wanted the solidity of family, an end to his own loneliness and passion in bed. He'd chosen her for those things because she'd been as anxious to give them as he was to take them.

It could be enough, or nearly enough. Her problem was, and continued to be, a quiet longing for more.

Shaking off the mood, she tried to picture him there in that room, alone, working, envisioning.

So much had been done here, she thought, so many hours creating, perfecting, experimenting. What made one man different from another in the way he saw and expressed what he saw? Crossing to his easel, she studied his work in progress.

A painting of Michael. The deep and simple pleasure of it had her hugging herself. There was a rough sketch tacked to the easel, and the portrait on canvas was just beginning to take shape. She could see that even since the sketch, which he'd drawn perhaps a week before, Michael had changed and grown. But because of this she would always be able to look back and see him exactly as he'd been in that one precious moment of time.

With her arms still crossed over her breasts, she turned to study the room. It was different without Gabe in it. Less... dramatic, she thought. Then she laughed a little, knowing he would hate that description.

Without him it was a wide, airy room, largely empty. On the floor were dried drops and smears of paint that could have been there for a week or a year. A small pedestal sink was built into one corner. She saw a towel tossed carelessly over its lip. There were shelves and a worktable with equipment scattered on them. Paints and bottles, jars crammed with brushes, pallet knives, hunks of charcoal and balled-up rags. Unframed canvases were stacked against the walls, much as they had been in Colorado. He hadn't hung anything here.

She wondered why she hadn't thought before to ask Gabe if he had anything she might hang in Michael's room. The posters she'd chosen were colorful, but one of Gabe's paintings would mean more. With that in mind, she knelt down and began to go through canvases.

How easily he drew out emotion. One of his pastel landscapes would make you dreamy. Next an edgy, too-realistic view of a slum would make you shudder. There were portraits, too—an impossibly old man leaning on a cane at a bus stop, three young girls giggling outside a boutique. There was a spectacular nude study of a brunette sprawled on white satin. Instead of jealousy, it raised a feeling of awe in Laura.

She went through more than a dozen, wondering why he'd stacked them so carelessly. Many were unframed, and all were facing the wall. Each one she held left her more astonished that she could be married to a man who could do so much with color and brush. More, each painting gave her a closer look at who he was. She could sense the mood that had held him as he'd worked. Rage for this, humor for that. Sorrow, impatience, desire, delight. Whatever he could feel, he could paint.

These didn't belong here, she thought, frustrated that he would close them up in a room where no one could see them or appreciate them or be touched by them. His signature was dashed in each corner, with the year just below. Everything she found had been painted no more than two years before, and no less than one year.

She turned the last canvas over and was caught immediately. It was another portrait, and this one had been painted with love.

The subject, a young man of no more than thirty, was grinning, a bit recklessly, as though he had all the time in the world to accomplish what he wanted to do. His hair was blond, a few shades lighter than Gabe's, and brushed back from a lean, good-looking face. It was a casual study, full-length, with the subject sprawled in a chair, legs spread out and crossed at the ankle. But, despite the relaxing pose, there was a sense of movement and energy.

She recognized the chair. It sat in the parlor of the Bradley mansion on Nob Hill. And she recognized the subject by the shape of the face, which was so much like her husband's. This was Gabe's brother. This was Michael.

For a long time she sat there, holding the painting in her lap, no longer hearing the storm. The lights flickered once, but she didn't notice.

It was possible, she discovered, to grieve for someone you hadn't even known, to feel the loss and the regret. That Gabe had loved his brother deeply was obvious in each brush stroke. Not only loved, she thought, but respected. Now more than ever she wished he trusted her enough to speak of this Michael, his life and his death. In the sketch of the baby Gabe had tacked on the easel she had seen this same kind of unconditional love.

If he was using the baby to help him get over the loss of his brother, should she begrudge him that? It didn't mean he loved their Michael any less. Still, it made her sad to think of it. Until he talked to her, opened up his emotions to her as he did in his work, she would never really be his wife and Michael would never really be his son.

Gently she turned the canvas back to the wall and replaced the others.

When the rain stopped, Laura decided to call Amanda and follow through with her decision to visit the gallery. If she wanted Gabe to take another step toward her, she would have to take another toward him. She'd avoided going to the gallery, not for all the reasons she had given, but because she hadn't felt comfortable in her role as wife to the public person, the well-known artist. Insecurity, she knew, could only be overcome by taking a confident step forward, even if that step took all the courage you could muster.

She'd grown, Laura told herself. In the past year she'd learned not just to be strong but to be as strong as she needed to be. She might not have reached the peak, but she was no longer scrambling for a foothold at the bottom of the hill.

It was as easy as asking. After her thanks were brushed aside Laura hung up the phone and glanced at her watch. If Michael stuck to his usual schedule, he would wake within the hour and demand to be fed. She could take him to Amanda—the first big step—then drive to the gallery. She glanced down at the dirt-stained knees of her jeans. First she had to change.

The doorbell caught her halfway up the stairs. Feeling too optimistic to be annoyed by the interruption, she went to answer it.

And the world crashed silently at her feet.

"Laura." Lorraine Eagleton gave a brisk nod, then strode into the hall. She stood and glanced idly around as she drew off her gloves. "My, my, you've certainly landed on your feet, haven't you?" She tucked her gloves tidily in a buff-colored alligator bag. "Where is the child?"

She couldn't speak. Both words and air were trapped in her lungs, crowding there so that her chest ached. Her hand, still gripping the doorknob, was ice-cold, though the panicked rhythm of her heart vibrated in each fingertip. She had a sudden, horrible flash of the last time she had seen this woman face-to-face. As if they had just been spoken, she remembered the threats, the demand and the humiliation. She found her voice.

"Michael's asleep."

"Just as well. We have business to discuss."

The rain had cooled the air and left its taste in it. Watery sunlight crept through the door, which Laura still hadn't closed. Birds were beginning to chirp optimistically again. Normal things. Such normal things. Life, she reminded herself, didn't bother to stop for personal crises.

Though she couldn't make her fingers relax on the doorknob, she did keep her eyes and her voice level. "You're in my home now, Mrs. Eagleton."

"Women like you always manage to find rich, gullible husbands." She arched a brow, pleased that Laura was still standing by the door, tense and pale. "That doesn't change who you are, what you are. Nor will your being clever enough to get Gabriel Bradley to marry you stop me from taking what's mine."

"I have nothing that belongs to you. I'd like you to leave."

"I'm sure you would," Lorraine said, smiling. She was a tall, striking woman with dark, sculpted hair and an unlined face. "Believe me, I have neither the desire nor the intention to stay long. I intend to have the child."

Laura had a vision of herself standing in the mist, holding an empty blanket. "No."

Lorraine brushed the refusal aside as she might have brushed a speck of lint from her lapel. "I'll simply get a court order."

The cold fear was replaced by heat, and she managed to move then, though it was only to stiffen. "Then do it. Until you do, leave us alone."

Still the same, Lorraine thought as she watched Laura's face. She spit a bit now when she was backed into a corner, but she was still easily maneuvered. It infuriated her now, as it always had, that her son had settled for so little when he could have had so much. Even in fury she never raised her voice. Lorraine had always considered derision a better weapon than volume.

"You should have taken the offer my husband and I made to you. It was generous, and it won't be made again."

"You can't buy my baby, any more than you can buy back Tony."

Pain flashed across Lorraine's face, pain that was real enough, sharp enough, to make Laura form words of sympathy. They could talk, had to be able to talk now, as one mother to another. "Mrs. Eagleton—"

"I won't speak of my son with you," Lorraine said, and the pain vanished into bitterness. "If you had been what he needed, he'd still be alive. I'll never forgive you for that."

There had been a time when she would have crumbled at those words, ready to take the blame. But Lorraine had been wrong. Laura was no longer the same. "Do you want to take

my baby to punish me or to bind your wounds? Either reason
is wrong. You have to know that."

"I know I can and will prove that you're unfit to care for
the child. I'll produce documentation that you made yourself
available to other men before and after your marriage to my
son."

"You know that's not true."

Lorraine continued as if Laura hadn't spoken. "Added to
that will be the record of your unstable family background.
If the child proves to be Tony's, there'll be a custody hearing,
and the outcome is without question."

"You won't take Michael, not with money, not with lies."
Her voice rose, and she fought to bring it back down. Losing
her temper would get her nowhere. Laura knew all too well
how easily Lorraine could bat aside emotion with one cold,
withering look. She believed, she had to believe, there was
still a way of reasoning with her. "If you ever loved Tony,
then you'll know just how far I'll go to keep my son."

"And you should know just how far I'll go to see to it that
you have no part in raising an Eagleton."

"That's all he is to you, a name, just a symbol of immortality." Despite her efforts, her voice was growing desperate
and her knees were beginning to shake. "He's just a baby.
You don't love him."

"Feelings have nothing to do with it. I'm staying at the
Fairmont. You have two days to decide whether or not you
want a public scandal." Lorraine drew out her gloves again.
The terror on Laura's face assured her that there was no risk
of that. "I'm sure the Bradleys would be displeased, at the
least, to learn of your past indiscretions. Therefore, I have no
doubt you'll be sensible, Laura, and not risk what you've so

conveniently acquired." She walked out the door and down the steps to where a gray limo waited.

Without waiting for it to drive away, Laura slammed the door and bolted it. She was panting as though she'd been running. And it was running that occurred to her first. Dashing up the stairs, she raced into the nursery and began to toss Michael's things into his carryall.

They'd travel light. She'd only pack what was absolutely necessary. Before sundown they could be miles away. Headed north, she thought quickly. Maybe into Canada. There was still enough money left to help them get away, to buy them enough time to disappear. A rattle slipped out of her hand and landed with a clatter. Giving in to despair, she sunk onto the daybed and buried her face in her hands.

They couldn't run. Even if they had enough funds to keep them for a lifetime, they couldn't run. It was wrong, wrong for Michael, for Gabe, even for herself. They had a life here, the kind she'd always wanted, the kind she needed to give her son.

But what could she do to protect it?

Take a stand. Ride out the attack. Not cave in. But caving in was what she'd always done best. Lifting her head, she waited until her breathing had calmed. That was the old Laura's thinking, and that was exactly what Lorraine was counting on. The Eagletons knew how easily manipulated she had been. They expected her to run, and they would use that impulsive, erratic behavior to take her baby. They thought that if she was too tired to run she would sacrifice her child to protect her position with the Bradleys.

But they didn't know her. They had never taken the time or effort to really know her. She wouldn't cave in. She wouldn't run with her son. She was damn well going to fight for him.

The anger came then, and it felt wonderful. Anger was a hot, animate emotion, so unlike the icy numbness of fear. She'd stay angry, as Amanda had advised, because angry she would not only fight but fight rough and dirty. The Eagletons were in for a surprise.

By the time she reached the gallery she was in control again. Michael was safe with Amanda, and Laura was taking the first step of the route she'd already mapped out to see that he stayed safe.

The Trussalt Gallery was in a gracefully refurbished old building. Flowers, neatly trimmed and still wet from the recent rain, were grouped near the main entrance. Laura could smell roses and damp leaves as she pulled the door open.

Inside, skylights offered an open view of the still-cloudy sky, but the gallery itself was brilliant with recessed and track lighting. It was as quiet as a church. Indeed, as Laura paused to look, she could see that this was a place designed for the worship of art. Sculptures in marble and wood, in iron and bronze, were placed lovingly. Rather than competing with each other, they harmonized. As did the paintings aligned stylishly on the walls.

She recognized one of Gabe's, a particularly solemn view of a garden going to seed. It wasn't pretty; it certainly wasn't joyful. Looking at it, she thought of the mural he'd painted for his mother. The same man who believed enough in fantasies to bring them to life also saw reality, perhaps a bit too clearly. They had that in common, as well.

There were only a few patrons here on this rainy weekday

afternoon. They had time to browse, Laura reminded herself. She didn't. Spotting a guard, she moved toward him.

"Excuse me, I'm looking for Gabriel Bradley."

"I'm sorry, miss. He wouldn't be available. If you have a question about one of his paintings, you may want to see Ms. Trussalt."

"No. You see, I'm—"

"Laura." Marion breezed out of an alcove. She was wearing pastels today, a long, slim skirt in baby blue that reached to her ankles, with a hip-skimming sweater in soft pink. The quiet colors only accentuated her exotic looks. "So you decided to pay us a visit after all."

"I'd like to see Gabe."

"What a pity." Without so much as a glance, Marion motioned the guard aside. "He's not here at the moment."

Laura curled her fingers tighter around the clasp of her purse. Intimidation from this quarter meant less than nothing now. "Do you expect him back?"

"As a matter of fact, he should be back before too long. We're booked for drinks in, oh—" she glanced at her watch "—half an hour."

Both the glance and the tone were designed to dismiss her, but Laura was far beyond worrying about games. "Then I'll wait."

"You're welcome to, of course, but I'm afraid Gabe and I have business to discuss. So boring for you."

Weariness was a dull throb at the base of her skull. She had no desire to cross swords now. Her energy had to remain focused for a much more vital fight. "I appreciate your concern, but nothing about Gabe's art is boring for me."

"Spoken like a little Trojan." Marion tilted her head.

There was a smile that had nothing to do with friendship in her eyes. "You're looking a bit pale. Trouble in paradise?"

And she knew. As clearly as if Marion had said it out loud, she knew how Lorraine had found her. "Nothing that can't be dealt with. Why did you call her, Marion?"

The smile remained in place, cool and confident. "I beg your pardon?"

"She was already paying good money for detectives. I only had a week or two longer at most."

Marion considered a moment, then turned to fuss with the alignment of a painting. "I've always thought time was better saved than wasted. The sooner Lorraine deals with you, the sooner I can get Gabe back on track. Let me show you something."

Marion moved across the gallery in a separate room, where the walls and floors were white. A sweeping spiral staircase, again in white, rose up in one corner. Above, balconies ran in a circle. A trio of ornamental trees grew under the staircase, fronted by a towering ebony sculpture of a man and a woman in a passionate, yet somehow despairing, embrace.

But it was the portrait that caught her attention, that drew it and demanded it. It was her own face that looked serenely back at Laura, from the portrait Gabe had painted during those long, quiet days in Colorado.

"Yes, it's stunning." Marion rubbed a finger over her lip as she studied it. She'd been tempted to take a knife to the canvas when Gabe had first unpacked it, but the temptation had faded quickly. She was too much a patron of the arts to let personal feelings interfere. "It's one of his best and most romantic pieces. It's been hanging only three weeks and I've already had six serious offers for it."

"I've already seen the painting, Marion."

"Yes, but I doubt you understand it. He calls it *Gabriel's Angel*. That should tell you something."

"Gabriel's Angel," Laura repeated in a murmur. The warmth spread through her as she took a step closer. "What should that tell me?"

"That he, like Pygmalion, fell a bit in love with his subject. That's expected now and again, even encouraged, as it often inspires great work such as this." She tapped a finger against the frame. "But Gabe's much too practical a man to string out the fantasy for long. The portrait's finished, Laura. He doesn't need you any longer."

Laura turned her head so that she could look directly at Marion. What was being said had run through her mind countless times. She told Marion what she had already told herself. "Then he'll have to tell me that."

"He's an honorable man. That's part of his charm. But once things come to a head, once he realizes his mistake, he'll cut his losses. A man only believes in an image," she said, with a gesture toward the portrait, "as long as the image is unsmeared. From what Lorraine tells me, you don't have much time."

Laura fought back the urge to turn and run. Oddly, she discovered it didn't take as much effort this time. "If you believe that, why are you taking so much trouble to move me along?"

"No trouble." She smiled again and let her hand fall away from the painting. "I consider it part of my job to encourage Gabe to concentrate on his career and avoid the kind of controversies that can only detract from it. As I've already explained, his involvement with you isn't acceptable. He'll realize that soon enough himself."

No wonder she had called Lorraine, Laura thought. They were two of a kind. "You're forgetting something, Marion. Michael. No matter what Gabe feels or doesn't feel for me, he loves Michael."

"It takes a particularly pitiful woman to use a child."

"You're right." Laura met her eyes levelly. "You couldn't be more right." When Laura saw that retort had hit home, she continued calmly, "I'll wait here for Gabe. I'd appreciate it if you'd tell him when he gets back."

"So you can run and hide behind him?"

"I can't see that Laura's reasons for coming to see me are your concern."

Gabe spoke from the entranceway. Both women turned toward him. He could read fury on Marion's face and distress on Laura's. Even as he watched, both women composed themselves in their own way. Marion lifted her brow and smiled. Laura folded her hands and raised her chin.

"Darling. You know it's part of my job to protect my artists from panicky spouses and lovers." Crossing to him, Marion laid a hand on his arm. "We're going to be meeting with the Bridgetons in a few minutes about the three paintings. I don't want you distracted and out of sorts."

He spared her only the briefest of glances, but in it Marion saw that he had heard too much. "I'll worry about my moods. If you'll excuse us now?"

"The Bridgetons—"

"Can buy the paintings or go to hell. Leave us alone, Marion."

She aimed a vicious glare at Laura, then stormed out of the room. Her heels echoed on the tile. "I'm sorry," Laura said after a long breath. "I didn't come here to make waves."

"Why, then? From the look of you, you didn't come to spend an afternoon in art appreciation." Before she could answer, he was striding to her. "Damn it, Laura, I don't like having the two of you standing here discussing me as though I were some prize to be awarded to the highest bidder. Marion's a business associate, you're my wife. The two of you are going to have to resolve that."

"I understand that completely." Her voice had changed, hardened to match his. "And you should understand that if I believed you were involved with her in any way I would already have left you."

Whatever he'd been about to say slipped completely away from him. Because he recognized the unshakable resolve in the statement, he could only stare at her. "Just like that?"

"Just like that. I've already lived through one marriage where fidelity meant nothing. I won't live through another."

"I see." Comparisons again, he thought. He wanted to shout at her. Instead, he spoke softly, too softly. "Then I've been warned."

She turned away so that she could close her eyes for a moment. Her head was pounding ruthlessly. If she didn't take the time to draw herself in, she would throw herself into his arms and beg for help. "I didn't come here to discuss the terms of our marriage."

"Maybe you should have. It might be time for us to go back to square one and spell it out."

She shook her head and made herself turn to face him

again. "I wanted to tell you that I'm going to see a lawyer in the morning."

He felt the life drain out of him in one swift flood. She wanted a divorce. Then, as quickly as he'd been left limp, the fury came. Unlike Laura, he had never had to prime himself for a fight. "What the hell are you talking about?"

"It can't be put off any longer. I can't keep pretending it's not necessary." Again she wanted to step into his arms, to feel them close around her, make her safe. She kept an arm's length away and stood on her own. "I didn't want to start what will be a difficult and ugly period without letting you know."

"That's big of you." Spinning away, he dragged a hand through his hair. Above him, her portrait smiled gently down. As he stood between them, he felt as though he were caught between two women, between two needs. "What in the hell brought this on? Do you think you can kiss me goodbye at the door, then talk about lawyers a few hours later? If you haven't been happy, why haven't you said so?"

"I don't know what you're talking about, Gabe. We knew this would probably happen eventually. You were the one who told me there'd come a time when I'd have to face it. Now I'm ready to. I just want to give you the option of backing off before it's too late to turn back."

He started to snap at her, then stopped himself. It occurred to him that what he had thought they were talking about, and what was actually being discussed were two different things. "Why do you need to see a lawyer in the morning?"

"Lorraine Eagleton came to the house this afternoon. She wants Michael."

No relief came at the realization that they weren't speaking of divorce. There was no room for it. He recognized a flash of panic before fury replaced it. "She may as well want the moon, because she won't have that, either." He reached out to touch a hand to her cheek. "Are you all right?"

She nodded. "I wasn't, but I am now. She's threatening a custody suit."

"On what grounds?"

She pressed her lips together, but her gaze didn't waver. "On the grounds that I'm not fit to care for him. She told me she'll prove that I was...that there were other men before and during my marriage to Tony."

"How can she prove what isn't true?"

So he believed in her. It was just that easy. Laura reached for his hand. "You can get people to do or say a great many things if you pay them enough. I've seen the Eagletons do that kind of thing before."

"Did she tell you where she was staying?"

"Yes."

"Then it's time I talked with her."

"No." She had his hand before he could stride from the room. "Please, I don't want you to see her yet. I need to talk with a lawyer first, make certain what can and can't be done. We can't afford the luxury of making a mistake in anger."

"I don't need a lawyer to tell me she can't walk into my house and threaten to take Michael."

"Gabe, please." Again she had to stop him. When her fingers curled around his arms, she felt the fury vibrating in him. "Listen to me. You're angry. So was I, and frightened, too. My first impulse was to run again. I'd even started to pack."

He thought of what it would have done to him to have come home to find the house empty. The score he had to settle with the Eagletons was getting bigger. "Why didn't you?"

"Because it wouldn't have been right, not for Michael, not for you or for me. Because I love both of you too much."

He stopped and cupped her face in his hands, trying to read what was behind her eyes. "You wouldn't have gotten very far."

The smile came slowly as she wrapped her fingers around his wrists. "I hope not. Gabe, I know what I have to do, and I also know that I can do it."

He paused, taking it in. She spoke of love one moment, then of what she would do, not of what they would do. "Alone?"

"If necessary. I know you've taken Michael as your own, but I want you to understand that if she pursues the suit it's going to get ugly, and what's said about me will affect you and your family." There was a moment's hesitation as she worked up the courage to give him a choice. "If you'd rather not be involved in what's going to happen now, I understand."

His choices had narrowed from the moment he'd seen her. They'd disappeared completely when she'd first put Michael in his arms. Because he didn't know how to explain, he cut through to the bottom line.

"Where's Michael?"

Relief made her giddy. "He's with your mother."

"Then let's pick him up and take him home."

Chapter 11

She couldn't sleep. Both memory and imagination worked against Laura as her mind insisted on racing over what had happened, and what might happen the next day. It was almost a year since she had fled Boston. Now, thousands of miles away, she had chosen to take her stand. But she was no longer alone.

Gabe hadn't waited to make an appointment with his lawyer during regular business hours. He had made a phone call and requested—demanded—a meeting that evening.

Her life, her child, her marriage and her future had been discussed over coffee and crumb cake in the parlor while a low, wispy fog had rolled in from the bay. Her initial embarrassment about speaking with a stranger about her life, her first marriage and her mistakes had sharpened painfully, then vanished. It had seemed as though they were talking about someone else's experiences. The more openly it was discussed, with details meticulously examined and noted, the less shame she'd felt.

Matthew Quartermain had been the Bradleys' attorney for forty years. He was crusty and shrewd and, despite his stuffy exterior, not easily shocked. He'd nodded and made notes and asked questions until Laura's mouth had dried up from answering.

Because he hadn't sympathized or condemned, it had become easier to talk plainly. The truth, spoken in simple, unemotional terms, had been easier to face than it had to keep hidden. In the end she hadn't spared herself or Tony. And in the end she'd felt a powerful sense of having been cleansed.

At last she'd said it all, put all the misery and pain into words. She'd purged her heart and her mind in a way that her lingering sense of shame had never permitted before. Now that it was done, she understood what it was to wipe the slate clean and begin again.

Quartermain hadn't been happy with her final decision, but she'd been firm. Before papers of any kind were served or answered, she would see Lorraine again, face-to-face.

Beside Laura, Gabe lay sleepless. Like her, he was thinking back over the scene in the parlor. With every word that played back in his head his fury inched higher. She had spoken of things there that she had never told him, going into detail she had glossed over before. He'd thought he understood what she'd been through, and he'd thought his feelings about it had already peaked. He'd been wrong.

She hadn't told him about the black eye that had prevented her from leaving the house for nearly a week, or about Lorraine explaining away Laura's split lip by speaking of her daughter-in-law's clumsiness. She hadn't told him about the drunken attacks in the middle of the night, the jealous rages if she'd spoken with another man at a social function, the threats of revenge and violence when she'd finally found the courage to leave.

They'd come out tonight, in excruciating detail.

He hadn't touched her when they'd prepared for bed. He wondered how she could bear to be touched at all.

What she had been through was all too clear now. How could he expect her to put it aside, when he was no longer certain he could? No matter how gentle he was, how much care he took with her, the shadow of another man and another time was between them.

She'd said she loved him. As much as he wanted to believe it, he couldn't understand how anyone who had lived through that kind of hell could ever trust a man again, much less love him.

Gratitude, devotion, with Michael as the common ground. That he could understand. And that, Gabe thought as he lay in the dark, was more than many people were ever given.

He'd wanted more for them, had been on the verge of believing they could have more. That had been before all those words had been spoken downstairs while the quiet spring breeze had ruffled the curtains.

Then she turned toward him, her body brushing his. He stiffened.

"I'm sorry. Did I wake you?"

"No." He started to shift so that they were no longer touching, but she moved again until her head rested on his shoulder.

The gesture, the easy, uncomplicated movement toward

him, tore him in two. The one who needed, and the one who was afraid to ask.

"I can't sleep, either. I feel as though I've run an obstacle course, and my body's exhausted from it. But my mind keeps circling."

"You should stop thinking about tomorrow."

"I know." Laura brushed her hair aside, then settled more comfortably. She felt the slight drawing away, the pulling back. With her eyes shut tight, she wondered if he thought less of her now that he knew everything.

"There's no need for you to worry. It's going to be all right."

Was it? Taking a chance, she reached through the dark for his hand. "The trouble is, different scenes keep popping into my head. What I'll say, what she'll say. If I don't..." Her words trailed off when the baby started crying. "Sounds like someone else is restless."

"I'll get him."

Though she'd already tossed the covers aside, Laura nodded. "All right. I'll nurse him in here if he's hungry."

She sat up and hugged her knees to her chest as Gabe tossed on a robe and strode to the nursery. A moment later the crying stopped, then started again. Under it, she could hear Gabe's voice, murmuring and soothing.

It was so easy for him, so natural. Sensitivity, tenderness, were as much a part of him as temper and arrogance. Wasn't that why she'd finally been able to admit that she loved him? There would be no cycle of despair, submission and terror with Gabe, as there had been with Tony. She could love him without giving up the pieces of herself that she'd so recently discovered.

No, he didn't think less of her. She couldn't be sure of all of his feelings, but she could be sure of that. It was just that he was as worried as she and felt obligated to pretend otherwise.

The light from the nursery slanted into the hallway. In it she could see Gabe's shadow as he moved. The crying became muffled, then rose in a wail. Recognizing the tone of the crying, Laura leaned back and shut her eyes. It was going to be a long night.

"Teething," she murmured when Gabe brought a sobbing Michael into the bedroom. Switching on the bedside lamp she smiled at him. All of them needed support tonight. "I'll nurse him and see if that helps any."

"There you go, old man. Best seat in the house." Gabe settled him in Laura's arms. The crying faded to a whimper, then disappeared completely as he suckled. "I'm going down for a brandy. Do you want anything?"

"No. Yes, some juice. Whatever's in there."

Alone, she held Michael with one arm and arranged her pillows behind her back with the other. It seemed so normal, so usual, just like any other night. Though there were nights when Michael was restless when her body craved sleep, there were others when she prized these hours in the middle of the night. These were the times she and Gabe would remember years down the road, when Michael took his first steps, when he started school, when he rode a two-wheeler for the first time. They'd look back and remember how they'd walked the floor, half dozing themselves. Nothing could change that.

They needed this, needed the normalcy of it. And, if only for a few hours, they would have it.

When Gabe came back in, he set her glass on the table

beside her. Smiling, she lifted a hand to his arm. "Can I smell your brandy?"

Amused, he tilted the snifter for her and let her draw in the scent. "Enough?"

"Thanks. I always loved the taste of brandy late at night." Lifting her juice glass, she clinked it against his snifter. "Cheers." He didn't join her in bed, as she'd hoped he would, but turned to stand by the window. "Gabe?"

"Yes?"

"I'd like to make a deal with you. You tell me what's on your mind, ask any question you need to ask, and I'll tell you the absolute truth. Then, in return, I'll ask you and you'll do the same."

"Haven't you answered enough questions for one night?"

So that was it. Laura set her glass aside before she gently shifted Michael to her other breast. "You're upset because of the things I told Mr. Quartermain."

"Did you expect I would take them with a shrug?" When he whirled, the brandy sloshed dangerously close to the lip of the snifter. Laura said nothing as he tossed back half the contents and began to pace.

"I'm sorry it had to be brought up. I'd have preferred another way myself."

"It's not a matter of its being brought up." The words lashed out. He drank more brandy, but it did nothing to soothe him. "My God, it's killing me to think of it, to imagine it. I'm afraid to touch you, because it might bring it back."

"Gabe, you've been telling me all along that it's over, that things are different now. I know they are. You were right when you said I compared you with Tony, but maybe you don't understand that by doing that I helped myself realize that things could change."

He looked at her then, only for a moment, but long enough for her to see that her words weren't enough, not yet. "Things are different now, but I wonder why you don't hate any man who puts his hands on you."

"There was a time when I wouldn't have let any man within ten feet of me, but I was able to start putting things in perspective, through therapy, listening to other women who'd pulled themselves out of the spin." She watched him as he stood in the shadow, his hands thrust in the pockets of his robe and clenched into fists. "When you touch me, when you hold me, it doesn't bring any of that back. It makes me feel the way I've always wanted to feel about myself, about my husband."

"If he were alive," Gabe said evenly, "I'd want to kill him. I find myself resenting the fact that he's already dead."

"Don't do that to yourself." She reached out a hand to him, but he shook his head and walked back to the window. "He was ill. I didn't know that then, not really. And I prolonged it all by not walking away."

"You were afraid. You had nowhere to go."

"That's not enough. I could have gone to Geoffrey. I knew he would have helped me, but I didn't go, because I was pinned there by my own shame and insecurities. When I finally did leave, it was because of the baby. That's when I began to get well myself. Finding you was the best medicine of all, because you made me feel like a woman again."

He remained silent while she searched for the right words. "Gabe, there's nothing either of us can do to change things that have already happened. Don't let it change what we have now."

Calmer now, he swirled his brandy and continued to look out of the window. "When you talked of lawyers in the gallery today, I thought you wanted a divorce. It scared me to death."

"But I wouldn't have— Did it?"

"There you were, standing under the portrait, and I couldn't imagine what I would do if you walked away. I may have changed your life, angel, but no more than you've changed mine."

Pygmalion, she thought. If he loved the image, he might eventually love the woman. "I won't walk away. I love you, Gabe. You and Michael are my whole life."

He came to her then, to sit on the edge of the bed and take her hand. "I won't let anyone hurt either one of you."

Her fingers tightened on his. "I need to know that whatever we have to do we'll do it together."

"We've been in this together right from the start." Leaning forward, he kissed her, while the baby dozed between them. "I need you, Laura, maybe too much."

"It can't be too much."

"Let me go put him down," Gabe murmured. "Then maybe we can continue that."

He took the baby, but the moment he eased off the bed Michael began to cry.

They took turns walking, rocking, rubbing tender gums. Each time Michael was laid back in his crib he woke with a wail. Dizzy with fatigue, Laura leaned over the rail, patting and rubbing his back. Each time she moved her hand away he cried again.

"I guess we're spoiling him," she murmured.

Gabe sat heavy-eyed in the rocking chair and watched her. "We're entitled. Besides, he sleeps like a rock most of the time."

"I know. This teething's got him down. Why don't you go to bed? There's no sense in both of us being up."

"It's my shift." He rose and discovered that at 5:00 a.m. the body could feel decades older than it was. "You go on to bed."

"No—" Her own yawn cut her off. "We're in this together, remember?"

"Or until one of us passes out."

She would have laughed if she had had the energy. "Maybe I'll just sit down."

"You know, I've been known to watch the sun come up after a night of drinking, card playing or...other forms of entertainment." He began to pat Michael's back as Laura collapsed in the rocker. "And I can't remember ever feeling as though someone had run over me with a truck."

"This is one of the joys of parenting," she told him as she curled her legs under her and shut her eyes. "We're actually having the time of our lives."

"I'm glad you let me know. I think he's giving in."

"That's because you have such a wonderful touch," she murmured as she drifted off. "Such a wonderful touch."

Inch by cautious inch, Gabe drew his hand away. A man backing away from a tiger couldn't have taken more care. When he was a full two feet from the crib, he nearly let out a breath of relief. Afraid to push his luck, he held it and turned to Laura.

She was sound asleep, in an impossibly uncomfortable

position. Hoping his energy held out for five minutes longer, Gabe walked over to pick her up. She shifted and cuddled against him instinctively. As he carried her from the room, she roused enough to murmur. "Michael?"

"Down for the count." He walked into their room, but rather than taking her to bed he moved to the window. "Look, the sun's coming up."

Laura stirred and opened her eyes. Through the window she could see the curve of the eastern sky. If she looked hard enough she could see the water of the bay, like a mist in the distance. The sun seemed to vibrate as it rose. And the echoes brought colors: pinks, mauves, golds. Softly at first, with the darker night sky still dominating above, the colors spread, then deepened. Pinks became reds, vibrant and glowing.

"Sometimes your paintings are like that," she thought aloud. "Changing, shifting angles, with the colors intensifying from the core to the edges." She nestled her head against his shoulder as they watched the new day dawn. "I don't think I've ever seen a more beautiful sunrise."

His skin was warm beneath her cheek, his arms strong, firm with muscle, as they held her to him. She could feel the light, steady beating of his heart. She turned her face toward his as the first birds woke and began to sing. When love was so easily reached, only a fool questioned it.

"I want you, Gabe." She laid her hand on his cheek, her lips on his lips. "I've never wanted anyone the way I want you."

There was a moment's hesitation. She felt it, understood it, then coaxed him past it. This wasn't the time to think of yesterdays or tomorrows. Her lips softened and parted against his and her hand slipped back to brush through his hair.

"You were right," she murmured.

"About what?"

"I don't think of anyone but you when we make love."

He hadn't meant to ask her for anything. He found there was nothing he couldn't ask.

She was so beautifully open. It made it possible, even easy, to put that part of her life that left him angry and bitter aside. That had nothing to do with where they could take each other. With his mouth still on hers, he moved to the bed. She wrapped her arms around him as he lay beside her. For a moment that was enough.

Morning embraces, sunrise kisses, after a long, sleepless night. Her face was pale with fatigue, but still she trembled for him. The sigh that passed from her lips to his was soft and drowsy. Her body arched, lazy, limber, at the stroke of his hands.

The dawn air was balmy as it fluttered through the window and over their skin. She parted his robe, pushed it back from his shoulders, so that she could warm his skin herself. Just as slowly, he drew off her nightgown. Naked, they lay on the rumpled sheets and made long, luxurious love.

Neither of them set the pace. It wasn't necessary. Here they were in tune, without words or requests. Demands were for other moments, night moments, when passion was hot and urgent. As the light turned gray with morning, desire was deliciously cool.

Perhaps the love she felt for him was best displayed this way, with ease and affection that lasted so much longer than the flare of a flame. She moved with him and he with her, and they brought pleasure to each other that came in sighs and murmurs instead of gasps and shudders.

She felt the roughness of his cheek when she stroked her hand there. This was real. Marriage was more than the band she wore on her finger or the coming together full of need and excitement in the dark. Marriage was holding on at daybreak.

He would have scaled mountains for her. Until now, somehow, the full extent of his feelings for her had escaped him. He'd recognized the need first, the love later, but now he understood the devotion. She was his in a way no other woman could ever be. For the first time in his life, he wanted to be a hero.

When they came together, full light was pouring over the bed. Later, still entwined, they slept.

"I know I'm doing the right thing." Still, Laura hesitated when they stepped off the elevator in Lorraine's hotel. "And, no matter what happens, I'm not going to back down." She caught Gabe's hand in hers and held it tight. Lack of sleep had left her feeling light-headed and primed for action. "I'm awfully glad you're here."

"I told you before, I don't like the idea of you having to see her again, to deal with her on any level. I can easily handle this on my own."

"I know you could. But I told you, I need to. Gabe..."

"What?"

"Please don't lose your temper." She laughed a little at the way his brows rose. The tension rising inside her eased. "There's no need to look like that. I'm only trying to say that shouting at Lorraine won't accomplish anything."

"I never shout. I do occasionally raise my voice to get a point across."

"Since we've gotten that straightened out, I guess the only thing left to do is knock." She felt the familiar flutter of panic and fought it back as she knocked on the door. Lorraine answered, looking regal and poised in a navy suit.

"Laura." After the briefest of nods, she turned to Gabe. "Mr. Bradley. It's nice to meet you. Laura didn't mention that you were coming with her this afternoon."

"Everything that concerns Laura and Michael concerns me, Mrs. Eagleton." He entered, as Laura could never have done, without an invitation.

"I'm sure that's very conscientious of you." Lorraine closed the door with a quick click. "However, some of the things Laura and I may discuss are private family matters. I'm sure you understand."

"I understand perfectly." He met her level gaze with one of his own. "My wife and son are my family."

The war of wills was silent and unpleasant. Lorraine ended it with another nod. "If you insist. Please, sit. I'll order coffee. The service here is tolerable."

"Don't bother on our account." Laura spoke with only the slightest trace of nerves as she chose a seat. "I don't think this should take very long."

"As you like." Lorraine sat across from them. "My husband would have been here, but business prevented him from making the trip. I do, however, speak for both of us." That said, she laid her hands on the arms of her chair. "I'll simply repeat what has already been discussed. I intend to take Tony's son back to Boston and raise him properly."

"And I'll repeat, you can't have him." She would try

reason one last time, Laura thought, leaning forward. "He's a baby, not an heirloom, Mrs. Eagleton. He has a good home and two parents who love him. He's a healthy, beautiful child. You should be grateful for that. If you want to discuss reasonable visitation rights—"

"We'll discuss visitation rights," Lorraine said, interrupting her. "Yours. And if I have anything to say about it, they will be short and spare. Mr. Bradley," she continued, turning away from Laura. "Surely you don't want to raise another man's child as your own. He hasn't your blood, and he only has your name because, for whatever reason, you married his mother."

Gabe drew out a cigarette and lit it slowly. Laura had asked him not to lose his temper. Though he wouldn't be able to accommodate her, it wouldn't do to let it snap so quickly. "You're very wrong" was all he said.

She sighed, almost indulgently. "I understand you have feelings for Laura. My son had them, too."

The first chain on his temper broke clean in half. The rage could be seen in his eyes and heard in each precise, bitten-off word. "Don't you ever compare my feelings for Laura with your son's."

Lorraine paled a little, but went on evenly. "I have no idea what she may have been telling you—"

"I told him the truth." Before Gabe could speak, or move, Laura put a hand on his arm. "I told him what you know is the truth, that Tony was ill, emotionally unstable."

Now it was Lorraine who moved, rising deliberately from her chair. Her face was flushed and pinched, but her voice was held at the same even pitch. "I will not sit here and listen to you defame my son."

"You will listen." Laura's fingers dug hard into Gabe's arm, but she didn't give way. "You'll listen now the way you never listened when I was desperate for help. The way you never listened when Tony was screaming for it in the only way he knew. He was an alcoholic, an emotional wreck who abused someone weaker than he. You knew he hurt me, you saw the marks and ignored them or made excuses. You knew there were other women. By your silence, you gave him approval."

"What was between you and Tony was none of my concern."

"That's for you to live with. But I warn you, Lorraine, if you open the lid, you won't be able to handle what comes out."

Lorraine sat again, if for no other reason than the tone of Laura's voice and the fact that for the first time Laura had called her by her first name. That one change made them equals. This wasn't the same frightened, easily pressured woman she had known only a year before.

"Threats from someone like you don't worry me. The courts will decide if some loose-moraled young tramp will have custody of an Eagleton or if he'll be placed with those who can give him the proper upbringing."

"If you refer to my wife in that way again you'll have more than threats to deal with." Gabe blew out a long, narrow stream of smoke. "Mrs. Eagleton."

"It doesn't matter." Laura squeezed his hand. She knew he was on the verge of losing control. "You can't make me cringe anymore, Lorraine, and you won't make me beg. You know very well that I was faithful to Tony."

"I know that Tony didn't believe that."

"Then how do you know the child is his?"

Absolute silence fell the moment Gabe spoke. Laura started to speak but was held off by the look in Gabe's eyes. Color flooded into Lorraine's face again when she found her voice.

"She wouldn't have dared—"

"Wouldn't she? That's odd. You intend to prove that Laura was unfaithful to your son, and now you claim she wasn't. Either way, you have a problem. If she had had an affair with anyone. Me, for example." He smiled again as he crushed out his cigarette. "Or haven't you wondered why we were married so quickly, why, as you've already asked, I accept the child as my own?" He let that thought take hold before he continued. "If she had been unfaithful, the child could be anyone's. If she wasn't unfaithful, you haven't got a case."

Lorraine clenched and unclenched her fingers on the arm of the chair. "My husband and I have every intention of determining the child's paternity. I would hardly take some-one's bastard into my home."

"Be careful," Laura said, so quietly that the words seemed to vibrate in the air. "Be very careful, Lorraine. I know you have no concern for Michael as a person."

Fighting for control she so rarely lost, Lorraine settled again. "I have nothing but the gravest concern for Tony's son."

"You've never asked about him, what he looks like, if he's well. You've never demanded to see him, even a picture or a doctor's report. You've never once called him by name. If you had, if I'd seen in you one ounce of love or affection for the baby, I'd feel differently about what I'm about to say." The courage came without the need to muster it. "You're free to draw up the papers and initiate a custody suit. Gabe and I have already notified our attorney. We'll fight you, and we'll win. And in the meantime, I'll go to the press with the story of what my life was like with the Eagletons of Boston."

Lorraine's nails dug into the material on the arm of the chair. "You wouldn't have the nerve."

"I have that and more when it comes to protecting my son."

She could see it, the calm, unshakable determination in Laura's eyes. "Even if you did, no one would believe you."

"But they would," Laura told her. "People have a way of recognizing the truth."

Lorraine's face was set when she turned to Gabe. "Do you have any conception of what this kind of gossip could do to your family name? Do you want to risk your reputation, your parents' reputation, over this woman and a child who isn't even of your blood?"

"My reputation can handle it, and, to be frank, my parents are looking forward to a fight." There was a challenge in his voice now that didn't have to be feigned. "Michael may not be of my blood, but he's mine."

"Lorraine." Laura waited until they were face-to-face again. "You lost your son, and I'm sorry for you, but you won't replace him with mine. Whatever the cost to protect Michael's welfare, I'll pay. And so will you."

Putting a hand under her arm, Gabe rose, keeping Laura beside him. "Your attorney can contact us once you've made your decision. Remember, Mrs. Eagleton, you're not pitting yourself against a lone pregnant woman. You're up against the Bradleys now."

The moment they were in the hall, Gabe pulled Laura

against him. He could feel the tremors coursing through her, so he held her a moment longer. "You were wonderful." He kissed her hair before he drew her away from him. "In fact, angel, you were amazing. Lorraine still doesn't know what hit her."

The flush of pride was as warm and satisfying as anything she'd ever felt. "It wasn't as bad as I thought," she said with a sigh, but she kept her hand in his as they walked to the elevator. "I used to be so terrified of her, afraid to speak two words. Now I can see her for what she really is, a lonely woman trapped by her own strict sense of family honor."

Gabe gave a quick, humorless laugh as the elevators doors opened. "Honor has nothing to do with it."

"No, but that's how she sees it."

"Tell you what." He pressed the button for the lobby. "We're going to forget about Lorraine Eagleton for the rest of the day. In fact, we're going to forget about her completely before long, but for now there's a little restaurant a few blocks away. Not too quiet, and very expensive."

"It's too early for dinner."

"Who said anything about dinner?" He slipped an arm around her waist as they walked out into the lobby. "We're going to sit at a table over the water, and I'm going to watch everyone stare at my gorgeous wife while we drink a bottle of champagne."

She loved him for that. Then her heart skipped a beat when he brought her fingers to his lips. "Don't you think we should wait to celebrate until Lorraine gives us her decision?"

"We'll celebrate then, too. Right now I want to celebrate being witness to an angel breathing fire."

She laughed and walked outside with him. "I could do it again. In fact…"

"What?"

She swept her gaze up to his. "I'd like to."

"Sounds as though I'm going to have to watch my step."

"Probably." She was giddy with success, but she was still practical. "I really shouldn't have champagne. Michael—"

Gabe kissed her, and signaled for his car.

Chapter 12

"You look exhausted." Amanda gave a quick shake of her head as she stepped into the house.

"Michael's teething." The excuse was valid enough, but more than a fretful baby was keeping Laura from sleeping at night. "He's been down all of ten minutes. With luck, he might make an entire hour straight."

"Then why aren't you napping?"

Since Amanda was already stepping into the parlor, Laura followed her in. "Because you called and said you were coming over."

"Oh." With a faint smile, Amanda took a seat, then tossed her purse on the table. "So I did. Well, I won't keep you long. Gabe's not home?"

"No. He said he had something to see to." Laura sat in the chair facing her and let her head fall back. Sometimes small luxuries felt like heaven. "Can I get you some coffee, or something cold?"

"You don't look as though you can get yourself out of that chair. And, no, I don't need a thing. How is Gabe?"

"He hasn't been getting a great deal of rest, either."

"I'm not surprised. No word from Lorraine Eagleton or her attorney?"

"Nothing."

"I don't suppose that you're able to take the attitude that no news is good news?"

Laura managed a smile. "Afraid not. The longer this goes on, the easier it gets to imagine the worst."

"And if she takes this to court?"

"Then we'll fight." Despite her fatigue, her newly discovered power came through. "I meant everything I said to her."

"That's really all I wanted to hear." Sitting back, Amanda adjusted the pin on her lapel. A little too thin, a little too pale, she thought as she studied Laura. But, all in all, she thought her daughter-in-law was holding up well. "When this is over, you and Gabe should be able to tie up a few loose ends."

Laura caught herself before she dozed off. "Loose ends?"

"Yes, little things. Such as what you intend to do with the rest of your lives."

"I don't know what you mean."

"Gabe has his art, and you both have Michael, and however many other children you choose to bring into the world."

That was something that made Laura sit up straighter. More children. They'd never discussed the possibility of more. As she began to, she wondered if Gabe even wanted any. Did she? She passed a hand over her now flat stomach and imagined it filled with another child—Gabe's child this time, from the very first moment. Yes, she wanted that. Glancing over, she saw Amanda studying her quietly and with complete understanding.

"It's difficult to make decisions with so much hanging over us."

"Exactly. But it will pass. When it does, what are you going to look for? Since I spent more than two decades under the same roof as Gabe, I know that he can, when the muse is on him, lock himself in his studio for hours and days on end."

"I don't mind. How could I, when I see what he can accomplish?"

"A woman needs a solid sense of accomplishment, as well. Children can be the best of that, but..." She reached for her purse, opened it and took out a business card. "There's an abuse clinic downtown. It's rather small, and unfortunately not well funded. Yet." She intended to correct that. "They need volunteers, women who understand, who know there can be normal life after hell."

"I'm not a therapist."

"You don't need a degree to give support."

"No." She looked at the card on the table as the idea took root. "I don't know. I..."

"Just think about it."

"Amanda, did you go to the clinic?"

"Yes, Cliff and I went there yesterday. We were very impressed."

"Why did you go?"

Amanda lifted a brow in a gesture Laura knew Gabe had inherited. "Because there's someone we both care about who we wanted to understand better. Don't get up," she said as she rose. "I'll let myself out. Give Gabe my love and tell him his father wants to know if they're ever going to play poker again. The man thrives on losing money."

"Amanda." Laura pushed off her shoes before she curled her legs up in the chair. "I never had a mother, and the one I always imagined for myself was nothing like you." She smiled as her eyes began to close. "I'm not at all disappointed."

"You're coming along," Amanda said, and left Laura sleeping in the chair.

She was still there when Gabe came in. He tilted the bulky package against the wall. When she didn't stir at the rattle of the paper, he walked over to the couch. He didn't even have the energy to wish for his sketch pad as he stretched out his legs and almost instantly fell asleep.

The baby woke both of them. Gabe merely groaned and pulled a throw pillow over his face. Disoriented, Laura pulled herself up, blinked groggily at Gabe, then put one foot in front of the other to get upstairs.

A short time later, he went up after her.

"My timing's good," he decided when he saw that Laura was fastening a fresh diaper.

"I'm beginning to wonder about your timing." But she was smiling as she lifted Michael over her head to make him laugh. "How long have you been home?"

"Long enough to see that my wife has nothing better to do than lounge around all day." He plucked Michael from her while she pretended to glare at him. "Do you think if we kept him awake and exhausted him with attention he'd sleep tonight?"

"I'm willing to try anything."

At that, Gabe sat on the floor and began to play nonsense games. Bouncing the Baby, Flying the Baby, Tickling the Baby.

"You're so good with him." Finding her second wind, Laura sat on the floor with them. "It's hard to believe you're new at this."

"I never thought about parenthood. It certainly has its compensations." He set Michael on his knee and jiggled him.

"Like walking the ten-minute mile at 2:00 a.m."

"That, too."

"Gabe, your mother came by."

"Should I be surprised?"

She smiled a little as she leaned over to let Michael tug at her hair. "She left a card—from an abuse clinic."

"I see." He reached over himself to untangle her hair from Michael's grip. "Do you want to go back into therapy?"

"No…at least I don't think so." She looked over at him. Michael was chewing madly at his chin. All the therapy she needed was sitting across from her. "She suggested I might like to volunteer there."

He frowned as he let Michael gnaw on his knuckle. "And be reminded day after day?"

"Yes—of what I was able to change."

"I thought you'd want to go back to modeling eventually."

"No, I haven't any desire to go back to modeling. I think I could do this, and I know I'd like to try."

"If you're asking for my approval, you don't need to."

"I'd still like to have it."

"Then you do, unless I see this wearing you down."

She had to smile. He still saw her as more fragile than she was or could ever have afforded to be. "You know, I've been thinking…with everything that's happened, and everything we've had to think and worry about, we haven't had much time to really get to know a lot about each other."

"I know you take entirely too long in the bathtub and like to sleep with the window open."

She took the stuffed rabbit Michael liked to chew on and passed it from hand to hand. "There are other things."

"Such as?"

"The other night, I said that you could ask me anything and I'd tell you the truth, and then I'd ask you something. Do you remember?"

"I remember."

"I never had my turn."

He shifted so that he could rest his back against the daybed. They were avoiding speaking of the phone call they were both waiting for. And they both knew it. Perhaps that was best, Gabe mused as the baby continued to rub his sore gums against his knuckles.

"Do you want to hear about my misspent youth?"

Though she was plucking nervously at the rabbit's ears, she smiled. "Is there time?"

"You flatter me."

"Actually, I'd like to ask you about something else. A few days ago, when it rained, I went into your studio to close the windows. I looked through some of your paintings. Perhaps I shouldn't have."

"It doesn't matter."

"There was one in particular. The one of Michael. Your brother. I'd like you to tell me about him."

He was silent for so long that she had to fight back the urge to tell him that it didn't matter. But it mattered too much. She was certain it was his brother's death that had sent him to Colorado, that was preventing him, even after all these months, from having a showing of his work.

"Gabe." She laid a tentative hand on his arm. "You asked me to marry you so that you could take on my problems. You wanted me to trust you, and I have. Until you can do the same, we're still strangers."

"We haven't been strangers since the first time we laid eyes on each other, Laura. I would have asked you to marry me with or without your problems."

Now she fell silent, as surprise ran through her, chased frantically by hope. "Do you mean that?"

He shifted the baby onto his shoulder. "I don't always say everything I mean, but I do mean what I say." When Michael began to whimper, Gabe stood to walk him. "You needed someone, I wanted to be that someone. And I, though I didn't know it until you were already part of my life, needed someone, too."

She wanted to ask him how he needed her, and why, and if love—the kind she'd always hoped for—was somehow mixed up with that need. But they needed to go back further than that if they were ever to move forward.

"Please tell me about him."

He wasn't certain he could, that he wouldn't trip over the pain, and then the words. It had been so long since he'd spoken of Michael. "He was three years younger than I," he began. "We got along fairly well growing up because Michael tended to be even-tempered unless backed into a corner. We didn't have many of the same interests. Baseball was about it. It used to infuriate me that I couldn't outhit him. As we grew older, I turned to art, and Michael to law. The law fascinated him."

"I remember," she murmured, as some vague recollection stirred. "There was something about him in an article I read about you. He was working in Washington."

"As a public defender. He set a lot of tongues clucking over that decision. He wasn't interested in corporate law or big fees. Of course, a lot of people said he didn't need the money, anyway. What they didn't understand was that he would have done the same thing with or without his stock portfolio behind him. He wasn't a saint." Gabe set Michael in the crib and wound up the mobile. "But he was the best of us. The best and the brightest, my father used to say."

She had risen, but she wasn't certain he wanted her to go to him. "I could see that in the portrait. You must have loved him very much."

"It's not something you think about, one brother loving another. Either it's there or it isn't. It isn't something you say, because you don't think it needs to be said. Then all you have is time to regret."

"He had to know you loved him. He only had to see the portrait."

With his hands in his pockets, Gabe walked to the window. It was easier than he could have imagined to talk to her about it. "I'd badgered him to sit for me off and on for years. It became a family joke. I won five sittings from him in a poker game. A heart flush to his three of a kind." The pain clawed at him, no longer fresh, but still sharp. "That was the last time we played."

"What happened to him?"

"An accident. I've never believed in accidents. Luck, fate,

destiny, but they called it an accident. He was researching a case in Virginia and took a small commuter plane to New York. Minutes after takeoff it went down. He was coming to New York because I was having a showing."

Her heart broke for him. This time there was no hesitation as she went to him and put her arms around him. "You've blamed yourself all this time. You can't."

"He was coming to New York for me, to be there for me. I watched my mother fall apart for the first and only time in her life. I saw my father walk through his own home as if he'd never seen it before, and I didn't know what to say or do."

She stroked his back, aching for him. There was no use telling him that being there was sometimes all that could be done. "I've never lost anyone I've loved, but having you and Michael now, I can imagine how devastating it would be. Sometimes things happen and there's no one to blame. Whether that's an accident or fate, I don't know."

He rested his cheek on her hair and looked out at the flowers she'd planted. "I went to Colorado to get away for a while, to be alone and see if I could paint again. I hadn't been able to here. When I found you, I'd begun to pull myself back. I could work again, I could think about coming home and picking up my life. But there was still something missing." He drew back and cupped her face in his hand. "You filled in those last pieces for me."

She curled her fingers around his wrist. "I'm glad."

When he held her, she closed her eyes. They would make it, Laura told herself. Whatever happened, they would make it. Sometimes need was enough.

"Gabe." She slid her hands down until they gripped his.

"The paintings in your studio. They don't belong there." She squeezed his fingers with hers before he could speak or turn away. "It's wrong to keep them there, facing the wall and pretending they don't exist. If your brother was proud enough of you to want to be there for one of your showings, it's time you had one. Dedicate it to him. Maybe you didn't say the words, but there can't be any better way to show that you loved him."

He had started to brush it aside, to make excuses, but her last words hit home. "He would have liked you."

Her lips curved. "Will you do it?"

"Yes." He kissed her while she was still smiling. "Yes, it's time. I've known that, but I haven't been able to take the last step. I'll have Marion start the arrangements." She stiffened, and though the change was only slight he drew her away to study her face. "Problem?"

"No, of course not."

"You do a lot of things well, angel. Lying isn't one of them."

"Gabe, nothing could please me more than you going ahead with this. That's the truth."

"But?"

"Nothing. All of this has really put me behind schedule. I need to give Michael his bath."

"He'll hold a minute." He kept her with him by doing no more than running his hands down her arms. "I know there's some tension between you and Marion. I've already told you there's nothing between us but business."

"I understand that. I've told you what I would have done if I thought otherwise."

"Yes, you did." Amusement moved over his face. She

would have packed her bags and headed for the door, but she would have gotten no more than five feet. "So what's the problem?"

"There is no problem."

"I'd prefer not going to Marion with this."

"So would I." Her chin came up. "Don't push this, Gabe. And don't push me."

"Well, well." He brought his hands to her shoulders as he nodded. "It's a rare thing for you to get that look on your face. Whenever you do, I have this deep-seated urge to drag you down on the floor and let loose." When color flooded her face, he laughed and drew her closer.

"Don't laugh at me." She would have twisted away, but his hands were firm.

"Sorry. I wasn't, really, more at the situation." He thought that perhaps delicacy was called for, but then he rejected the idea. "Want to fight?"

"Not at the moment."

"If you can't lie better than that, we'll have to keep you out of poker games," he murmured, and watched her eyes cool. "I overheard your discussion with Marion at the gallery."

"Then you obviously don't need me to spell things out for you. She believes I'm going to hold you back, prevent you from reaching your full potential, and she took steps to stop it. I realize that the Eagletons would have found us, probably in a matter of days, but I won't forgive her for calling them. The fact that you're associated with her gallery means I have to be polite to her in public, but that's the extent of it."

His hands had tightened on her shoulders, and all amusement had been wiped from his face. "You're telling me that Marion called the Eagletons?"

"You just said you'd heard us, so—"

"I hadn't heard that much." Deliberately he relaxed his hands, then took a step back. "Why didn't you explain this to me before so that we could have told her to go to hell?"

"I didn't think that you—" She stopped and stared at him. "Would you have?"

"Damn it, Laura, what more do I have to do to convince you that I'm committed totally to you and Michael?"

"But she said—"

"What difference does it make what she said? It's what I say, isn't it?"

"Yes." She folded her hands but didn't lower her gaze. It was what he said. And not once had he ever said he loved her. "I didn't want to interfere when it came to your work."

"And I won't tolerate Marion interfering in my life. I'll handle it."

"How?"

Exasperated, he tugged his hand through his hair. "One minute you talk of my work as though I had an obligation to mankind to share it, and the next you act as though I'd have to go begging to find another gallery."

"I didn't mean... You'll take your paintings out of Marion's gallery?"

"Good God," he muttered, and took another turn around the room. "Obviously we need to talk—or maybe talking's not what's called for." He took a step toward her, then swore when the phone rang. "Stay here." With that he turned on his heel and strode out.

Laura let out a long breath. He'd said something about

dragging her to the floor and letting loose. That was what had been in his eyes a moment before. And what would that have proved?

She moved to the crib to hand a fretful Michael his favorite rabbit. It would only have proved that he wanted and needed her. She had no doubts about that. Why shouldn't she be surprised that he would cut himself off from Marion for her? But not for her, really, Laura thought as she leaned over to nuzzle the baby. For himself. Marion had made the mistake of interfering.

Reasons didn't matter, she told herself. Results did. A great deal had been accomplished here this afternoon. He'd finally trusted her with his feelings about his brother. She'd been able to say the right things to convince him to show his work, and Marion was out of their lives.

"That should be enough for one day," she murmured to Michael. But there was still an ache in her heart.

She wouldn't think about the Eagletons.

"He needs us, Michael." That, too, should have been enough. Perhaps they were a replacement for someone he had loved and lost, but he had already given the baby unconditional love. He had given her a promise of his fidelity. That was more than she'd ever had, more than she had come to believe she would ever have. And yet it wasn't enough.

"Laura."

She turned, annoyed because she was feeling weepy and dejected. "What is it?"

"That was Quartermain on the phone." He saw the fear come first, then saw it vanish to be replaced by determination. "It's over," he told her before she could ask. "The Eagletons' attorney contacted him a few minutes ago."

"Over?" She could only whisper. The strength she'd built up, layer by layer, began to slip.

"They've pulled back. There'll be no custody suit. Not now, not ever. They don't want anything to do with the baby."

"Oh, God." She covered her face with her hands. The tears came, but she wasn't ashamed of them, not even when Gabe gathered her close. "Is he sure? If they change their minds—"

"He's sure. Listen to me." He drew her back, just a little. He wasn't entirely certain how she would feel about the rest. "They're going to file papers claiming that Tony wasn't Michael's biological father. They want him cut off legally from any future claim to the Eagleton estate."

"But she doesn't believe that."

"She wants to believe that."

She closed her eyes while relief and regret poured through her. "I would have tried to be fair, to let them see Michael. At least I want to believe I would have tried."

"He'll lose his heritage."

"The money?" When she opened her eyes, they were dark and damp. "I don't think that will matter to him. It doesn't to me. As far as family goes, he already has one. Gabe, I don't know how to thank you."

"Then don't. You were the one who stood up to her."

"I did." She brushed the tears away, and then there was laughter as she threw her arms around him. "Yes, I did. No one's ever going to take him away from us. I want to celebrate. To go dancing, have a party." She laughed again and squeezed him hard. "After I sleep for a week."

"It's a date." He found her lips with his, then held them there as she melted into him. Another beginning, he thought, and this time they'd take the first step properly. "I want to call my parents and let them know."

"Yes, right away." She pressed against him for a moment longer. "I'll give Michael his bath, and then we'll be down."

It was nearly an hour before she came downstairs, bringing a more contented Michael with her. The baby, fresh from his bath, was awake and ready to be entertained. Because her jeans had gotten wet, she'd changed into a pale lavender shirt and slacks. Her hair was loose around her shoulders, and both she and Michael smelled of soap and soft talc. Gabe met her at the foot of the stairs.

"Here, let me have him." He curled his arm around the baby and tickled his belly. "Looks like you're ready to go field a few grounders."

"So do you." Envious, Laura muffled a yawn. "You haven't had any more sleep than I have. How do you manage it?"

"Three decades of clean living—and a body accustomed to all-night poker games."

"Your father wants to play. Maybe Michael could sit in."

"Maybe." He tipped her chin up with his finger. "You really are ready to drop, aren't you?"

"I've never felt better in my life."

"And you can barely keep your eyes open."

"That's nothing five straight hours of sleep wouldn't fix."

"I've got something to show you. Afterward, why don't you go up and take a nap? Michael and I can entertain ourselves." His thumb traced along her jawline. Until Laura, he hadn't known that the scent of soap and powder could be arousing. "Once you've rested, we can have our private celebration."

"I'll go now."

He laughed and caught her arm before she could start back up. "Come see first."

"Okay, I'm too weak to argue."

"I'll keep that in mind for later." With the baby in one arm and the other around Laura, he walked into the parlor.

She'd seen the painting before, from the first brush strokes to the last. Yet it seemed different now, here, hung over the mantel. In the gallery, she had seen it as a beautiful piece of work, something to be studied by art students and patrons, a thing to be commented on and discussed, dissected and critiqued. Here, in the parlor, in the late afternoon, it was a personal statement, a part of all three of them.

She hadn't realized just how much she'd resented seeing it in Marion's gallery. Nor had she known that seeing it here would make her feel, as nothing else had, that she had finally come home.

"It's beautiful," she murmured.

He understood. It wasn't vanity or self-importance. "I've never done anything in my life that compares to this. I doubt I will again. Sit down, will you?"

Something in his tone had her glancing over at him before she settled on the couch. "I didn't know you intended to bring it home. I know you've had offers."

"I never had any intention of selling it. I always meant it for here." Resting the baby on his hip, he walked over to the portrait. "As long as I've lived here, I haven't done anything, or found anything, that I wanted to hang in that spot. It goes back to fate again. If I hadn't been in Colorado, if it hadn't been snowing, if you hadn't been running. It took what had happened to you, and what had happened to me, to bring us together and make this."

"When you were painting it, I wondered why you seemed so driven. I understand now."

"Do you?" With a half smile, he turned back to her. "I wonder just what you understand, angel. It wasn't until a little while ago that I realized you have no idea what I feel for you."

"I know you need me, me and Michael. Because of what happened to all of us, we're able to make things better."

"And that's it?" He wondered if he was pushing too far, but he thought that if he didn't push now it might be too late. "You said you loved me. I know gratitude's a big part of that, but I want to know if there's anything more."

"I don't know what you want me to say."

"I want you to look." He held out a hand. When she didn't move, he walked over to her and drew her to her feet. "Look at the portrait and tell me what you see."

"Myself."

It seemed to be the day for showdowns, Gabe thought. He quickly carried the sleeping Michael upstairs to the nursery and put him in the crib. Going back down to Laura, he took her by the shoulders and, holding her in front of him, made her face the portrait. "Tell me what you see."

"I see myself as you saw me then." Why was her heart hammering? "I seem a little too vulnerable, a little too sad."

Impatience had him giving her a quick shake. "You don't see enough."

"I want to see strength," she blurted out. "I think I do. And I see a woman alone who's ready to protect what's hers."

"When you look at her eyes. Look at them, Laura, and tell me what you see."

"A woman falling in love." She shut her own. "You must have known."

"No." He didn't turn her toward him. Instead, he wrapped his arms around her so that they both continued to face the portrait. "No, I didn't know, because I kept telling myself I was painting what I wanted to see. And what I was feeling myself."

Her heart leaped into her throat and throbbed there. Whatever he could feel, he could paint. That had been her own conclusion. "What are you feeling?"

"Can't you see it?"

"I don't want to see it there." She turned to grip the front of his shirt. "I want to hear it."

He wasn't sure he had the words. Words came so much less easily than emotion. He could paint his moods, and he could shout them, but it was difficult to speak them quietly when they mattered so much.

He touched her face, her hair, then her hand. "Almost from the first you pulled at me in a way no one ever had before and no one ever will again. I thought I was crazy. You were pregnant, totally dependent on me, grateful for my help."

"I was grateful. I'll always be grateful."

"Damn it" was all he could manage as he turned away.

"I'm sorry you feel that way." She was calm now, absolutely, beautifully calm, as he glared at her. She'd remember him like this always, she thought, with his hair tousled from his hands, a gray shirt with the sleeves shoved up to the elbows and his face full of impatience. "Because I intend to be grateful for the rest of my life. And that has nothing to do with my intending to love you for the rest of my life."

"I want to be sure of that."

"Be sure. You didn't paint what you wanted to see, you never do. You paint the truth." She took one step toward him, the most important step she'd ever taken. "I've given you the truth, Gabe. Now I have to ask for it. Are your feelings for me tied up in that portrait, in that image, are they an effect of your love for Michael, or are they for me?"

"Yes." He caught her hands in his. "I'm in love with the woman I painted, with the mother of my child, and with you. Separately and together. We could have met anywhere, under any circumstances, and I would still have fallen in love with you. Maybe it wouldn't have happened as quickly, maybe it wouldn't have been as complicated, but it would have happened." She started to move into his arms, but he held her back. "When I married you, it was for purely selfish reasons. I wasn't doing you any favors."

She smiled. "Then I won't be grateful."

"Thank you." He lifted her hands to his lips, the one that wore the old wedding band, then the one that wore the new. "I want to paint you again."

She was laughing as his lips came down to her. "Now?"

"Soon."

Then his hands were in her hair, and the kiss became urgent and seeking. It was met equally as her arms went around him. Love, fully opened, added its own desperation.

There was a murmur of pleasure, then a murmur of protest as he drew her to the floor. Her laugh turned to a moan when he unbuttoned her blouse.

"Michael—"

"Is asleep." He dragged her hair back, leaving her face unframed. Everything he'd wanted to see was there. "Until he wakes up, you're mine. I love you, Laura. Every time you look at the painting, you'll see it. You were mine from the first moment I touched you."

Yours, she thought as she drew him back to her. Gabriel's angel was more than a portrait. And she finally belonged.

* * * * *

Two classic tales of love and fate from
#1 *New York Times* and *USA TODAY*
bestselling author

NORA ROBERTS

IRISH REBEL

From the moment she met him, Keeley Grant knew there
was something wild about Brian Donnelly. He dared
to ignore everything that said a poor Irish rogue shouldn't
touch her, and battered down every wall she threw at him.
But a wild thing by nature cannot be contained, not by
convention or fences or even by love. Could she give him
everything if he was just going to walk away?

SULLIVAN'S WOMAN

Colin Sullivan had a vision—the painting of his career,
with Cassidy St. John as his model. She would be a
challenge to paint, with her passion for life and a beauty
that captivated him. But as she stood in front of him every
day, Colin began to realize that the real challenge
wouldn't be to capture her image…but her heart.

Read both unforgettable stories, collected in

Irish Dreams

Coming in September 2011 from Silhouette Books!

PSNR151BCCTR

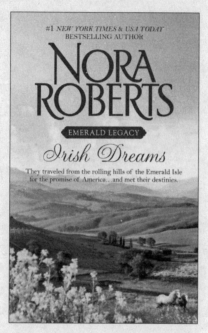